something like... stories
volume one

D1738624

Jay Bell Books
www.jaybellbooks.com

Did you buy this book? If so, thank you for putting food on our table! Making money as an independent artist isn't easy, so your support is greatly appreciated. Come give me a hug!

Did you pirate this book? If so, there are a couple of ways you can still help out. If you like the story, please take the time to leave a nice review somewhere, such as an online retail store (my preference), or on any blog or forum. Word of mouth is important for every book, so if you can recommend this book to friends with more cash to spare, that would be awesome too!

Something Like Stories: Volume One © 2015 Jay Bell / Andreas Bell
ISBN: 978-1515109945

Cover art by Andreas Bell: www.andreasbell.com

Something Like Stories
Volume One

by Jay Bell

Foreword

You hold in your hand a collection of short stories that I hope you'll find both wondrous and strange. I've always felt a short story should be free of the burdens of continuity, allowing a new reader to decide if they enjoy an author's style or not. In that way, the stories contained in this book make for a very poor introduction. They rely too heavily on events that have already transpired on other pages. If you're as spoiler-phobic as I am, then this is easily the worst *Something Like...* book you could start with. I highly recommend that—before proceeding—you have already read the first six books in the series. That's *Summer* all the way through *Thunder*. Bonus points if you've read books of mine outside of this series. You'll get more out of this collection than other people will, and between you and me, I love you just a little bit more for it. You'll also find some bonus material at the end, such as a guide to all the characters and a timeline of key events. I greatly enjoyed putting this compilation together, enough so that I'm hedging my bets and describing this as the first volume. If you enjoy it too, hopefully you and I will meet again in the next installment. Until then!

-Jay Bell, November 2015

Table of Contents

———————

Something Like Yesterday

by Jay Bell

———————

Austin, 2001

"Count your angels. The more you can name, the more will come to your aid. They can light up the dark, chase away any shadow. There's nothing they can't protect you from. Nothing at all. Listen now. Let me teach you their names. We'll practice every night, and by the time we're through, you'll never be frightened again."

Eric Conroy's eyes shot open, his heart racing. The breath he pulled into his lungs felt hot and sharp as razor blades. He only wished that fear could be so easily tamed, or pain so effortlessly vanquished. Lately fear and pain were his constant companions, although a third member of the trio was doing all it could to keep the other two in check. Eric turned his head and saw a figure half-hidden by an easel. Love. His pulse slowed, the ache subsiding enough to allow him to croak out one word.

"Tim."

The man behind the easel froze. Then he sprang into action, setting aside the brush to fetch a glass of water from the nightstand. He carefully angled the straw so Eric's lips could meet it, bringing much needed moisture to his throat. As Eric drank, he stared up at the man performing this act of kindness: silver eyes tense with concern, an attractive face despite its troubled expression, and thick black hair to compliment the bronze skin. Tim was just as handsome and youthful as the day—two years ago—when he showed up on Eric's doorstep. But back then he had only perceived the most superficial side of Tim's beauty. The rest had come later.

After swallowing a few times, Eric moved his head away from the straw to nod at the easel. "What are you doing?"

"Painting you."

"Like this?" Eric tried to picture himself, shriveled and fading, lost among the sheets in a bed that was too large for one person. The image would have been sad if he didn't find it so ironic. To think his final days would not only end like this, but be preserved on canvas as well. "You're cruel."

"I promised I would paint you," Tim said, the emotion

evident in his voice. Sorrow with a trace of barely subdued anger—grieving the inevitable and yet still raging against it.

Eric broke eye contact momentarily. "That's right. Make me a king, surrounded by beautiful young men."

This brought a hopeful smile to Tim's features. "I'll make you an emperor with no clothes."

Eric chuckled in appreciation and was rewarded with pain. He squeezed his eyes shut, willing it to stop, but his body had long ago ceased responding to his wishes. "Time for more of those poppies, Dorothy."

Tim seemed to share his pain, frowning with discomfort, but did as he was asked. He traded the drinking glass for a brown bottle and medicine dropper, neither of them acknowledging that Tim filled it with twice as much medication as the hospice nurse recommended. The morphine wouldn't kill Eric, but if it did, it would only beat cancer to the punch. Eric opened his mouth, trying to ignore the sickly sweet flavor intended to mask the bitter taste. Tim knew the routine, holding the drinking glass close so Eric could sip from it again.

"Need to answer Mother Nature's call before that stuff kicks in?"

Eric shook his head, hating how age and illness had returned him to the role of a child, no longer even capable of using the restroom alone. He only needed help getting there, but he knew that would change when things got worse.

"How about some soup? You need to eat something."

"Just keep working," Eric replied. "I like the sound of the brush."

He shut his eyes, feeling the mattress shift as Tim stood. He listened to the paintbrush slide off the easel, wood against wood. Then came the gentle noise of wet paint spreading across dry canvas, like the ocean lapping against the beach. Like moist lips pressing against sun-baked skin. Eric laughed softly at the thought.

"Morphine kicking in already?" Tim asked.

"Not quite yet."

"You should try to get some sleep."

Eric opened his eyes in protest. "All I do is sleep. I'm sick of it."

A concerned gaze met his briefly, then returned to their task. "Talk to me then. Tell me your life story."

"What, all of it?"

A shrug. "Why not?"

"When you get to be my age, that can be a daunting task. I'm not sure there's enough time left."

The paintbrush stopped moving. "Don't say that."

"It was a joke," Eric said, mostly for Tim's benefit, but part of him also wanted to believe that time was no longer a precious commodity. Once all he really had was time, but now… "The highlights of my life, perhaps. What do you want to know?"

"Uhhh. What were your parents like?"

"Oh." He'd been asked to recount his own life, and now he was being asked to sum up two more. No easy task! "My father's name was Maxwell, but everyone called him Mac. He was a businessman. That was his main focus, but his passion was for his family. Mac loved us, and when he wasn't distracted, he was attentive. Usually though his mind was elsewhere, even while he was sitting at the dinner table. I never held it against him, since he worked hard to provide for us."

"And your mom?"

"My mother?" Eric smiled, warmth slowly seeping into all the places where pain had invaded, soothing them temporarily. His vision blurred, and he saw instead a woman with bleached-blonde hair, ruby red lipstick, and eyes that always seemed to smile. "My mother was wonderful. The absolute best."

*

Rain pattered against the window, a brief flash of light making the drops of water glow. Then a pause before a grumble of thunder confirmed Eric's fear. Rain he could deal with, but not a full-blown storm. He pulled the sheets up to his neck, the ones with the Wild West theme that he'd begged his grandmother to buy. Sometimes he would climb beneath them, pretending he was a native chief in his tipi, which always made him feel courageous. He did so tonight, reminding himself that he was nearly seven years old. He was no baby! A storm shouldn't scare him anymore. He tried to ignore the distant rumbles, but a vicious blaze of lightning—so bright it illuminated his make-believe shelter—sent him running for the door.

Eric didn't feel too good about the dark hallway either. He hurried down it to the closed door of his parents' bedroom. Despite his fear, he paused there, listening to his mother's husky chuckle. She always laughed more when his father was in town. She seemed happy even when he wasn't home, but somehow less complete. He tried the knob and found it locked, the rattling noise causing the voices beyond to go quiet. After some murmuring and a rustle of blankets, the door cracked open.

"Baby boy," his mother said, a silky robe covering her slight frame. "What's the matter?"

"The thunder woke me up," he lied. In truth he had lain awake to see what sort of storm it would be.

"Thunder? I didn't hear any thunder."

Eric responded with pleading eyes.

Gina looked over her shoulder. Then she slipped into the hall. Just knowing he wouldn't have to make the return trip alone made him feel better. A gentle hand on his back guided him down the hall and to his room. Once there, Eric climbed into bed, but remained sitting up. He watched his mother go to the window, lightning briefly chasing away the shadows on her face. Then she closed the curtains and returned to his bed, turning on the side-table lamp. Eric had been tempted to do so himself, but his father was always strict about the electricity bill.

"You can leave it on tonight," his mother said, recognizing his relief. "Try to get some sleep now. Okay?"

"Wait! Can't you stay until I fall asleep? Or can I sleep with you and Dad?"

His mother smiled and sat on the edge of the bed, but he could already guess the answer to both questions. "You're too big. There's no room. I need to get sleep too, honey. What are you so scared of? That storm won't come inside. No one invited it."

"Please stay," he tried.

His mother took a deep breath. "You know what you can do? Count your angels. Do you remember how?"

Eric nodded. All he had to do was remember their names and they would come to protect him. Admittedly, this usually made him feel better, but not as much as his mother's presence did.

"Go on then," his mother urged.

"Michael," he said, starting with the easiest. "Um… Ralphie."

"Raphael," his mother corrected. "That's two. Who else?"

"Gabriel. I don't know any others."

"Uriel. You say it."

"Uriel."

"There. That's four, one for each bedpost. I think I can see them there now. Can you?"

"No. What do they look like?"

"Oh. Well, Michael has long wavy hair. He's very handsome. Raphael has a really big nose. The other angels always tease him about it."

"Really?"

"I'm afraid so. Gabriel has wings of gold, and Uriel has eyes like fire. No one would dare mess with any of them."

"What if they're late? How long does it take them to get here?"

"Only an instant. They're already here. You're safe now, honey." His mother kissed him on the forehead. "Good night."

"Wait! What if they leave while I'm sleeping?"

"That's not what angels do."

"How do you know?"

Gina stood, lifting the sheets so that he would lie down. Then she tucked in the covers around him all the way up to his neck. "In this life, you can either believe the good things, or you can believe the bad. It's really up to you, but I promise that one will make you happier than the other. So are you going to believe that the storm can hurt you, or are you going to believe that the angels will keep you safe?"

"The angels," Eric said.

"That's my little man. Should I leave the light on?"

Eric squinted at the nearest bedpost, trying to see the angel there. Maybe he just needed to have faith. "No," he said.

"You make me proud. Sweet dreams, darling."

Gina turned off the lamp and left the room. But Eric didn't close his eyes. He stared out the window, at the gap of black sky where the curtains didn't meet. He waited for the next flash of light, the next ominous rumble. When they finally came, he refused to be afraid of either.

* * * * *

Eric snorted, a sharp intake of breath that for once didn't hurt. His head still hummed, the morphine keeping him from feeling anything but good. He blinked a few times, then turned his head to see Tim still laboring behind his canvas.

"I must have dozed off. How long was I asleep?"

"Just a few minutes," Tim replied, leaning to the right to

consider him, eyes sparkling in amusement. "You weren't making a lot of sense."

"I wasn't?"

"No. At first, yeah, but then you started talking about Michael."

"*Michael*?" Eric asked in disbelief.

"Uh-huh. That was the guy, wasn't it? The one from your fraternity days?"

"Yes. I'm surprised you remember."

Tim grunted. "Kind of hard to forget that story. Besides, I hate his guts."

"Why?" Eric asked.

Tim shook his head and resumed painting. "You know why."

"He wasn't that bad. Not at the beginning, anyway. People change. Sometimes for the worse, sometimes for the better."

Tim was silent, probably wondering which category he fell into.

"He was nothing like you." Eric said.

More silence.

"Fine," Eric said with a sigh. "I'll let you judge for yourself. If you think you can handle more incoherent rambling."

"I'll never get tired of hearing you talk," Tim said, but he remained hidden behind the canvas, the terseness of his voice enough.

"Very well. Try not to fall off that stool, because for this story, we're going all the way back to my junior year in college."

"Let me guess, the eighties?"

Eric fanned himself, as if flattered. "If you weren't already in my will, you would be now. No, I'm afraid we'll have to travel all the way back to nineteen sixty-five."

*

The theater interior was dark, the rows of seats empty except for one other person. Not that audiences here were ever large. The little art house cinema had only one screen; its maximum capacity no more than fifty people. Still, only two of those seats being occupied was pretty bad. Eric had struggled to find any theater that was screening the film, and as weird as Austin was, even its laid-back population wanted nothing to do with the controversial content of *Inside Daisy Clover*. Only this one independent theater had been bold enough to show the film. Judging from the low turnout, the other theaters had been right to act so prudently.

Still, Ruth Gordon was a delight, and Robert Redford was hunky enough, although starring in this flop would probably mark the end of his blossoming career. Eric tried to lose himself in the plot, but he kept finding himself pulled out again by the other patron, who wouldn't stop clearing his throat. Eric shot a glare down the row to where the man was sitting, surprised when this was taken as an invitation. The man rose and moved down the aisle to sit closer, leaving only one empty seat between them. His expression was worried and framed by dark wavy hair, but he managed something close to a smile before speaking in a whisper.

"Hey."

"Hello," Eric said, not bothering to be quiet. When the other man grimaced, he added, "I don't think the others will mind us talking."

The man glanced around, then remembered they were alone. He chuckled and held out a hand. "I'm Michael."

Still confused by the situation, Eric accepted it and offered his own name.

"Some film, huh?" Michael said, jerking his head at the screen. "I thought it would be... racier."

"Me too," Eric said, considering the moving images briefly. "I can't think of any other film with a bisexual character. I mean, there are some where it's pretty obvious, but regardless, I thought this one would be more rewarding."

"Rewarding?" Michael said, but he flashed an understanding smile.

Eric stared, taken in by the even features, the strong jaw, and the skin partially hidden by a paisley dress shirt, the top button undone. "He's homosexual, you know," Eric said. "Robert Redford's character. In the book, he's not bisexual."

"You've read it? Is it... racier?"

Eric laughed. "A friend of mine read it, so I don't know. I always meant to pick it up, but seeing the movie seemed easier."

Michael looked him up and down, no doubt seeing the dark hair he had inherited from his father and the slight build that— sadly—a genetic roll of the dice had decided should come from his mother. Michael didn't seem too disappointed by what he observed, because he licked his lips and said, "Wanna get out of here?"

"To do what exactly?" Eric asked, even though he had a pretty good idea.

"To go somewhere more private. Unless you think—" Michael glanced around, then up at the projector room. "No, not a good idea."

Eric breathed in, caught a whiff of cologne, and nearly gave in to temptation. He had done such things before, loitering around the right public restrooms or getting into strangers' cars at remote parks. Those experiences had been fun. Thrilling! In the beginning anyway. While his hormones still tormented him every day, he found other parts of himself impossible to satisfy. Some itches couldn't be so easily scratched, but lately he had an idea of what he wanted, and it sounded even more daring than sex with another man.

"I'll let you take me to dinner," he said.

Michael's eyes widened. "What if someone sees us?"

Eric shook his head in amusement. "I know this is hard to believe, but men do sometimes dine together. Even normal ones."

This last statement proved that Eric understood exactly what was being suggested. He wasn't naïve enough to think he was just making a new friend. He was one of society's forbidden little secrets.

Michael still seemed hesitant, so Eric tried again. "I know a barbeque place not far away. It's terrible. We'll probably be the only ones there."

"Think so?"

"If not, I'm sure we'll find somewhere else."

"That a promise?"

"Sure."

Michael smiled. Then he stood. "Let's go."

*

The barbeque restaurant wasn't quite as empty as the theater had been. A family celebrated a birthday toward the front of the dining room, two tables pulled together to accommodate them. An older couple was seated by the window, eating in silence. Eric requested a table in the far back corner, where they were unlikely to be overheard. Despite this, Michael remained hesitant to speak until the waitress had delivered their drinks and food.

"I'm pretty sure we're in the clear," Eric teased.

"This is wild," Michael said in a whisper. When Eric made an impatient expression, he cleared his throat and spoke at a normal volume. "But it's kind of nice."

"Isn't it? We can actually get to know each other first. I think I've seen you around before. On campus."

Michael studied Eric's face. Then he blanched. "Oh geez!"

"What?"

"I *know* I've seen you before. I remember now. You're in Alpha Theta Sigma."

"Gosh, I feel like a celebrity. How did you know?"

"I was one of the failed pledges last year. If I'd recognized you sooner, I never would have… Oh man!"

Eric laughed. "Relax. I'm not going to rush back to the frat house and tell them I got cruised while at the movies."

"I guess not," Michael said. "You're so lucky! I really wanted to join."

"Well, maybe you should try again."

Michael perked up. "Think you can help me?"

Eric hesitated. "Yes, but not because of what's going to happen later. I don't want you to think you need to… Ahem."

"Oh I want to do that!" Michael said with a wild grin. "I was willing before I found out who you were."

The front of Eric's jeans felt tighter. Maybe they could skip dinner. But no, he knew that past the release of endorphins, he would be left feeling hollow. "Tell me more about yourself."

"What do you want to know?"

"The prerequisite question. The one everyone seems more concerned with than learning someone's name."

"What's your major?" Michael rolled his eyes, but he seemed amused. "I'm going to be a teacher."

"Really? You enjoy college so much you don't want to leave?"

"I'm aiming for a younger audience. I'm an only child, and I always wanted brothers and sisters. It's not like I'm going to have kids of my own because, uh… I don't think I can fake it. I tried once. With a girl. Total disaster."

"Couldn't manage a salute?"

"Exactly. I love kids though. Not in a creepy way!"

Eric felt annoyed by the implication, but he had heard it often enough. Gay people are after your children! Lock them up! Keep them safe! Ridiculous.

"I figure this is the best way of having that family," Michael continued. "I'll treat those kids like they're my own."

Eric resisted a sigh. "That's very endearing."

"Thanks. What about you?"

Eric chuckled nervously. "My plans aren't so noble. I'm a business major. Money makes the world go 'round."

"Oh." Michael looked somewhat disappointed, turning his attention to his food.

"My father provided a good life for us. My mother, sister, and I had everything we ever needed. When it came time to plan my future, I decided to follow in his footsteps. Hopefully I'll be able to do the same for my own family some day."

"Wife and kids?" Michael asked, tearing a barbequed rib off the rack.

"Maybe, although lately I've been wondering if there's another way."

Michael made a face as he chewed, showing he didn't understand.

"What if," Eric said carefully, "two men decided to live their lives together. Disregarding the obvious limitations. I agree that kids seem unlikely, but I like your solution. What if, at the end of a long day of teaching, you didn't return home to an empty house."

He expected the suggestion to cause bewilderment, but when this didn't happen, Eric concluded there was hope for them both. His elation was short-lived.

"It won't work," Michael said. He sucked reddish-orange sauce from his fingers, then shook his head as he wiped them on a napkin. "I knew a couple of guys who tried."

Eric leaned forward. "Really?"

"Yeah. Tom and Jerry, and no, I'm not joking. Those were their names. This was in San Marcos, my hometown. I don't know how long these two knew each other. I didn't notice them until our senior year of high school. All Tom and Jerry did was spend time together, but that's not so unusual. Guys are best friends with guys, but they were a little too... I don't know. They just looked at each other with this longing sometimes, like they couldn't help it. People noticed, and they talked, but it was just gossip. When prom came around, Tom and Jerry weren't dumb enough to go to the dance. They went out to Spring Lake and parked. At night. The only people who did that were there to make out. If that's all they had done, I doubt anyone would have noticed. Instead they had the car doors open, music playing on the radio. They stood beside the car, dressed in tuxedos, holding each other and slowly turning to the music. Their own little prom. Maybe they thought everyone else was at the dance, giving them privacy. They were wrong." Michael averted his eyes, jaw clenching. "They didn't see us coming."

"You were there?"

"Yeah. I didn't do anything to them personally. They got off pretty easy—a black eye and a bloody lip—because they were smart enough to get in the car and hightail it out of there."

"What happened then?"

"Jerry got a girlfriend quicker than you would believe. Tom stopped coming to school after that." Michael frowned. "I made sure to be more careful."

"We aren't in high school anymore."

"You think that matters?"

Eric swallowed. He had spoken to men caught in compromising situations, one who had scars to prove the violence he had suffered. "It's always a risk," he said, lowering his voice. "Every time we meet a stranger, even at the usual places, we never know if they are an undercover cop or someone who hates our kind. Even when you approached me in the theater, you couldn't have known. If you had gotten it wrong, and I *was* the sort of person to tell the fraternity, think how bad that might have turned out for you."

"I know," Michael said. "And that's why—"

"—that's why it's smarter to be in a relationship. To be with someone you can trust. If we keep taking risks with strangers in public, chances are it will end badly. Eventually. And maybe that relationship can become more than just physical. Have you ever longed for that?"

"Yes," Michael said, voice hoarse.

The waitress chose that moment to check on them, and Eric waited impatiently for her to go away. When she did, he leaned forward. "A small house. Just me and you."

"People would notice. Eating out together is one thing, but two adults—single men—who live in the same house? No way."

"Fine," Eric said, refusing to be discouraged. "Two hopelessly single men too wrapped up in their careers for romance, who live in a duplex."

Michael thought about this. "The same duplex?"

"Neighbors," Eric said. "Same house, different halves of the building. That wouldn't be so strange, and I doubt anyone would notice one man sneaking over in the middle of the night."

Michael's eyes lit up. "Maybe we could have some sort of secret passage. Or a simple door, like adjoining hotel rooms. That can't be too hard to install, right?"

"Whatever works for you. So is that a yes?"

Michael appeared hopeful. And interested. He shook his head and laughed. "You're too much! We don't even know each other!"

"Then let's change that." Eric motioned to the waitress. "Check, please!"

*

Michael had a last name (Schwartzer), a pair of pet mice he had smuggled into his dorm room (Howdy and Doody), and a fantastic dick (six and a half inches) that never seemed to tire. He had a passion for geography that was contagious—no matter how unlikely that sounded—and he tended to get quiet when he felt insecure. That's probably why the brothers of Alpha Theta Sigma had overlooked him during the previous pledge drive, but Eric rectified that situation during the next one. He didn't vouch for Michael, rather he coached him behind the scenes and gave him advance notice on the challenges he would face.

Michael rose to the occasion, took the solemn oath, and moved into the fraternity house as a fully-fledged brother. Eric had dreamed of sharing a room with him, but his current roommate said that he would never want to switch because he was "living with the nicest person ever." That's what being cordial had earned Eric. Michael's roommate was also unwilling to trade, out of laziness instead of loyalty. So the secrecy went on, their relationship squeezed into spaces both dark and solitary, which was thrilling but also tiresome. Eric yearned to be open, no matter how unrealistic that wish.

Reprieve came during the summer break. The nice weather didn't open any minds to the idea of one man loving another, but at least Eric had a safe place to go, and he intended to take Michael with him.

"When did you tell your parents?" Michael asked from the passenger seat. His right arm rested in the open window, a finger repeatedly tapping the side of the car like Morse code for "I'm nervous, I'm nervous, I'm so freaking nervous!"

"When I was eighteen and about to go to college. I figured if they reacted badly, at least I wouldn't be living there anymore. I told my best friend when I was fifteen."

"That you're queer?"

"Homosexual. And yes. I don't think she really understood. I told my sister the next year, part of me hoping she would blab to our parents. If they got upset, I could deny it. If they were okay with it, I would have admitted it. Unfortunately, she decided to keep my secret. Only time in her life she ever did!"

Eric laughed, but Michael continued his agitated tapping.

"How did they react?"

"My parents?" Eric breathed out. "Okay, I guess. My mom wanted me to talk to our minister, who was surprisingly relaxed about it all. He even winked at me, which I try not to think about."

"Was he hot?"

"No. Not that it would have mattered. He's a holy man!"

"Wouldn't have stopped me," Michael said, regaining some of his confidence. "So your mother was okay after that?"

"More or less."

"And your father?"

"The topic came up only once." Eric chuckled. "Naturally he found a way of working it into a business context. Apparently it's useful to have a wife and children, rapport and such, so he was concerned I wouldn't have that advantage and encouraged me to come up with alternative strategies."

"He sounds square," Michael said. "But also open-minded. I don't get it."

"He's a practical man. Religion and politics aren't for him."

"Lucky you. That's all my father talks about, usually over food. My shoulders still tense up whenever I sit at a dinner table. So uh… Do your parents know about me?"

"No," Eric said. "I was tempted, but I figure that's your choice. Do you want me to tell them?"

Michael was silent before he answered. "Not really. Not yet. I'd rather they get to know me first. Besides, I don't want them listening for any creaking bed springs. They aren't light sleepers, are they?"

"I'm sure we'll manage," Eric said. "We always do." He bit his bottom lip when he felt a hand sliding up his leg. "Stop! I'm trying to drive."

"Sorry."

"Are you?"

"Not really."

"Do you ever think about telling yours?"

Michael inhaled. "There's no point in telling my folks. Maybe I'm more like your dad than I care to admit because I'm always thinking of my career. An openly gay school teacher? It'll never happen, so I've made my peace with this being a permanent secret."

"Oh."

"Do you like me less because of it?"

"No," Eric said. "Of course not. You're simply being practical. I just wish the world was a different place."

"You and me both."

When they arrived at Eric's childhood home, Gina greeted them at the front door. She offered handshakes instead of hugs, probably assuming that Eric would feel embarrassed. He knew correcting her would only embarrass her instead, so he let it stand. She ushered them into the dining room where the table was already set with a pot of coffee, clean cups, and her famous apple crisp pie. Eric's father sat at one end of this spread. Mac set aside his newspaper and offered a nod and a handshake to Michael. He hugged Eric, not sharing his wife's reservations.

"Have a seat," he said. "I've been staring at that pie for the last hour and resisting temptation."

Eric noted that his father's breath smelled like alcohol. That wasn't so unusual. In the evenings and on weekends, drinking was his favorite way to unwind. Currently he was on a rum kick, which should complement the pie nicely.

"Do you drink coffee?" Gina asked, smiling at Michael while she casually assessed him. "If not, we have some tea the neighbors brought back from England."

"I'm fine," Michael said, smiling his appreciation. "The only thing I love more than coffee is pie."

They all sat, and soon Eric relaxed as he listened to his parents interview Michael. What was he studying, what occupations did his parents have, what did he think of the most recent game? Michael handled all of this with ease, only shooting the occasional confused glance at Eric when he didn't understand a reference. Then Eric would interject. By the time the coffee pot was empty and all but one slice of pie consumed, the vibe felt much more laidback.

"I'll help," Eric said when his mother rose to clear the table.

"Me too," Michael said, starting to rise.

"How much do teachers earn on average?" Mac asked.

Michael hesitated and sat again. "Depends on if it's private or public school."

"What's the difference?" Mac asked. "I can guess which pays more, but is it a significant amount?"

"You stay and relax," Eric said quietly when collecting Michael's plate.

He left his boyfriend and his father to talk business. Eric was happy to escape into the kitchen with his mother and help her with the dishes.

"He's very handsome," she said, as if this was cause for concern. Gina had her back to the sink, not interested in working.

"I think so too," Eric said, setting plates on the counter.

"Doesn't that make things difficult for you? Too tempting?"

Eric laughed. He couldn't help it. "Yes. He's very tempting."

Gina took in his happy expression. Then her face lit up. "He likes you in return! Is that true?"

Eric forced down his smile. "He's not as open as I am about these things, so please, don't broach the subject with him. Okay?"

"But you're happy?"

Eric nodded. "I'm very happy."

His mother leaned around him to look into the dining room. "I always knew you were surrounded by angels."

"What do you mean?"

"Michael! Have you forgotten their names?"

Eric laughed in surprise. "No. I haven't forgotten. I just didn't make the connection." Not to mention that Michael was no angel. Thank goodness for that.

"Wavy hair and everything, although I always pictured it being longer. And blond."

"You're a silly woman," Eric said warmly.

"I'm not. Do you love him?"

That took Eric by surprise. Their arrangement had been ongoing for six months, and while sex might have been their priority at first, what Eric really enjoyed now was when they walked around campus, hiked along the Colorado River, or just stayed up late at the fraternity house together. Always talking. Conversation after conversation, or in rare instances, a mutually content silence. Sex was a crucial part of their relationship, but their intimacy wasn't limited to the physical.

"Maybe I do," Eric confessed.

Now his mother hugged him. "I'm happy for you," she said. "Be careful out there, but I think this is a good thing."

"So do I."

Gina pressed a hand to his cheek. Then she sat at the small kitchen table, looking pale. "I'll help in a bit," she said. "I just need to catch my breath."

Eric supposed his news was shocking for her, no matter how positive. He filled the sink with soapy water and got started on the dishes, but when he looked over at his mother, her eyes were closed, her complexion waxy. "Are you okay?" he asked.

"Just getting old," Gina said, rising and grabbing a dish towel. "I'll be fine."

*

The beer-scented breath on Eric's ear was warm. He leaned toward the voice, needing time to digest the words that had been spoken.

"It's snowing outside?"

Michael nodded. "Uh-huh. Come see."

"You're full of it."

"Come see," Michael repeated.

Eric's eyes darted around the room. The Christmas party was in full swing, the actual holiday a week away. The frat house had been decorated with surprising finesse—under Eric's guidance, of course. This included garlands, wreaths, mistletoe, and strings of light. Stockings hung from the fireplace mantle, presents nestled beneath the tree. The wrapped boxes appeared innocent enough, but when opened later would reveal smutty gifts typically purchased by boys trapped in the bodies of men. Two kegs had already run dry and the night had just begun. Oh how he loved a good party!

His fraternity brothers were in high spirits, few of them without dates. Even Parker was in a good mood, having raised a beer bottle in Eric's direction earlier in the evening. Coming from him, that was almost a warm hug and a kiss on the cheek. Parker had hated Eric since their first fraternity mixer. They had invited over the girls of Beta Delta Omega, and Eric had singled out one he liked. Elegantly dressed, she had a contagious laugh and a sharpness to her stare that promised intelligence. Ideal company to while away the evening with. Parker had noticed her too, although probably for her long legs and ample breasts. They had both vied for her attention, and for whatever reason, Eric had won out. That had resulted in a stimulating conversation and a very charming slow dance. Plus endless glares from Parker, who didn't have any luck that night.

That had been two years ago. Eric couldn't even remember the woman's name. Jennifer? Janice? He doubted Parker could remember it either, but that hadn't stopped him from holding a grudge. Perhaps he had finally gotten past it. Or maybe he was just drunk. Eric was a little lightheaded himself, and from the way Michael swayed slightly, he wasn't alone.

"The gazebo," Michael said, flashing a grin. "Five minutes. I'll meet you out there. Don't let me freeze to death!"

Eric snorted. "Somehow, I think you'll survive the cold. One part in particular, anyway."

Michael leered in response, then checked the crowd for any witnesses before disappearing into it. Eric watched him go, breath short and heart pounding. Then he went to refill his beer, chugging it down for courage. He mingled, teasing his brothers or smiling at women as he slowly made his way toward the rear of the house. Then he slipped outside while patting his pockets, as if searching for a lighter and cigarettes, even though he didn't smoke.

He laughed at this little ruse as he moved away from the light of the house. Night had fallen, and the moon was high in the sky, illuminating the world in a cold white glow. Eric saw no sign of the snow Michael had promised, but it felt like winter regardless. Eric tugged at his shirt sleeves, wishing he had put on a jacket before coming outside. He hurried to the edge of the property, where a wooden gazebo overgrown with vines sat in one corner. A shadowy figure occupied it, and once certain it was Michael, Eric picked up his pace. Normally he avoided the gazebo, since in the warmer months it was filled with spiders and bugs, but hopefully they were all hibernating now. Or dead.

By the time Eric stepped onto the wooden floor, he was shivering. Only one available cure for that. He threw himself into Michael's arms, appreciating the warmth the larger man provided.

Michael chuckled in response. "It's not *that* cold. You're too skinny."

"Shut up and hold me, you brute!" This summoned another laugh, but Michael did as he was told, embracing Eric and squeezing him close. "At least we know we're alone. No one else is stupid enough to be out in this weather."

"Their loss," Michael murmured, one of his hands sliding down to grab a butt cheek.

"Hey!" Eric protested.

"Hey yourself. I'm horny. I've been saving it up."

Eric swallowed. "Really?"

"Yeah."

"For how long?"

"Three days."

Eric laughed. "And that's supposed to be impressive?"

"For me it's a new record! I should be in all the newspapers. On the front page."

"Now that I would like to see."

Michael's only response was a kiss that neither of them wanted to end. They were forced to break it off to check their surroundings. Once certain they were still alone, Michael started undoing his belt.

"Here?" Eric asked in disbelief.

"We've done it in places more public than this."

"But it's freezing!"

"Then we better hurry. Get on your knees."

Eric had his dignity, but in some situations it went flying out the window. Michael had his cock out, hard as steel and practically steaming with heat. Eric glanced around once more, then dropped to his knees, taking it in his mouth. He knew Michael would keep lookout, so Eric closed his eyes, enjoying the tactile sensation across the surface of his tongue, Michael's gentle moaning, the light musky scent in his nostrils... He was so lost in the moment that he gasped when Michael pulled him to his feet. He allowed his jeans to be undone, eager for the favor to be returned. Instead, Michael spun him around, exposing his butt to cold air.

"What are you doing?"

"I think you know," Michael said, slipping a finger between his cheeks.

"I'm pretty sure it's your turn to play that role."

Michael's breath was a huff against Eric's neck. "You keep track?"

"Yes. And we're not doing this here. We don't even have—"

A spitting noise cut him off, followed by something wet and warm poking his rectum.

"Don't," Eric said, but with less conviction.

"I'll be gentle. I promise."

Michael reached around and took hold of Eric, silencing any more protests with gentle caresses. Surely this was impossible, right? Taking him wasn't easy in the best of circumstances. Maybe being drunk helped, because Michael was making steady progress, and so far it didn't feel too bad. In fact, it was feeling pretty good.

"You okay?" Michael whispered.

"Yeah," Eric said. A wave of pleasure washed through him. "Just go easy."

"I will. I promise."

Eric stifled a moan. "I love you."

"I love you too," Michael said, placing a kiss on his neck.

Eric leaned forward, taking hold of the gazebo railing. He gripped it tightly, pain competing with the pleasure now, but he could handle this. For Michael.

"Dave!" a stranger's voice declared. "You were supposed to meet me by the rose bushes!"

The newcomer was female and intoxicated. Michael froze at the same time her unsteady footsteps stopped, the mutual intake of their breath audible, but none so much as the young woman. Her eyes darted over their bodies, unable to rest at any one spot as she struggled to make sense of what she was witnessing. Her gaze settled on Eric's face, which winced in response.

"Oh my god!" she whispered. "Oh, Jesus!" Then she spun around and ran toward the house.

"Wait!" Eric called out.

"Don't tell her to wait," Michael hissed, pushing him away. "Damn it! Pull up your pants."

Eric didn't need to be told. He quickly got himself in order, making eye contact with Michael repeatedly as he did likewise. They shared the same panic, both silent as they tried to figure out what to do.

"Let's just go," Eric said. "We'll hop the fence, grab the bus, and take it downtown."

"They'll notice we're gone!"

"So? Not everyone is here. Toby left an hour ago and John—"

"Is out of town. It won't be hard for them to figure out who's missing, and when they were last seen." Michael shook his head. "We need to get back inside."

"Seriously?"

"Yes! She was looking for someone. He could be out here, and even if he isn't, as soon as that girl starts blabbing, it's going to be a manhunt! I don't plan on being on this side of it."

"But she saw us! If we go back inside—"

"It's dark," Michael said. "She was drunk. She won't be able to single us out, unless of course we look like we just came back inside. Let's go. Around front so they won't catch us on the way in."

Eric nodded his agreement, despite feeling uneasy with the plan. They jogged around the house and, as quietly as possible, snuck in through the front door. The entryway was empty, the sound of the party continuing uninterrupted. Michael nodded to one wing of the house and headed for the kitchen. Splitting up made sense. Eric moved through dark rooms, touching his cheeks to make sure they weren't red with cold or embarrassment. They felt a little warm, but that could just as easily be from drinking.

He rejoined the party, grabbing a beer and seeking a conversation partner. His roommate. No! What if people thought *they* were the two who were screwing? Eric looked around, trying to find an available woman. Where were the wallflowers when you needed one? Then he spotted the girl who had caught them. She was talking with friends who wore slightly skeptical but clearly disgusted expressions. The girl kept looking around the room. Eric followed her gaze. Michael! His lover was jostling another guy, grinning like he didn't have a care in the world. Eric looked back at their witness, who shook her head and kept searching.

He should leave. He knew he should. Michael was safe, so if he went now, maybe no one would believe such a crazy story. Eric wouldn't hide. He could return to his room, pretend to be passed out. All he needed was someone to vouch for him should his absence be noticed. Eric walked over to his roommate, poking him in the chest with a finger and making sure to slur his words. "I'm... sofuckindrunk. Imma go lay down."

"Maybe you should," came the amused response.

"WHAT?"

The voice boomed through the room; every head turned.

Rick, the president of the fraternity, was attracting all the attention. He was an okay guy. Usually. He could be a hothead when drinking, but that might work in Eric's favor. Currently Rick was shaking his head at their witness and her small group of friends.

"Bullshit!" Rick declared. "No way!"

"I'm not a liar!" the girl said, offended by his disbelief. "I saw it with my own—" She turned to look through the crowd again, her luck instantaneous. "Him!"

She pointed, and people moved out of the path of her accusing finger. Eric wished he had been smart enough to do the same. Instead he stood there, face burning, mouth hanging open. He felt his head shake in denial, which was stupid because the accusation hadn't even been made yet. He should have looked puzzled. Instead, even without seeing himself, he knew how hopelessly guilty he must have appeared.

Rick's brow furrowed, his own head shaking, not wanting to believe the truth. He was joined by someone else. Eric's stomach sank at the sight of him.

"What's going on?" Parker asked.

The girl started repeating her story. Eric was unable to hear the details until someone decided to kill the music.

"—in his butt. Like he was pretending to be a woman."

Rick scowled. Parker's expression was much more gleeful. Eric marched over, but he had done so too late. He tried to make himself indignant, considered feigning ignorance, and remembered he was supposed to be drunk. He had no solid strategy. He was a mess, and Parker seemed to sense his weakness.

"What did you do, Eric? Were you out there fucking some poor guy?"

"No," the girl said, "he was the one... um."

"Oh!" Parker laughed. "Of course. *You* were getting fucked! How long have you been a queer, Eric?"

"I'm..." The denial caught in Eric's throat, unwilling to

manifest. "You don't know what you're talking about. *I* don't know what you're talking about!"

"Is this true?" Rick asked, still scowling but willing to believe otherwise.

"I don't know what she thinks she saw—"

"She saw you getting fucked," Parker said, projecting for the entire room now. "She saw a filthy queer getting fucked up the ass."

"She's wrong!" Morally wrong, at least. She shouldn't have called him out on this.

"Oh really?" Parker swept his gaze across a gathering audience. "Did anyone see Eric go outside recently?"

The crowd murmured. Then someone called out that yes, he had been seen going out, probably just to keep the drama going.

Eric snorted. "I can't step outside my own fraternity for some fresh air?"

"Not to have faggot sex, you can't!"

"That's enough," Rick grumbled. "We have a reputation to uphold."

"It's that reputation I'm trying to protect!" Parker declared, turning to gather support from the crowd. He got it. Heads were nodding, wanting more.

"It's her word against mine," Eric snapped. "You're really going to believe an outsider over your own brother? Have you forgotten the pledge you took?"

Parker glared. Then he got another idea. "I know how we can settle this. If Eric isn't queer, then surely he's slept with one of you ladies before. Right? Speak up! Don't be shy. If you've slept with Eric Conroy before, step forward."

Everyone remained where they were. Even if he had slept with someone here, no self-respecting woman was going to admit it publically. Especially not now. When your reputation got rolled in the mud, no one wanted to risk getting dirty by association.

"No?" Parker said. "Okay then. If any of your *friends* have slept with Eric, then speak up now. Even if they aren't here. Hell, if you've ever heard of Eric sleeping with *any* woman anywhere on this entire planet, please tell us about it!"

The silence was thick. Eric only needed one person to lie on his behalf, to spare him this humiliation, but he knew it wouldn't happen. He could feel his own doom like lead lining his stomach.

"I don't like this," Rick said, but he was glaring at Eric now. "I don't remember seeing you flirting with a woman before."

"That's not entirely true," Eric said. "Is it, Parker?"

Parker bared his teeth. "Who were you with? Who's your queer little friend? Let's hear what he has to say about this!"

Eric clenched his jaw. His instinct was to turn to the crowd, seek out Michael for support, but he knew how damning that would be. "I don't know what you're talking about."

"Who was he with?" Parker asked, turning to the witness.

"I'm not sure," the girl said. "I think I saw him earlier. Um…"

She started searching the crowd again. This time she would get it right. The intensity of the situation had sobered up Eric. No doubt it had done the same for her. She would look again, maybe recognizing some trace of fear on Michael's face, and that would give him away.

"He's gone," Eric blurted out.

Rick narrowed his eyes. "What?"

"He's gone. I met him out back. I wasn't stupid enough to invite him to the party."

"No," Parker replied, grin victorious, "but you were stupid enough to get caught."

"I guess so," Eric said.

"Get out." Rick said this so quietly that it was hard to be sure he spoke at all.

"I'm still your brother—" Eric tried.

"Get out!" Rick growled. "This is not who we are." He clenched his jaw, then addressed the crowd. "He does *not* represent Alpha Theta Sigma. We are not… We aren't faggots!"

The silence in the room was complete. Parker's lips curled back as he regarded Eric with disgust. The crowd mirrored his expression. Mostly. Eric also saw fear, and sympathy, but too few and meek to stand with him.

"You heard what Rick said." Parker grabbed Eric's shoulder. "Leave!"

"Get your hands off me!" Eric said, knocking his arm away.

Parker brought it around again, a hand cracking him across the face.

Eric wanted to fight back, but he was outnumbered and Rick was past the boiling point.

"GET OUT!" the chapter president roared.

Eric clenched his jaw. Then he turned and took one step before he was shoved. He shot a glare over his shoulder and was pushed again. He felt more hands than just Parker's as he stumbled forward. He fell once, trying to ignore the slurs being hissed from all directions. Someone tried to kick him while he was down, but Eric was moving faster now, refusing to run but wanting to. His anger was gone. He felt afraid. Vulnerable. He wanted Michael, wanted to hear his voice shout in protest, wanted to feel those arms wrap around him protectively and guide him to safety. Eric wouldn't allow himself to look. He couldn't. At least one of them was safe.

He collided with the door when someone decided to shove him against it. He scrambled to get it open, but he wasn't moving fast enough for them. Hands grabbed Eric, lifting him carelessly. He was horizontal to the ground, his nose just inches from the stone walkway. They were going to throw him in the street. Like a drunk in a movie. Like Fred Flintstone tossing Dino outside the front door. Eric almost found it comical. Then he recognized the shoes to one side of his head. They were Michael's.

"Close enough," a voice said. Parker, of course. "Ready? One, two—"

Eric was swung backward, then forward. He was thrown, feeling relief at no longer being held captive, even as he sailed into the air. Then he hit the concrete sidewalk and rolled off the curb. He lay still, fearing what might come next. Drunken laughter receded into the distance. Eric raised his head, skin stinging as he pushed himself upright and watched silhouettes disappear back into the house. The last one he saw go was the most familiar, but Michael didn't even turn around to make sure he was all right. Not even when he closed the door.

*

Eric stood in front of another door. This one opened onto a sanctuary. He wouldn't be thrown out of here because of who he loved. Or who he had been stupid enough to think he loved. He refused to believe it now. If their love had been real, Michael never would have stood silently by while Eric was tormented. Even if that's what Eric had wanted. And he certainly wouldn't have helped carry him to the sidewalk and—

Eric rubbed his bruised elbow, still unable to move it freely, the skin on his forearm scraped raw. Then he forced down the tears. He'd done enough crying on the way over. He wouldn't let this ruin Christmas for his family. This wasn't their burden to bear. He fumbled with the key, trying to get it in the lock. The door swung open. His father stood there, baseball bat in hand.

"Easy now!" Eric said, backing up a step.

"You can never be too safe." Mac peered at him. "Looks like someone already took a bat to you. What happened?"

Eric touched his swollen cheek self-consciously. "You know how clumsy I am."

"Been drinking?"

"Yeah. Got attacked by a tree. Never saw it coming."

His father stood aside so he could enter. "We weren't expecting you until tomorrow."

"I know."

"No bags?"

"They're in the car," Eric lied. In truth, he had no idea how he was going to get his possessions out of the fraternity house, including the presents he'd bought for his family. He didn't want to return there. Not ever. "Where's Mom?"

"She's sleeping."

Eric checked the glass clock on the living room shelf. "It's only nine-thirty! She's a night owl!"

Mac didn't reply. Instead he turned and walked into the kitchen. Eric followed him and sat down at the table when he realized his father intended to make them both coffee. He didn't feel like he needed to sober up, but having a warm mug in his hands sounded heavenly. He watched his father work, noticing how his shoulders were slumped. The kitchen was messier than usual. Come to think of it, the living room hadn't looked very neat either. After pouring the coffee into two mugs, Mac opened a cabinet and took out a glass bottle. He turned and held it up in offering.

Eric nodded. His father laced their coffee with whatever it was, then brought the two mugs to the table and sat.

"Thanks," Eric said.

Mac nodded, looking him over again. "Must have been some tree."

"I'll live."

"Your mother hasn't been feeling well," Mac said quickly and with finality, as if it was the end of the conversation.

That's not how Eric saw it. "She's sick?"

"That's what I said."

"For how long? Is it serious? When I called three weeks ago, you said she couldn't talk. Was she—"

"That's enough," Mac said, waving a hand. "Let it go."

Eric shook his head, not understanding. "I'm concerned! Of course I'm not going to let it go! Can I see her? When did she go to sleep?"

"Around six."

Eric stared. That wasn't normal! "What's wrong with her? A flu? Something worse?"

Mac took a swig of his coffee, grimacing at the taste or the heat. "She didn't want you and your sister knowing. Not until after the holidays."

"What? Tell me!"

Mac shook his head. Then he spoke.

"Cancer."

* * * * *

Eric swallowed, the pain more than physical this time. Not because of what had happened at the fraternity so many years ago. Those events he had set behind him. But watching his mother's battle with cancer, seeing her suffer, and now experiencing first-hand what she had gone through...

"I would have fucking killed them."

Eric turned his head. Tim was glowering, paint brush trapped in one fist. Then the fingers unclenched, his anger turning inward.

"Not that I can talk," Tim continued. "I shouldn't judge because I'm just as bad."

"Nonsense," Eric said warmly. "You were younger than them. You might have been too closeted to make your love for Ben public, but you wouldn't have stood by and let others hurt him. And you certainly wouldn't have participated."

"No," Tim said grudgingly. "I wouldn't have. There was this one time, after we had split up, that Benjamin started smarting off to the biggest guy in school. Ben was like Scrappy Doo. Remember him? The little cartoon dog always trying to pick a fight? Well, that day he got one, and I hate to think what would have happened if—"

Eric started coughing, interrupting the story. Tim wasn't

offended. His face showed pure concern as he set aside the paint brush and sat on the bed's edge.

"I'm okay," Eric managed. He drank from the glass again, resisting the urge to ask for more morphine. Not because he was worried about getting addicted. He was dying. What did it matter if he ended his days as a junkie? Except it did, because he didn't want Tim to think less of him. "What happened? Did Ben get hurt?"

"A little," Tim said. "He did all right considering the monster he was up against. I had his back, but I'm no hero because I should have always been there for him. And I wish I could have been there for you. I would have beaten your fraternity brothers to a pulp. Wait, are any of them still alive? Maybe it's time for some payback!"

Eric chuckled. "They aren't worth your time. Besides, if it wasn't for that dark night, I wouldn't have met the love of my life."

"Gabriel?"

"Yes."

Tim's brow creased. "He's not on my good list either."

"He should be," Eric said, patting Tim's hand. "And if it wasn't for Alpha Theta Sigma, I never would have met you. They sent you to my door as a joke, asking for pledge money. For all their ill intent, that fraternity is responsible for sending two wonderful men my way."

Tim's eyes searched his. "I think I might be jealous of Gabriel."

"You're trying to flatter me. Regardless, I don't want you to think poorly of him. Chances are you'll be meeting him soon. When you do, I'd like you to understand how much he helped me. Between losing my first boyfriend, getting thrown out of a fraternity—literally, and learning that my mother was seriously ill, I wasn't a very happy person. But then, I met him…"

*

Eric dug into the pockets of his jeans for a third time, certain two dollars had been there when he entered the grocery store. He had found one of the bills, but the other had disappeared before he could spend it. The cashier cleared her throat, then looked meaningfully at the line behind him. Eric did the same and met a number of stares. One was more intense than the others. A guy in a brown suit just a shade darker than his skin. His black hair was short and neat, matching the rest of his tidy appearance. He was close enough that Eric could smell his aftershave. The man might have been a lawyer if not for his youth. He was around Eric's age, which would explain why his lips were downturned. No doubt he—like everyone—had heard what had happened. Over the last month, the stares and comments had only increased.

"Sir?"

Eric looked back at the cashier and then his items. A gallon of milk, a pack of gum, and a newspaper. He was only ten cents short. Normally this wouldn't be an issue. His mother always made sure that he had enough money, but she wasn't doing well, and his father had more pressing concerns. Something would have to go. The milk they needed at home. As for the other two, he debated between having good breath and being entertained.

"I guess I don't need this."

He picked up the gum so he could return it to the rack. The young man was partially in his way, but he didn't move. Instead he held out his hand for it.

Eric stared, then placed the pack of gum in his palm. "Thanks."

Cheeks burning for reasons he wasn't sure of, he took his measly five cents in change, grabbed the milk and newspaper, and hurried outside. He had reached the end of the block when a voice called out.

"Hey! Excuse me."

Eric turned around, seeing the young man from the store. He took in the perfectly straight tie and polished shoes, and wondered if he was about to receive a pamphlet on religion. He checked the man's hands, finding only a folded newspaper in one.

The man gestured at him with it. "You're that guy, aren't you? The one who got kicked out of the fraternity."

Eric rolled his eyes. "Yes, but I'm not signing autographs today. Goodbye." He turned to leave, tensing when he felt a hand on his shoulder.

"I'm on your side."

The words were friendly. The man wasn't interested in mocking him, so what did he want? A casual encounter? Eric turned around, looking at the deliciously thick lips, the chestnut brown eyes, and the slim build beneath the pristine suit. Eric's body started to react, but his heart got in the way. He still missed Michael. Eric didn't want him back. He just wished he could turn back time to when everything had been good between them.

"I'm not interested," he said. "Sorry."

The man looked amused. Then he smiled. "I'm no stranger to rejection, but normally it comes after I've made an offer. All I'm interested in is conversation. I'm Gabriel Porter. Have you heard of me?"

"Eric Conroy," he replied, "and no."

Gabriel sucked in air and shook his head. "Today has not been good for my self-esteem. Tell me, Eric, are you political?"

"You make it sound contagious."

Gabriel's gaze was intense. "It can be. I saw Dr. Martin Luther King Jr. speaking last year, and it changed my life. Before that day, I was sleepwalking through the world. I accepted what black people go through as an immutable fact. The world was built in a certain way, and the idea of taking it apart and rebuilding it hadn't even occurred to me. Not anymore. If you don't like the house you live in, then it's time to renovate."

"Or you can move," Eric said. "That's what I've been thinking about."

"You can't outrun hate," Gabriel said with a shake of his head. "It won't even bother chasing after you because hate will already be waiting at your destination. There's no escaping it."

"Cheerful. It's been nice talking to you, but I have to go."

"Are you ashamed of being queer?"

Eric clenched his jaw. "I don't like that word."

"Why not? I'm black and I'm queer. No sense in denying it. That's who I am, and I can't change either fact, so that leaves me with one option: I can change other people's minds. Make it so they don't hate me."

"That's simply who they are," Eric said. "They can't be changed any more than you or I can."

"People aren't born that way. A baby doesn't hate someone else because of how they look or who they love. All that bullshit comes later, taught to them by ignorant adults. Those lessons can be unlearned. All it takes is effort from people willing to stand and fight." Gabriel cocked his head. "Or you can run away and pretend to be someone you're not."

"I'm not ashamed!" Eric snarled.

"Do your parents know?"

"Yes!"

"And your friends?"

The fight left Eric. "I don't have many left. Or any, in fact."

Gabriel nodded. "Then it sounds like you could use some new ones. There's a book club I'm a member of. We meet every Wednesday at the Lukewarm Café. Five in the afternoon. It would be good to see you there."

"What are you reading at the moment?"

"Everything." Gabriel smiled. "We read anything we can get our hands on, then meet up and share that information with each other. We're staying informed. It's intense. I think you'll like it."

"What makes you say that?"

"Because you chose the newspaper instead of the gum. Speaking of which—"

Gabriel reached into his pocket and pulled out a small rectangle—the pack of gum Eric hadn't been able to afford. Then he offered it. "I'm sorry about what happened to you. I really am."

"Thanks," Eric said as he accepted the gift. "I didn't mean to be so standoffish with you. It's just been really hard lately and—"

"I get it," Gabriel said. "Trust me, I really do. Will we see each other again?"

Eric felt short of breath, so he simply nodded.

Gabriel did the same. Then he turned and walked away.

*

The Lukewarm Café was aptly named, because that's exactly how Eric felt about the place. The floors were sticky, the furniture old, mismatched, and painted in a rainbow of colors. Eric sort of liked the thriving green plants crowding the front window. The patrons he was less sure about. He saw a number of tie-dye T-shirts and guys with long hair. In addition to the fragrance of coffee was the pungent smell of body odor with a hint of marijuana. In one corner, a man played guitar while a woman sang, but not on stage. The guitarist sat in a chair, the singer on the table.

Eric found this bohemian lifestyle appealing, but knew he would never embrace it. He was much too organized and fond of schedules and grooming. He had assumed Gabriel was the same way and wondered if being sent here was a joke since the man was nowhere in sight.

No one offered to seat him, so Eric walked up to the counter. A woman stood behind it, tongue sticking out one corner of her mouth as she worked on a charcoal etching. The wooden counter top was her canvas.

"Excuse me," he said. "I'm looking for a... book club?"

"The enlightened," the woman said, not even glancing at him. "You have to travel to a higher plane to find them."

Eric considered her, trying to decide if she was high or insane. Then he turned slowly, scanned the room, and noticed the stairs on the far wall. No doubt they led to a higher plane. He nearly left the café, not in the mood for further riddles, but the idea of seeing Gabriel again encouraged him to venture up.

To his relief, the place was much quieter upstairs. Dirtier and less organized too. The room was dusty and grey, nothing having been painted in bright colors, but that made the people stand out more. They sat in a circle, and like the chairs downstairs, none of them seemed to match. Gabriel was there, dressed in the same suit but with a pale green shirt. Next to him sat an Asian man in a tennis outfit. An older woman, eyes crinkled in amusement, helped fill the circle, as did a hippie with a bushy beard that covered most of his torso. All eyes were on a young woman who was speaking in rapid-fire French, gesturing so emphatically with her cigarette that she dropped it.

"She says," Gabriel said, extending a foot to stamp it out, "that the French Resistance movement during World War II used a number of tactics we could employ today. Some of them sound too violent but— Ah! Here he is! I told you all about Eric?"

Five heads turned to consider him, and Eric felt himself being judged. Or maybe they were just trying to figure out if he fit their group, which would probably mean that he needed to not fit in at all. Currently he was wearing jeans and a T-shirt, both tight enough to show off his figure, just in case Gabriel felt like looking.

"Hi," he managed.

All eyes returned to Gabriel, seeking an explanation. "Okay, maybe I forgot to mention him. This is Eric. He's queer. *Homosexuel*," he added with a French accent. "Please, have a seat."

Eric sat, still feeling uneasy. There wasn't a book in sight. "So," he said. "What were we discussing?"

"How to stick it to the man!" the hippie said.

"How to initiate progress," Gabriel amended. "Changing minds and thus changing the world. Like we talked about the other day."

Eric tensed. "This isn't a reading group at all. You're with the—what's it called? Students for a Democratic Society."

"Ha!" The French woman said. "They are too *conservateur*."

"Conservative," Gabriel clarified. "The SDS is too right-wing for us."

Eric's jaw dropped. "The people protesting the war, the ones who burn their draft cards, are too conservative?"

"They don't welcome women's liberation," said the older woman. "They only concern themselves with the problems of men."

"Not including queer men," Gabriel said, "and their understanding of black civil rights is flawed. No, the focus of the SDS is much too narrow. What we're trying to accomplish here incorporates *everyone* who is marginalized. If we can band together into a single force—"

Eric stood. "Best of luck, but this isn't for me. I'm not an anarchist."

"Nor am I." Gabriel addressed the group. "Keep exchanging ideas. I'd like to talk to Eric alone. If that's okay?"

This last sentence was addressed to him. Eric nodded. Gabriel rose and led him to a back corner, where he brushed a thin layer of dust off two wooden chairs. Then he offered one.

"I'm sorry," he said. "I know the surroundings aren't great, but we needed a safe environment." He sighed. "You know that Martin Luther King lecture I went to? I was scared. So scared I was shaking. Malcolm X had recently been assassinated, and I was fascinated that ideas could be worth killing over. I don't agree with such methods of course, but Malcolm's death triggered my curiosity. What sort of knowledge could be so upsetting, so powerful, to drive other people to murder? I went into that Martin Luther King lecture knowing I would be changed, but also fearing for my life. I can only assume that you feel equally unsettled now. Here we are, a group of people casually talking about revolutionizing the world as we know it. But the old regime—"

"I keep thinking about my father," Eric interrupted. "If you want to know the truth, that's my problem here. He couldn't be a bigger part of—I guess you would call it the establishment. He pays his taxes, votes Republican, buys only American products. You would probably hate him, but he's always provided for my family. When he found out about me, he could have pushed me away or treated me differently, but he didn't. And now my mother—his wife—might be dying, and he's forced to take care of her in a way he's not used to. He's learning how to nurture, just for her. So when you talk about fighting against people like him, it feels wrong. It *is* wrong."

Gabriel's tone was gentle when he responded. "No one is talking about putting the old regime behind bars or punishing them in any way. If anything, your father is proof that people can change for the better. He obviously loves you and your mother very much. He made his feelings for you a priority over his political affiliations. But many people don't have a queer son or a sick wife who needs them. Without love to change their opinion—or to challenge their beliefs—they remain set in their ways. More often than not, that means spreading hate and fear, or infringing on the personal freedom of others. That's what we're trying to solve here. How do we reach out and help people on either side of that situation?"

Eric sighed. "What do you want from me? Why did you invite me here?"

"I want to hear your story."

"My life hasn't been interesting. I guess besides— Oh. You want to know what happened at the fraternity."

"Yes. I'm not interested in gossip or rumor. I want to hear your side of the story. The truth." Gabriel gestured to one of the chairs again. "Please. Sit down."

Eric sat, and Gabriel pulled his chair around so they were facing each other. Then Eric started talking. First about Michael, but then he backtracked to how he had struggled with his sexuality in his youth, and how he had fought to accept himself. He spoke about his dreams, his wish for a normal relationship. A marriage like his parents had. This led again to Michael and the ugly way their relationship ended. Despite the pain this summoned, Eric found that the words came easily. He had needed someone to talk to about it. He hadn't told his parents, wanting to spare them from such unpleasantness. They didn't know he had been kicked out of the fraternity. He had used his mother's illness as an excuse to move back home, promising to help take care of her. He felt doubly guilty now because most of the time he couldn't face her condition. He found himself talking about that too. Eric had to force himself to stop speaking before even more of his feelings came pouring out.

"I'm sorry," Gabriel said, leaning forward to clamp a hand on Eric's shoulder. "You don't have to face this alone. I want you to know that. You have a friend. If you want me, I'll be there."

"Thank you," Eric said, his voice strained.

Gabriel patted him, then leaned back. "I think more people should hear your story. I write for *The Daily Texan*."

"The student newspaper?" Eric said in disbelief.

"Yes, and before you say no, just listen. People already know about you. The secret is out, but all they hear are the rumors and lies. You got caught screwing at a party and were thrown out of the fraternity. We both know there's more to it than that, but nobody else will unless we tell them. I can publish your side of events and set the record straight."

Eric swallowed, feeling disappointed. "So that's what this is really about. You're just chasing down a story."

Gabriel shook his head adamantly. "I meant what I said. I want to be your friend, no matter what your answer is. If you told me no right now, it wouldn't change a thing."

"No."

Gabriel shrugged. "Okay. No problem. I respect your decision."

Eric took a deep breath. "Fine. You can write the story, but I want to read it before you hand it in or whatever."

"That goes against the rules," Gabriel said, "but considering that we're friends now, you've got a deal." He was classy enough not to grin in delight. Instead he remained somber. "I know what it's like to lose a parent. I hope you don't experience that anytime soon. I also know what it's like to love another man, and to fear losing him."

"You do?"

"Yes." Gabriel looked back at the group, at the Asian guy in particular. "Robby and I celebrate our one year anniversary next week."

"Oh. Great."

Gabriel raised an eyebrow. "I thought you weren't interested?"

Eric blushed. Then he laughed. "I *might* have given you a chance. Maybe. Now we'll never know."

Gabriel smiled. "I'm flattered, but would you really have wanted to move on so quickly?"

"No," Eric admitted. "I just hate the idea of being alone."

Gabriel's eyes darted over him. Then he winked. "Something tells me you won't have to worry about that for long."

Eric sighed. "I hope you're right."

*

"We need to talk."

The phrase was enough for Eric to know who had snuck up behind him at night in the campus parking lot. *We need to talk* summed up Gabriel completely, because that's all he seemed to do—talk about causes and perspectives and tactics and hope. The man had an intellect matched only by his drive, and as much as Eric admired this attribute, it had also put an end to any fledgling crush. He couldn't imagine Gabriel silencing his mind long enough to allow his body to take control. In fact, he couldn't imagine Gabriel having sex at all. Maybe he just talked during the entire process. *I'm invading you now just like the Romans did Britain, only to meet guerilla resistance from Welsh tribes, which draws interesting parallels to the current war in Vietnam. Are you close? I'm close.*

"Something wrong?" said the real Gabriel, who wore his patented determined expression.

"Just thinking about the war," Eric said. "What's up?"

"Our article won't be appearing in *The Daily Texan*. The editors rejected it."

"Oh," Eric said. And then, in the name of solidarity, he added, "Those bastards."

"I'm sorry."

"It's not your fault."

"This your car?" Gabriel nodded to the Volkswagen Beetle they were standing beside. More than ten years old now, the vehicle was rust-colored, but not because of the paint. Once it had been white. Probably. Eric had never seen it new, but after working a summer job before he started college, it was all he had been able to afford.

Eric held up the keys. "She's all mine."

"Maybe you should invest in some Turtle Wax." Gabriel pointed. "That one's mine."

The vehicle was impossible to miss. Not only was it ostentatious with a white convertible top and aqua paint, but the wicked tailfins made it appear like it belonged in the sea. Eric looked back and forth between the car and its supposed owner. Then he laughed. "Almost had me there."

"What?" Gabriel said with a straight face. "You think I can't afford it?"

"That's not…" Eric shook his head. "I just pictured you having an environmentally friendly bike, or maybe a van equipped with megaphones on the roof."

"Oh, I get it." Gabriel made a face. "I'm more than just my politics, you know."

Eric grinned. "Prove it."

Gabriel matched his expression. "Okay. Let's go for a drive."

A few minutes later, Eric was gripping the seat edges in fear. "Slow down!"

"This *is* slow," Gabriel said, peering into the rearview mirror. "Just wait until we leave the city limits."

He slowed down anyway, which was good since Eric no longer needed to press himself against the seat back. "What kind of coffin is this exactly?"

"A '57 Chevy. I love this car. Made a lot of memories in it."

"Such as?"

"The first time I ever messed around with another man. Tobias Fowler, my best friend's cousin. He was visiting from Colorado and couldn't take his eyes off me. We were sitting in this car when he said he'd never seen a black guy's…"

"What?" Eric pressed, despite knowing the answer.

"Credentials."

Eric laughed. "So you showed him?"

"I had never seen a white guy's, so it made sense to ah, compare notes."

Eric resisted the urge to adjust himself. "And then?"

"Use your imagination."

"I will. Later. When I'm alone."

Gabriel chuckled, then shot him a glance. "What about you?"

"My first?" Eric looked out the window as they crossed over the Colorado River, the Tom Miller Dam in the distance. "Some guy in a park. To be honest I was terrified we'd get caught, and everything was rushed. I didn't really enjoy it."

Gabriel grunted. "Someday it won't be like this. We'll fall in love and ask our crushes to the homecoming dance, just like anyone else. We won't be fumbling around in the bushes anymore. Not on the first date, anyway." He turned down the heater. "Feeling cozy?"

"Yes. It's a nice car."

"It belonged to my father," Gabriel said. "I was never into cars like he was, or had his special touch when it came to machines. He was a great mechanic. The whole neighborhood would come to him because they knew he wouldn't overcharge like the repair shops. People started bringing by their vacuum cleaners, lawn mowers—just about anything with a motor inside." He laughed, but the sound was tinged with sorrow.

"What happened to him?"

Gabriel frowned, the vehicle coming to a stop. He didn't answer until they had made a right turn. "Uncle Sam needed him to fix his tanks and planes." He clucked his tongue and shook his head. "I'm being dramatic. My father mostly worked on Jeeps, but also a few helicopters. He wasn't there to fight. He went through the same training as everyone else, but he wasn't meant to be in the line of fire. He wasn't a soldier. Not really. He just fixed things."

"I'm sorry," Eric said.

Gabriel remained grim. "I won't go. When we graduate and this stupid war is still raging, I'll burn my draft card. I refuse to put my mother through losing both a husband *and* a son."

"For what it's worth, I'm not fond of the draft either. It should be a choice."

Gabriel didn't respond. He was hunched forward, looking out the windshield. The roads here curved continuously, travelling upward as they did. When they rounded a corner, the Austin skyline sparkled in the distance. Gabriel pulled off the road, parking the car beneath a tree.

"If you brought me out here for some necking…" Eric said, but he couldn't finish the sentence because he wasn't against the idea.

"Robby would kill me," Gabriel said. "He may look small, but that tennis grip of his is vicious."

"You speak from experience?"

Gabriel nodded, turning on the radio and adjusting the dial. Through the static they heard snippets of ethereal songs and voices until one came out loud and clear. A Spanish guitar was plucking out a happy little tune.

"*Concrete and Clay,*" Gabriel said. "I love this song."

Another surprise, since the lyrics were hopelessly romantic and not at all realistic.

"Dance with me."

Eric's head whipped around at the invitation. Gabriel was smiling, one hand on the handle, ready to open the door. He thought about Michael's ill-fated couple who had been caught doing something similar. Then Eric imagined an Asian guy attacking him with a tennis racket. "What about Robby?"

"He never dances with me."

That's all the convincing he needed. Eric opened his own door, the volume of the song increasing as Gabriel cranked it up before he too stepped out. They met in front of the car, illuminated by headlights. The rhythm was meandering. It wasn't the sort of song that would make them break a sweat. Instead they rolled their shoulders and shook their hips, laughing as they moved in front of each other, coming close but never quite touching. Sadly, it wasn't a very long song, but they were in luck. No annoying DJ interrupted with an announcement. One song ended and then the next began. *Do You Wanna Dance* by the Beach Boys. This was a song they could really move to! The lyrics were disturbingly appropriate, the questions the song posed hitting close to home. Two people could do more together than just dance, and if it weren't for a certain tennis player, Eric would risk making a few a suggestions.

When the song ended, he stopped, but not because he was winded. Eric just didn't see the point in getting worked up any more than he already was. Gabriel didn't complain. He was all shining white teeth as he returned to the car to lower the radio's volume. Something caught his eye on his way, and he gestured for Eric to join him. "Get a load of that!"

Eric glanced up the hill, seeing first the glowing windows and the edge of a roof that had caught the moonlight. Even in the limited illumination, he could see that the house was huge and perched on the edge of a hill like an ancient fortress.

"Now that's a home!" Gabriel declared.

"I don't know," Eric replied. "Seems a little decadent."

Gabriel continued to stare with shining eyes. "Someday I'll own it. I won't be alone though."

"Robby?"

"My mother."

Eric laughed. "You've seen *Psycho*, right?"

"Not like that. I'm going to get rich and buy it for her. No way is she going to spend the rest of her life cleaning up after white people. No offense."

"None taken. What does she do exactly?"

"Maid. She has an education. She's too smart for that kind of work, but you know."

Eric didn't, but he could guess. "Politics pay well. I'm sure you'll be able to help her out."

"Not politics," Gabriel said. "Sure, there's money to be had there, but only if you make it to the top. I'm not taking any chances. She's made too many sacrifices to put me through college. That's why I'm majoring in economics."

"Ah. I'm a business major."

Gabriel looked over in surprise. "Really? I figured it would be something softer. Rehabilitating woodland creatures maybe."

Eric snorted. "Then I guess we both had the wrong first impressions. I never would have guessed you liked to dance. I couldn't even imagine you… Never mind."

Gabriel looked confused. Then amused. "Maybe I've never felt so amorous that I needed to do it in a gazebo, but I promise you, I've had no complaints in that department."

"Prove it," Eric said, feeling daring. Hey, it had worked the first time!

Gabriel seemed tempted. Then he looked back at the house on the hill. "Ask Robby if you want details. Just make sure I'm in the room when you do. I love seeing him blush."

Eric laughed, but what he really felt was jealousy. If only he had met Gabriel instead of Michael, and if only they had both been single at the time. Still, at least he had a new friend he could trust. "Thanks for bringing me out here. This is fun."

"Feels good getting away from it all," Gabriel agreed. He exhaled, as if decompressing. "Sometimes you've got to leave all the bullshit behind."

"Sorry about the article."

"It's fine."

Eric leaned against the car. "It probably wouldn't have made a difference anyway. People love a scapegoat."

"They do, but you're wrong." Gabriel turned to face him. "This article needs to get published. It *will* make a difference."

"How?" Eric asked. "I don't mean to bring you down. I just don't see what good it will do."

"Other people will read what you went through, and many will either relate or sympathize. The rest can go to hell, but we need as many people on our side as we can get."

"We'll always be outnumbered," Eric said, shaking his head. "How many homosexuals do you really think there are?"

"Have you read the *Kinsey Reports*?"

"No."

"I'll buy you a copy. The short answer is more than you think."

Eric wasn't convinced. "If there are so many of us, then why are we so repressed? Why isn't there—I don't know—a homosexual civil rights movement?"

"That's exactly what I'd like to see!" Gabriel said. "Even if there aren't many people like us, there are plenty of minorities. Black, Hispanic, queer, Asian. You add up all of those minority groups, plus our allies, and you know what you end up with? A majority!"

Eric smiled. "It's a nice idea, but women make up just over half the population. Are you telling me they aren't repressed?"

"It's not just a numbers game," Gabriel said, his confidence unwavering. "Attitudes need to change too. The rest will fall into place. Stick with me and you'll see."

Eric wasn't convinced. He couldn't imagine a world without racism, sexism, and prejudice, but the request was easy to follow. No matter what shape their relationship took, or how limited it may be, he planned on sticking by Gabriel for as long as possible.

*

"You're surrounded by angels."

Eric furrowed his brow at this, unsure what his mother meant. Was she referring to Gabriel's visit? That had been over a week ago. The man might not be going into politics, but he still behaved like a politician, visiting families, kissing babies, shaking hands. He was just that kind of guy. He hadn't needed to meet

Eric's family. The two of them weren't an item, but Gabriel had insisted it was important.

Gina had loved it, amused that Eric had found another angel to add to his collection. She had been clear of mind that day, shining with an inner light. Since then she hadn't spoken much or made sense when she did. At the moment her face was constricted, her eyes unfocused. She was in bed, of course. Eric couldn't remember the last time she had left it. He didn't think she ever would again. Not while living.

He swallowed against the lump in his throat and placed a hand over hers, even though they were now clammy instead of warm, boney instead of soft. At times he resented her. The little boy inside of him still expected her to take care of him. Their roles shouldn't have reversed. He hated sitting next to her bed like this, the room smelling faintly of urine no matter how many times they aired it out or made sure the sheets were clean. Mostly he just felt sad. Frustrated too, because no noble sacrifice would save her. He could do nothing at all except sit there and wait.

His father took care of the really unpleasant things. He'd enter the room with a bowl full of sudsy water or new diapers or more medicine. Then, his breath laced with rum, he would ask Eric to leave the room. The excess drinking was understandable. Hell, his father could burn down the house and half the neighborhood along with it, and Eric wouldn't need to ask why. His wife, the mother of his children, was dying. What greater justification for madness could there be?

Eric lacked any reprieve from the pain. He had tried drinking but only made himself sick. He had attempted to stay away from the house, deny any of this was happening like his sister did, but guilt had brought him back. He had even asked the hippie in Gabriel's group for some pot, but all he got out of that was a coughing fit. So he sat there and waited, wishing for his mother to die because her lingering in this condition made God seem cruel. Sadistic. If angels really existed, they should have taken her with them weeks ago.

Gina opened her mouth, but no words came out. Her eyes moved around the room. Then she saw him and tried harder to speak. When this failed she slid her hand away and steepled it together with the other. Like she was begging. Or maybe she wanted him to pray. He could do that. Eric had a few choice words for God, none of them kind. But instead of speaking them, he would plead once more for God to be merciful.

Eric got down on his knees, elbows on the mattress, and placed the tips of his fingers together. He closed his eyes, tears spilling down his cheeks. Then he prayed.

*

The world had changed. Shortly after Eric's mother died, all hell broke loose. Activists like Gabriel were everywhere now. The lawns of the University of Texas campus were filled with war protesters. Citizens and police clashed in the downtown streets. The Black Panthers. Students for a Democratic Society. Groups of female students who were starting to be called Women's Libbers. Everyone, no matter which cause they were linked to, was itchy with indignation, spewing out opinions with indiscretion. Except Eric. He didn't care about any of it. Not the University of Freedom movement, or Gentle Thursday, or any of the other new movements. His mother had died. Ten days of unconsciousness. Ten days of withering away until almost nothing was left. Then release. His mother was gone.

His father was gone too, because the drink that Mac had relied on to get through those dark days was still needed. Even more so. Who did he have to be sober for? Eric and his sister were both adults. What did he have left but to chase after his wife in the only way he knew how?

Eric coped by different means. He studied, trying to fill his head with so much knowledge that there wasn't room for anything else. When his mind became too tired for that, he visited art galleries, losing himself in painted worlds. He almost felt disappointed when he graduated because it left him with too much time to think. Empty hours had become his enemy. He sought employment without much luck. He attended Gabriel's meetings, the upstairs room at the Lukewarm Café now crammed with angry bodies. Eric liked seeing Gabriel in action—how he had finally found the audience he had always needed. Sometimes this was even enough to make Eric smile.

But not today. This was the last time he would attend such a meeting. Once everyone had spoken and decided on a new course of action, the upstairs room slowly began to clear. The music and voices downstairs got louder. Eric waited, watching Gabriel shake hands with the newest recruit, a young girl bristling with idealism. Gabriel caught him staring, then gently guided the girl toward the stairs before approaching. They sat together, quite possibly in the same dusty chairs where Eric had poured out his heart at the beginning of the year. That seemed an eternity ago.

"I've got good news," Gabriel said. "Remember the article I wrote about you? The one *The Daily Texan* rejected?"

"Don't tell me," Eric replied. "You sold the film rights. I'm going to be famous."

"Not quite. You've seen *The Rag*, the underground newspaper?"

"Hard to miss," Eric said. "One issue had a naked woman on the cover."

"Er, yes." Gabriel appeared appropriately embarrassed. "Anything to get people's attention. Anyway, they've asked me to write for them. They want a black man's perspective, but I told them I wanted to start with something more subversive."

Eric's eyebrows shot up. "Me? I'm subversive now?"

"Talking openly about queer issues is definitely subversive. So what do you think? Are you excited?"

"I'm excited for you," Eric said carefully. "And relieved that I'm no longer a student here."

"I wish I could say the same," Gabriel murmured. "Are you okay? You're putting on a brave face. I can tell. You don't need to do that for me."

Eric sighed. "I have news of my own."

"What?"

Eric pulled a folded piece of paper from his back pocket. He thought about handing it to Gabriel but worried he might destroy it. Instead he unfolded the paper and held it up.

Gabriel's eyes moved over the words. Then his jaw clenched. "You've been drafted?" He sneered. "Didn't take them long. Freshly graduated! Time to send all that education to the frontline so it can go to waste. Don't worry, Robby and I have been talking about this. We're defecting to Canada. We need to graduate first, but there's no reason you can't go now. I have a contact up there and he—"

"Gabriel."

"—has helped a few other people I know. Until then you can—"

Eric sighed, making sure it was loud enough to be audible.

Gabriel stopped rambling and focused on him. Then he looked angry. Furious, actually. "You're not serious!"

"It's my decision," Eric said softly. "I need you to respect it."

"No!"

"No you won't respect it or—"

"You can't go," Gabriel said. "Please! Why would you even consider?"

Eric took a deep breath. "Maybe I need to witness it for myself. People are either denouncing the war or supporting it, but most of them haven't seen what's happening with their own eyes."

"I can tell you exactly—"

Eric held up a hand. "Or maybe I need to witness something so horrific that it lets me forget what I've seen in my own town. In my own home."

"Your mother?"

"And Michael and all the rest of it. I'm done, Gabriel. I'm tired. I need to go somewhere else and do something new, because whatever I need to feel better, it isn't here."

Gabriel's nostrils flared. He looked skyward, shaking his head. He clenched his jaw, struggling with his thoughts. Then he grabbed Eric's hands and stood, pulling them both to their feet. The draft card took flight, swooping in short arcs until landing on the floor, but none of that mattered because Gabriel pulled him close, his thick lips pressing against Eric's. It wasn't exactly the kiss he had been dreaming of. More like the clumsy smooch of a child, mouths mashing together without finesse. Eric savored it anyway. When they pulled away, he saw wet streaks gracing Gabriel's cheeks. Tears, just for him.

"Don't go," Gabriel said. "I'll make you happy again. I don't know how, but I will. Just please don't leave."

Eric smiled gently, then broke physical contact. "If I asked you for what I really want, you would never be able to respect me. Not truly."

"Robby?" Gabriel asked.

"I know you love him. It's okay."

Gabriel looked pained, but he nodded.

"He's lucky. Maybe I will be too someday."

"My father died over there."

Eric swallowed. "I know. My mother died over here. I don't

know what to tell you. I can't make sense of the world. I only know one thing. This is what I need."

"I love you," Gabriel said. Then he looked bewildered. "I can't tell you how exactly. A friend, a brother, or something more. Just remember that when you're over there, okay? Someone back home loves you."

"Thank you," Eric said, and it was all he could manage without crying himself. Besides, Gabriel already knew how he felt. That kiss, which had been meant to anchor him here, wouldn't have happened otherwise. He loved Gabriel, but now it was time to say goodbye.

* * * * *

"I didn't know you were a soldier," Tim said, standing behind his canvas again. "You never talk about it."

"I was lucky to be accepted into the Army." Eric rolled over onto his side, which took more effort than it should have. Pain came with the relief, but he tried to ignore both. "If the recruitment officer had heard the gossip about me, even as desperate as the military was then, I wouldn't have been accepted. I was prepared to insist I was a different Eric Conroy entirely, but fortunately for me, the recruitment officer wasn't an avid reader of *The Rag*."

"How come you never bored me with old war stories?" Tim teased.

"It's a difficult thing to discuss with someone who hasn't been there. With other veterans, yes, but not you. I hope you never know the horrors of war. What I'm putting you through now is bad enough."

Silver eyes appeared over the top of the canvas, questioning him. Eric thought of his mother, of the pain of watching her wither away, reduced to a shadow of her former self. Death's hand touched more than just those whose life it took. Eric's darkest years had begun with her passing, and he feared the same would be true for Tim. Eric had intended to send him away, to hire the help he needed and to find some pretense for them to no longer see each other. That would have been the kindest course of action, but Eric had felt afraid to face the end alone. Not without someone who truly cared about him. "I'm sorry," he said.

"For what?" Tim asked.

"All of this. It's going to get much worse."

The eyes disappeared behind the canvas again. "I don't care."

Brave words. Uninformed and soon to be proven wrong. At least he would be rewarded for what he was about to go through. Eric had seen to that.

"You've got me liking Gabriel," Tim said. "Didn't think that was possible, but he seems all right. Back then, anyway. Did he really run away to Canada?"

"Oh yes, he and Robby both. We lost touch for many years. I didn't think I'd ever see him again." Eric coughed, but turned it into a chuckle. "Then, nearly a decade later, one of nature's greatest forces reunited us."

"Love?" Tim asked.

"Ha!" Eric replied, rolling onto his back again. "No, not love. Greed!"

*

The house was silent. Empty. Eric walked from room to room, part of him searching for any scuff marks that needed to be polished off the wooden floors, any smears on the windows that needed to be wiped away. The rest of him was caught up in memories. His childhood bedroom; the bathtub he had shared with his sister when they were little; the kitchen counter where he sat as a child, watching his mother cook. Mostly though, he thought about his father, remembering the man who had been so steadfast and certain, and the stranger he had become on his way toward self-induced oblivion.

His death had been easier. Eric hated to admit it, but Mac had been incomplete after Gina had died. Eric had known widows who thrived after losing their husbands, but men rarely did the same. "We're all just boys in need of our mothers," he said, voice echoing in the empty master bedroom. He performed one last cursory inspection, then walked toward the front of the house. An unexpected knock on the door stopped him short.

A concerned neighbor? Or someone interested in buying the house? That would be odd because the realtor's "for sale" sign was still sitting in the garage. The knock came again, followed by a tilted face appearing in one of the windows to the side. They stared at each other, Eric's throat constricting with emotion. Then he rushed forward to open the door.

"What are you doing here?"

Gabriel smiled and opened his arms wide — an invitation Eric couldn't refuse. He allowed himself to be embraced, marveling that someone could still smell the same after so long. The cologne was different, or perhaps it was the aftershave, but beneath it all was the unmistakable scent of a man he had never stopped loving.

"Look at you!" Gabriel said, stepping back and doing just that. "The military suited you well, I see. Are those muscles?"

"One or two," Eric said sheepishly. "I never managed to put on much weight but—"

"Stop being modest. You look great, although I was expecting a crew cut, not feathered bangs."

Eric ran a hand through his hair, wishing he had it cut recently. Then again, trim and orderly wasn't exactly *en vogue* these days. "I like the mustache."

"Thank you," Gabriel said, running a finger along the pencil-thin line. "Robby talked me into growing it."

Robby. Of course. Not everything had changed then. "I'm thrilled to see you, but again, what are you doing here?"

"Ah," Gabriel said. "Well, I didn't have your address. The last letter I got from you said you were moving and starting a consulting business, but you didn't give me a new address. I've been trying to track you down, and I thought your father might know where to find you."

Eric didn't respond in words. His emotion came unbidden. Gabriel read his face, then glanced over his shoulder at the empty interior.

"I'm sorry. I didn't realize—"

"It's fine," Eric said. "Come in."

Once inside, he realized he couldn't offer Gabriel anywhere to sit or anything to drink except water directly from the tap. They ended up in the kitchen anyway, Eric leaning against one of the counters, arms crossed over his stomach.

"What happened?" Gabriel asked.

"He drank himself to death," Eric said. "It's not that I didn't see it coming. I'm just glad I made it back home before it happened. Funny how things turn out. My mother died and it sent me running to the ends of the earth. Then I come back only for my father to die. I guess that's my lesson. There's no escaping death." He laughed humorlessly and shook his head. "I'm not normally so bleak, don't worry. I saw enough during the war to realize how precious life is, and how good we have it here. I won't take that for granted."

"That's good," Gabriel said with a nod. "You've been through enough. You deserve to be happy."

"What about you?" Eric asked. "Just visiting? Last I heard you and Robby were in Calgary."

"We're back," Gabriel said. "Moved home last week. Carter pardoned all the draft dodgers. Didn't you hear?"

"I don't pay attention to the news," Eric said. "I'm tired of conflict. Let me live in ignorant bliss."

"Not while I'm around," Gabriel teased, reaching out to jostle him. "I'll make an activist out of you yet!"

His touch felt good. Eric wanted to lean into it, step forward into another hug. He wanted to be held and to feel safe again. Perhaps Gabriel sensed this, because he moved closer, resting his back against the counter so their shoulders brushed against each other.

"How's your mom doing?" Eric asked.

"Great! She finally got away from that maid job. Works in a nice office now. Technically she's a secretary, but from what I've heard, she practically runs the place. I still intend to buy her a house and let her retire. That's why I'm here, in fact."

"Should I give you a tour?"

"Not like that," Gabriel said. "I don't have any money. All I've got is an economics degree that I haven't used since graduation. The war and the president I protested against are both gone, and I find myself lacking a purpose."

"I can't offer you a job," Eric said. "Business is mediocre at best. I barely scrape by. I don't have any staff. Not even a secretary. I'm a one-man show."

"But at least you're still performing," Gabriel said emphatically. "I'm out behind the theater, digging around in the trash cans."

"That bad?" Eric asked.

"Nearly," Gabriel said, his frustration palpable. "I haven't come begging though. I bring opportunity. I ran into a friend of mine the other day. Do you remember Marcello?"

Eric shook his head. "I don't think so."

"Remember the campus love-ins? Marcello sometimes organized them and was always in the middle of each. Big guy, curly hair, gets a little touchy-feely when he's high."

Eric had a vague memory of an inappropriately long hug and the smell of tobacco. "Smokes like a chimney?"

"That's the one."

"Didn't he get expelled?"

"The authorities tried, but I'm not sure he was even enrolled." Gabriel shook his head. "Anyway, he has a small nest egg he's looking to invest."

"Send him my way." Eric reconsidered. "Wait, you need this more than me. It sounds like the perfect opportunity for you to get a new start."

"I'm out of touch," Gabriel said, spinning around to face him once more. "I don't know the market, but you've got your finger on the pulse. That's why I thought we could do this together."

"I haven't made anyone rich," Eric said dismissively. "Then again, I haven't had much to work with. How much is he looking to invest?"

"Ten grand."

"That's..." A number of possibilities flashed through his mind. "That's not bad!"

Gabriel grinned. "Are you in? We're going to do this together?"

Eric took one look at those twinkling brown eyes and nodded. "Together."

*

Eric reported to work the next day, mind buzzing with potential. The office he rented was one of many in a two-story building. Most of the other tenants shared the same air of hopeful desperation. The stock market was not a happy place. Ever since the crash a few years back, it had been a bear market with most stocks steadily losing value. This meant very few investors were willing to gamble their hard-earned money.

Today would be different. Eric made sure his desk appeared organized, stacking papers or shoving them into drawers. When this revealed a number of coffee stains, he went to the restroom down the hall to get something to wipe up with. When he returned to his office, he found it occupied. A large man stood at the desk, riffling through a stack of papers. Eric stopped and stared, wet paper towels dripping in one hand. Then he cleared his throat.

"Can I help you?"

The man spun around, looking him up and down. "My sentiments exactly."

His suit was tan, the pants tapering outward at the ankles. A burnt orange shirt struggled to conceal a prominent belly while the collar allowed more freedom, the top buttons undone to reveal a hairy chest. The man's dark hair was slicked back, a few curls having broken free. Gold jewelry accentuated all of this. Even on casual inspection, Eric could tell that most of it was fake.

"Marcello," he guessed. He had seen this man before, albeit in a tie-dyed robe large enough to be used as a tent.

"A pleasure to make your acquaintance," Marcello said, pausing to suck on a cigarette. "I was searching for an ashtray, but to no avail."

"I don't smoke," Eric said, then added pointedly, "Especially not in here."

"There's no time like the present." Marcello spotted an empty coffee mug and ashed into it. "Necessity is the mother of all invention."

"And manners maketh the man," Eric said without thinking.

"Ah, the wit and wisdom of bygone days," Marcello said. "I was thinking recently how entire conversations could be conducted using nothing but famous quotes. No paraphrasing either! That would ruin the challenge. This sounds simple enough at first, but how would you order at a restaurant? An apple a day? Parsley, sage, rosemary, and thyme? One would soon end up starving. I don't suppose you have anything stronger?"

The cigarette was held aloft. Was he asking for drugs? The man seemed like he was already on more than enough. "Sorry, but our appointment wasn't until this afternoon."

"I'm aware of that," Marcello said easily. "I'm already acquainted with Gabriel. You, on the other hand, I'm not familiar with. If I am to trust you with a significant portion of my money, I need some sense of you as a person." He glanced around the office critically. "Does success elude you, or are you the sort of man who can tame it, have it come at your beck and call?"

Eric struggled to find a suitable answer. "Such concerns are usually addressed during a presentation, which is exactly what Gabriel and I were going to finish working on today."

"A presentation. I see. I'm imagining impressive equations supplemented by graphs and pie charts."

"Exactly."

Marcello ashed again. "I'm not interested in such things. If I were, I wouldn't need you."

Eric clenched his jaw. "Then what exactly do you need?"

"To know what sort of man you are."

"Well, I graduated from The University of Texas with a GPA of—"

"That's your education," Marcello interrupted, exhaling smoke. "Who are you?"

"Eric Conroy," he answered, feeling exasperated. "I'm a financial consultant."

"I already know your name and occupation. It's taped to the door, rather than stenciled. What I'm asking, is who you *are*. What makes you tick? What sort of person—"

"Fine!" Eric snapped, his temper breaking. "I'm a war veteran who hates fighting, a businessman who can't seem to find work, a compulsive planner even though life is impossible to predict, and I'm queer, but I don't know why I mention that, because I can't remember the last time I shared my bed with anyone. Who the hell are you?"

Marcello pulled deeply on his cigarette, not at all shaken by this outburst. Instead he calmly sized Eric up, shrugged, and answered the question as if it were obvious. "I'm Marcello Maltese."

Eric felt like shouting and crying at the same time. He'd blown it. No doubt about that. Say goodbye to that ten grand, because he had lost his cool and alienated their client. Not that Marcello seemed upset. Maybe it wasn't too late. "I can make you money," Eric spluttered. "I know it might not look like it. I know how dire the financial forecasts are right now, but give me a chance and you won't regret it. I swear!"

Marcello stubbed out his cigarette in the coffee mug. Then he nodded. "Let's talk business."

A few minutes later, they were seated at the desk. Eric had poured two coffees in fresh mugs and ducked next door to borrow a real ashtray. He felt as classy as a used car salesman and was breaking out in a sweat, so he tried to calm down and focus on the numbers.

"Gabriel really should be here for this," he said before beginning.

"I'm well aware of his situation," Marcello said, "and his

current lack of expertise. You can bring him into the fold later. It's *you* who possesses the knowledge I need. Or so I was told."

"I've got it all right," Eric said, flipping over a page. "Take a look. I've put together a collection of stocks and bonds that I feel will yield a slow but steady return high enough to offset inflation and—"

Marcello coughed, but not because of the fresh cigarette he had lit. "We continue to misunderstand each other. Capital losses, algorithmic trading, purchasing power parity—none of these things interest me."

"You certainly seem familiar with the subject matter."

"Enough to know when to pass the buck—so to speak—to someone with a greater love of numbers. I am not a cautious man. Life is meant to be lived, and that means taking action, not idly standing by and hoping for the winds to blow in my favor. When it comes to money, I either spend it or put it to work for me. That is why I am here today. I need this capital to generate a stream of revenue large enough to allow me to continue manifesting my personal vision."

"Manifest your personal vision?"

"To do as I please," Marcello clarified.

Not that it helped Eric understand. He tried to keep his expression neutral, wishing more than ever that Gabriel were here. At the very least, maybe he would be able to interpret. "If you don't mind me asking, how did you earn the money you intend to invest?"

"Sign a non-disclosure agreement and I would be happy to tell you."

Eric laughed. Marcello did not.

"Um." Eric flipped through more pages, seeking an answer he already knew wasn't there.

"Let me ask you this," Marcello said. "My understanding is that your father recently passed away. My condolences. If I'm not mistaken, his untimely death means there is a house on the market."

"You're surprisingly well-informed."

"You'll get used to it." Marcello leaned forward. "I assume there will be some form of financial inheritance for you, or profit from the sale of the house. I'd like to know what you—a financial consultant—plan to do with that money."

"Nothing."

"Nothing?"

"Half the money goes to my sister. The rest I'll put in a savings account with an acceptable interest rate."

Marcello leaned back again. "I'm disappointed. I thought you would invest in some hot little stock or relatively unknown enterprise."

"It's not my money," Eric said, feeling testy again. "My parents worked hard their entire lives, and I'm not about to risk any of it, no matter how strongly I believe an investment would be a good one. My father never asked me to do such a thing while he was still alive. It's not what he wanted."

Marcello shook his head. "I disagree. It *is* your money, both legally and literally. Regardless, pretend for a moment that your father had indeed asked you to invest it for him. What then? Where would that money go?"

"Technology."

"Such as?"

Eric took a deep breath. "Electronics. Computers."

"Computers," Marcello repeated, not sounding enthused. "Calculators the size of refrigerators with a television screen attached."

"They've come a long way," Eric said. "The Apple II just hit the market last week. I saw it at a tradeshow. The screen can display color now!" This failed to impress Marcello so he tried another tactic. "You mentioned a calculator. I'm assuming you have an electronic one?"

"Yes. Is that the sort of computer you mean?"

"Kind of. Since you bought that calculator, how often do you sit down and do math by hand? Good old fashioned pen and paper. How often?"

Marcello thought about it. "Almost never."

"I worked with computers in Vietnam. We used them to process information. Platoon movements, casualties, civilian data. The learning curve wasn't easy, but once you start using computers, they become indispensible. Just like your calculator. I'll take a computer over a filing cabinet any day. Even the White House has one installed."

"A computer or a filing cabinet?" Marcello joked, but he was clearly interested.

"We had electronic calculators in the Army, years before they hit retail. Now home computers are being introduced too, and it might be a niche market to start, but I don't think it will stay that way."

"This sounds like a long-term investment."

"It is," Eric said. "If you want instant results, take a trip to Las Vegas. That's the quickest way to gamble. If you want to yield the biggest crop, you've got to plow the field, plant your seeds, and wait."

Marcello stubbed out another cigarette. "Is this what you and Gabriel intended to sell me?"

"No. I wanted to offer you something safe. Something proven."

"That wouldn't have seduced me. No, I much prefer this new idea."

"It's just a dream," Eric said warningly. "I think it's going to come true, but I can't promise you anything."

"A dream?" Marcello said. "I can't imagine a more worthwhile investment. You've convinced me!"

Eric perked up.

"Nearly."

He slumped again.

Marcello took a checkbook from his jacket pocket. "I'm willing to entrust my money to you, all ten thousand dollars, on one condition."

Eric's mouth went dry. "What?"

"That you do the same. Take the money your father left you and do something with it."

"That's really none of your business."

"Perhaps not, but if you worked hard to provide a living for your children and had left them some money, wouldn't you want them to be happy?"

"Of course, but—"

"And would you dictate what form that happiness takes?"

"No."

"There you have it." Marcello flipped through the book to reach a blank check. "As passionately as you just spoke about computers, I can only assume it would bring you joy to invest in them. And what better way to convince me to take a leap of faith than by jumping off the cliff first?"

He was right. Eric wanted to take that leap. Maybe he wouldn't use all of his inheritance, but some—just a little—could be used to invest in his own happiness.

*

The office was dark except for light from the desk lamp and, thanks to a small window on the far wall, much less smoky. After Marcello left, Eric had started planning. Gabriel arrived an hour later, which didn't slow his pace at all. He simply kept working while trying to fill Gabriel in on what needed to be done. This took little effort. Gabriel was still sharp, despite not having used his economics degree. Calls were made, papers were drawn up, reports were compiled, numbers were crunched. Anyone else would probably find this tedious, but Eric enjoyed every minute.

"I've never seen you this way before," Gabriel said from next to Eric as he helped rearrange papers. "I'm jealous."

"Jealous?" Eric asked. "Of what?"

"All those times I tried to get you fired up about different causes, all the speeches I gave that worked on everyone but you... I should have been talking to you about money instead."

"It's the challenge," Eric said with a chuckle. "I admire your convictions, but I've always felt powerless when it comes to politics. Here I can actually do something."

"You're definitely in your element," Gabriel commented, surveying their work. "I have to admit I'm enjoying it too. What did you make of Marcello?"

Eric grimaced. "Him, I'm not so sure about."

"No?"

"He's nosey, bossy, and has a few screws loose. Scratch that, he's *missing* a few screws. Some gears as well."

Gabriel laughed. "You'll grow to love him."

"Any idea where he got all this money? He was tight-lipped about it."

Gabriel looked uncomfortable and checked his watch instead of answering. "Looks like we've been having a little too much fun. It's past nine. We missed dinner."

"Robby won't be happy. Where did you leave him anyway? Are you staying with your mother?"

Gabriel seemed puzzled. "Robby?"

"Your ball and chain," Eric teased.

"Not since last year. We split up."

"What?" Eric blinked. "But you said… When I asked if you were still living in Canada, you said *we're* back. Both of you."

"We are, but he moved a few months earlier than I did. We're still friends. We're just not together anymore. What about you? I figured there was some lucky soldier with a heart-shaped locket around his neck."

"No," Eric said. "There's no one. I'm free for the taking."

They stared at each other. Then they looked at the desk, which was covered with immaculate stacks of paper in carefully paper-clipped sections. Gabriel swiped his arm across these, clearing the surface. Then he grabbed Eric's shoulders and spun him around so his back was to the desk. Eric started backing up onto it, his lips meeting Gabriel's. This time the kiss wasn't hampered by reservations or prior promises. Their mouths met with hunger as their bodies carefully inched onto the desktop. Eric lay flat, Gabriel's body pressing against his, grinding against him. This wouldn't be gentle and tender or long and leisurely. Their need was too strong.

Eric reached down and nimbly undid a button before swiftly unzipping the rest. Something hard and hot tumbled out, falling directly into his hand. He was amused that Gabriel hadn't been wearing underwear, but his thoughts soon turned to other matters—namely shimmying down the desk so he could get that thing in his mouth. He took a good look as he did, admiring the dark skin and how it curved to the right. Then he stopped gawking and went to work. Gabriel's moans started quietly, then grew louder as Eric did his best to impress. He hoped they were the only ones working late tonight, or else there would be some serious gossip around the water cooler tomorrow.

"Get back up here," Gabriel said, rolling to the side.

Eric complied, already intent on getting his own pants open. Then he lay back and closed his eyes, feeling wet warmth envelop him. He moved his hands over Gabriel's hair, letting his fingers brush across his face. This was real. He delighted in that. A decade-long fantasy was finally coming true! Gabriel sat up on his knees, staring at Eric's face and voicing similar thoughts.

"I waited a long time for this."

"Me too."

"Just tell me it's not going to be the last time."

Eric shook his head emphatically. "Definitely not."

"In that case… Race you to the finish line!"

Gabriel grasped himself and started pumping. After a moment of confusion, Eric laughed and did the same. He too got on his knees, each of them on one end of the desk and facing each other. His fantasies had never gone quite like this, but seeing Gabriel's muscles tense and in motion—just getting to witness him do something so intimate—was hot as hell. Eric was about to suggest they start touching each other again when Gabriel's lips pulled back, his expression primal. That pushed Eric over the edge. A place normally reserved for paper and ink was transformed into a fountain, if only for a few seconds.

Afterwards, panting and more than a little delirious, they started laughing.

* * * * *

Eric sucked in air, his eyes shooting open. His entire body felt dried out, like meat left on the sidewalk to roast in the sun. Tim was quietly working his canvas, the light of day having taken on the intensity of afternoon.

"How long was I out?" he rasped.

"Half an hour, maybe."

"Where did I leave off?"

"Uh." Tim stayed behind the canvas. "It sounded like you and Gabriel were about to get it on."

Eric sighed in relief. "At least my inability to stay awake spared you the details."

"So I take it you guys were an item from then on?"

Eric meant to answer. Instead all he could do was wince, but he did so quietly, waiting until the pain released him enough that he could speak again. "What time is it?"

Tim understood what this meant. It's not like Eric had appointments he needed to keep. He set down the paintbrush and filled the water glass, then administered another medicine dropper full of morphine. "You need to eat."

"I'm fine."

"You're not."

Tim stood and left the room. Food. Eric tried imaging hamburgers and pizza, steaks and soups, but nothing sounded good. Lately it never did. He dreaded whatever dish Tim would bring back into the room and hoped too much effort wouldn't be put into its preparation. When Tim returned he was holding an ordinary bowl, and when he sat on the edge of the mattress, Eric saw what was inside. Cereal. The kind with marshmallows in it. One of his guilty pleasures.

"Come on," Tim said, holding up a spoonful. "You said that medicine tastes like crap. This will help."

In truth, even marshmallow-laced cereal didn't sound good anymore, but the gesture was too kind for him to refuse. Tim raised spoonful after spoonful to his mouth, naming a marshmallow with each. "Orange stars. Blue diamonds. Green clovers." They had just reached pink hearts when he had to decline.

"That's all. Thank you."

Tim shrugged, then started eating the cereal himself. Eric laughed and felt another burst of affection for him. Love. Hard to say which kind. If they had met in another time—and hadn't been born in two very different decades—then maybe their love would have been of the romantic variety. Instead... Eric never had children and couldn't say for sure how parenting felt, but occasionally he wondered if he was experiencing something similar.

"I hope you find someone," Eric said. "Eventually."

"Already have," Tim said dismissively. "Speaking of which, I officially like Gabriel. A lot. I didn't think that was possible."

"I'm sure I've told you these stories before."

"Some of them, but not in so much detail."

"The painkillers make me ramble." Eric leaned back, staring off into the past. "Gabriel was a good man."

"Back then."

"Even now."

Tim tilted the bowl to his mouth and drank the milk. Then he set it aside and wiped his chin. "So that's how you and Gabriel got rich? Investing Marcello's money?"

"Not entirely. Gabriel and I became partners. Not just in business. After our—ahem—passionate encounter in the office, I brought him home with me. We took turns holding each other that night, and we got very little sleep because all we wanted to do was talk, confessing feelings that had begun developing a decade earlier. From that day on, we were inseparable. Gabriel was always better with people than I was. He found the clients and did a much better job of convincing them of my schemes.

Investing is a long game, so it wasn't until three years of this that we started truly reaping the benefits."

*

Eric dabbed the corners of his mouth with the cloth napkin and tried to feel comfortable. Lighting in the restaurant was high, illuminating the white table cloths, the immaculately polished cutlery, the glasses so spotless they were nearly invisible. And of course him. He felt like his every move was being monitored and analyzed by the waiters, who were never far away, always watching. He supposed they were only being attentive to his needs, but their good service made him uncomfortable.

He wasn't used to places like this. He had shared the same one-bedroom apartment with Gabriel for years now, pinching every penny to make ends meet. This meant shopping for the cheapest groceries and preparing meals from scratch, which he had learned to enjoy. These days he loved cooking so much that even when their fortunes improved, they still didn't eat out much. Nor had they upgraded the apartment, since they spent most of their time in the office. Splurging on a meal like this went against his instinct, but then again, this was a special occasion, and they did have an important client to impress.

Marcello seemed to share none of his discomfort. The large man surveyed their surroundings with a pleased air and consumed his food with surprising delicacy, as if he had been born into such an environment. Perhaps he had, since Marcello remained vague about his past. Wherever he came from, the highlife seemed to suit him just fine. He had even, halfway through the meal, waved over the handsomest of the waiters and insisted he try some of the food. The poor young man had obeyed and was spoon-fed a bite of smoked veal.

"Delicious," Marcello declared at the end of the meal, placing his hands over his belly, which appeared considerably smaller than last time. He was dressed in a white suit that made him blend in with their surroundings, although the plum dress shirt with the butterfly collar kept him from disappearing entirely. "An absolute delight!"

"I'm happy you enjoyed it," Gabriel said warmly, nodding in thanks as the serving staff cleared the table. "We've been looking forward to this evening."

"You still haven't told me what all this is about," Marcello said.

"We were saving that for dessert," Eric replied, sliding the ashtray across the table.

"No, no," Marcello said, raising a hand. "I'm done with such things. My body is a temple. I met the most adorable Buddhist monk a few months back, and he's been teaching me how I can free myself from the chains of the physical world. I've been trying to free him from that alluring robe he wears, but alas, with little success."

"I believe Buddhist monks take a vow of celibacy," Eric said.

"Nonsense!" Marcello declared. "He's simply playing hard to get, but he has been generous in his advice. I'm a new man."

"You look good," Gabriel conceded. "Hopefully your new worldview doesn't require you to renounce material gain."

"Ah," Marcello said, a gleam in his eye, "would it not greatly benefit you both if I suddenly needed to be rid of my money? No doubt you would gladly invest it for me. I assume that's what this meal is about. There's another prospect you would like me to consider?"

"No," Eric said, reaching down to grab his briefcase. He placed it on the freshly cleared table, despite the face one of the waiters made. Nothing was going to stop him from enjoying this occasion. He clicked open the latches and pulled out a stack of papers, but all that mattered was the top page. He handed this to Marcello, feeling giddy. "Thank you for trusting us with your money."

The paper was taken and carefully considered. As much as Marcello professed to hate such things, Eric had learned over the years what a keen mind for numbers he possessed. The man ran his own business, which had been steadily rising in success over—

"Six figures," Marcello breathed. "I promised myself when I was younger… I thought maybe by the time I retired…"

"Lost for words?" Gabriel asked. "I never thought I'd see the day!"

Marcello laughed, his whole body shaking. Then he wiped at his eyes and handed the paper back. "You've done well."

"Thank you," Eric said, feeling pleased. "*You've* done well!"

"I hope I'm not alone? You stayed the course with your own investment?"

"Yes," Eric said. "I'm grateful you pushed me to do so. If I hadn't—well, I'd still be happy right now. But mostly just for you."

"My baby is brilliant," Gabriel said, signaling the waiter. "We're both very lucky to have him in our lives."

"Indeed," Marcello said. "And what a fabulous way of celebrating! Let me pay, I insist."

"Not a chance," Gabriel said. "Besides, we're not done yet."

Two waiters arrived, one with a silver tray and glasses, the other with bottle of champagne tucked into a bucket of ice. The beverage was presented, opened, and poured with great ceremony. Then they were left alone to toast. Gabriel, as usual, found the perfect words.

"To combining business with pleasure, and to the limitless love of friendship."

"Here, here," Marcello said, but he set down his glass.

"You're not going to drink?" Eric asked.

"My little monk would be so disappointed, but please, go ahead. I'll enjoy watching you."

"It's just champagne," Eric replied. "It's not like you're going to get addicted."

"He's got a point," Gabriel said. "How many homeless guys do you see on the street guzzling Laurent-Perrier?"

"I've never been one for drinking," Marcello said, "I've always preferred more enlightening substances."

"A sip won't do any harm," Eric pressed. "It'll be our little secret."

Marcello appeared amused. "I *do* have a soft spot for peer pressure. Very well. Gentlemen, to our mutual success! May it continue to soar skyward!"

They lifted their glasses and took a sip. Eric and Gabriel did, anyway. Marcello started to tilt his glass away, then changed his mind and guzzled most of the contents.

"How very—" He covered his mouth and burped discretely. "Excuse me. It certainly is refreshing!"

"Not only that," Gabriel said, offering a refill, "but it makes good news sound better, and bad news almost forgivable."

"Meaning?" Marcello asked.

Eric exchanged a glance with Gabriel. He thought they were saving the announcement for another day. He preferred to keep tonight's spirits high, but Gabriel gave him a "Why not?"

expression. He knew Marcello best, so maybe it wouldn't be a big deal after all.

"We want to take our business to the next level," Eric said.

"Oh?"

"Austin isn't exactly the financial capital of the world," Gabriel explained. "Most of our work is done remotely, which slows us down and means our information is often out of date. Eric has some really clever ideas. He's been investing in the raw materials computers and electronics require, and we're already seeing— I know these things bore you, but trust me, it's where we need to be."

"Not to mention the sort of clients we could find there," Eric added.

Marcello looked between them. "Where exactly?"

"New York," Eric replied sheepishly.

"The Big Apple," Gabriel said with much more bravado. "Once we're in the thick of the action, we can give you even better results."

"I'm less concerned about the money," Marcello replied, "than I am about saying goodbye to friends." He sniffed. "Then again, when you say better results…"

Gabriel laughed and pointed. "I *knew* you'd be okay with this!"

Marcello kept a straight face, but only just. "I didn't say I was okay with your decision, but we survived Canada, didn't we?"

"That we did."

"You know, I've been meaning to visit Studio 54." Marcello's eyes twinkled. "Maybe I'll buy it! Ha ha! Promise me you'll get an apartment with better insulation. Your place in Calgary was so cold that my nipples were hard for two weeks solid."

Gabriel cackled. "That had nothing to do with the cold, and everything to do with me!"

"You *were* at your sexiest when you were a draft dodger," Marcello purred. "A modern day outlaw! I was tempted to enlist just so I could go AWOL and join you in the Frozen North. Whatever happened to those two Eskimo boys?"

Eric felt left out of the conversation, but not in a bad way. He hadn't understood their friendship at first. Gabriel was classy and upfront in his opinions. Marcello could be evasive and manipulative, but what they had in common was their causes. The idealist protests of the sixties had given way to a much more pragmatic approach in the seventies. Money made the world go 'round and was the most effective catalyst for change. Gabriel and Marcello had both figured that out, and each diverted a significant portion of his success into the change he wanted to see. For Gabriel this was most often on a political level. Marcello was more grassroots, focusing directly on individuals. That seemed to be his primary interest in life. People. Men in particular.

"Seven figures!" Marcello declared. "Nothing less will justify you leaving me behind. Make me a millionaire, and you'll have my blessing."

Gabriel looked at Eric with absolute glee. "Well? Think we can do it?"

Eric took a deep breath. "Why not?"

"Excellent!" Marcello said. Then he raised a hand to get the waiter's attention before gesturing to the champagne bottle. "My good man, we're going to need another of these!"

*

Ten years together. Twenty if counting back to when they had first met. While they hadn't been together romantically, their love had blossomed into existence then. Two decades. How far they had come! Their feelings for each other had survived war and separation. Then they had plunged into the challenge of cohabitating while forging careers together. Success had been the only result. When he and Gabriel teamed up, the world's obstacles fell away. Mostly. They had money. They had reputation. What they had very little of, was time.

Eric checked his watch, then looked at the front door of the condo again. From the inside. He was still at home, waiting and willing for Gabriel to arrive. He turned away from it, pacing back and forth, then forced himself to stop. Instead he stared out the floor-to-ceiling windows at the twinkling lights of the New York skyline. He wanted everything to be perfect for their anniversary. He had gotten a fresh haircut, was wearing his favorite suit, and had even been watching his figure over the previous month. A little cologne, dinner reservations, and the perfect present. Where the hell was he?

The front door swung open. Finally! Gabriel strolled in. He smiled, kissed Eric, then went to the kitchen for a glass of water.

"Where have you been?" Eric asked. "We have reservations at *Exquis*."

"Oh," Gabriel said, sipping from a glass before setting it on the counter. "Did you make the reservation for four? I didn't plan on spending so much on the Petersons, but that could work."

"The Petersons," Eric repeated, following Gabriel into the bathroom.

"Yes. You didn't forget, did you?" Gabriel checked his teeth in the mirror. "I'm over the wining and dining thing, but you know they have more money than sense. If we don't get there first—"

"Did *I* forget?" Eric said incredulously. "I'm not the one who forgot! When did you make this appointment?"

"Last week." Gabriel washed his hands. "You look nice. Ready to go?"

Eric clenched his jaw. Then he let go of the anger. He didn't want to fight. Not today. "There's something I wanted to talk to you about. It's important."

"We're short on time." Gabriel sprayed on another puff of cologne, then headed for the front room. "Tell me in the car. I'll call the Petersons from there and let them know where to meet us."

Eric reached into his suit jacket and fondled the envelope hidden in the inside pocket. He was tempted to leave it behind. The night was ruined. Better to save it for a different occasion. "Can you cancel?" he asked. "Please."

"The Petersons," Gabriel repeated. "Do you know what Mr. Peterson asked me the other day? He wanted to know if gold was worth more than silver, then he tried convincing me that platinum was the Latin term for silver, because *clearly* they look the same. If we don't help them invest their money, they're going to get robbed blind. At least I'm only interested in a cut."

"Why do you need more money?" Eric said. "Don't we have enough already?"

"No." Gabriel opened the front door and gestured for Eric to exit. "Hurry up. I hate being late."

They rode the elevator down without speaking. Gabriel hummed happily. Eric quietly seethed. They stopped at the ground floor, then walked outside to hail a taxi. A white limousine occupied much of the curb, which was annoying because now they would have to walk to the corner and—

Gabriel went right to the limousine and opened the rear door.

Eric stared. Then he smiled. "You son of a bitch!"

"What?" Gabriel said innocently. "I thought a limo would impress the Petersons."

Eric wasn't falling for it anymore. He trotted forward, kissed his lover on the cheek, and slipped inside. The interior was filled with bouquets of white flowers. Roses, peonies, orchids, and daffodils. Eric laughed happily. "I feel like it's my wedding day."

"If it were up to me, it would be." Gabriel slid inside beside him and nodded to the driver. Once the car was in motion, he took Eric's hand in his and murmured, "Happy anniversary, baby."

Time. So absolutely precious. Eric intended to enjoy every second of the evening. He was happy when they got stuck in traffic. At the restaurant, he didn't mind when the kitchen took longer than normal to produce their order. Once they were served, Eric ate at a leisurely pace. His entire focus was on Gabriel. This made him even more confident about the gift he had chosen.

"Are you happy with our lives?" Eric asked.

"Why wouldn't I be?" Gabriel said, swirling his glass of wine. "I've got everything I could ever want. Wait, are you happy?"

"Nearly," Eric admitted. "We don't see much of each other."

"We work together!"

"Yes, but we're too busy to interact. Some days I talk to the doorman more than I do you. I'm starting to feel like I'm in a relationship with him instead."

"How old is Stanley, anyway? Eighty-five? Whatever floats your boat, I suppose." Gabriel took in his expression and grew more serious. "Yes, I wish we had more time together. We're in our prime though. We're working toward our retirement."

"We're already rich!" Eric said with a mad chuckle. "We won't live long enough to spend half this money."

"You never know. With inflation or another stock market crash—"

"Yes, I do know," Eric interrupted. "Few are in a better position than us to know these things. Our money is safe. We've made sure of that."

Gabriel cocked his head. "What are you getting at?"

"This." Eric slid the envelope from his suit pocket and pushed it across the table. "An old forgotten dream."

Gabriel took the envelope and opened it, his eyes on Eric instead, searching for a hint. Then he focused on the paper, his confusion turning to amusement. "You bought us land? In Austin!"

"In West Lake Hills. Do you remember?"

Gabriel shook his head.

"We took that drive out there—"

"The night we danced together!"

"Under the stars." Eric smiled. "There was a house on the hill, and you talked about wanting to buy it for your mother. I actually tried to buy that exact one, but it isn't for sale."

Gabriel laughed. "You sure have a good memory! Or maybe not. My mother already has a house. We saw to that."

"I know, but it was a nice dream, and I thought… We've worked hard. Let's enjoy the fruit of our labors. Who knows what the future holds, or how much time anyone has left?"

Gabriel appeared concerned. "Are you sick? Is there something you're not telling me?"

"I'm fine, but how many friends have we lost to AIDS? None of us saw that coming, and nobody knows where it will end, or what might be next."

Gabriel's mouth tightened, his expression vulnerable. "I miss Robby. I still think of him every single day."

Eric sighed. "I know. I'm sorry."

"Monogamy probably saved our lives. Do you ever think of that? Our love for each other kept us safe."

"We were lucky, and I don't want to take what we've been given for granted. We can't predict the future, but we can hedge our bets." Eric reached across the table. "Think of it as another business venture, except with time instead of money. I want to invest all that I have in you."

Gabriel took his hand and searched his eyes. "Don't you like it here?"

"Yes. Most of the time. The hectic pace gets to me."

"And our careers?"

Eric used his thumb to stroke one of Gabriel's fingers. "Our careers can wait. Maybe in ten, fifteen, even twenty years we'll get bored. Then we can decide what to do with ourselves. Remember your causes, how you were doing all this so you could help others? When's the last time you were able to focus on that? I know you donate a lot when Marcello has his events, but wouldn't you like to take a more active role? You can still work with clients from a distance, like we used to."

Gabriel's forehead creased. He stared at his wine glass, lost in thought. Then his eyes focused again and he nodded. "Okay."

"Really?"

"Yes. I mean… I think so." Gabriel laughed nervously. "We'll need more than just a plot of land. Unless our new lives involve camping."

"That brings us to your anniversary present for me," Eric said with a wink. "You're buying me a house!"

* * * * *

"I freaking love this house." Tim stood up, tilting his head left and then right to stretch his neck. "You always say you wish you were an artist, but look around. You designed all of this, and it *is* art."

"I merely dreamed up a few ideas," Eric said dismissively. "The true talent came from people with years of training. I loved the process though. Even at the beginning, when we really did camp here."

"Seriously?"

"For a few weeks, yes. The happiest years of my life, they all took place right here."

Tim frowned. "But this is where you guys…"

Eric nodded in understanding. "Nothing lasts forever, Tim. I know that's an unpleasant thought, and it feels nicer to cling to an impossible ideal, but one way or another, everything has its time and comes to an end. That's nothing to grieve. It simply makes way for new beginnings."

"Are you sure?" Tim asked, clearly uncomfortable with the idea. "If two people meet and are made for each other, like soulmates, couldn't they stay together?"

"Yes, but only until they are forced to part. People get old and die, and rarely at the same time." Eric sighed. "Maybe the next world is different. Perhaps the ultimate promise isn't just eternal life, but eternal love as well."

"Do you think there's an afterlife?"

"I certainly hope so!" Eric said. "Ask me again in a few weeks and I'll have a much more informed opinion."

"That's not funny!"

"It's the truth."

Tim's face was flushed as he sat back down in front of the canvas. He chose, like so many young people, to focus on anger instead of sorrow. "Gabriel shouldn't have taken you for granted," he grumped. "How long did you two make it here?"

"Nearly seven years. My mother used to say that was a lucky number. I don't regret any of it. Not one single day. Well… That's not entirely true. There's no sense in dwelling on the negative, although it does demonstrate the point I was trying to make. As some stories come to an end, new ones begin."

*

Paradise.

Eric scoffed at himself and shook his head. As a teenager he had turned up his nose at the *Donna Reed Show, Leave it to Beaver*, and other wholesome television programs that portrayed picture-perfect families and the innocuous adventures of white middle-class America. These usually involved a pearl-necklace-wearing housewife obsessed with keeping her home clean and her family fed. Occasionally she might put her hands on her hips and shake her head ruefully at the antics of her husband and children, but rarely did life get more heated than that.

Eric's father, oddly enough, had been the one who insisted on watching these shows, perhaps enjoying how the husband was always depicted as king. Eric took no pleasure in them, knowing he would never have that sort of life. No wife and kids for him. Rather he imagined himself more like James Bond, who never seemed to have a home. Instead Bond travelled the world, staying at tropical resorts or snowy lodges while seducing beautiful women. Or men, in Eric's fantasies. That's what he had planned on, but if he was honest, it wasn't what he wanted.

Eric walked along the upstairs hall of his house, peeking into each room and still feeling just as satisfied as when it was new. Even more so, since time had allowed for little personal touches and memories to be made here. The walls were covered with his favorite art, the shelves contained souvenirs of all the adventures he and Gabriel had shared. This was his home, and he couldn't be more content. He was Donna Reed, always cooking, always caring for his man. Only the children were missing, but recently that had changed too. He and Gabriel had children now. More than a dozen of them.

Eric reached the stairs, his socked feet silent on each carpeted step. He didn't want to interfere, but he enjoyed looking in on them. All of this was relatively new. During the last year, Gabriel had become restless. Initially he had been happy with their new lives in Austin, but slowly his discontent expressed itself in a myriad of ways. He didn't smile as much, he tended to be moodier, and he would invent tasks to occupy himself, like when the pool had been installed. Gabriel had micromanaged every aspect, overseeing every shovel of dirt and the placement of every tile. Eric had tipped the construction workers generously for tolerating this behavior.

Gabriel clearly required more than remote business transactions or house projects. He needed a sense of purpose. He had regained some of his old fire during the Gulf War, his eyes lighting up when he saw students protesting it on campus. Naturally he had also criticized their methods.

"Why not offer them the benefit of your experience?" Eric had responded.

Gabriel had balked at the idea. "What? Like get involved?"

Convincing him had taken ages, but with the looming Senate elections and some disaster involving a healthcare bill, Gabriel finally agreed. Now he was the organizer of a student movement. The old campaigner was back on the trail! Eric stuck his head into the living room, first checking to make sure the snacks he had whipped up hadn't been depleted yet. He noticed with some pleasure that they had been. Then his attention focused on the group, twelve or so young people, many of them slack-jawed at the heated debate. That was no surprise, considering the participants. Zachary was a hothead. A sophomore in college, he was passionate about politics. Eric had never heard him talk about anything *but* politics, even when answering the door. No "Hello, sir, can Gabriel come out and play?" Instead he would start off with "The Republicans are on the move," or "This country is on the brink of disaster unless we act." Eric never knew quite how to respond, so he always hurried to fetch Gabriel. Not that Gabriel seemed to fare much better. He and Zachary were constantly yelling at each other, going into such detail and depth that Eric found it difficult to follow.

Occasionally he would sit in the room and try. Zachary wasn't just a hothead. He was hot. Chestnut brown hair that matched his eyes, lightly tanned skin, and lips that were luscious even when pulled back in a sneer, which was most of the time. Some faces were made handsomer by anger. Zachary's was one of them. His body was pleasing too, upright and tight, although Eric couldn't imagine him working out. Maybe the constant tension kept his body trained.

"Perfect for politics," Gabriel had commented once. "That face will win over most people from the get-go, and his mind will conquer the rest. If I can get that temper of his under control, the kid will go far. But first he'll have to start listening to me."

This was said with both exasperation and faint amusement. Gabriel had found a worthy sparring partner. Their heated debates left him content and amorous. All Eric had to do was sit back and await the benefits. And avoid letting it all give him a headache.

"This isn't the sixties!" Zachary snarled. "We can't sit on the university lawn with flowers in our hair and expect anything to change. Those tactics didn't work even back in your day!"

"Now wait just a minute," Gabriel said, index finger wagging. "What we initiated back then was a cultural upheaval, a paradigm shift that eventually—"

Eric rolled his eyes and turned toward the kitchen, intending to refresh the snacks. He found the room unexpectedly occupied by someone who was examining the little plates of *insalata caprese*.

"Chocolate syrup?" Marcello asked, poking at a slice of mozzarella.

"Balsamic syrup," Eric corrected. "Try a bite."

"Perhaps later. Care to join me for a drink?"

Eric looked at the clock. Four in the afternoon. Close enough! He fetched the bottle of champagne from the refrigerator, considering Marcello as he opened it. "Does Gabriel know you're here?"

"No."

"House key?"

"Yes," Marcello replied. "Best Christmas present I was ever given, although I do miss sneaking in the back door. No pun intended. Gabriel and I never—"

"I know," Eric said, trying to banish the image from his mind. He popped the cork—which didn't help—and carefully poured two glasses. "You'll be waiting a long time to see him. The last meeting like this lasted until eight at night, although only Zachary and Gabriel were there for the final two hours."

"I'm here to see you, actually," Marcello said.

"Oh? What for?"

"We're friends, aren't we?"

This wasn't a rhetorical question. Marcello's gaze was probing. He continued speaking before Eric could answer.

"Business was the genesis of our relationship, and I know that for some time, any semblance of friendship was born out of us wanting to please Gabriel."

"Yes," Eric said, "but only because we needed time to get to know each other. I like you. We're definitely friends."

"That's precisely what I'm here to assert," Marcello said. "My fondness for you isn't reliant on any other association. Quite simply put, I like you too."

"Okay," Eric said a little uncertainly. "Well... I'll drink to that. Here's to friendship!"

They clinked glasses, then eyed each other while taking sips.

"You're a good man," Marcello said. "Gabriel once said that he and I were lucky to have you in our lives. If anything, that has only become more true with each passing year. Only a fool wouldn't recognize your value."

Eric took another sip and swallowed. "This is doing wonders for my self-esteem, but I feel like you're going somewhere."

Marcello shook his head as if he'd been silly. "Sundays always make me sentimental. Pay me no heed."

Conversation was easier to follow after that. Marcello talked about his business and the woes of his love life, then showed polite interest in the food Eric had prepared. By the time they reached the bottom of the bottle, they were laughing and gossiping about people they both knew.

"Ah," Marcello said, checking his watch. "I must go. I have a dinner date with... someone. I can't remember his name, only the brand of jeans he wears and how they cup his bottom so exquisitely."

"Best of luck," Eric said. "Not that you'll need it. Should I call a taxi?"

"For me?" Marcello said, pressing a hand to his chest. "I've never felt more sober in my life! All the more reason to rush home and open another bottle."

"Drive safely," Eric stressed.

At least Marcello didn't have far to go. Traffic in their neighborhood was minimal. After saying goodbye, Eric felt his stomach growl. Time to see about feeding himself, although he was a little too hungry to start cooking now. Perhaps Gabriel could drive them into town for a bite to eat.

Eric remembered the meeting and went to see if congress was still in session. He didn't hear any shouting. He found the living room mostly empty. Only Gabriel and Zachary remained, which wasn't unusual. What *was* different was the way their voices murmured softly. Eric leaned against the doorway to observe. They were sitting on the couch, turned toward each other, a respectable distance between them. The topic remained the same, neither of them ever tiring of politics, but the anger was gone. Zachary was smiling, which was a sight to behold. Not just because of its rarity. He truly was a beautiful young man. Gabriel's expression was hard to see from where Eric stood, but his husky chuckle sounded warm, and when he heard Eric and turned around, his eyes were still shining. Then that light flickered, the smile fading.

"Dinner time already?"

"Yes," Eric said. He looked to Zachary. "Care to join us? You must be hungry."

"No." Zachary shot to his feet, not making eye contact. "I already ate so many of the snacks you provided. Thank you. That was very thoughtful."

"My pleasure," Eric said, feeling amused by his excessive politeness. He watched them say goodbye and shake hands like they had reached an agreement. Then Zachary showed himself out, sparing Eric a quick glance and another thank you on his way. "I'm starting to feel jealous," Eric joked when they were alone.

"Why?" Gabriel asked, missing the attempt at humor.

"I'm not getting any younger. Maybe I should dye my hair."

"I like the gray. It's distinguished."

"Distinguished," Eric repeated. "Gosh. Thanks. Try not to tear off my clothes or anything."

Gabriel didn't seem to hear, gathering up his notes. Once he had, he looked up. "Did you cook?"

"No, I thought we could grab a burger. There's a new place in town. You'll have to drive. Marcello paid a visit."

Gabriel laughed. "Are you drunk?"

"Just a little. Let's go."

When they reached the downtown area, he gave directions,

paying close attention to Gabriel's reaction when they parked in front of the restaurant.

"Lukewarm Café!" he said, getting out of the car.

No evidence of the old establishment remained. The café had closed down long ago, replaced by a copy shop. Now it had changed owners again and become a small bar and grill. They gawped when they entered, searching for any signs of multicolored chairs or smoke-stained windows, but the whole place had been renovated. The upstairs area was now for staff only. Food was being carried down the steps, suggesting a kitchen had been installed there.

"I'm a little disappointed," Gabriel said. "They should have kept a few things the way they were."

"I'm grateful they didn't," Eric said. "Despite the memories we made here, it was never the sort of place where I wanted to eat."

They let the waiter seat them, then reminisced while waiting for their order. As they dined Gabriel talked about the most recent meeting, which was fine. Eric liked seeing him so passionate.

"There's a convention in Connecticut next week," Gabriel said once their plates were empty. "Not the national convention, but in the same spirit, run by young political hopefuls. I'd like to take Zachary there, let him make some connections and meet people his own age. It's all very last-minute, but I managed to get him registered."

"Next week?" Eric asked.

Gabriel gave a curt nod. "Over the weekend, yes."

"Well, okay. I just hope the weather isn't still bad up there. I don't miss the snow!"

Gabriel was quiet.

Eric stared. "You don't want me tagging along?"

"The subject matter doesn't interest you."

"No, but I can visit a few art museums during the day and meet you both for dinner. Or I'll just spend time in the hotel. A change of scenery sounds good."

Gabriel's jaw flexed. "We can take a trip together afterwards. There's no sense in you going because I'll be busy until late in the evening. You know how these things are."

Eric studied him. "No, but I'm beginning to get the picture."

Gabriel sighed. "It's not like that."

"Are you sure? Because lately, all you do is talk about him. Remember what we promised? We said we would be honest with each other. If I'm wrong and there's nothing between you two, say so and I'll believe you. That's all I need."

Gabriel scratched at a dimple in the table's wooden surface, not speaking, not looking up.

"Jesus," Eric breathed. "How far has this gone?"

"It hasn't," Gabriel said. "I swear. Nothing has happened, but if you want the truth, I care about him. I like him. A lot."

"Enough that you wanted to be alone with him? What did you have planned?"

"Nothing," Gabriel said, "but I won't deny part of me secretly longs for more, and yes, at the moment what I want most is to spend time with him. Alone."

Eric shook his head, despite being able to relate. He still noticed other people. For a brief period he had even developed a crush on the mailman, who always stopped to chat, but Eric had never taken things this far. He had never planned a romantic getaway. "You're being awfully presumptuous. What makes you think Zachary would be interested? You're twice his age! Is he even gay?"

"He tried to kiss me."

Eric's jaw dropped. "What?"

"He tried to kiss me."

"In the middle of a meeting? In my own home?"

Gabriel shook his head. "We went out for lunch—"

"When?"

"—and nothing happened. I didn't let it."

Eric closed his eyes and willed his head to stop spinning. He'd been foolish, had never seen this coming. "I won't force you to be with me," he said, opening his eyes. "I won't hold you prisoner. There's no point. Go to your stupid convention, and while you're there, figure out what you want because I won't play second fiddle to some boy fresh out of high school, and I sure as hell won't be a victim of your midlife crisis!"

"This isn't a midlife crisis," Gabriel snapped. Then he exhaled. "I'm sorry."

"Don't be sorry," Eric muttered under his breath. "Just make up your god-damned mind!"

*

Paradise lost.

Eric walked through his house, no longer satisfied, comforted no more. His picture-perfect world had been nothing but a delusion. He had worked hard to build this life, feeling confident in its resilience, not realizing how fragile it all really was. His happiness hinged on one person, and now Gabriel was... Well, that remained to be seen. Perhaps this was all a crisis of faith, a skipped heartbeat before their relationship would resume its steady rhythm. Or maybe it was the beginning of the end.

Eric walked through the house, waiting for it to no longer to be empty. When he heard the front door open, he hurried to the couch, not wanting to appear desperate. He sat on the cushion that had separated Gabriel and Zachary that day, like a belated effort to keep them from getting too close.

When Gabriel entered the room and Eric saw his expression, he knew it was too late.

"We need to talk."

Eric had once welcomed those words. Now he dreaded them, because they wouldn't lead to good news.

Gabriel sat down, his expression guarded. "I need more time to explore this."

"You haven't decided?" Eric asked, feeling irritated.

"I mean time apart. I won't cheat on you, and before you ask, nothing happened. But I don't think I'll be able to keep that promise. Not for much longer."

Eric swallowed, fear coursing down to his belly. Faced with the idea of losing Gabriel, he found himself panicking and willing to compromise. "An open relationship," he blurted out, "or we could take a break, maybe just for a month to get these urges out of your system. A threesome? He's a nice kid. I'm sure I could —" Eric grimaced.

Gabriel noticed. "I know you don't want any of those things."

"Of course I don't!" he shouted. "What I don't understand is what you want! Sex I can understand, but are you seriously thinking of dating this person? What could you possibly have in common?"

"Everything!" Gabriel snarled. "He reminds me of myself when I was that age! I can help him avoid making the same mistakes."

"Is that what I am to you?"

"No." Gabriel clenched his jaw, then shook his head wearily. "But our careers were a mistake. I should have done something more meaningful."

Their careers were a major part of their relationship, so it hurt to hear Gabriel regretted them. "You haven't thought this through. What about twenty years from now? You'll be sixty years old. He won't even be our age yet! How is that going to work?"

"I *have* thought ahead." Gabriel put a hand over Eric's. "I don't want to see you get old. I don't want to be there when you die. I've been through that more times than I can stand. Losing my father was bad enough, but being there for Robby, watching him waste away... You know what that's like."

"I do," Eric said, a lump in his throat, "but I don't care. I would suffer that again a million times over, just for you. I don't care how bad it would hurt me."

Gabriel's hand withdrew. "I always said you were stronger than me."

"Fuck you," Eric spat. "Get out!"

Gabriel rose, then quietly left the room. Eric held it in. He waited until certain that he wouldn't be heard. Then he started crying.

*

"You knew."

Eric marched up the long drive to a palatial house, which only made him angrier because the wealth that financed this home wouldn't exist if not for him. And this is how he was repaid? He should tear it all down, brick by brick! Or just rip the owner to pieces. Marcello must have installed the new security system he'd been talking about because he was standing outside the front door when Eric reached it, unshakeable as always, even though Eric was clearly enraged.

"You knew!" he repeated.

Marcello raised his hands, showing his palms. "I suspected, and when I asked Gabriel the truth, he confessed his feelings. That's when I—"

"What?" Eric snarled. "Bragged about your own exploits? Encouraged him to live the way you do? I hate you!"

Eric wanted to punch Marcello, slam that serene face with a fist just to see his expression shift. He wasn't a violent man.

Eric had purged himself of that during the war. Still, he couldn't help lashing out. He pounded his fists against Marcello's chest, growling in an effort to hold himself back. Marcello allowed himself to be pummeled briefly, then grabbed Eric's wrists with surprising ease and clenched them tight. All that weight gave him an advantage. Eric squirmed against his grasp, unable to pull free.

"I told Gabriel he was making a mistake," Marcello said, "that he would spend the rest of his life regretting the day he lost you. I have no doubt that he will. It pains me to learn, from your reaction, that he didn't take my advice to heart."

Eric stopped struggling. "Why did you come to the house the other day? Not to warn me, because you didn't say a damn thing! You got me drunk and acted like we're best friends, and for what? Because you're hoping to be next in line?"

Marcello released him and held his head high. "Make no mistake! I love you, but not in that way. I feared Gabriel's indiscretion would rob me of your friendship, and yes, I did consider warning you. But if Gabriel had changed his mind and didn't act on his impulses, anything I said could have been equally damning. I'm sorry that you're in pain. The last thing I wanted to see was you get hurt. You're better than him, Eric. He never deserved you."

"But I wanted him," Eric said, chin starting to tremble. "I still do. I want him back."

"I know." Marcello stepped forward and opened his arms, wrapping Eric in them protectively. "I wish there was something I could do. I tried to make him see reason. I'll try again, but as much as Gabriel and I respect each other, we've always had our own minds."

Eric pressed his face against Marcello's chest to hide his tears. "It hurts. More than I imagined it ever could."

"That will change," Marcello said, his embrace constricting. "Not today, and not tomorrow, but eventually the pain will fade away. You'll find someone worthy of your affection. I promise you that."

Eric couldn't reply. All he could do was squeeze his eyes shut against the aching in his heart and let his friend shield him from the world.

* * * * *

Eric returned from the realm of hazy memory to find a hand

on his own. Like the hug from Marcello so long ago, the grip was almost painful in its strength, but the reassurance it gave mattered more. Tears were on Tim's cheeks and his jaw kept flexing.

"I don't want to lose you," he croaked. "He was an idiot to walk away."

Eric managed a smile. "I'm glad he did. If Gabriel hadn't left me, my friendship with Marcello wouldn't have become as close as it did. Even more unthinkable, I might not have met you."

But Eric wasn't entirely pleased with the way things had worked out. Gabriel should be the one sitting at this deathbed, having already suffered through the experience twice before. He had no more innocence to lose. Tim's greatest problems involved accepting himself and getting over his failed relationships. Challenging, but nothing like looking death in the eye. That was a rite of passage everyone faced, and life was never quite the same afterwards. Eric hated putting Tim through that. Of all the things he sometimes dreamed they could be to each other, he had never wanted this.

"I'm tired," he said truthfully.

Tim didn't move. "Do you need a drink? More medicine? Maybe we should—"

"There's nothing more I need," he interrupted gently. "Except maybe to see that painting. Show it to me."

"I'm not done yet."

Eric slid his hand free so he could pat Tim's. "Then you better get to work."

Tim rose and returned to his canvas. Eric closed his eyes and tried to sleep, but he still found himself lost in memory. The lonely difficult years of bitterness. The acceptance of what was lost and a new appreciation for all he still had. The day he had opened the door to find two young men standing there, one with the most striking silver eyes. What followed was a happiness he had scarcely known before. Eric lingered in those memories, replaying comfortable conversations or basking in moments of shared solitude.

"Eric!" The voice sounded distant, but it brought him back to the present. Tim was shaking him awake, then he hurried back to his easel to turn it around. "Look!"

The image was truthful. Eric wasn't young. He wasn't free

of this bed. He was old, sick, and dying, but more than that, he was surrounded by colors. Light wove around him, the different shades of his story, the people who had been characters in his play. Rainbows encircled him in these final moments and somehow made what he was going through okay. Perhaps because all that effort Tim had put into the painting proved to Eric—beyond any reasonable doubt—that they truly did love each other.

"You made me beautiful."

Tim shook his head. "You've always been beautiful."

Eric looked at him, wondering if this young man would come out of the experience unscathed after all. Maybe his youthful optimism was strong enough to remain intact. He hoped so, because Eric adored Tim this way, standing there with his chest heaving as he radiated hope. He closed his eyes, wanting to hold on to the image. He held it in his mind for as long as he could, even when darkness started to encroach on the edges.

"I love you," he said, the image fading.

Then there was nothing left to see. Just calm oblivion, but he didn't feel afraid. Just weary. He could rest here. If only it wasn't so cold! With this thought came light. Dim at first and from above, like a sun shining weakly through a storm. Then the brightness increased, bringing warmth. Eric turned his attention upward, the breath catching in his throat.

An angel with wings of gold, the sight both beautiful and terrifying. His fear didn't last long because comfort radiated from this being's presence. The angel's bare feet touched ground that Eric couldn't see and its arms opened, eyes questioning, as if asking what he needed most.

"Let me sleep, Gabriel," he said. "I'm tired."

The angel slowly got to its knees and sat, offering its lap. Eric crawled forward, resting his head there. No more pain, no more fear or uncertainty or guilt. Just peace. His breathing slowed, steady and deep, quiet and content, before shuddering once more and never again.

Something Like Fall

by Jay Bell

———————

Part One: Jace
Missouri, 2003

———————

Hey, Allison! Wish you were here. As you can tell from the back of this postcard, Missouri is called the Show-Me state. I'm pretty sure that's meant ironically, since there isn't much to see here. Or maybe people are desperate to see anything besides flat land and bleak highways. Show me... anything! I hope Warrensburg will be more exciting. If you don't hear from me again, it's because I died of boredom. Your soon-to-be-dead best friend —

"Honey buns."

Ben looked up from the postcard he was scrawling on. Outside the passenger window of the rental car, a handsome man approached. Ben smirked. "I told you never to call me that. Not in public."

Jace grinned, blue eyes sparkling. "I never do, but I think I'll start." The happy expression remained. Jace seemed thrilled to be here, as if they had pulled up to a tropical resort instead of some anonymous gas station on a pockmarked highway. Jace stood by the window, brandishing pastries sealed in shrink-wrapped plastic. "Honey buns," he repeated. "I didn't know they made these anymore."

Ben accepted one tentatively. "You always take me to the nicest places."

"And you always bite your nails and expect disaster. How many times have I told you not to judge a place from the highway? At least wait until we arrive."

"So Warrensburg is going to be amazing?"

A grimace broke free across Jace's face before he reined it back in. "I'll make it amazing." He leaned forward, stuck his head in the window, and transformed concrete and the smell of gasoline into a little slice of heaven.

By the time their lips parted, Ben was sold. He signed the postcard, then added at the very bottom: *PS- Never mind. I love it here!*

Jace walked around the rental car to the driver's side and got in. In the cup holders he set the milk he had bought for himself and the Coke that Ben had requested. Then his long fingers partially unwrapped one of the pastries. He took one bite, then another, making happy little noises as he ate. Ben observed this, feeling ridiculous that something so simple could make him love Jace even more.

This trip might turn out to be good for them both. Not that they were having problems. College was finally over, and even better, Ben's enormous mistake was fading to distant memory. They were healthy and… Happy didn't quite describe it, not for Ben anyway. Jace always had a bounce in his step because his life was neatly organized. Flight attendant extraordinaire. A self-described astronaut of the stratosphere. He had an identity, a job to keep him occupied. All Ben had was a degree in English. A stupid useless degree that the temp service he worked for never once asked to see.

Allison had recently suggested he work at the hospital, in some sort of speech therapist position that had recently opened up. Not because he had majored in English Literature, but because he could sing. He was still trying to wrap his head around that one, but she had given him a look that said, "Don't question me, I know what's best for you!" He had avoided giving a definitive answer by saying he would think about it while on this trip. Maybe he actually would and finally figure it all out in the modest land of Missouri.

"Show-Me state," he mumbled as they resumed driving. "Okay. Show me what I'm supposed to do."

"Hm?" Jace said, reaching over to take his hand. The gesture would have been more romantic if his fingers weren't still sticky from the pastry. Jace seemed aware of this, because he held on tighter when Ben tried to pull away, laughing mercilessly. Not that Ben really minded or struggled much. He might not be content with the rest of his life, but in his relationship, he couldn't imagine being happier.

As they reached their destination, he felt much more optimistic. Warrensburg had small-town charm, the buildings worn down like comfortable furniture, the old trees stretching their branches wide, showering sidewalks and streets in crimson, orange, and gold.

"I miss the leaves changing colors," Jace said, sounding wistful. "We get that in Austin, but not like this."

"It's nice," Ben conceded. "Winters must be different too."

"Those I don't miss," Jace said, "although I didn't mind so much as a kid. Sledding was fun, and so was building snowmen with Dad. He always insisted on dressing them up so they wouldn't get cold. I was in my early teens before I stopped thinking that made sense. I always felt bad for the snowmen other people built because they were naked."

Ben chuckled along with him, but soon grew more somber. He was nervous, and probably without justification, because surely Jace's parents were just as wonderful as the son they had raised. Regardless, this was a major event, and one long overdue. Over the last three years, Jace had offered to introduce Ben to them many times and had even booked flights on two separate occasions, only for fate to intervene. On the first attempt Jace was called into work, having to cancel one flight so he could get on another. The second attempt was interrupted by Ben's mother needing emergency surgery. His father had asked him to come help take care of her, not knowing that she had already asked Ben to help take care of her husband. Life kept getting in the way, often enough that he nearly expected their flight today to be hijacked, just to prevent this meeting.

And yet here they were. Jace was pointing through the windshield at invisible memories—a bike wreck on a street corner, a dog that always chased him if he tried crossing the property, and a creepy house that was purportedly haunted, although now it had been replaced by a block of apartments. Ben tried to pay attention and nodded to show he was listening. In truth his thoughts were racing. Jace's parents would be good people, but what if they thought he wasn't? Jace was so damn perfect. Would they also expect him to be?

He was about to find out. They drove through a sleepy neighborhood, cruising around a lake to get there. Jace pulled over briefly, nodding across the water to a valley where a number of houses were perched on the sloping land.

"That one right there," he said.

The house was three stories high with a large wooden deck that jutted out. Huge trees surrounded it, producing the autumn leaves that were tumbling gracefully through the air. Perfection.

The entire house and the family within were perfect, Ben felt sure of it. He broke out into a light sweat as they parked in the driveway. Two people appeared at the front door. Jace's parents were older. Ben knew that from photographs he had seen. Mrs. Holden had silvery hair gathered in a single braid that rested over one shoulder. She was tall and thin, like a graceful goddess. Mr. Holden was pudgier and mostly bald on top, thick glasses perched on the end of his nose. He didn't appear perfect from the outside, but he probably spoke ten languages and possessed an encyclopedic knowledge of wine and classical music.

Jace was already out of the car. Ben unbuckled his seatbelt with numb fingers, opened the door, and stumbled to his feet. He watched Jace hug his parents, the exchange of happy words lost on him as he tried to find his own. Something that would impress them. A quote? From literature! Hey, maybe that English degree wasn't so useless after all! "I am only human," he blurted out, "although I regret it."

This was met with a puzzled silence.

"Mark Twain said that," Ben supplied helpfully.

"Only human," Mr. Holden repeated, offering him a hand. "I'm glad to hear it. We were starting to worry Jace would marry that cat of his."

"Don't be ridiculous," Jace retorted. "Samson is a confirmed bachelor. That's the lifestyle he has chosen for himself. Besides, who said anything about marriage?"

Ben relaxed somewhat. Jace might be perfect, but he was also weird, meaning Ben's little outburst probably wouldn't be remembered. Hopefully. "I'm Ben," he tried again. "Nice to finally meet you."

"I'm Serena." Jace's mother stepped close, placing her hands on his shoulders as she looked him up and down. He saw no criticism in her eyes. Only delight. "I've waited so long for this!"

"You and me both," Ben said with a chuckle. He opened his arms to hug her. A moment later, he was pulled aside so Jace's father could do the same.

"I'm Bob," the man said after releasing him. "Do you eat meat?"

Ben blinked. "Yeah. Of course!"

"I told you!" Bob waggled a finger at his wife. "Just because he worked at a vegetarian restaurant doesn't mean he *is* one!

Now we're stuck eating bean balls for lunch."

"Falafel," Serena corrected, arching one of her eyebrows slightly. Ben knew that expression. It was the same one Jace used when Ben was acting up. "Please, come inside."

Bob put an arm around Ben's shoulders, guiding him in. "Welcome home, son."

"We're not married yet!" Jace complained from behind. "And you wonder why it took three years for this to happen?"

Ben was ushered into the dining room, and once seated at the table, it really was like being part of the family. When he asked for ketchup, instead of anyone leaping up to fetch it for him, he was sent to dig around in the refrigerator and get it for himself. Formality and friendliness rarely coexist, and it was clear which Jace's parents valued more. Conversation was casual and easy, Ben treated like he'd always been a member of the family. By the time dinner was over, he felt comfortable in Bob and Serena's presence and eager to prove himself worthy. He hopped up to clear the table. Jace helped and followed him into the kitchen. They worked together at the sink, standing side by side.

"What do you think?" Jace asked when passing him a freshly rinsed dish.

Ben placed it in the dishwasher. "I think I'm in love."

"With me?"

"With the whole package. You, the town, your family... Let's pack our bags and move!"

"Easy now," Jace said, handing over a drinking glass. "Give it a few days. My parents are fine, but you might want to hold off on saying nice things about the town."

"What's so bad about it?"

Jace shut off the water and turned to lean against the counter. "There's never anything to do, so chronic boredom is an issue, but what really bothered me was—" He struggled to find the exact reason, his smile subtle when he spoke again. "You weren't here. That's why I had to leave. I was looking for you."

"So romantic!" Ben said breathily as he shut the dishwasher. Then he pretended his legs were weak, swaying like he was losing his balance. "I might need smelling salts!"

"Too much?" Jace asked. "I was trying to woo you."

Ben grew serious. "There's no such thing as too much. Not when it comes to you."

"That's good," Jace said, pulling him close, "because we're sleeping on the couch tonight and it's going to be a very, *very* tight squeeze."

As if to demonstrate this, Jace squeezed him, hard enough that Ben cried out.

"Actually," Serena said, "your sister's old room is now a guest room."

Ben yelped in surprise, not having noticed her arrival. Jace relaxed his grip. Ben tried not to blush as he moved away. He failed.

"It's very private," Serena continued, seeming amused by this display. Then as an aside, she added, "Thank goodness for that."

Jace looked puzzled. "I thought we'd stay in my old room."

Serena shook her head. "That's your father's new office."

"He took over my old bedroom?" Jace said, nearing a whine.

Ben tried not to laugh. He knew all too well how easily parent and child roles reasserted themselves. "I'm not picky. All I need is a couch and a blanket."

Jace continued to pout. "What does he need an office for? He's retired!"

"You know how your father is," Serena said, sounding slightly exhausted. "He likes to keep busy, and I need his mess confined to one room."

"What about my old things?"

"They're in the closet. You didn't leave much here." Serena pursed her lips briefly. "You're a grown man now. I didn't think you'd mind."

"Of course not," Jace said, shooting Ben a self-conscious gaze. Then, as if trying to save face, he added, "I just wish you had waited until I was here. I could have helped move the heavier items."

"Somehow we managed," Serena replied. "I'm going to fix myself a coffee. Would you like one?"

"No, I thought I'd drag Ben out into this gorgeous weather and show him the lake. Do you mind?"

"Not at all. There aren't any plans until tomorrow when your sister and her family arrive. You boys have fun."

"We always do." Jace grabbed Ben by the hand, leading him toward the back door. "Come along, honey buns. If we don't go fishing, there won't be anything to eat for dinner."

* * * * *

First impressions are of the utmost importance, which always seemed weird to Ben, because he found them so unreliable. The lake was a perfect example. Up close the body of water was much less impressive than from far away. In fact, it was barely more than a pond. Jace didn't grow up waterskiing or sunbathing on the deck of a yacht. Only the smallest of fishing boats could navigate this lake comfortably, and that would first require traversing one of the decayed wooden docks.

Similarly, the home of Jace's parents wasn't illustrious or excessive. Sure, the house was spread out over three stories, but the interior was of fairly average size. The rooms contained within were all practical and necessary, or at least would have been for parents raising two kids. Few families had a valley and lake behind their home, but these too were likely chosen with children in mind, since they made a nice playground. Jace's parents didn't seem the type to worry about their image or social status.

The lake was equally humble. Only the shore closest to the neighborhood was maintained. The far side was overgrown, forcing them to walk slowly and choose their steps carefully. Jace filled this time by sharing more childhood memories, such as learning to ice skate on the lake's frozen surface. His father had taught him how, his mother constantly worried about the ice not being thick enough. He was in the middle of describing a nasty fall he'd taken when they reached the edge of the forest. There they paused. Jace grew silent, his story forgotten as he stared into the dark depths.

"What's in there?" Ben asked.

"Ghosts," Jace answered. "Maybe even a werewolf."

"Sounds like fun," Ben said, taking a step forward.

Jace grabbed his shoulder. "It'll be dark soon. We better not wander too far."

His advice was sound. The sun had set by the time they finished circling the lake and returned inside. Jace had been joking about needing to fish, but Ben wasn't too concerned either way. Lunch had been late, and he dreaded the idea of packing in another meal. Evidently he wasn't alone in this feeling, because only light snacks had been prepared and set out on the coffee table in the living room. The family gathered there, the vibe casual, everyone engaged in their own task while still interacting. Jace flipped through channels on the TV, making fun of local commercials. Serena brushed a cat on her lap, another one taking its place when the first hopped down. Bob browsed a newspaper, reading aloud whenever he found something interesting. The mood was made even more mellow when Bob poured three glasses of whisky, Serena opting for wine.

Ben was content to ignore his drink and quietly observe everyone, deciphering which traits Jace had inherited from which parent. The good looks came from his mother, thankfully, although Ben amused himself by imagining Jace going bald and donning a pair of thick spectacles like his father. A love for animals and a graceful nature came from his mother too. All the eccentric stuff and a love of reading came from Bob. Jace was lucky, having gotten the best of both worlds. Heck, *Ben* was lucky, because he got to spend his life with this man.

He looked over at his boyfriend, who raised his empty glass, jangling the ice. Ben had barely touched his, not really enjoying the taste. He made a pleading face and—making sure they weren't being watched—exchanged his glass for Jace's. Of course when that one was emptied, another round was poured. Once again Jace was drinking for two, but he seemed to handle it well. Mostly. He was a little wobbly when they finally decided to retire. The guest room was on the bottom floor. Jace collapsed onto the bed, then propped himself up on his elbows to look around.

"Michelle's old room. I wish they had left it the way it was." He turned his head to the high-set window and chuckled. "You have no idea how many boys snuck in through there at night."

"For her," Ben said.

"Unfortunately. Although there was this one guy..."

Ben took in the shit-eating grin and shook his head. "You're drunk. I'm going to get ready. Then we're going to bed."

"Sounds like a plan," Jace said, still leering at him.

Ben waited until he was in the connecting bathroom before allowing himself a smile. This should be an interesting evening. He'd never seen Jace so intoxicated. Maybe it would add extra spice to their sex life. Ben made sure he was squeaky clean, even flossing and using mouthwash before he returned to the bedroom. When he did, he found it empty.

He waited, thinking Jace had gone for a glass of water or

something. After ten minutes passed without his return, Ben decided to investigate. The house was dark now. Ben felt like one of those boys sneaking in the window for love. That brought back a few memories of his own, but he shoved them aside as he went upstairs. Kitchen, dining room, and front room were all empty. The next set of stairs led to a hallway. He hesitated, because one of these doors opened to the master bedroom, and if he chose wrong, the situation would be really awkward. "Hello again, Mr. and Mrs. Holden. Just wanted to say goodnight!" Right.

He nibbled on a fingernail, considering each door until he noticed a sliver of light from the closest one. Seeing that it wasn't completely shut, he crept forward to peek inside. The trappings of a messy office met his eye, as did familiar blonde hair over the edge of a desk, partly concealed behind a stack of paper. He pushed the door open and entered. Jace was sitting on the floor, surrounded by a number of items he had dragged from the closet. Ben was about to speak when he heard a sniff. The wet kind, normally reserved for a bad cold. Or crying. Jace wasn't sick, so...

"You all right?"

Jace hurriedly wiped at his face, then looked over his shoulder and forced a grin. "Yeah. Just going through some of my old stuff."

Ben approached and looked over his shoulder. In a battered shoebox was a notebook, a carving of a wooden lion, and a handful of photos. Jace was holding one of them, and after hesitating, he held it up so Ben could see. The picture revealed a punky guy who was pulling on a cigarette, his amused eyes reflecting the burning ember.

"Is that him?" Ben asked, sitting on the carpet. "Is that Victor?"

Jace looked over in surprise. "You remember his name?"

"Hey, I pay attention when you talk! This guy was like your Tim, right? The lesson you had to learn." He reached for the photo.

Jace handed it to him. "Yeah. That's him."

"He's cute," Ben said, ignoring a stir of jealousy. They were both allowed to have a past, and considering what he'd done in their present a few months back, Ben definitely wasn't one to judge. It's just that Jace had gotten weepy while looking at this photo. "Punks are hot. I dated a guy in Chicago sort of like this. Right before we met, but he wasn't as— Hey! Are his eyes mismatched?"

Jace smiled. "Yeah. I thought it was freaky when I first met him. I grew to love it."

Love. Strong word. Ben handed back the photo and reached for the others. "Do you mind?"

"Go ahead."

Most were of Victor from different angles. Always in the same jacket, always with a cigarette hanging out of his mouth. With one exception. In that one he was grinning, the expression matched by the lanky guy with shoulder-length hair who was standing next to him. Ben stared. Then he started laughing. "Your hair!"

"Shut up," Jace said, trying to swipe the picture from him, but his drunken reflexes were too slow.

"It's so pretty!" Ben said, still laughing. "Holy crap. You must have spent an hour each morning just brushing it!"

"*He* liked it," Jace taunted.

"I like it too," Ben lied.

"Good, because I'm growing it out again."

Ben blanched. "Uh…"

"That's what I thought." Jace managed to snatch away the photo and brought it close to his face. "The nineties," he said, shaking his head while staring at his younger self. Then his eyes moved to Victor, and he grew solemn again. He dropped the photo in the box and dug around, pulling out an old Zippo lighter. "So dumb," he mumbled, seemingly to himself.

"What is?"

"This!" Jace gestured to the box. "It's all that's left. This and a Halloween mask back home. Don't throw it out if you ever find it."

Ben furrowed his brow, still not understanding. "How much did you drink, exactly?"

Jace flicked open the lighter, one finger spinning the wheel, but it no longer sparked. "He was an important person to me. Now he's just a box of junk. Makes you wonder if we all end up that way."

"I'm already multiple boxes. You should see how much stuff Allison saved from when we were younger. She could open a museum, not that anyone would want to…" He trailed off because Jace was wiping his eyes again. One tear managed to break free, a wet streak trailing down his cheek. Ben struggled to remember if he'd ever seen Jace cry, even during a movie. "Hey, it's okay! It's not junk, and it's not dumb. These things help you remember. It's the memories that count. You've got yours, and Victor has his. Hell, I bet he has a box full of Jace paraphernalia. Ever give him a lock of your hair?"

Jace spluttered laughter and shook his head. "No."

"Well, don't worry. I'm sure on occasion he drinks too much whisky and gets all emotional about you too."

Jace met his eye. "I get it now. What you did. I understand why it happened."

Ben swallowed. He knew exactly what Jace was talking about, but he asked anyway. "Why I did what?"

"Why you cheated on me. With Tim."

Ben's throat constricted. "Technically we were taking a break when that happened. But I'm sorry. I wish I could undo it all. I hate that it still—"

Jace raised a hand to stop him. "Don't feel bad. Those first loves, they get in deep. Like a tattoo. They get under your skin, and no matter how faded they grow over time, no matter how much the edges blur, they're still there when you look down. And sometimes you remember how vibrant they used to be."

Ben groped around in his mind for a response, but couldn't find words among the growing clutter of jealousy and insecurity. He knew he deserved this because he had been reminded of that vibrancy when he met Tim again and acted on those feelings. Doing so had put Jace through hell, but somehow he was able to forgive. Now Ben knew why, and he supposed he was okay with it, but nothing prepared him for what Jace said next.

"I want him back."

As a friend? As a lover? Did he want to *be* with Victor again? Ben couldn't deny him that. Fair was fair, but it would mean they would have to take another break, and the thought alone made his chest ache. "Are you unhappy with us? With me?"

Jace looked surprised. "I don't mean it like that." He tossed the lighter back in the box. "I just wish he was more than these, these… *things*. I wish he was still part of my life." He reached for the lid, closed the box, and stood. With his foot he nudged it back into the closet. "Enough. Let's call it a night."

Ben rose and followed him out of the office and back

downstairs. Jace collapsed onto the bed after Ben helped him get undressed. Once they were both beneath the sheets, Jace threw an arm around him and promptly fell asleep. Not Ben though. His eyes remained open for quite some time, staring unfocused at the shadows on the wall.

Ben was mostly silent during breakfast the next morning, providing Jace with the opportunity to clarify last night's discussion. Now that he was sober, maybe he would make more sense. Or at least chase away the concerns gnawing at Ben's insides. Jace didn't speak much as they showered together, and at the breakfast table he ate slowly, wincing occasionally. A hangover. Did that mean he had been too drunk to remember anything?

"Quite a night," Ben said as he helped Jace carry dishes to the kitchen. "Last night," he added, just in case there was any confusion.

"I overdid it," Jace admitted. Nothing else though.

"You seemed pretty emotional before bed."

Jace blinked a few times. "Did I?"

"Yeah. Remember?"

The doorbell rang, causing Jace to grimace. "That can't be my sister already."

Loud voices soon confirmed it was. Ben kept watching Jace, who seemed to think the conversation had reached its natural conclusion. So maybe he didn't remember. Was that a good thing? Alcohol tended to strip away the layers, revealing what lurked beneath the surface. The fact remained that Jace still loved Victor. That was okay. That he wanted him back, was so distraught over it… *That* was cause for alarm. Ben understood though. He still thought of Tim, probably more often than he should, but he had taken Jace's advice. Tim was part of his past now. Ben had made his peace with that.

The noise from the front room invaded the kitchen, a hyperactive five-year-old barreling into Ben's legs and then Jace's. This was Preston's version of a hug, and it only lasted the briefest of seconds. Then he noticed a cat and chased it down the stairs to the family room. Emma arrived next, chubby cheeks rosy as she smiled at them. Her mother, Michelle, was right behind her, holding a sleepy three-year-old boy.

Jace's sister, nephews, and niece. Ben had met them before, since they lived in Houston. He had worn himself out playing with the kids every Fourth of July, except last year, when busy schedules and relentless rain had put a damper on their plans. Seeing how big the kids were getting reminded him of how long it had been.

"Hi, Uncah Ben," Emma held out her arms for a hug, and Ben was happy to comply. Still, she was eight, a little old to still have pronunciation issues. While hugging her, he glanced up at Michelle, who seemed somewhat embarrassed.

Emma went next to Jace, repeating the ritual with the same strange pronunciation. *Uncah.* Then she went to the door leading to the deck, turning to tacitly seek permission from her mother.

"It's lovely out today," Michelle said. "Let's all go."

A moment later they were seated on the wooden deck together and enjoying the morning sun. Everyone but Jace, who was shielding his eyes.

"I should have warned you," Michelle said, tittering. "Dad pours them extra strong these days."

"You're not kidding." Jace looked pale, then a little green when Preston decided to crawl over him and ended up kneeing his stomach.

"Greg blacked out last time we were here," Michelle said. "Ended up in your old room, like you two were having a sleepover."

Ben looked to Jace, searching for a reaction. A triggered memory.

Instead, Jace winced when one of the kids started yelling. "How did you get here so early?" he murmured. "Did you fly?"

"We drove. We got into town late last night and went straight to the Trout house."

Ben chuckled at the name, glancing across the valley at a house perched on the opposite side. That's where Greg grew up—Jace's best friend, and the person who eventually married his sister. How quaint was that? Michelle had literally married the boy next door. Or at least the one across the valley.

"Just be glad they have lots of space over there," she continued. "Otherwise we'd all be stuffed into my old bed."

Jace didn't respond, more concerned with stopping Preston from clambering over him a second time. He grabbed his nephew under the armpits when he got close, lifted him up and set him on the other side of his lawn chair. This instantly became a game, with Preston wanting to be lifted back and forth. After a few minutes of this, Jace rose.

"I think I'm going to lie down again. Just for a little while."

"Headache or hangover?" Michelle asked.

"Both." Jace paused, looking at Ben. "You'll be all right?"

"Around your family? God no!"

Michelle laughed. Jace seemed relieved. Then he left.

"Wow," she said. "I haven't seen him that wrecked since we were teenagers."

"Did he drink a lot back then?" Ben asked, already knowing where he intended to steer the conversation.

"Not too much. We used to steal Dad's whisky. Which was *disgusting!*" Michelle added when she noticed Emma listening. "Honey, go watch out for your brothers. Make sure they don't wander too far."

Emma shrugged as if it was no concern of hers, but she went to find the boys anyway.

"Did you guys ever have parties?" Ben asked. "Like with lots of friends?"

"No, not really. I had some birthday parties, but not what you're thinking. Jace mostly just had Greg. Does two dorky guys running around the woods and playing Rambo count as a party?"

"No," Ben said, smiling at the image. Then he swallowed. "What about Victor?"

"Victor!" Michelle said, indecipherable emotions playing across her face. "He was more of a boyfriend."

"Yeah," Ben said, trying to find the right question. Instead he just stared.

Michelle noticed. She dealt with troubled kids every day in her line of work, ones much more practiced at hiding their emotions than Ben was. "Has he been talking about Victor lately?"

"Sort of," Ben said. "Last night, actually. When he was drunk. He even dug out some old photos. I don't mind. I know how important he was to Jace. Kind of cute too, in his own way. Um..."

"You're not jealous of him," Michelle said, a note of disapproval in her voice.

"No. Well, maybe."

"Seriously," Michelle said. "It's not like he's going to show up and steal Jace away. I don't see how you could feel threatened by—"

"Jace said he wanted Victor back," Ben said, getting defensive. "When he was drunk. Not just like, 'Oh, I wonder what ever happened to him, it would be fun to catch up.' More like it pained him that they weren't together anymore."

Michelle's eyes were wide. She considered this in silence. Then she exhaled. "Jace has talked to you about Victor, right? Before last night. You know about him."

"Yeah. He was an important part of Jace's life. I know all that."

Her expression said he didn't. "Communication is crucial. Relationships can survive a lot. Infidelity, doubt, lies, ebbing passion—that all comes with the territory. But if there's one thing I've seen destroy relationship after relationship, it's communication shutting down. That's a death sentence right there."

Ben sat up straight, his muscles tense. "You're freaking me out."

"Good!" Michelle said. "I like you. No, I *love* you. I want you to be my brother-in-law some day, so if I'm scaring you, that's good, because I know you're smart enough to fix this."

"To fix what?"

"Communication," Michelle repeated, crossing her arms over her chest. "Not with me. With him."

He opened his mouth to respond, then shut it again because she was right. The person he should be talking to was inside the house, trying to sleep off a hangover.

"How you doin'?" said a loud voice, the kind Jace wouldn't be able to handle right now.

Ben liked it though, since the voice belonged to a great guy. Greg was at the kitchen counter, flipping steaks back and forth in flour.

"They've got you on cooking duty?" Ben asked, moving closer to investigate.

"Yup! We're going to grill us up some food, Mizz-ur-rah style!"

Ben laughed, then quickly looked away when Greg pushed the pan to the side and turned to face him.

"How are things back home? We haven't seen you lately. Been busy? Find a job yet?"

Ben studied the kitchen floor. "No. Still temping. I hate it."

"That's rough." Greg walked around him to rinse his hands in the sink. "You should try real estate. People like you. That's half the battle right there. I think you'd be good at it."

"Not really my thing."

"Uh huh."

Ben noticed how scuffed the linoleum was around the stove, probably from so many people standing in that spot when cooking. "How are you?"

"Fine."

"Good."

"Yup." Greg cleared his throat. "Can I ask you something?"

"Sure!"

"Do you have issues about making eye contact? Because I saw you talking to Michelle, and you were looking right at her. But with me, it's like I scare you."

Ben felt his cheeks flush. He forced himself to raise his head, eyes traversing over the person he was speaking with. Freaking Greg! Why'd he have to be so handsome? Brown hair and eyes, which normally wouldn't be exceptional if not for the killer body, lopsided grin, and easy charm—like scientists had distilled all the best traits from a slew of frat boys and removed the drunk asshole gene, creating the perfect guy. Except Ben already had the perfect guy. Who knew there could be two?

"It's the muscles, isn't it?" Greg said, making them bounce. "Go on, admit it."

Ben covered his eyes and groaned in embarrassment. "It's hard not to stare because, yes, you're good looking and I don't want to creep you out and I'm totally madly completely in love with your best friend so don't get the wrong idea. Please! But yes, it's a little awkward."

Greg guffawed. "I'm used to it from Jace, don't worry."

Ben lowered his hand. "Really?"

"Yeah! Occasionally I'd catch him looking at me that way. Especially after he came out. He'd practically start panting, then his eyes would reach my face and he'd look a little nauseous. Instant cold shower."

"You've got a great face!"

"Thanks, but I think it's because I'm *me*. You know? My body is one thing, but he's definitely not into me. Still, I always found it flattering. I can't remember the last time I caught him doing that, but it doesn't make me uncomfortable. Feel better?"

"Barely," Ben admitted.

"I'd rather you check me out than feel like you can't look at me."

"I'll try to keep my eyes above your shoulders."

"Your loss," Greg teased. "Wait until Jace hears about this!"

"I'd bribe you to keep silent, but I'm totally broke."

Greg chuckled again, turning to open cabinets until he found some spices. "So what do you think of my hometown?"

"I like it," Ben admitted. At least he had until the recent mystery. He realized it was cheating, but if anyone knew Jace's deep dark secrets, one of his closest friends would. "Then again, I feel a little left out. Everyone seems to know more about what's going on than I do."

"I hear you," Greg said. He was back at his steaks, shaking some kind of powder over them. "When I first moved to Houston, I felt completely lost. Like one of the Beverly Hillbillies. All it takes is a little time."

"Yeah, but small towns have more secrets."

Greg looked at him. "Do they?"

"You tell me."

He seemed to think about it. Then he leaned forward and spoke in a soft voice. "Don't tell anyone, but I'm sleeping with my best friend's sister."

Ben felt disappointed but forced a smile. "Did that cause tension between you two?"

"Naw," Greg said, resuming his work. "You know how Jace is. He's a laid-back guy. Doesn't have any demons. You can trust him."

Greg put enough emphasis on this to prove the conversation hadn't gone over his head. Ben was glad for the reassurance, but that wasn't the issue. The real question was if Jace felt like he could trust Ben.

Family is great, especially during reunions when everyone is chirping nonstop like a tree full of birds on the first day of spring. But all that togetherness meant private time with Jace was difficult to find. Anxiety had settled in Ben's stomach and refused to leave. He was eager to dispel it, so when the afternoon rolled around and Michelle and her family returned to the house across the valley, Ben casually pulled Jace into the hallway.

"Can we talk?"

"Sounds like we already are," Jace said, flashing him a smile.

"Feeling better?"

Jace nodded. "Yeah. Mostly. You know how when you drink too much, you crave the grossest food the next day? I need a gas station burger. Let's go get one."

Ben didn't hide his concern. "Are you sure your stomach can handle that? You barely touched lunch."

"I know it's counterintuitive, but it's exactly what I need. What did you want to talk about?"

"This and that. We can talk on the way."

"Sounds good." Jace patted his pockets to find the car keys. Once he had them in hand, he led the way to the front door. "There's someone else I want you to meet while we're out."

"Really?" Ben said, his mouth feeling dry. "Who?"

"Someone important to me. It's a surprise."

Victor. Who else could it be? Making an issue of him now — just before they were about to meet — would be beyond awkward. Ben avoided the subject once they were in the car and instead asked about Jace's childhood. This led to more stories from his youth, but Ben found these difficult to concentrate on, paying only enough attention to listen for one name in particular. That was silly though, because all he had to do was stop playing games and ask.

"Jace—"

The car took a sharp left turn as they pulled into a parking lot. "Here we are!" Jace was grinning like mad. "I hope he's working today."

"The person we're supposed to meet?" Ben asked incredulously.

"Yup!"

"He's in *there*?"

Jace laughed. "Don't sound so nervous. He's family. Come on."

Oh. Okay. Not Victor, unless that's how Jace described their closeness these days. When they entered the store, Ben scanned the interior for a dark mohawk and mismatched eyes. He didn't see anyone matching that description. A loud greeting and happy laughter drew his attention. Jace was hugging someone, and he definitely wasn't Victor. The man was old, his black skin leathery, his hair white and thin. He was wearing a pair of overalls that were filled by a big belly. Even after the hug ended, he still held Jace's hand a moment, eyes shining as he looked him over.

"What a nice surprise," the man said. "Don't tell me, you've finally decided to accept my offer. You'll move home and run the store?"

"Afraid not," Jace said. "My work is in the sky, and my home—" He turned and nodded at Ben. "—is with this guy."

The older man noticed him, face lighting up. "This is him? This is Ben?"

"Hi," Ben said sheepishly, offering a hand.

"Nice to meet you, son! I'm Bernard."

"You can call him Bernie," Jace said, an edge of teasing in his voice. "That's the name on the store outside. Must be there for a reason."

"Call me whatever you like," Bernard said easily. "I just hope you've heard half as much about me as I have you."

Ben racked his memory. "Didn't you drag him out of a river once?"

"Like a cold dead fish!" Bernard laughed, patting Ben's hand a few times before finally releasing it. "You should have seen his face. I made him take a shower when I got him back to my camper, mostly because I was certain he had shit himself."

"You see?" Jace said. "This is why he's family. Only relatives can humiliate each other with such swift precision."

"We are indeed family," Bernard said, "although you'd never guess it to look at us."

Ben smiled. Jace went to get his microwave burger, leaving them alone.

"Memories can make the past seem so near to us," Bernard said. "Seems like yesterday he was just an ornery, messed-up teenager, but when I see the man he's become, it feels like a million years have gone by."

"I wish I could see him like that again," Ben said. "It's hard to imagine. Jace has it so together."

"I'm glad to hear it, but he's had his rough times, just like we all do. And look at you!" Bernard patted him on the shoulder. "I think Jace has finally found his happily ever after! Am I right?"

"I hope so," Ben replied, face flushing a little. "I'm trying not to mess it up."

"You better not. You hear me?" Bernard's eyes—faded with age—were dead serious.

"Geez, no pressure!" Ben said, chucking to relieve tension.

Bernard laughed with him to show he'd only been kidding. "No pressure at all. Just know that I'll be at your wedding. Have you set a date yet?"

"Why does everyone keep talking about marriage?" Jace hollered from the other side of the store. "This microwave is filthy, by the way. I never let it get this dirty!"

"You know what to do!" Bernard replied, seeming pleased when Jace went through a door marked *Employees Only*.

"He used to work here?"

"Oh yes," Bernard said. "Although sometimes he got paid for standing around and socializing with that friend of his."

"Greg?"

"Victor. Eventually he started working here too. Victor never worried about the microwave getting dirty though. Too lost in his own thoughts. I always liked that about him. Not good for the business, but the world needs dreamers."

Great. Victor had punky sex appeal, had been Jace's first love, and was a thinker. He probably had a cool artistic job, like writing plays or managing bands. "What's he do these days?"

Bernard appeared startled. "Victor?"

"Yeah. Assuming he doesn't work here anymore."

"Son, Victor passed away a long time ago. I'm surprised you didn't know that."

A pit opened in Ben's stomach, more than one emotion plummeting into the depths. He felt foolish for not knowing, wounded that Jace had never confided in him, and sad for a man he had never met. While not proud of it, he also felt a sting of animosity. Victor had been the first to win Jace's heart—would always have a place there—and that was okay. But now he knew that Victor's name was carved into Jace's heart, his death cutting deeper emotionally than Ben ever could. Jesus, had they still been together when it happened?

"Death always comes as unwelcome news," Bernard said, studying him, "even years after the fact. Must be hard for Jace to talk about. I'm sure he'll tell you in his own time. Best to let it happen that way, if you understand what I mean."

Ben did. He wasn't supposed to know about this yet. But when would Jace tell him? Wasn't three years enough to establish trust? How long was Jace going to wait? Still, none of this was Bernard's fault. Getting mopey about it now would be rude.

"I don't know if you'll thank me for this," Bernard said, "but you're welcome to any food in the store. If you're hungry."

"I'd rather hear more stories about Jace when he was a teenager," Ben said, spotting him returning from the back room. "The more embarrassing the better."

"Oh, I've got a few of those. Like the time I got a call from one of my regulars that I needed to hustle to the store because something was wrong with my clerk. It was around midnight if I remember correctly, and I show up in a fit to find Jace draped across the counter, snoring his head off."

"What are you talking about?" Jace asked, working on cleaning the microwave.

"Nothing!" Bernard lowered his voice. "Lord knows how long Jace had been sleeping, but there was a small pile of cash next to him with notes from customers, saying what they had bought. God bless this town! You'll never find more honest people. Imagine what would happen in Houston if people walked into a gas station and found the clerk asleep."

"Clearance sale," Ben said. "The kind where everything is free. So nobody tried to wake him?"

"At least one person did, but he had taken sleeping pills—"

"No you don't!" Jace said, hurrying over, the microwave humming behind him. "I'm not letting you tell that story. You make it sound bad, when it just so happens I had been studying *really* hard."

"And staying out late," Bernard said helpfully.

"Anyway, I had a headache and so—"

"And so this genius helps himself to the sleeping pills." Bernard jerked his thumb at an endcap full of medicine.

"They were aspirin," Jace said. "And yes, sleeping pills too. The box said 'P.M.' on it, and I thought it meant they worked better at night. Somehow."

"Makes perfect sense," Ben said, trying not to laugh. "Still, are they really that strong?"

"If you take double the recommended dose," Bernard supplied.

"It was a bad headache!" Jace said. "I did sleep really well. And I got paid for it, so the joke's on you, old man."

"The joke is watching the old security footage of you drooling on the counter."

Jace stiffened and his eyes went wide, just as the microwave dinged. "There were security cameras? Seriously?"

"Judging from that guilty expression," Bernard said, "I can only imagine what else you got up to. And no, there weren't cameras, but now I wish there had been."

Ben laughed, feeling more relaxed. Bernard kept telling stories, most of them harmless, because Jace clearly had a good life while growing up. Maybe that made talking about the darker moments more difficult. Ben would wait, but until Jace decided to open up to him, he would still feel like they were both haunted by Victor's ghost.

Ben adopted the thinker pose, matching the sculpture by Rodin, as he often did when in this room. He wondered if Rodin had come up with the idea while seated on the toilet himself, because it sure suited the occasion. Ben took his time, enjoying the solitude, having grown weary of the constant social interaction after another night with his potential in-laws. The idea made him smile, even though that future now seemed less certain.

When finished, he checked himself in the mirror, washed his hands, then went into the upstairs hallway where he had retreated for extra privacy. Not that he really needed it. Jace and his parents were out on the balcony, soaking up the sun. A family ritual, it would seem. That's why he felt puzzled when hearing the shuffling of paper in Jace's old room. Ben poked his head inside and found a little girl seated at the desk, her face solemn as she brought piles into order.

"Emma? What are you doing here?"

"I'm playing president," she replied.

He walked into the room. "Is your mom here?"

"Nope."

"Your dad?"

"Nuh-uh."

"Does anyone know you're here?"

"No. I walked over by myself. I needed alone time."

He could relate to that.

"You can stay," she added. "I like you, Uncah Ben."

He perched on the edge of the desk, watching her move papers around. "So what are you doing? Signing bills into legislation? Repealing laws your predecessor worked hard to enact?"

"Is that what presidents do?"

"When not telling the military to blow things up, yes."

"Then that's exactly what I'm doing."

Ben tapped an old water bill. "Sign here, please. And here."

As they whiled away the time in this manner, Ben observed Emma when she was distracted. She was a little overweight for her age, and sometimes solemn when around her brothers. But otherwise, she was bright and talkative. Speaking of which... "What am I to you?" he asked. "Me and Jace. What are we?"

"My uncahs."

Ben nodded. "Right. But it's actually said differently. Uncle. You say it."

"Uncah."

Demonstrating the proper pronunciation of the word obviously wouldn't be enough or someone would have already corrected her. "What's a solider do in battle?"

"Fight."

"And sometimes in the really bad battles he has to..."

Emma caught on. "Kill."

"Which is sad," Ben said, "because someone probably loved the person who was killed, making them wish it could be undone, so that the dead guy could be un-killed."

Emma made a face. "Is that a real word?"

"If we want it to be. You say it."

Now Emma looked offended.

"Un-kill," Ben tried. "I'm un-kill Ben. Get it?"

Emma sighed. "I know how to say uncle."

Ben's jaw dropped. "Then why don't you?"

"Because it's cute. Everyone makes a big deal when I say it all dumb like that."

"So you've been playing us this whole time?"

Emma returned to signing random pieces of paper. "People like it when I'm cute."

"Okay," Ben said. "Fair enough. Um... You know my sister? Your Aunt Karen."

Emma made a repulsed face.

"Exactly. My mom used to put a bow in her hair when she

was little. A great big red thing the size of her head. I've seen photos, and sure, it was cute. She must have gotten a lot of praise for that bow, because she kept wearing it. Into her teens. Imagine Karen in glasses with braces and pimples, *fifteen years old*, and she still has this stupidly huge bow in her hair. Instead of people thinking she was cute, they started making fun of her. Enough that she finally stopped. Maybe Karen actually liked the bow, because let's face it, she's got bad taste. But if you're only talking a certain way so people will like you, try being yourself instead. In the end, that's what people will respect most. They'll like you for being who you really are."

Emma studied him briefly, then continued playing with her papers. He wasn't sure if any of his lecture had sunk in. Not until they decided to join the others on the back deck. Emma greeted her grandparents first, then she turned to Jace.

"Uncle Jace!" She said. "I'm the president now!"

Jace appeared startled. Then delighted. He picked up Emma and swung her around, kissing her face until she started laughing and protesting.

"He'd make a great father," Serena murmured from next to him. "You both would. Do you ever think about having children? Is that something you want?"

"Eventually," Ben said. "I still have to get my own life figured out and find a real job first." He watched how happy Jace seemed, how his eyes sparkled as he continued to tease his niece. "Maybe someday."

"Wanna go for a walk?"

Ben looked up in surprise at the offer. Jace's expression was pensive. Perhaps because it had been another full day. Michelle and Greg had come searching for Emma once they noticed her missing, bringing the two boys with them. Greg's parents stopped by soon with food. After hours of conversation and eating, all Ben wanted to do was bask in the silence now that everyone had gone. The house was finally quiet. Even the television was off. All he could hear were the sounds of whisky on ice and the occasional turning of a magazine page as Jace's parents unwound. Ben was playing on his laptop, but his boyfriend's eyes were hopeful and waiting for an answer.

"Okay. Let's go."

The sun was already setting as they walked down to the

lake. Ben imagined they would sit on the dock and listen to the sounds of nature. Instead they skirted around the water's edge and entered the woods.

"Do you know where we're going?" Ben asked, blinking in the increasing gloom.

"Of course," Jace said. "Don't worry. You're safe with me. I won't let any bears get you."

"Ha!" Ben walked a few more steps, then glanced behind him when he heard the underbrush rustling. "There aren't any bears in Missouri. Are there?"

"Only one way to find out."

Jace seemed confident, never hesitating as he guided them deeper into the woods. Eventually they reached a clearing, the open sky above them burnt orange, the first stars already twinkling from trillions of miles away. Jace walked slower, as if inspecting his surroundings, but Ben couldn't see much of anything. Just leaves and dirt. Jace spotted something though, and bent to lift a thick branch, brushing away debris and revealing torn canvas tied around one end.

"I wonder if someone knocked it down," Jace said. "Or maybe it was the weather."

"Did you have a tree house here? Or a fort?"

Jace seemed surprised by Ben's presence. He dropped the branch and stood upright. "I'm sorry about the other night," he said. "That must have been uncomfortable for you."

Ben swallowed. "I wasn't sure you remembered."

"It's blurry," Jace said. "I believe I got upset about Victor being nothing more than a box. Am I right?"

"Yeah." Ben tried to smile reassuringly, but Jace looked so solemn that he didn't manage. "What is this place?"

"This is Victor," Jace said, gesturing around him. "Not that box. Not those trinkets. This is where he really is. This pile of wood used to be a shelter. The original one was on that side, actually. Victor would camp out in this clearing. His way of being close to me. A lot happened here. This is where I came out to Greg, but only because Victor forced me to. Asshole." He said this with warmth in his voice, and a subtle smile. "This clearing is where I first confessed my feelings, first kissed another boy, and uh… Everything. It happened right here. This is even where I said goodbye."

Jace turned to face him, half his face glowing orange from the last light of the day, the rest lost in shadow. His voice wavered when he spoke. "This is Victor's final resting place. He died a long time ago, Ben."

He didn't know how to respond. No words seemed adequate. He felt like taking Jace into his arms, but not here. Somehow it was too sacred. He felt as though he was trespassing.

Jace turned away, scuffing at the ground with his foot, still digging for the past. "I never told you because I didn't want it to be true. The first time you asked me a question about Victor—I don't even know what it was anymore. Nothing unusual, but you phrased it like he was still alive, and I didn't want to contradict you. I wanted to believe it was true. To pretend."

Ben swallowed. "What happened? Am I wrong to ask?"

Jace took a deep breath and exhaled. Then he told Ben everything. At first he talked about the good times, like he was still denying anything had ever gone wrong. Then he spoke about their time apart, and how they had found each other again. The story was familiar in many ways, not so different from Ben's own. Except the end was ugly. Jace cried as he revealed the details. Ben joined him because he could only imagine that level of pain. For one fleeting instance, he wished he could check on Tim. Not to chase after any unresolved feelings, but just to make sure he was okay, that he was still flashing his winner's smile and behaving like the world belonged to him. But mostly Ben hurt for Jace, knowing no way to comfort him. Some pain is permanent. And deep.

Ben looked around the clearing, trying to imagine everything that had happened there. "Where is he buried?"

"Not buried," Jace said. He crouched, touching the tips of his fingers to the leaves. "I scattered his ashes here. No one else knows that. Not my family, not Greg. Just you. I thought telling you might make up for having kept so much secret. And because I have a request."

Ben clenched his jaw, but not because he was angry. "What?"

"If anything ever happens to me—"

"Okay," Ben said, holding up a hand to stop him. "I get it. You don't have to say it out loud."

Jace studied him. "You'll do it?"

"Yes. Now can we please go somewhere else so I can kiss you?"

"What's wrong with here?"

"It seems… disrespectful."

Jace smiled. "Because of Victor? Are you kidding? He would love it!"

Ben made a face. "Seriously?"

"Yup. I'll spare you one of his lectures, because basically they all boiled down to giving in to your feelings instead of denying them."

Ben held out his hand. "Sounds like my kind of guy."

Jace came close, took Ben's hand, and pressed it to his heart. "I love you, Ben. More than anything. I hope you know that."

"I love you too."

A moment later, all the negative emotions that had clung to Ben fled, chased away by a single kiss.

The car was blissfully silent as they drove through Warrensburg, neither of them speaking until they reached the city limits.

"Funny how these visits work," Jace said. "We have our own lives now, but whenever we want, we can return home and rediscover the past. Like a museum where most of the exhibits are broken, dusty, or straight-up missing, but there's still enough there to remind you of how it used to be. Once it gets too painful or boring, you get to leave it all behind again."

"Not all of it," Ben said mysteriously. He didn't clarify, not even when Jace shot him a questioning expression. In one corner of his suitcase was an old shoe box. In it rested a wooden lion, a notebook, some photos, and a battered Zippo lighter. They were taking Victor home with them. A little piece of him, anyway. He hoped Jace would discover the box someday and feel glad about it. Until then, Ben would set it next to a box of his own, one that also held trinkets belonging to a dusty corner of his heart.

"So you liked my parents?" Jace asked. "They didn't drive you crazy?"

"I love them! Your whole family, actually. I wouldn't mind becoming an official member." Ben cleared his throat. "Somehow."

Jace grinned. "Why does everyone keep talking about marriage? We've got a few adventures left before that happens. Open the glove box."

Now it was Ben's turn to look puzzled.

"Go on," Jace prompted. "Otherwise I'll forget they're in there, and someone from the rental company will get a paid trip to… You'll see."

Ben opened the glove compartment and found a pair of airline tickets. They weren't for the flight home to Austin. He read the destination and came close to crying. "Paris?"

"Yup."

"As in France?"

"I don't mean Paris, Texas!"

"But we always said…" Ben trailed off, not wanting to jinx it.

"Said what?" Jace asked, focusing on the road. "We take an international trip every spring. That we eventually visit Paris was inevitable. Right?"

"Yeah," Ben said, reaching over to take his hand. "It's definitely meant to be."

A lonely flight. Then a rental car, the interior silent. GPS and a map were his guide now, instead of a comforting presence behind the wheel. Ben cruised down time-worn roads, passing a rickety gas station where an old man polished the glass door, his back to the street. He continued through neighborhoods filled with small homes and narrow yards, the memories that had been made there no longer spoken aloud. When Ben reached the lake he stopped, not daring to enter the subdivision where he might be recognized. He walked along the far edge of the shore where no houses were built. Overgrown brush and muddy ground made this difficult, but he pressed on. The woods were dark when he entered, more than one ghost needing to guide him if this was going to happen. If he found it, it would be a sign. If not…

Ben stepped into the clearing. He wasn't sure at first. So many years had gone by, and it had been just one hour among all the others they had shared together. He took off his backpack and carefully set it on the ground. Then he walked around the edges of the clearing, getting on his hands and knees to be sure. There it was. The broken remnants of a shelter.

He walked to the center of the clearing and knelt in front of the backpack, feeling guilty when his fingers touched the cardboard box which held a sealed bag. Not where the ashes normally resided, but he had to fly and the airlines had guidelines about such things, which was maddening. All of this felt so crazy that he considered gathering everything up and heading home. But he knew why he really wanted to leave. His reasons were selfish.

"I'm sorry it took me so long to do this," Ben said. "I didn't want to let go of you. I still don't."

He waited for a response, or maybe some ghostly apparition to appear. When neither of these things happened, he opened the box and tore open the bag inside.

"I don't know how you want me to do this. I wish I had been braver and let you tell me. The thing was, back then it was so unthinkable that I'd ever be standing here. Still is. It's been years, Jace. You've been gone for years."

Ben hung his head and let the sorrow pass through him, feeling a weird sort of panic when he saw that some of his tears had created wet indentations in the ashes. Then again, maybe that was appropriate. One last union between them on the physical plane. He tilted the bag, carefully pouring the ashes on the ground, forming a circle. No beginning and definitely no end. "Forever," Ben said, placing an open hand in the middle of the circle, his palm flat on the ground. That's when he heard it, the echo of words spoken long ago and nearly forgotten. He repeated them, just so they never would be. "I love you. I hope you know that."

He remained still, lost in memory, until he grew cold. Then he picked up his things, leaving behind only that which now belonged there. He experienced a moment of concern, worrying about Jace being alone, but then remembered he wasn't. This clearing wouldn't be a lonely place for him or for Victor, now that Ben had finally kept his promise.

He walked back to the car, got behind the wheel, and collected himself enough that he could drive away. But before he turned the key to the ignition, he noticed the phone on the passenger seat, a blinking icon informing him that he'd missed a call. Ben looked at the name, feeling uncomfortable about seeing it here. Then he pushed a button and pressed the phone to his ear, listening until ringing was replaced by a familiar voice.

"Hey!" Tim said. "Tomorrow's the big day. Our first house!"

"I'm aware of that."

"Are you okay? I know you wanted the day to yourself, but

I had this feeling like…"

"Like what?" Ben asked.

"Like maybe you needed me."

Ben smiled and shook his head ruefully. "Maybe I do."

"Yeah? Do you miss me?"

"Yeah."

"Really? How much?"

"A lot less than a few seconds ago," Ben said testily.

"Okay, okay," Tim said hurriedly. "Sorry. I'll let you have your space. Just promise me you'll be there. Tomorrow."

"Don't worry," Ben said. He looked out across a lake, at woods where love had been made, stories had been told, and dreams were laid to rest. Then he started the car. "I'm coming home."

Part Two: Tim
Texas, 2008

Are you with me?

Such a loaded question. How could four simple words carry so much weight? Ben stared at the cell phone screen, then looked out the car window, subconsciously tapping one corner of the device against his chin. Are you with me? Yeah, of course! At times the thought made Ben happier than he had been in years. At others he was conflicted. If only he could seek permission, reach across the void to ask one last question. Ben looked again at the phone and did a quick search. Sure enough, a ouija board was available as an app. He allowed himself to consider the possibility, then laughed. If communicating with the dead was that easy, the world would be a different place. And besides, Jace *had* given him permission before the very end. Just not for this person in particular.

Are you with me?

Ben shook his head. "Stop being so damn dramatic," he murmured to himself. It's not like Tim was questioning his loyalty. When the message was read in its entirety...

I know we have a lot to do today, but there's no rush. We can move our stuff in whenever we feel like it. I thought we'd go over to the new house just you and me and check it out. No stress. Just fun. Are you with me?

Ben grinned and texted back. *I'm already there.*

What? came the startled response. *Seriously?*

I'm parked out front. Ben looked over at the house. He might be experiencing pangs of doubt, but he loved this place. That's why he'd made the drive out here, hoping it would steel his resolve. The phone chimed, attracting his attention again.

I'm on my way!

He had a flash of a car wreck, one so vivid it made him wince. *Drive safe. Remember your promise.*

I will. Don't worry. I'm invincible. I'm Iron Man!

"You're a dork," Ben said out loud, a welcome emotion stirring in his chest.

He got out of the car and considered his future home. The house had a lonely vibe, not unlike a certain teenager he had once met and fallen in love with. Located on the edge of Austin, the property was easy to miss, situated on a road that wound through a wooded area. The narrow driveway cut through unmaintained land and ended in a loop that swept in front of the house before backtracking again, as if scared to commit. Two stories: the ground level a rectangle, the second floor a combination of triangles. A separate garage sat to one side. The place had been on the market for years, probably because it didn't make much of a first impression. Or because it was so secluded, but Ben liked that about it.

He spun around, considering the land. And the silence. Here he could easily pretend that all the crazy events leading up to now were some sort of fevered dream. A plot that had jumped the tracks and lost itself in the wilderness. Here he could let go of it all, and maybe find the same focus he had once possessed. No more divided heart. Just a burning certainty that would drive him to do anything in the name of love. If ouija boards were real, the second person he'd like to contact would be a ghost of the past—his teenage self, because that guy seemed to have had it all figured out.

Not possessing a key, Ben walked around the side of the house. No need for a privacy fence here. They were unlikely to ever spot their nearest neighbors, although Tim was already talking about building a fence so Chinchilla could roam the yard freely. Maybe Samson would like that too. Ben reached the stone patio in the backyard, trying to imagine the future. At times it was crystal clear. Today it remained surreal. He knew from experience that creating a home took time, even if the building was already there. When he and Jace had finally scraped together enough cash to buy their house, it was a good six months before…

Ben clenched his jaw against the flood of memories. He cherished them, but they were double-edged, picking him up and knocking him down at the same time. He had thought his trip to Warrensburg the day before would help, since there was one person who wouldn't be making the move with them. He just hoped he had done the right thing.

"Doubt," he said to the yard, rolling his eyes. "What a useless sensation." He turned to consider the house. "What about you? Any misgivings? You must have had a nice family living in you once. Maybe the people who built you. You must have relied on each other, and I bet you didn't see the end coming. It's hard to get over something like that. Impossible, as far as I can tell. So maybe you're not completely sure about us either."

The house didn't respond. Probably for the best, Ben thought, or he would be moving into a mental health ward instead. When the sun broke from behind a cloud and warmed the stones beneath his feet, Ben carefully stretched out on the patio, enjoying the heat. He cleared his thoughts, listening to the sound of bird song or the occasional whisper of a gentle breeze. Oh yes, he liked this place very much. Enough that when he heard the growl of an engine, he hopped to his feet and rushed to the front of the house wearing a smile.

Tim matched it, climbing out of his ridiculously expensive car, his silver eyes shining. He was always like this when they met, his expression filled with awe, like Ben was a beautiful vision. Tim wasn't so bad himself; the naturally dark skin, the jet-black hair, the toned body that had brought Ben so much pain and pleasure. Even seeing him now made Ben's chest feel tight.

They realized they were standing and staring at each other. Ben was the first to laugh. Tim grinned in response and swaggered over, a set of keys dangling off one finger. Ben ignored them, focusing instead on that smile, watching it come close and finally disappear so it could be replaced by a kiss.

"Miss me?" Tim asked.

"It was one day," Ben replied.

"You didn't answer the question."

"Maybe."

"Well I sure missed you." Tim nodded toward the house. "Can you believe it? That's ours! It belongs to us. We're going to live there. Maybe forever!" He glanced back at Ben, no doubt noticing how the blood had drained from his face. "Try to contain your excitement."

"I'm overwhelmed," Ben said. "But not in a bad way. Everything has changed so quickly."

"It has," Tim agreed. "Like I said, there's no rush. Today we'll just explore the house again. All the moving stress can wait. We have time, right?"

"Yeah," Ben said, feeling grateful. "We do."

"Okay. Let's do this!" Tim strode toward the front door, fumbling with the keys until he found the right one and got it unlocked. Then he opened the door, but instead of walking through it, he turned around and extended his arms. Not for a hug though. He looked like he wanted to pick Ben up.

"What are you doing?" Ben asked, backing away.

"I'm going to carry you over the threshold."

"What? You can't do that!"

Tim made a face. "Why not?"

"That's like—" Ben grasped for words. "—marriage stuff."

"Is it?"

"Yes!"

Tim halted. "One of us is getting carried over that threshold. It's bad luck otherwise."

"You aren't carrying me. I won't let you."

Tim shrugged and turned around, his back toward Ben. "You leave me no choice." He spread his arms wide and started leaning backward. Then he was falling. "Trusting!" he called out.

Ben barely had time to react, rushing forward and wrapping arms under Tim's armpits. Even then Tim nearly hit the ground. All that muscle weighed a ton, and Ben needed every ounce of his strength to keep him upright. Or horizontal to the ground, because that's all he could manage.

"Nice save," Tim said. "Now get me inside."

"You can't be serious," Ben said, still straining.

"It's just like when you broke my ankle and had to carry me home. You can handle it."

"That's not quite how it happened," Ben said, but he walked in a circle, turning them away from the house. Then he lurched backward, dragging Tim along with him. He made it to the door before his arms began shaking. They were barely over the threshold when he buckled and fell, landing on his ass.

Tim seemed content to lie there, perfectly snug in Ben's arms. "See? I knew you would manage."

Ben collapsed backward and tried catching his breath, which wasn't easy because he couldn't stop laughing. Eventually he got himself under control and tried to push away the body pinning him down. After making him beg first, Tim finally rolled off, then rose to help Ben to his feet. They stood together in the entryway, considering their new home.

"Remember my dad's den?" Tim asked, striding forward into the biggest room. "That's what I'm thinking of here. A killer television, some obnoxious speakers, a ridiculously huge couch—"

"Bookshelves," Ben said, gesturing at the walls. "With actual books on them. Not just novels but art books too."

"Eric has a lot of those."

"Good. Reading chairs over there and a table. I want this to be a social room, not just a movie theater."

"It can be both. Right?"

"Yup."

A door to the left led to a long kitchen, the floor covered in curious blue tile. Ben loved that detail. Tim seemed content to let Ben make decisions there, having more opinions about his vision for the backyard.

"A pool for sure, but not back here. At my current place, I always worry about Chinchilla falling in by accident. So maybe an area for grilling and a fence that reaches the tree line. No, a little beyond it so we can still enjoy them."

Ben nodded in agreement. Upstairs was more challenging, since they had four rooms to figure out.

"A guest room," Ben said. "Uh, I've thought about this, and I think my current bed should go in there. For obvious reasons."

Tim gave him a blank expression.

"You and I can't sleep on the bed where Jace and I... You know."

Tim tried to appear understanding but ended up laughing. "You think of the weirdest stuff! But that's fine with me. Especially since you and I have already—you know—in mine."

"I don't want to know that bed's history," Ben said, shoving him playfully.

Tim brushed a hand down his back affectionately. "We can buy completely new mattresses if that's what you need."

Ben shook his head. "I don't want to waste money. You're bringing a lot more to the table than I am. In fact, I crunched some numbers, and after the mortgage is paid off, I'm mostly breaking even. The house didn't sell for as much as I'd hoped."

"I'm not worried about the money," Tim said. "What about this room? The light is good. Studio?"

"Fine by me. That means the room across from the bathroom could be an office, which just leaves—"

"Master bedroom!" Tim said, grabbing Ben's hand and dragging him inside.

The space was large, with a private bathroom and a generous walk-in closet. The room didn't have much to offer presently, but Tim was looking around with a grin plastered on his face. Or was he leering?

"Wanna give it a spin?" he said.

"Feel free," Ben said, heading for the hallway. "I'll wait downstairs."

"Hey!" Tim caught his arm, the confident grin shifting to something more vulnerable. "I'm serious. Why not?"

Ben turned to face him, his body reacting instantly. His heart was pretty interested too. Only his brain got in the way, hurriedly scribbling a list of concerns. "You said we have time."

"We do," Tim said. "I guess I just don't get… If you're not in the mood, that's fine. But it's not like we haven't already, um, when we were in Mexico."

"I know," Ben said, filling with longing at the memory.

"Right, so uh… If this is something else, we should probably talk about it."

"It's hard to put into words," Ben said, breaking eye contact. "I still have a house across town, and it's full of old things. I've said goodbye to a lot of them, which was really *really* difficult. Especially yesterday. And you still have your house, and I know it's been sold, but we had a false start there once. I need us to do this right. A clean break from the past. Otherwise we might find it tripping us up again."

"Okay," Tim said, hands held up in surrender. "We'll wait until we're settled before things get too heavy."

"Thanks," Ben said. "Geez, when did you get so mature?"

"Just don't test me," Tim said with a nervous chuckle. "I'm about two seconds away from whipping it out, whether you're willing to lend a hand or not."

Ben laughed. "I really can wait downstairs."

"Nah," Tim said. "I'll get myself under control. But remember when I said we could take our time when moving in?"

"Yeah."

"That's before I knew the circumstances. If we hurry, we should still be able to rent a moving truck."

Ben smiled. When he saw Tim wasn't kidding, he nodded. "Okay. Let's put those muscles to work!"

* * * * *

Despite Tim's determination, the move ground to a halt. He only had himself to blame. Ben's house was full of packed boxes and a slightly confused cat. Tim didn't seem to understand the concept of moving. Or packing. Whenever Ben pointed out all the clothes that still hung in the closet, or the computer that was still plugged into the wall, or the kitchen that was fully stocked with pots and pans of every conceivable variety—none of which had been disturbed—the response was always the same. "I'll just throw them in the car and drive them over."

This excuse was pushed to its limit on the second day. They stood before a huge object, Ben with his hands on his hips, his eyebrows raised. "Well?"

Tim squirmed visibly. "I'll just drive it over."

"It's a grand piano!"

"Baby grand piano," Tim corrected, "and it's got wheels. Maybe I can tow it."

"There's no room in the new house," Ben said. "Even if you managed to get it over there, we'd have to put it in the backyard. Unless you've taken lessons during our time apart, you can't even play. Can you?"

"No."

"Could Eric?"

"No, but he used to throw these epic parties, and that's when—" He noticed Ben's glare. "What?"

"I'm trying to be patient, but I don't feel like you fulfilled your end of the bargain. We're combining two households, and yours is huge. You should have gotten rid of most of this junk already."

"I know," Tim said, "but it's not junk. It's Eric's possessions. They belonged to him."

Ben exhaled, regretting his choice of words. He understood Tim's struggle because he'd gone through it himself. The only unusual part of this situation was the sheer size. Most people had a memory box; Tim had an entire house.

"We have to pick and choose," Ben said carefully. "If Eric didn't play the piano, then it seems like this should be an easy piece to let go of."

Tim was silent. He stared at the instrument, then raised his head to consider the rest of the room. "I feel like I'm taking him apart. Dismantling him."

"Eric?"

Tim nodded. "He put these things where they are. He consciously decided where it all should go. Once I move everything, it can't be undone."

"That's why you haven't packed?"

"I guess so. Don't kill me, but I'm thinking about keeping this place. Maybe we could rent it out, like a vacation home. Or I saw this show on TV about recording studios. Artists need quiet space to work, so maybe we could make something of it."

"The house already sold," Ben said. "Didn't it?"

"I could buy it back. Maybe." Tim hung his head, then shook it. "Sorry. I know I'm being ridiculous."

"You're not. Hey, I know what we'll do. Before we move anything else—" He pulled out his cell phone. "—we'll make a video of it all. Like a visual record of everything Eric surrounded himself with."

Tim looked up, considering the idea. "Okay. Let's do it. I'll make one too."

Ben exhausted the free space on his phone before he captured it all, but between them, they recorded most of it. After that, moving went smoother. They still had a lot of work to do, but working alongside Tim, sharing a common goal, made it much easier to simply enjoy being in his presence again without any pressure.

None at all. Since the discussion at their new home, Tim had gone full-on platonic. No propositions, no kisses, not even hand-holding. At first Ben had found this off-putting, but at least he was no longer on the defensive, or trying to silence his own uncertainty every time they got close. Instead he found himself watching Tim from afar. Admiring him. Wishing more would happen. Back to basics. All the way back to the very beginning. Once Tim had been an impossible dream, but now Ben knew he could—and had—won his heart. For some, this would be enough to make the flames flicker and die. Ben checked his own emotions and felt nothing but heat. He still loved Tim. A little more time wouldn't change that, so why wait? Ben didn't know the answer to that question. He just knew that he needed to.

Six days. That's how long it took to move. Most of that time was spent helping Tim get his house in order. Ben would wake up, report to work at the hospital in the morning, then drive over to Tim's house in the afternoon to help him pack. Or find someone willing to buy or take the things they couldn't keep. At night Ben would return home, trying to comfort Samson before eventually falling asleep.

Now they had finally done it. With help from Allison and her husband, they got the larger pieces of furniture moved in. The sun had set and they were exhausted, but at last their labors were complete. But were they home?

"Sure feels good," Ben said, trying to sound positive.

They were sitting in the living room. The couch was where it should be and functional, but the television was somewhere in the kitchen, the coffee table buried beneath boxes, and the entertainment center was turned on its side and blocking a window.

"It feels totally weird," Tim replied.

Ben didn't betray his true feelings yet. "Weird?"

"Yeah. You don't think so? The entryway is so stuffed full of crap that we have to walk sideways just to get to the front door!"

Ben relaxed. "It does feel super weird," he admitted.

"We'll get it figured out eventually," Tim said. "First we'll have to play Tetris. Why don't you Texans have basements? Drives me crazy. We could really use the space."

"There's a shovel in the garage," Ben said. "Start digging."

"I'm half-tempted." Tim stretched out on the couch. He seemed about to rest his head on Ben's lap, but remembered that they were still hands-off. He propped himself up on an elbow instead. "You know how when staying at a hotel, you wake up feeling all confused?"

"Yup. I never sleep good on the first night."

"But after a few days it gets comfortable. I figure that's what's ahead of us."

Ben yawned. "Sleep does sound good."

"So does a shower."

Ben nodded and stood. "You go first. I want to check on Samson."

Currently the cat was shut in the guest room since they weren't quite ready to introduce him to Chinchilla. Ben found Samson hiding under the bed, unwilling to come out, so apparently he was content to remain confined for the night. Ben coaxed him out anyway, gave him love and made sure he ate a little. By the time he reported to the bedroom, Tim was already beneath the covers. Ben took a quick shower, his back aching from all the lifting. When he was toweling off, he considered the bed. He could put on pajamas, but he'd have to go digging for them first. Or he could do what he normally did and sleep naked.

Tim's back was to him. He was probably already unconscious, considering he'd done more than his share of hauling stuff around. Kind of a shame, because seeing those muscles strain all day long, sweat soaking his shirt, had Ben eager for a different sort of exercise. He let the towel drop to the floor, shut off the lights, and slipped into bed. The sheets had remained on the mattress when they moved it, meaning they smelled like Tim. Ben buried his head in a pillow and breathed deeply.

This scent brought back memories, many of them centered around stolen hours late at night, their voices kept low so as not to wake anyone. There had always been parents to worry about disturbing, or Ben's sister, or most recently Tim's grandmother when they were in Mexico. That had been out of respect and nothing more, but perhaps this history is what made their time together now so strange. Ben didn't associate the feeling of home with Tim. That honor belonged to another man. And yet, in rare exceptions of perfect solitude, such as when Tim's parents had been out of town, Ben had basked in the fantasy that they did live together. He had played house while yearning for a future like this one, when they would always have privacy and never need to lower their voices or withhold a single touch. He had practiced for this by playing house with Tim as a teenager. Now he was the only obstacle to that dream coming true.

And why? Ben had needed to mourn. He had done so in more ways than he ever guessed possible. Just when he thought he had finished and moved on, he would find a new way. Maybe that would never change. Other things had though. The home he had once known was gone. He supposed it had been ever since Jace died, but their old house had remained a shadow of it—the shape reassuring despite not being substantial. Now that too was gone, leaving him with two choices: Remain homeless, or allow that comfort to grow again. Maybe it wouldn't exist right away. Maybe it wouldn't grow at all, but he was determined to fight. It's not like Ben needed to force himself. He knew what he wanted.

Time to start living again.

Ben scooted over, trying not to wake Tim as he nestled up against him. A sharp inhalation of breath broke the silence. Tim hadn't been sleeping after all. That was good. Ben let one hand explore, pushing it under an arm, over a ribcage, and across a chest, but all he felt was soft cotton, leaving him puzzled. "Are you wearing pajamas?"

Tim's response was husky. "Yeah."

"Why? They only get in the way."

Before Tim could respond, Ben slipped a hand beneath the cloth, his palm touching Tim's bare stomach. He rubbed up and down. Tim remained motionless. Poor guy probably couldn't keep up with the rules anymore. Ben wasn't sure he understood them either. He pulled on Tim's hip, rolling him over, then slid his hand into his pants. Hot, hard, and delightfully familiar. Ben felt like he was shaking hands with an old friend as he started pumping, the thought making him laugh.

"What?" Tim said defensively.

"I'm just happy."

"Yeah?"

"Yeah. You can touch me too, you know."

Tim rolled over, holding himself above Ben, their lips meeting. He paused only to peel off his shirt. Then he returned for more kisses, but the pajama bottoms remained, so Ben scooted downward, kissing Tim's neck, licking a nipple, letting his tongue dart into his belly button. Then he pulled the pants down and opened wide.

Tim started thrusting, his groans like a siren song that urged Ben's head to rise up and meet him, his throat taking a pounding a few times, but he loved it. Tim stopped suddenly, remaining perfectly still, but Ben didn't relent. He wrapped an arm around Tim's waist and kept bobbing his head.

"No no no!"

Too late. Warm liquid shot into his mouth, Ben savoring the taste. Tim didn't seem quite so pleased, rolling off to one side.

"Fuck! Sorry. What was that, three minutes? I haven't been jacking off because I didn't know when this might happen, but it's all I could think about and… This is so humiliating."

"It's fine," Ben said, scooting up again to be on the same level. "I liked it. I've been with you enough times to know sex usually lasts longer.

"Oh. Okay."

"There's no way that was three minutes though. More like two."

Tim groaned, but in embarrassment this time.

"I also know from experience," Ben said, tiptoeing his fingers over Tim's chest, "that it doesn't take you long to bounce back. Or was that just when we were teenagers?"

"Only one way to find out," Tim said.

Now it was his turn to dive beneath the sheets. Ben soon understood his lack of control, but he'd always possessed a fair amount of self-control. He was glad he managed to resist going over the edge, because after experiencing mind-numbing pleasure, Tim climbed back on top of him. He put one of Ben's legs over his shoulder first, and when their lips met again, the position made clear his intent.

"Really?" Ben asked.

"I'm willing if you are." Tim leaned forward, poking him in the butt. "*And* I'm able."

"Lube," Ben said, not hiding his eagerness. "Where the hell is the lube?"

"In the box by the toilet?"

"No. That's the wrong one because when I went looking for conditioner, I discovered it's full of paint tubes."

Tim turned to consider the room. "Does that mean it's in the studio?"

"Or in the entryway with everything else."

"Do we really need it?"

"I'm not going without!" Ben said incredulously.

"Without lube or without my cock?"

"Either," he admitted.

They scrambled out of bed and started digging through the unpacked boxes, ending up downstairs. Soon the house resembled the aftermath of a police raid.

Tim found the lube first, holding it aloft like a baton in a marathon and streaking by Ben on his way to the stairs. "Come on!"

Naturally this got Chinchilla excited and she gave chase. After a moment, Ben did too. He leapt over the dog on his way down the hall, leaping into bed right after Tim did. Bulldogs aren't made for jumping, but she tried her best, front legs pawing at the mattress. Then she grumbled and stood by their bed before finally giving up and returning to her own. Tim rolled over onto his back, pantomiming squeezing lube over his entire body, like he was a giant hotdog. Neither of them were hard at this point, feeling too silly from their jaunt through the house.

They soon found the mood again. Ben swung a leg over Tim and sat on him, letting his fingers trace lines across his chest, gently moving his hips until he got the reaction he wanted. The rest was like falling back into a wonderful old habit. Tim's fingers explored before he slipped inside, Ben navigating a narrow line between pain and pleasure until it became only the latter. Then he rolled over, relinquishing control.

Their motions remained slow, perhaps compensating for the previous early finish. Or maybe just to prove what Tim had been saying all along: They had time now. At last. Each dance between them had once been fleeting, but this one could last forever. Ben grabbed Tim and pulled him close, staring into his eyes and hoping they would never part ways again. Tim nodded as if sharing this sentiment, his body moving above Ben in gentle motions, carrying him through the night on currents of tender perfection.

"Think this is a good idea?" Tim asked, shifting uneasily from foot to foot.

"Sure," Ben said. Then he coughed nervously. "Have you unpacked the oven mitts yet?"

"Nope." Tim knelt down to pet Chinchilla. "I wish I could find her leash."

"It'll be fine. What's the worst that can happen?"

"When a dog meets a cat?"

"Hmm." Ben looked down the hallway at the closed bedroom door. "Point taken. Still, I don't see how keeping them separate any longer will help."

For the past two days, Samson had taken up residence in the master bedroom. Ben had it mostly organized, and while Chinchilla didn't like having to sleep away from them at night, she had the run of the house besides that room.

As Ben walked down the hall, Tim remained at the opposite end. Chinchilla perked up, like she knew something exciting was about happen. "Here goes," Ben said.

He opened the bedroom door. At first nothing occurred.

Samson was on the bed, seemingly content to stay there. Then he rose, stretched, and hopped off the bed. He went a few steps down the hallway before he spotted Chinchilla and froze. The dog stood, head cocked, but she remained calm.

"Samson," Ben said, "this is Chinchilla, your new..." He looked up at Tim for help.

"Roommate?"

"Yeah. Roommate. Maybe even your friend."

Both animals remained stationary.

Tim grinned. "I think we're okay!"

That's when Chinchilla took off down the hall, running straight for Samson. Now Ben froze. Should he dive in front of the cat to protect him? Or tackle the dog or—too late! Like a rocket-propelled sausage, Chinchilla was just inches away, mouth opening, like she'd discovered a delicious morsel to devour.

Yipe!

Samson struck so fast that the motion was difficult to see, his paw whipping forth with claws extended, hitting Chinchilla on the nose. Then he hissed for good measure, but that wasn't necessary because the dog had already reversed motion and retreated down the hall. Chinchilla didn't stop until she had taken shelter behind Tim's legs. She peeked around them with a baleful expression.

"Jesus!" Tim said. "Did you see that?"

"Barely," Ben said.

"What a right hook!"

Ben laughed. He couldn't help it. "He gets that from his dad."

Tim rubbed his jaw. "Don't remind me. What a beast."

"Jace or the cat?" Ben asked, still laughing. "Either way, they only attack when provoked."

Samson sauntered down the hall, stopping halfway and sitting, tail flicking back and forth.

Tim crouched, trying to comfort Chinchilla. "This is one fight you can't win," he said to her. "Trust me. I speak from experience."

Ben walked through the house, poking his head into each room and feeling pleased. Only one week since moving in and the house already felt more comfy. No more blank white walls, thanks to some serious hammering and hanging, and while there were still unpacked boxes, Ben had managed to hide most of them behind furniture. Today he had the place to himself. Tim was working at the gallery. Ben had enjoyed the time spent together, but he'd been living alone for years. He was no longer used to having a constant companion. Now he planned on relaxing. No music, no television, just a long lazy day spent reading in the sun. He grabbed the book he had foolishly packed when first preparing to move. Now he would finally get to continue the—

Ben stopped in his tracks. Through the window, he could see someone sitting in the very deck chair he had imagined himself occupying. Judging from the rapidly balding head visible over the chair's back, this person wasn't Tim or anyone else he knew. He hadn't heard the doorbell ring or anyone knock. Who would come all the way out here just to hang out in their yard? The former occupant, maybe?

Chinchilla had failed in her duty as guard dog. She sat next to the stranger, staring up at him. A hand appeared—a number of jewel-encrusted rings on the fingers—and reached for her with sinister intent. Then it pet her on the head. Gently. That gave Ben pause. Still, no sense in taking any chances. He went to the kitchen and picked up his phone. Funny that the dog seemed so at ease. She had barked like mad when the mailman rang the bell yesterday. Ben bit his bottom lip. Why was that hand vaguely familiar? Perhaps the police weren't necessary just yet. Setting the phone down, he grabbed instead one of the heavy cast iron skillets that had belonged to Eric.

When he opened the back door, he tried to do so quietly. Then he crept forward.

"Lovely!" the man declared suddenly.

Ben leapt away, felt something touch his back, and then really freaked out. The frying pan slipped from his hands and clattered noisily to the ground. Ben spun around, realized he had only bumped up against the house, and turned around again defensively. Chinchilla was spooked and had retreated to the grass, but she was looking to him as the villain, not the man in the chair who remained motionless.

"Simply lovely," the stranger said, as if nothing had happened. "When Tim told me you were moving out here, well, I thought he was mad. I might not live in the city, but I made sure to have a view. To keep an eye on things, you might say.

Now I'm beginning to see the appeal of such peaceful solitude."

"That was the idea," Ben muttered. He walked a wide circle around the chair to see who he was dealing with. The man was large, but not menacing. A Hawaiian shirt was stretched across his large belly, the pattern consisting of pineapples and hula girls. No, hula boys! The white pants and sandals gave the appearance of someone on permanent vacation. The man's heavy features lit up in surprise when taking him in.

"Ah! You haven't aged a day! Handsome as ever."

"Thanks," Ben said, still peering at him. "I know you."

"Even I wouldn't make that claim," the man replied. "I remain an enigma, even to myself."

"Marcello," Ben said, still working it out. "I was at your birthday party once. You rented an entire water park, and that was when... Wow."

"A memorable day? I'm delighted to hear it. I try to make all my birthdays remarkable. You should come to the next one. My fiftieth! We'll have to find some special way of celebrating. Anyway, I did have the pleasure of making your acquaintance in more recent times. The Eric Conroy fundraiser? I'll never forget you and your husband on the dance floor. Such an enchanting evening!"

Ben swallowed. "That's right. Sorry I didn't recognize you at first. I just never expected to find you in my backyard."

"I'm sure that will change," Marcello said. "Oh, we have so much catching up to do! Please, pull up a chair. Be my guest."

"I think you've got that backwards," Ben said, but he did what he was told, dragging a chair around so they were still facing each other. "Are you here to see Tim?" he asked as he sat. "I know you two are close."

"Thick as thieves, and no, I knew he wouldn't be here. That's precisely why I came. I'm eager to hear how you are doing. It's so much easier to be honest when there aren't extra ears around. That's always been the court system's greatest flaw. A jury? Who wants to publically confess their dirty little secrets to a row of grim-faced strangers? No, the Catholics got that one right. A dark closet in which to whisper our equally dark deeds, and a solitary man who can plead with God on our behalf."

"Not to be rude, but you *are* a stranger. To me, anyway."

"Then let's change that." Marcello leaned forward. "Your

life has undergone quite a few changes recently. How have you been holding up?"

"I'm fine," Ben said, still trying to make sense of the situation. Tim and Marcello knew each other. They were friends, he supposed. Maybe this was the equivalent of Allison backing Tim against a wall and telling him not to mess up. "You're here because you're worried I'm going to hurt him."

Marcello leaned back again and studied his nails. "One of the many flaws we men are burdened with is our love for the hunt. We have centuries of primitive instincts to purge from our systems, so we still enjoy chasing rabbits through the underbrush like the dogs we are. Tim adores you enough not to make you pursue him. The memory of you alone caused him to turn away more than one suitor. He is, quite literally, willing to give everything to you. I don't think there is a request you could dream of that he would find too ridiculous to fulfill. So yes, I do worry about how vulnerable such a stance makes him. I've seen his generosity rewarded with greed, his faith repaid with betrayal."

"Ryan," Ben said.

"You're familiar with him."

"I helped scare him away."

Marcello looked into the distance. "Indeed you did. I must be slipping. Or sober. Do you have anything to drink?"

"I appreciate what you're trying to do," Ben said, "but you've got nothing to worry about. I love him."

"Of course," Marcello said, waving a hand dismissively. "It's just that when I mentioned your husband, I thought I saw a shadow cross your features."

Ben studied him, temper rising. "You really want to go there? If you expect me to not have feelings for someone I love, and *lost*, then you're not nearly as clever as Tim says you are."

"How flattering," Marcello said, but his gaze was steady. "Death and I are old acquaintances. I've seen how it can cause those left behind to behave as if they too had died."

"I've already been through that phase."

"And how it can cause us to romanticize those people, to deify them, so they become beyond reproach. How could mere mortals possibly compete?"

"Jace was perfect while he was alive, and I still managed to want Tim anyway, so you can stop worrying about that."

"And then there is guilt," Marcello continued. "The nagging question of what that departed person would want, were they still here to tell us."

Ben wished he had a snappy comeback. Instead he remained silent.

Marcello nodded, as if understanding. "We can never know for sure. That's what makes death so frustrating. But if your roles had been reversed, had it been you who undertook that journey first, would you have expected Jace to wait for you?"

"No," Ben said instantly. "I would have hated that."

"And if he found comfort in someone from his past, would that in any way cause you distress? Perhaps you would prefer it if he found someone new instead."

Ben shook his head, throat feeling tight. "I wouldn't, because there's no replacing the comfort of a familiar body. It would take time before someone new could be trusted, or for the love to grow. I would want Jace to find any happiness he could, and that would be the quickest way."

"Then it seems to me, considering how well you knew Jace, that you can speak with some authority on how he would feel about this situation."

Ben breathed out. "He'd be fine with it. It's just—"

"Yes?"

"If there is an afterlife, and Tim and I are going to be together until we die, what then?"

Marcello smiled. "I have a very distinct vision of what Heaven would be like, but sharing it with you in the midst of this tender moment hardly seems appropriate. Let's just say I feel that everyone will find their proper place. And position. Ha ha."

"If that's all you're concerned about," Ben said, "then I don't think you need to be. I won't take Tim for granted, or turn my back on him because of any sort of guilt."

"Good," Marcello said, seeming satisfied. "You've set my mind at ease. Thank you. Now then, do you have any concerns?"

"About you? Plenty!"

Marcello chuckled. "About Tim. Any lingering doubts that I can help banish?"

"No," Ben said. Then he hesitated. "You mentioned that he had turned guys away because of me. I have a question I've been meaning to ask him, but it's hard, because if he answers one way he might find it embarrassing. If he answers the other way, he might think I'm judging him, and I'm totally not."

"You're wondering if he slept with other people while you were apart. Would it bother you if he had?"

"No," Ben said. "Not at all. I'm also curious if he dated anyone besides Ryan. I hate the idea of Tim remaining single just to honor my memory or whatever."

Marcello's eyes twinkled. "How silly that would be."

"Exactly. I never wanted that."

"Tim was aware of your true wishes. That motivated him, on occasion, to venture out into love's murky waters. To my knowledge, none made it past the first date. I believe he would compare any suitors to you, and when they invariably didn't measure up, he would dismiss them entirely. That hardly seemed fair, but I'm beginning to understand his fascination. So no, no true relationships since Ryan. A few lucky souls were allowed to spend the night with him, but that was all."

Ben felt oddly conflicted. Part of him was flattered; the rest wished Tim had someone to love him during those interim years. A guy like Jace. At the very least, he clearly had someone looking out for his best interests. "You really care about him, don't you?"

"Eric loved him," Marcello said. "With the entirety of his being. We would have lost Eric sooner if not for that. When he did pass away, I suppose that was my inheritance. His love for Tim."

"You know," Ben said musingly, "You're not such a bad guy. You just have a terrible reputation."

"I wouldn't have it any other way."

They smiled at each other.

"Want a tour of the house?" Ben asked

"I'd be delighted," Marcello replied. "We can begin with the kitchen. The refrigerator, to be precise. I believe you'll find a chilled bottle there."

"The champagne?" Ben asked. "I thought Tim bought it for a special occasion. I keep waiting to be surprised."

Marcello spread his hands wide, as if presenting himself.

A special occasion? More like a weird occurrence. Definitely a surprise though, and hopefully the last for quite some time.

Housewarming. Ben had always liked that term. He found

it to be accurate. A house didn't become a home until memories were made there. Only then did warmth fill the rooms. When the guests had arrived and the party truly began, he made sure to give a complete tour of the place. This took the better part of an hour, since everyone kept stopping to mingle, whether that meant gossiping while in the office or joking around when stuffed into the downstairs bathroom.

Now they were in the backyard, free to spread out, feast on salads and grilled meats, or cool off with a drink. Ben glanced around. Michelle, Greg, and their three children. A pair of nurses from the hospital, and some colleagues from the theater, including Allison's husband. Ben's parents had even made the drive out and would be their first overnight guests. Tim's invite list was notably shorter. Just one person in fact, although perhaps to compensate, Marcello had brought along not one but two dates, a handsome guy on each arm as he toured the yard. That was causing quite a few stares, which Marcello clearly enjoyed.

Funny how Tim had run with the popular kids in high school, had joined a prominent fraternity in college, and yet always ended up on his own. A loner. Ben always had friends. Maybe not many, but they made up for in loyalty for what they lacked in numbers. The best of them, Allison, was currently taking care of his boyfriend, providing Tim with a familiar face amongst the sea of strangers. Ben felt a rush of affection for her as he watched them talking. At the moment, Allison was laughing at something Tim had said, then she responded, wearing a teasing expression. She must have noticed Ben staring, because she turned to look at him, patted Tim on the arm, and walked across the yard alone.

"How's it going?" Ben asked when she was near.

"I think your boy has had one too many," she said with a grin.

"That's all right. He was nervous about being around everyone."

"Some things never change."

Ben chuckled. "Think how hard it is for us to be around our families. He didn't have much practice growing up, so…"

Allison nodded. "Fair enough. I like the new house."

"Thank you," Ben said. "For everything."

Her eyes widened. "I'm not the one paying for it!"

"I know. I mean thank you for tricking me into meeting Tim

again. I was okay before, but it was a hollow sort of happiness. I kept smiling, hoping the rest of me would buy the act and really feel that way."

Allison nodded. "Some people enjoy being single and are stronger on their own. You've always been strong, no matter what, but you're not made to be alone. You've been looking for someone to put a ring on that finger since the day I met you."

"Since before then. I owe you so much. Things are good. Now when I wake up in the morning—"

"I don't want to know," Allison said.

"Liar! You always loved hearing the details."

They matched each other's grins. Then, like facing a mirror's reflection, their faces became puzzled at the same time. Loud voices were booming from the center of the yard. They turned to discover two muscle-bound idiots: Ben didn't usually think of them that way, but both Tim and Greg had beer bottles in their hands, chests puffed up like roosters trying to intimidate each other.

"He's not married!" Tim was shouting.

Greg jabbed a finger at him in response. "Marriage is a promise! You're making it impossible for him to keep that promise. He already belongs to someone!"

"He doesn't belong to anybody!"

"Ever heard of wedding vows?" Greg bellowed.

"Yeah," Tim spat. "How about 'until death do us part'? Or are you forgetting that Jace is—"

"Don't you fucking say it!"

"I'll say whatever the hell I want!"

The beer bottles hit the grass like gauntlets being tossed to the ground. Then fists started flying. Both men were big enough to dish out serious damage and remain standing while taking a beating. They'd probably come close to killing each other, but Ben was already striding across the lawn, scowling and grinding his teeth, fighting the temptation to throw punches of his own. Seeing Greg get slugged in the nose and Tim knocked in the jaw purged those feelings. Instead he just kept walking, straight into the middle of the action. If they wanted to hit someone, let it be him.

That seemed likely. He found himself between two heaving chests, heat radiating off arms that still grasped at each other.

Ben turned, making eye contact first with Greg. Then he looked at Tim. The fight went out of those silver eyes and was replaced by shame and sorrow. Tim shook his head, clenched his jaw, and turned to walk toward the house.

Ben watched him go, then rounded on Greg.

"What are you doing?"

"Looking out for you," Greg said.

"Looking out for me? Or for Jace?"

Greg shrugged. "Same thing. There's no difference in my mind."

That might have been endearing under other circumstances, but Ben was still pissed. "Jace told me, before he died, that he didn't want me to be alone."

"Yeah," Greg said, gesturing toward the house. "But *him*? You think Jace would be okay with that?"

Ben was suddenly grateful for that conversation with Marcello. Otherwise this might have tripped him up, caused a crisis of faith. "Do you know what Jace wanted for me? Can you say, with *absolute certainty*, that you know?"

Greg struggled internally. "No."

"Neither can I. All I've got to go on is what *I* want. You can either respect that or you can—" He glanced over and noticed Emma standing not far away, her face still pale with shock. Ben returned his attention to Greg and lowered his voice. "I'm my own man. Understand?"

Michelle walked up then, putting a gentle hand on his shoulder. "I can take it from here. You might want to get a fresh set of charcoals hot. That way I can shut my husband's head in the grill."

Greg winced, adopting a hangdog expression. "Oh man…"

Ben took a deep breath, gave Michelle an expression of gratitude, and headed for the house. One down, one to go. He went from room to room, worrying that Tim had gotten in the car. He shouldn't be driving. Not in his current condition. This thought spurred him upstairs, breath tight until he found Tim sitting on the guest room bed.

He didn't look up. His attention remained on his hands, one of which was pink around the knuckles. "I blew it, didn't I? After all these years I finally got you back, and it took me—what? A month to ruin it all?" Tim raised his head. "If there's anything

I can do… Hell, I'll beg if that's what it takes. I don't care. Just don't make me leave!"

Ben resisted a sigh because chances were it would be of the dreamy variety. "You're not going anywhere. I love you, even when you're stupid."

Tim stood, "Really, because I—"

Ben raised a hand to silence him, catching sight of the ring he still wore on his finger. "This is confusing," he admitted. "For all of us. It's only natural for there to be some tension. I'm not mad at Greg because I know he said those things out of love for Jace. Not because he hates you."

Tim glowered. "I'm not so sure about that."

"I am," Ben insisted. "I'm also not mad at you because you love me. And you were right. I don't belong to anyone."

"You might not," Tim said, "but I do. I belong to you. I'm happy to admit it, and no amount of right hooks from Jace or his posse will change how I feel. I'll never stop loving you. Even if it ends up killing me."

Ben smiled. "First Jace, then his cat, now his best friend. What were the odds?"

"Yeah," Tim said. "How many more friends and relatives does he have? I might need to hire a bodyguard."

"I'll protect you." Ben sat on the edge of the mattress and took Tim's hand. "I'm not totally against the idea of belonging to you. But I love you enough not to want to own you. I still want you to do what's best for you. I hope that will involve us staying together. If not—"

"Then I'll fight." Tim met his gaze, eyes intense. "I won't be the one to quit. Not ever."

Ben thought of a few responses to that, but the most suitable didn't involve words. He leaned forward and kissed Tim. He tasted like beer, which wasn't bad, and probably explained why the kiss tried to evolve into something more.

"Easy now," Ben said, placing a hand on Tim's chest to push him away. "I'm not going to reward negative behavior with nookie."

Tim moaned in disappointment. A few seconds later, he smiled. That made it harder to resist the idea, so Ben looked away. At the dresser, in fact, where something had caught his eye during the tour earlier. He stood to fetch it.

"What's this?" The object was flat, perfectly square, and gift-wrapped. "Did you buy my parents something?"

"No," Tim said. "Sorry. I found that while making sure the drawers were empty for them to use. It's nothing. I meant to throw it away."

"But it hasn't been unwrapped."

"Yeah, well..."

Ben grinned. "Is it for me?"

"Kind of. It's for your birthday."

"Wow." Ben looked down at it. "Talk about an early start! My birthday is still months away."

Tim broke eye contact.

"You *do* know when my birthday is."

"October 27ᵗʰ," he said instantly.

"Then why—" Ben brushed at the wrapping paper, noticing the thin layer of dust. "When did you buy this?"

"A few years ago."

Ben scrunched up his face. "We weren't even talking then."

Tim shrugged sheepishly.

"You bought me a present when we weren't together?"

"I was at a flea market when I found it, and it just happened to be your birthday. Seemed appropriate. I didn't think I'd ever see you again, but I still wanted to get you something."

"That's..." Either sad or sweet. Ben couldn't decide. "Can I open it?"

"Sure."

He tore away the paper. A vinyl record. He wasn't completely surprised, suspecting as much from the shape and feel, but the cover got his heart thumping. Roberta Flack, sitting behind a piano. Or so it appeared. A cardboard flap opened, revealing the opposite side of the piano but Roberta remained where she was, now standing and singing. His eyes moved to the album title. *Killing Me Softly*. He flipped it over to confirm it contained the song of the same name. Then he looked up.

"Do you remember singing that to me?" Tim asked. "Back when we were teenagers."

"Yeah," Ben said, his throat tight.

"Good, because I don't remember. Maybe you could remind me."

"Nice try."

"I mean it," Tim said. "First song on the album. That's the one."

Ben remained where he was. "I don't have a record player."

"Now I know what to get you for your actual birthday."

"This is already enough. It's very sweet of you. Just tell me you didn't buy other presents for me while we were apart."

Tim averted his eyes. Then a different idea occurred to him, because he rubbed his jaw where Greg had punched him. "Ow!" he declared. "I sure am in a lot of pain here! If only there was something you could do."

Ben laughed. He set the record on the dresser, plopped down on the mattress, and didn't mind at all when Tim rested his head in his lap. Then Ben gently stroked his face, strumming his pain as he began to sing.

Ben carefully lowered the vinyl disc onto the turntable. With reverence he guided the arm to the first groove, placing the needle there, which seemed like a terrible idea. Needles scratched things, didn't they? Regardless, he'd seen this same ritual played out on television more than once. He took a step back and waited.

"Now what?"

"I don't think it's voice activated," Tim said helpfully.

"Did you really have to get a vintage record player? If it was new there would probably be an app or something."

"I thought an old one would be charming. Is that why you waited so long to—"

"No!" Ben said, cutting him off. "I've just been so busy. I blame the holidays. Ever feel like there are too many? We took that trip for my birthday—"

"—which also involved Halloween."

"Right. Then there was Thanksgiving with my family, followed by Christmas and New Years, which are like a sharp turn on the edge of a steep cliff. Just when you've recovered from plummeting over the side and have climbed back up—bam! Valentine's Day hits you straight on."

Tim rolled his eyes. "I like the holidays. Especially this year. V-Day was awesome."

"Me too. I just wanted to firmly establish my excuse for not having used your ancient and slightly musty gift until now."

"It's vintage," Tim countered, pushing a few buttons

experimentally. "And it's in great condition." He sniffed. "It does smell like someone's garage. If you don't like it—"

"I do! I mean, I think I will. People always say vinyl sounds better."

"It can't," Tim said. "No way. That's gotta be nostalgia."

"Probably. How about this one?" Ben flipped a silver switch. The record started spinning, sluggishly at first, but soon it reached a steady rhythm and the first song began.

"Nice," Tim said, putting his arms around Ben. "How does it go again?"

Ben turned around, singing the first verse. Then he stopped, wanting to hear Roberta's voice instead of his own. Tim pulled him closer as they swayed. Ben nestled his head against Tim's chest, enjoying the warmth of his body, losing himself in the moment. There had been so many like this lately. Their life had hit a stable rhythm, even the doubters having made their peace with his decision. This was love.

The song came to an end, and Tim pulled back slightly. "Are you thinking what I'm thinking?"

"I can feel what you're thinking," Ben said. His phone rang, the digital ringtone a stark contrast to the music they were listening to. "Sorry," he said, disentangling himself.

"Saved by the bell," Tim murmured.

Ben shot him a glance that promised he wouldn't have to wait long. Then he answered the phone. "Hello?"

"Hi. Uh. Ben?"

The voice was unfamiliar to him. Maybe a temp working at the hospital. "Yup! Who's this?"

Hesitation. "You don't know me, but I was hoping you could help. I'm trying to reach someone named Jace. He's your husband, right?"

What a question! Ben looked over at Tim, whose attention was on the record player as he turned it down. Ben hurried to the kitchen before answering.

"Yes, he's my husband."

"Oh, good. Do you have a number for him? Or if he's there, could I speak to him?"

Obviously this person didn't know Jace well or he would have heard the news by now. A bill collector, maybe? "Sorry, but who am I speaking to?"

"My name is Jason. Uh, I met your husband once a long time ago. His sister was my caseworker back when I was in foster care. He said I could call if I ever... So..." The voice croaked and went silent.

"You met Jace?" Ben asked. Jason calling for Jace. This was like something out of the *Twilight Zone*. Wasn't there an episode where a woman got a call from the dead? "Listen, what's the best number to reach you at? And your last name. Please."

"Oh, okay. My name is Jason Grant. My number is—"

"Hold on." Ben jerked open a drawer and scrambled for a pen and paper. "Okay, go ahead." He listened to the number, scribbling it down. Then he repeated it just to make sure he had it right. "Wait, isn't that a Houston area number?"

"Yeah. That's where I live."

"All right." Jace had also lived in Houston but a long time ago. The person on the line didn't sound very old, his tone of voice too casual, like he hadn't quite mastered adult formalities. "You really met Jace?"

"Yeah. He looks just like his sister."

Ben laughed. "Yeah. He certainly... Yeah. Listen, I'm going to have to give you a call back, okay? It's not a good time right now, but I'll definitely call you back."

"Okay." Jason sounded like he'd given up, as if Ben was brushing him off. "No problem." The line clicked and went dead.

Ben stared at the phone, then set it down. When he turned around, he found Tim standing there, arms crossed over his chest. "Did you hear all that?"

"Your half. Who was it?"

"I don't really know."

"This is about Jace, isn't it. He's coming back into our lives again."

Ben didn't answer.

Tim stepped forward. "It's fine," he said. "Whatever it is, I'm okay with it."

"Really?"

Tim hesitated. "Probably." His expression appeared vulnerable, before it became determined. "For sure. One thing though. You said that you're his husband."

"You heard that?"

"Yeah. And I get it. I think. But does that mean— If there was ever someone… I have this friend of a friend, and he was talking about marrying you some day. I know, right? Who does this guy think he is? But if he heard what you said now, he'd probably be wondering if that was ever possible. Eventually. Maybe."

Ben smiled. "If there's one thing I've learned from all our time together and apart, it's that the rules don't apply to us."

"So anything's possible?"

Ben opened his arms wide. "Absolutely anything."

Part Three: Jason
Texas, 2009

This is about Jace, isn't it? He's coming back into our lives again.
The words weren't his own, but they echoed Ben's thoughts.
He had spent years going over the memories made with Jace,
flipping through photos of their time together, staring at every
scrawled letter he'd had the foresight to save. When all that
remained was the past, the only option was to repeat it over and
over again, like a favorite music album, even though doing so
slowly wore down the novelty. Not unlike the vintage record
still playing in the house. No one was listening to it now. Ben
needed fresh air, so he retreated to the backyard, almost afraid
to consider the possibility. What if an extra song was on that old
favorite album, one he had somehow overlooked? What if more
of Jace was out there for him to discover?

Ben paced on the patio, occasionally looking to the yard in
an attempt to focus on the present. Tim was throwing a ball for
Chinchilla, even though she had no idea how to fetch. Instead she
would race to the spot where the ball landed and turn, panting
happily while she waited for Tim to follow, pick the ball up,
and throw it again. They patrolled the length of the newly-built
fence while doing this, concern etched on Tim's features despite
the frivolous activity. Eventually he abandoned this game and
walked over to where Ben stood.

"Do you think he has a kid?"

Ben shook his head, not understanding. "What?"

"Jace. Maybe he got some girl knocked up when he was a
teenager and never told you about it. Maybe that's who this Jason
Grant person is."

Ben considered the idea and laughed. "No."

"How can you be so sure?"

Because he and Jace didn't keep secrets from each other.
Maybe at first, but by the end nothing had separated them

anymore. They were one person. "He never had sex with a woman. We talked about it."

"His loss," Tim murmured to himself.

"Hey!" Ben swung at him, slow enough for Tim to easily dodge.

"Krista Norman," Tim said wistfully, laughing at the glare Ben shot his way. Then he grew serious. "Why don't you call Michelle and find out? She was his caseworker or whatever, right?"

"That's what he said."

"Then what are you worried about?"

"I'm not worried." But that wasn't the complete truth. What if Jace *did* have a secret that challenged what Ben thought he knew about him? What if they weren't as close as he'd thought?

"You sure look worried," Tim pressed.

Ben pulled out his phone, navigated the menu to find Michelle's work number, and scowled until Tim resumed his game with Chinchilla, giving him privacy. Then he counted the rings, feeling more apprehensive with each.

"Michelle Trout."

"You've got your business voice on."

After a pause, the voice sounded much happier. "Ben! How are you? Why are you calling me at work?" She gasped. "Is this what I think it is?"

"I'm not looking to adopt," he said. "Not unless you want to give Emma to me."

"Never," Michelle said firmly. "Take Preston. Did I tell you he bit another student? When I asked why, Preston said he was being bullied. I'm glad he stood up for himself, but who bites another person?"

"Zombies," Ben said. "Or rabid dogs. Maybe you should have him tested."

"You might be on to something." Michelle sighed wearily. "Please tell me you're calling with good news. I could use it."

"Oh. I'm not really sure. I got a strange call today. Have you ever heard of a Jason Grant?"

"Jason Grant!"

Ben held the phone away from his ear. She was either very excited or extremely upset. "I'll take that as a yes. He says you used to be his caseworker."

"I am! I mean, I was. Oh my gosh… Is he okay? Why would he call you?"

"I was hoping you could tell me that. He was trying to reach Jace."

The line went quiet a moment. "Oh."

Ben's mouth went dry. "What?"

"I introduced them. Jason was one of my trouble cases. He was going through a hard time, and I thought it would help if Jace gave him a pep talk."

"That must have been years ago."

"It was."

"So why is he calling now?"

"Maybe he wanted advice." Michelle's voice was terse, like she was holding something back. "I hope he's okay."

"Who exactly are we dealing with here? You said he was a trouble case."

"Jason? He was a good kid. One of my favorites. Finding a family for him wasn't easy. He was terrible at first impressions, which is often all you get in this business. He wasn't exactly forthcoming with his feelings either. Not until I gained his trust."

Ben's eyes flitted to Tim. "I can imagine that making life difficult for him."

"Mm-hm. He was stubborn too, not unlike someone I know. Always had to have things his own way. And he was proud."

"Proud," Ben said, picking up on the implication. "Jason is gay?"

"Yup. That's one of the reasons I wanted Jace to talk with him. They hit it off too. We went out to lunch, saw a movie. It was a good day. Jace never told you any of this?"

Ben struggled to remember. "I'm not sure."

"Hm. It worries me that Jason is calling after all this time."

"He did sound a little down."

"Do you have his number?" Michelle's business voice was back in full force. "Jason wasn't the type to ask for help. He might need me."

Ben gave her the number. Then he ended the call so she could get the answers both of them needed.

"Well?" Tim asked, approaching cautiously.

"I don't know," Ben said. "Michelle had asked Jace to talk to this kid before. 'Everything will work itself out.' That sort of thing. That still doesn't explain why Jason is calling now."

"Or why he would have your number."

Ben looked down at the phone. "That *is* weird."

"Michelle's taking care of it?"

"Yeah."

"So problem solved."

Ben looked up to find Tim grinning. "I guess."

The happy expression remained. "Wanna go back inside?"

"Why?"

"Music, dancing, romance... We kind of got interrupted."

"Oh."

Tim leaned forward to kiss him. Ben reciprocated, but his heart wasn't in it.

Tim must have noticed because he pulled back first. "Maybe later," he said.

"Sorry." Ben gestured at his head. "It's all still buzzing around in there."

"Yeah. I get it." Tim took a step back. "I think I'll go for a run."

"Are you mad at me?"

"No." Tim broke eye contact. "It's been a weird day. No one is to blame for that. Right?"

Before waiting for an answer, he went inside. When Ben followed a few minutes later, he found the house empty, the record no longer playing.

When Tim returned from running, he offered Ben a sheepish smile. Judging from the sweat drenching his clothes, he'd pushed himself hard. He'd obviously found peace while out there because he no longer seemed tense. Or maybe he'd stopped in the woods somewhere and jacked off. The thought was erotic enough to get Ben in the mood again, as was the manly scent radiating off Tim's heated body as he came near, but then of course the phone chose that moment to chime.

Just a text message. It could wait. Probably. Unless the message really was urgent. Ben glanced at the phone, just to see who it was from.

Tim noticed this and detoured, moving toward the stairs. "I need a shower," he explained.

Follow him... that's what Ben should do. That's what he

would do. But the message was from Michelle, and he was dying to see what it said.

Hi! Talked to Jason. Wanna Skype?

Odd. They never Skyped. Emma was fond of it and often contacted him that way, but he and Michelle stayed in touch through other means, mainly phone calls and texts. Ben knew from previous conversations that she used video conferencing at work since it helped to see the facial expressions of the people she was dealing with. Why would she need to see his? Unless the news was bad.

Sure. Just give me a moment.

He sent the text and went upstairs to the office, the shower forgotten until he heard the water running. Too late now. He'd already agreed to make an appearance. A few minutes later, he was staring at a pixilated and poorly lit version of Michelle.

"Hi!" she said, sounding a little too cheerful.

"I hate suspense," Ben said. "Cut to the chase."

"Okay. Jason is doing all right. Nothing too serious. I lost touch with him after Jace died and I took all that time off from work. Jason sort of disappeared around then, so it's a huge relief to finally speak with him again. He dropped out of high school, which I'm not happy about, but at least he got his GED. He's been working and trying to build a life for himself, but lately things haven't been going well. Lost his job, can't make rent. Jace offered…" Michelle nibbled her bottom lip. "Jace said if he ever needed help, that Jason should call. That's why he did."

"Jace gave him my number?"

"Yes."

"Okay." Ben leaned back. No big deal. "So what's he need? Money?"

"That solves most problems," Michelle said. "What's good for him is a little more complicated. At work, teenagers are always pushed my way. No one wants to deal with them because their cases either seem hopeless or pointless. Why bust your butt trying to find a home for a sixteen-year-old? They'll be on their own soon enough. But think about when you were in your early twenties and something went wrong. Who did you turn to?"

"Jace," Ben answered immediately.

Michelle smiled. "And if you hadn't been lucky enough to have him in your life?"

"My parents."

"Exactly. Adults need a support network too. That never changes, so even though he's eighteen years old, I'd still like to find Jason a family."

Ben turned around to make sure Tim wasn't standing behind him. And so he could slyly make a panicked expression. "So," he said, facing the camera again. "Uh."

Michelle grimaced. "I know I'm asking a lot. I haven't done Jason any favors by describing him as troubled. He's a really sweet guy."

"He doesn't have anyone?" Ben asked. "No distant relatives, no matter how incompetent? No friends he can move in with?"

Michelle shook her head. "Nobody. And for the record, Jason didn't ask for anything. When he called, he just wanted advice. He didn't have anyone else to turn to."

Ben tried to imagine that, picturing the darkest days of his life without Allison or his mom or Jace. Or even Karen, who wasn't the best sister, but she had made sure he was fed and safe when forced to babysit him. "Okay."

"Sorry?"

"He can come live with us."

Michelle wasn't cheering yet. "I need both of you to be okay with this. You don't need to answer right away. Talk it over with Tim, sleep on it, make sure this is something you are—"

"He needs someone. I could probably pay his rent and help him find a job, but you're right. He needs a safety net. I can be that net. Er... I think." Ben winced. "He's eighteen? If he calls me dad it's going to be *really* awkward."

Michelle laughed. "This isn't foster care. He's no longer in that program. There won't be any papers to sign, or inspections. Likewise, you can't have any expectations. You won't be in charge of him, and he won't have to answer to you."

Ben raised his eyebrows, as if offended.

"Sorry. You wouldn't believe some of the people I deal with. I know you'll do fine. No weird parental vibe or obligations. Just be his friend and help him get his life on track."

"The answer is yes," Ben said, "but I'll talk to Tim about it and get back to you."

"You're the best!" Michelle said. "Thank you!"

"It's nothing," Ben replied. "I'll let you get on with it. Send the family my love. Save a little for yourself too."

They said their goodbyes and ended the call. Then Ben turned around to consider the door and the hallway beyond. He might have told Michelle the decision was nothing, but explaining the situation to Tim wouldn't be so simple.

"What if he steals our stuff?" Tim asked, ignoring the plate in front of him.

Ben cursed himself, wishing he had waited until they had finished dinner before broaching the subject. Otherwise he could have heated up a frozen pizza instead of working so hard on the grilled salmon and steamed vegetables.

"If he steals our things, we'll kick him out." Ben took a bite, hoping to lead by example. He tucked a chunk of broccoli in one cheek so he could keep speaking. "It's not like you can't afford to buy more."

Tim glanced over at Chinchilla, who was begging at his side. "What if he's mean to the animals?"

Ben chewed and swallowed while shaking his head. "Michelle would have mentioned that. They have files about such things. She says he's a good person."

"What if he kills us in our sleep?"

"Good person," Ben repeated. "She wouldn't ask us to take him in if she thought our lives, pets, or possessions were in danger."

Tim frowned and considered his plate. "He'll have to get a job. And pay rent. No freeloading."

"God forbid," Ben said. "Could you imagine some rich guy letting a young person live in his giant house for free? That would be madness!"

The point wasn't lost on Tim. Eric had once done the same for him. Check and mate. Or so he thought. Tim huffed and stabbed at the fish. Then he looked up. "These things don't always end well."

Ben shook his head, not understanding.

Tim didn't answer, focusing instead on feeding a bite to Chinchilla, her little teeth gently scraping along the fork to get the food. Tim then used it to feed himself. Ben had seen this display enough times that it no longer fazed him.

Time to play the big card. Ben just hoped it wouldn't backfire. "Your parents weren't always there for you. Remember how hard that was? What if they hadn't been there at all?"

Tim brightened. "Could you imagine? Just think how much sex we could have had!"

"And then imagine you never met me," Ben said. "No house either. Just you, trying to make ends meet without anyone to bail you out when you made mistakes."

Tim thought in silence. At least he was eating now. When he set down the fork, his silver eyes locked on to Ben's. "Why are you doing this? What's your motivation?"

Ben had to search himself for the answer. Was this about Jace? A little. But more than that… "We've been lucky. Sure, our lives haven't been perfect. We've both lost people we love. Everyone does eventually, but how many of them walk away from the experience with financial independence, or reunited with their high school sweetheart?"

"I love it when you call me that," Tim said. "Makes me want to put on my old baseball uniform."

"You still have that?" Ben asked, on the verge of drooling. Then he shook his head, refusing to get sidetracked. "My point is that our lives could have been different. Hell, I was struggling before we met again, but when I was late on house payments, I had people I could ask for help. The same with you. If Eric hadn't left you what he did, you still had other options. This kid doesn't. That alone makes me want to help him, but I also feel like I have a debt to pay off. The world has been good to me. It's time to give back."

"That's noble," Tim said. "Way better than my reason. I'm only saying yes because it'll make you happy."

Ben smiled. "So we're doing this?"

Tim nodded. "Yeah. We are. Aren't you a little freaked out though? We're letting a total stranger move in with us. We don't even know what he looks like."

"Yes," Ben conceded. "I'm nervous, but I'm not the one forced to start over and put my faith in complete strangers. Considering what Jason is going through, I'll bet he's twice as freaked out as we are."

The SUV cruised down the driveway, coming to a stop in front of the house. Ben watched through the front window. His heart was thudding like he'd just run a few laps. He peered at the car and tried to catch sight of the passenger. Greg was driving and Michelle was riding shotgun, but Ben couldn't see anything of interest from here. He reached for the doorknob and hesitated. He'd slept badly, all his dreams variations of this moment. The car would pull up and out would hop Jace, looking younger than Ben had ever seen him in real life, his hair just as long as in those old photos. In some of the dreams Ben would open the front door to find him already standing there, or discover him sitting in front of the television, playing video games. Ben had felt thrilled by this each time, but also confused, because eighteen was too young for him. He wanted the old Jace back, not some half-baked version.

Now that he was awake, Ben wasn't expecting either. Of course not. He had briefly entertained the notion of reincarnation, even doing online research about it before deciding such concepts weren't for him. But he still wondered if this meeting had some special significance. Only one way to find out.

Ben opened the front door and stepped outside, eyes on the vehicle. Greg met him first, clapping him on the shoulder. Then Michelle approached with words of gratitude. Ben waved them away, turning toward the car. He spotted Emma in the backseat, conversing with the person sitting next to her. All he could see was dark brown hair. Then Emma nodded in his direction and the head turned.

The boy's gaze was both guarded and probing. Eyes are said to be the window to the soul, but these were more like one-way mirrors. Nothing was getting through them. Not from this side. Ben offered a smile, and while the expression wasn't returned, this encouraged Jason to open the car door and get out of the vehicle. Emma appeared from around the other side of the SUV, demanding Ben's full attention. He hugged her, then looked at Jason again.

His hair was messy and without style. It covered his forehead and tangled around his ears. He wasn't a model by any means, but he was good-looking enough that finding love shouldn't prove much of a challenge, if such things interested him. Right now, he seemed rather uncomfortable, so Ben extended a hand. That struck him as too formal, so he dropped it, then realized a hug was probably too familiar at this point.

"Um. Welcome home." he said. Wait, was that presumptuous? "You are staying, aren't you? Or do you want to look around first, inspect the premises?" He turned to Michelle for guidance. "Is there a checklist or something?"

Jason must have found this funny because he laughed. His

blue eyes lit up for the briefest of moments, convincing Ben that everything would be all right. He offered his hand again, this time keeping it extended. "I have no idea what I'm doing," he admitted. "Let's start with the basics. I'm Ben."

Their hands met. He braced himself, breath catching in his throat, but only in anticipation. He felt no spark, even though the single word that was spoken next caused a longing in his heart.

"Jason."

"Jason," Ben repeated. The same name as his husband, even though everyone called him... "Do you go by anything else? I mean, I'm really a Benjamin, but pretty much everyone just calls me Ben."

"I've never had a nickname in my life."

"Oh." Time to let go of silly notions. "Okay. Jason it is."

"He did have a nickname," Michelle corrected. "At the group home, the staff used to call him Jason the Gypsy because he couldn't settle down."

"Really?" Jason seemed genuinely surprised, his guarded expression vanishing when he turned to Michelle. "I never knew that!"

"You never knew, because I would have twisted their heads off if they called you that to your face."

Jason smiled at her, and this time the expression remained. "Oh I don't know. I sort of like how it sounds."

"In that case..." Ben gestured grandly to the front door. "Jason the Gypsy, come and see your new wagon!"

He led the way inside, always feeling a mixture of happiness and agitation when inviting so many people into his home. Normally the environment was so serene. Ben didn't have to worry about dodging around people or making sure everyone had what they needed. Tim didn't require much, having lived on his own long enough to be self-sufficient. Seeing their peaceful paradise invaded—Greg flopping down on the couch, Emma digging through the refrigerator for a drink, Michelle casually doing a home inspection out of habit—made him a little jittery. Then again, a full house was a happy house. Later, once everyone had gone, Ben would no doubt miss the more hectic pace.

Of course this time, one of their guests wouldn't be leaving. He looked at Jason, who didn't seem to know what to do with himself and hadn't said more than two sentences since entering the house. Everyone else had settled down and seemed at ease. Maybe a little time alone together would help break the ice. "Do you want to see your room?"

Jason glanced at Michelle, as if seeking permission.

She raised her hands. "You're on your own. I'm your friend, not your caseworker."

"Oh, right." Jason looked embarrassed. "Old habits die hard."

They walked together in silence through the living room and were halfway up the stairs when Ben paused and turned around. "Is this move a good one or a bad one for you?"

Jason shook his head. "Huh?"

"I'm just thinking of the different times I've moved." Ben slowly continued his way up the stairs. "When I first went to Chicago for college, I couldn't wait. I wasn't sad at all, because I'd been in the same town and same house for so long. Once I actually got there... Well, things were a little run-down compared to The Woodlands. I learned to love it there, but I was happy to move back to Texas where my best friend and I got a duplex together. I really liked living with her. Once we graduated, that time came to an end. I was mostly living with Jace by then anyway, but when we hauled all our stuff out of there, cleaned up, and were about to turn out the lights... There might have been a few tears."

They were in the hallway now, Jason smiling at the story. "I was living with my best friend too. Steph was awesome. We had so much fun together in that apartment, but in my situation, she was the one who fell in love and left to go live with the guy."

"Did you feel betrayed?" Ben said, putting on a guilty expression. "Allison was cool about me ditching her, and I bet you were too nice to say anything, but Steph and I totally betrayed you guys. Am I right? Do you secretly hate us?"

Jason laughed. "No. In her case, she was moving really far away. Before she went, she even said I could come live with them, but her boyfriend didn't like me. It would have been awkward. Three's a crowd anyway. Um."

"You're not a third wheel," Ben said reassuringly. "We're happy to have you here. Really."

Jason nodded his appreciation, still looking uncomfortable. "I guess maybe I should have called her when I started having trouble, but we lost touch and uh... I'm sorry if I'm a burden."

Ben made a face. "Are you serious? We were bored out of our minds before you came along. You're the one doing *us* a favor."

Jason seemed appeased. "I don't believe you, but thanks."

Ben resumed their tour, Jason overwhelmed by the different items Ben had bought in preparation. He politely declined most of them. Jason seemed to be a man of humble means, which Ben could appreciate, because it was only recently that his own living situation had improved. When they reached the master bedroom, Ben couldn't help but entertain one last hope. Jason was absolutely thrilled to discover Samson. Maybe the cat would recognize in Jason something Ben couldn't see, but the cat reacted like he did with most strangers, cautiously sniffing the newcomer before deciding to ignore him.

Jason was thrilled regardless, even more so when he found out they had a dog. A fellow animal lover. That was good. They returned downstairs so Jason could meet Chinchilla. There they parted ways, Jason going out into the backyard to be with the dog. Emma was out there too and would be good company.

"What do you think?" Michelle asked, joining him at the back door.

"I like him," Ben said. He watched Jason drop to his knees on the grass so he could interact with Chinchilla better, his face gleeful as he received a barrage of licks. At the moment he seemed much younger than eighteen. "It's a little surreal to think he'll be staying with us. I'm glad, but it'll take some getting used to."

"No more strutting around the house naked," Michelle said. "I'll need to make sure all electrical outlets have safety plugs in them too."

Ben turned to her to make sure she was joking. "I guess this feels like an average work day to you."

Michelle shook her head. "It feels like a second chance. I never should have taken time off work. Not when there were kids who needed me."

"Your brother had just died. You needed time to heal. I did too. There were days when I thought I'd die from grief. How can anyone be expected to function normally at such times?"

They stood in silence, remembering how it had felt then, and sometimes still did.

Ben nodded toward the kitchen. "I guess I should get started on dinner."

"I'll be sous-chef!"

They reported to the kitchen but ended up talking instead of working. Michelle told him about her kids' latest exploits, especially the boys, who were at home in Houston with a babysitter. Ben listened while setting out ingredients on the counter. Then he asked a thinly veiled question.

"How's Greg?"

Michelle sighed. "Still being an idiot about the whole thing. Yours?"

"The same."

"I saw Tim on the riding mower. At least he's here this time."

Ben nodded. "I'm hoping he'll come inside. I didn't buy any beer though. I figure we shouldn't tempt fate."

"Speaking of which, maybe I should keep an eye on him. Cover your ears."

Ben did so, wincing anyway when Michelle shouted her husband's name. Greg showed up soon after, followed shortly by Emma, Jason, and Chinchilla. The kitchen was large, but felt cramped with everybody present, hungry eyes watching his every move. Jason leapt in to help, chopping onions and deseeding chili peppers. He seemed much more at ease.

"You like to cook?" Ben asked him.

"I prefer to be on the receiving end," Jason said. Then his cheeks flushed. "That sounds weird."

Ben laughed. "I understood what you meant. Here." He rolled a zucchini toward Jason, then ended up blushing too. "Oh! Bad timing. I wasn't trying to imply... Geez."

Now Jason chuckled. "Who knew that food could be so awkward!"

"Hurry up and chop it," Ben said. "The sooner it's in slices, the sooner we can forget about this."

"There should be a gay cooking show," Emma chimed in. "*Cooking With Innuendo.* Could you imagine? Bananas dipped in chocolate. Sausages stuffed into buns. The possibilities are limitless."

"You're grounded," Greg said.

"Mushroom caps," Michelle said. "Filled with cream cheese."

"You're grounded too," Greg responded. "And divorced."

"Tuna tacos," Emma said.

Ben and Jason exchanged a look of revulsion.

"Peaches drizzled in honey," Emma continued, clearly inspired. "Melons covered in whipped cream. Steamed clams!"

Greg groaned. "I'll never eat again. You guys are ruining food for me. Remember whose fault it is when I starve!"

They all laughed, Jason included, which was good. If he shared their sense of humor, he would do just fine. Ben was turning around to fetch a frying pan when he noticed a figure in the doorway.

"Tim! Hey!"

He was covered in sweat from being out in the sun, but Tim making an appearance at all felt like progress, even though he kept his attention trained on Ben. The one exception was when his focus shifted to consider Jason.

"Hey," Tim said in greeting, nodding upward.

"Hi," Jason replied.

They stared at each other, the atmosphere in the kitchen growing thick.

"Dinner is almost ready," Ben said, hoping to dispel the tension. "Care to join us?"

Tim gave a barely perceptible shake of the head. "I have some work at the gallery. I was just about to head over there."

"Big surprise." This came from Greg, who earned himself an elbow in the ribs. Michelle had him under control, but it was too late. The two men glowered at each other.

Emma saved the day by clearing her throat. This got Tim's attention, his mood improving considerably. "Hey! What are you sitting there for? Come give me some sugar!"

"But you're disgustingly sweaty," Emma said. She hopped off the stool anyway and went to him, suffering a soggy hug and doing her best not to laugh as Tim rocked her back and forth.

Ben's smile matched Tim's. Moments like these made him wish he could get pregnant. Tim would be a good father, he was sure of it. Those shining eyes met Ben's as he let go of Emma, like he was sharing the same thought. Then he looked at Jason and seemed much less certain, before he nodded and left the room.

"Ow!" Greg said. "What? I didn't say anything that time!"

"You were going to," Michelle replied.

"Work has been really busy for him lately," Ben said. "Normally he wouldn't miss my enchilada casserole for the world."

Everyone was gracious enough to accept this excuse without

questioning it, although Jason was more somber now, as if starting to feel out of place. Or maybe he was struggling with disappointment, which would be understandable, because Ben felt the same way.

"The first few days are always rough," Michelle said, helping him at the kitchen sink. Greg was in front of the television again. Emma and Jason had decided to walk around the property. That left them alone, which was good, because Ben had one burning question.

"What if this doesn't work out?"

"I won't let him end up on the street," Michelle said. "Jason can come live with us, if need be."

Ben rinsed a plate and handed it to her. "That would have been easier than relocating him here."

"You don't have to do this."

"We're doing it! I'm not backing out. I just wonder why you chose me. I don't have any experience. Is it the gay thing?"

"No." Michelle put a fistful of knives and forks into the dishwasher. "You really don't remember when Jace went to Houston for a few days? That's when he met Jason."

Ben snapped his fingers. "I do remember! Greg came to Austin and crashed at our place. The next morning they left together. I remember feeling relieved because I'd been taking care of Jace nonstop. This was after his first aneurysm, right?"

"Right."

Ben shut off the water. "I remember I had tons to catch up on, but I ended up sleeping most of the day. I was exhausted. Emotionally more than anything."

"And I was glad to have the extra time with him," Michelle said. "I loved having Jace stay with us. When he returned to Austin, he didn't mention anything unusual?"

"Unusual?" Ben shrugged. "He didn't always make sense. He did once he recovered more, but I learned to pay attention to his actions more than his words. Why? What would he have said?"

Michelle closed the dishwasher and leaned against the counter. "I didn't tell you because I didn't want it to influence your decision. Or make you feel pressured. I'm not completely innocent, because when I introduced them, I hoped for a particular outcome. And I got it."

"What?" Ben asked. "Tell me!"

"They really hit it off. Enough that Jace told Jason he could come live with you guys. I think it took all of twenty minutes, although I didn't find out until later that night when Jace shared the details. Jason said no. He was still shaken up from the previous foster family, but Jace made it an open offer. That's why Jason had his number. Yours too. I think Jace gave it to him just in case he..." Michelle swallowed. "You know."

Ben stared at her. Then he laughed, which probably seemed crazy, but he only did so because he was happy. *This* is what he'd been waiting for. A sign of some sort, a connection back to the man he loved.

Michelle seemed to understand and offered a tentative smile. "In a way we're fulfilling Jace's wishes. That's a good thing, isn't it?" The smile faded, her chin trembling.

Ben couldn't find words. All he could do was hug her as they both did their best not to cry.

"This is Jason's home now," he said once they disengaged. "Don't worry about him fitting in. I'll make it work, no matter what it takes. This is where Jason belongs."

Michelle nodded and grabbed a tissue to dab at her eyes.

They would make this work. They would become a family. All Ben had to do was convince Tim of that.

When the sun began to set, Michelle and her family started the long drive back to Houston. That left Ben and Jason alone, which isn't how it should have been. They felt comfortable enough in each other's presence, but *two* men had invited Jason into their home. Tim was a part of that decision and should be present. Ben sent him a text, letting him know the coast was clear. Greg was gone, and yet Tim continued to stay away. The hours dragged on until finally Jason excused himself and went to his room. Ben remained where he was, sitting sideways on the couch, eyes locked on the front door until it finally opened.

Tim froze when seeing him, then sighed and shut the door. "Hey," he said when he was near, bending over the couch for a kiss. Ben allowed this, mostly to determine if Tim had been drinking. His breath tasted neutral.

"Did you eat? I can reheat some leftovers."

"I'm fine. Really." Tim remained aloof, not making eye contact.

"I've been waiting for you."

"Sorry. It's just that…" Tim looked around the room as if making sure it was empty. "You know."

"You can't avoid him every time they come to visit. Seriously. He's a part of my family. I know Greg isn't blood, but that doesn't matter. Call a truce or something. For me."

Tim clenched his jaw. "I don't get why you care."

Ben refused to dignify that with an answer.

Tim read his unhappy expression and sighed again. "I'll try. Let's not argue, okay?"

"No one is arguing. I just don't understand you sometimes. Where were you? They left more than two hours ago. Didn't you get my text?"

"At the gallery. And yeah, I did."

"So why didn't you come home sooner?"

Tim flopped down on the couch, his face angled away.

Ben nudged him to get his attention. "You never work late. It's not just Greg you were avoiding, is it?"

"This is your thing," Tim replied.

"We talked about this! You said we would do this together!"

"I know, but you can handle it. I thought about it today, and I think it's better for everyone if I stay out of the way."

Typical. That was always Tim's solution. When things get uncomfortable, run away. Ben stood and headed for the kitchen.

"Hey!" Tim twisted around. "Where are you going?"

"To get a drink. When I come back, you better have a damn good reason for what you just said. Or better yet, a change of heart."

He stood in front of the refrigerator, letting the door remain open, the cool air soothing his hot cheeks. Why did everything have to be so complicated? Ben grabbed a Coke and returned to the living room, ready to give Tim an earful.

"My parents."

These words stopped Ben in his tracks. "Your parents?"

"Yeah. Look what a great job they did with me." Tim's expression was one Ben had seen often when they were teenagers: anger mixed with hurt. Then he shook his head, as if trying to banish the feeling. "The thing is, I don't know how to do it right. I can't raise a kid."

"He's turning nineteen!" Ben said incredulously. "He's already grown up. He doesn't need a dad."

"Fine," Tim said. "What about Ryan?"

Ryan? Ben walked over to stand in front of the couch. "What does he have to do with any of this?"

"He was about Jason's age. Look what a great job I did with him. The kid ended up in the emergency room."

Ben felt like kicking himself. Of course! He should have seen this coming. Tim had made a comment about such arrangements not always working out. He wasn't stingy. Tim had generously welcomed a teenager into his home before. The result had been theft, property damage, and a drug overdose.

"This is different," Ben insisted. "Jason is nothing like Ryan."

"You don't know that," Tim said, eyes pleading for him to understand. "Ryan was a perfect little angel when I first met him. By the time we separated... Well, you saw for yourself."

"It's not the same, and I doubt Ryan was that innocent when he met you." Ben put the Coke on the table and sat on the couch, reaching over to touch Tim's shoulder. "So all of this is because you're worried about screwing up?"

"I'm not worried," Tim said. "I *know* I'll fuck this up. You won't though. You'll know exactly what to— Hey, I'm trying to talk here!"

Ben leaned forward. "And I'm trying to kiss you."

Tim pulled back, still skeptical. "I thought I was in the dog house."

"You might be still. But you being worried about doing a good job is sweet. Sweet enough that I'll give you something to smile about while in the dog house."

"Punishment accepted. Uh, where is he?"

"Upstairs. I think he's asleep."

"Okay."

Tim's lips met his, and he placed his hands on each side of Ben's cheeks. He seemed hungrier than usual. Ben struggled to understand why. Then he realized how long it had been. More than a week, which didn't seem like much, but the call from Michelle had interrupted them. Since then he had been preoccupied, getting the guest room ready for Jason's arrival, shopping for extra supplies, reading the book on foster care from front to back, just to be prepared. Ben's behavior wasn't exactly self-centered, but he hadn't made much time for Tim, who hadn't complained once. Sure he had avoided Greg today. Jason too, for very different reasons, but in a way, Tim had taken all these changes in stride. He deserved a reward.

"Seriously?" Tim whispered, eyes wide as Ben fumbled his jeans open.

"Yeah," Ben said, reaching inside and grabbing more than a handful. "Tonight is all about you. Anything you want."

"How about some privacy?" Tim asked, looking toward the stairwell. Then his eyelids fluttered and closed as Ben pumped his hand up and down. "Or just keep going." He gasped a moment later when Ben buried his face in his lap. "Yeah. That'll do just fine!"

Ben greeted the morning with some anxiety. Michelle had joked about not strutting around the house naked, not realizing how often hormones got the better of them. What if Jason had come downstairs in the night, maybe for a drink of water, and saw them going at it? Ben was tense when his new ward arrived at the breakfast table, searching his face for any sign of distress. Jason seemed tired and in serious need of caffeine, but that was all.

Tim had already left for work, getting an earlier start than normal despite their talk last night. Obviously they still had unresolved issues. Ben tried to put this out of his mind. He had taken the day off, and once Jason was showered and dressed, they drove into town for a shopping trip. Ben hadn't been able to decide on everything Jason would need before he moved in. This seemed the smartest way of dealing with it. Besides, what better way to bond than by blowing through cash? They were in the car, a question on Ben's lips, one he had promised himself not to ask too soon, but he couldn't resist.

"So, you met Jace?" Ben asked.

Jason nodded. "Yeah. I was going through a hard time, and Michelle thought it would cheer me up."

"Did it?"

"Definitely." Jason sounded upbeat. "Most adults try to offer solutions, but he was more about telling me he'd been there, gotten through it, and found his dream guy."

Ben grinned. "Really? He said that?"

"Yeah. He talked about you a lot."

Warmth filled his chest. "Really really?"

Jason seemed amused. "Really for real. Are you so surprised? I mean, the guy married you, right?"

"I know." Ben seriously considered pulling over to the side

of the road because his eyes were threatening to tear up. "It's just nice to hear it again, like getting a message from him after all these years."

"I'm sorry," Jason said. "About what happened, I mean."

"It's fine." Ben took a deep breath and sighed. "Actually, it's not. Jace dying will never be okay, but accepting that has helped a lot. I've learned I can still feel happy along with the sorrow. And that I can still love others without having to stop loving or missing him." He glanced over to make sure he hadn't confused Jason. "Listen, Michelle told me that Jace invited you to come live with us. I want you to know that he meant it. I don't remember him mentioning it to me, but at the time he was struggling with memory problems. He didn't forget people though, just details, and I don't want you to think he forgot about you. Or that he used an empty promise to make you feel better."

Jason shook his head. "I never thought that. The truth is, I turned him down. I'd gone through an ugly situation with my previous foster family and decided that I was done trying to fit in where I didn't belong. As much as I liked Jace—and I really did—I just wasn't ready. I told him that too. I'm guessing that's probably why he didn't mention the idea to you."

"Okay," Ben said. "That makes sense. I was constantly worried back then, and I'm sure he didn't want to add to that. Still, I'm surprised you were able to resist his charms."

Jason chuckled. "Only because I was shell-shocked. I ended up calling him eventually, didn't I?"

"True. If you don't mind me asking, what exactly happened with you and your last family?"

"It's a long story," Jason replied.

Ben pulled into the mall parking lot, noticing a free spot. "I've got time."

Jason was silent, even once the car was parked and the engine turned off.

"Sorry," Ben said. "Was the question too personal?"

Jason unbuckled his seatbelt but didn't reach for the door. "I get that you're trying to show interest. The thing is, I have more experience at these sorts of things than you do. I've been in more than twenty foster homes, and what people want most is for you to act grateful about the present. They never appreciate hearing how ugly the past was. You're a good person for taking me in, and chances are you have this rosy picture about how the world works. There's nothing wrong with that, but you don't want to see the world through my eyes. Trust me."

"He died in my arms," Ben said.

Jason's head whipped around. "What?"

"Jace. He was having an aneurysm. He'd been through one before and survived, but this time he wasn't willing to fight. He wouldn't let me call an ambulance. He just wanted to be held, and don't think that was a rosy moment, because death isn't soft or gentle when it comes. So while I might have had a good life, I've seen a few hard times myself."

"Sorry," Jason said, cheeks flushed. "I didn't mean—"

"It's fine," Ben said reassuringly. "I want to get to know you. The *real* you. I don't want to have a superficial relationship. I know such things can't be forced, but if you ever feel like confiding in me, then just know that I'm open. Good or bad, I'm willing to listen."

Jason nodded, face a little slack. He didn't have anything to say though.

Ben was the first to get out of the car, hoping that shopping could break the ice again. They were halfway across the parking lot when Jason spoke.

"I loved my mom. You know that time between spring and summer, when things are really starting to warm up?" Jason's eyes sparkled as he stared straight ahead. "Dandelions and freshly mowed grass. Somehow I associate those with her. I think we spent a lot of time in the front yard. I remember my grandma had a chair by the front door, a big jug next to it we made sun tea with. Anyway, they were my family. My real family."

"What about your father?" Ben asked, holding open the door of the department store for him.

"My dad died when I was young. It wasn't a tragedy. Not for me at least. He enlisted shortly after finding out my mom was pregnant, but not to support us. He wanted out."

"Sorry," Ben said.

"Don't be. My mom was all I needed. She was my best friend. We'd always go to the public pool, and when we got snow cones, she would let me choose the flavor for her. I made a mix each time, like any kid does, and honestly some of them tasted pretty gross, but she always raved while eating hers, like I was some sort of master chef. She made me feel like I could do anything. She even taught me how to play guitar. I had a friend who threw a fit each time he had to go to his piano lessons. I never understood that because my mom made it so fun. We'd sit on the couch, passing the guitar back and forth. Once I got the hang of it, she'd croon along, sounding like Janis Joplin. She was raised as a Jehovah's Witness, but when it came to music, she preferred a little fire and brimstone." He laughed.

Ben joined him. "She sounds amazing."

"She was." Jason's grin faded away. He stopped to look at the dress shirt a mannequin wore, tugging the sleeve down so it was closer to the plastic wrist. "Everything changed when my grandma died. I liked her too, but she was old and tired. I cried, but my mom took it really hard. I guess I didn't understand how much support she had gotten from her. She started drinking—"

"No longer a Jehovah's Witness then."

"No," Jason confirmed, continuing to stroll. "I guess not because she never tried passing that on to me. My grandmother talked about it *all the time* before she died. That's why I remember. I was only six, so some of this stuff I pieced together later, like the funny little flask that my mom and Hank were always sipping from. I didn't know what that was until later."

"Hank?" Ben asked.

"My mom's boyfriend. I really liked him at first. More than I should have. He was a coach of some sort. PE maybe? He had these big pale muscles and dark-red hair. Great teeth too. God I loved his smile." Jason looked over at Ben as if embarrassed. "I guess he was my first crush, but at that age, it's not like I wanted to kiss the guy or do anything sexual. I just really admired him. A lot."

"I know exactly what you mean."

"Oh. That makes me feel more normal. I definitely thought Hank was awesome. He had this station wagon and we went everywhere in it. I don't mean travelling really. It just seemed like any time spent with Hank was in the station wagon. I always sat in the far back, which was like my own little room. He'd pick up my mom for a date, swing by a toy store, and let me choose one thing. Whatever I wanted. Then I'd be in the back of the car, pretending it was my own private little world. I'd play with my new toy or eat McDonalds. We went to a lot of drive-thru places.

Drive-in movies too. In retrospect, I think this made it easier for them to drink. Maybe that was the reason. They didn't have to worry about being kicked out of a movie theater or restaurant for getting loud and weird, and believe me, they did."

"Was that scary for you?"

Jason shook his head, glancing at displays of men's cologne without interest as they neared the mall corridor. "I thought it was funny. When Hank moved in with us, that's when it got scary. He had a lot of rules, but you had to guess them, because there were no second chances. If you messed up, even the first time... I don't have scars or anything. I met kids later who had gone through way worse than I did. My home life wasn't that bad. Things weren't exactly great either. I remember limping to school one morning, and there was also a week when I couldn't sit down without crying, because it hurt too bad, but I had to anyway."

Ben tried to stay calm. Imagining what had led to these conditions made him sad, but sorrow never lasted long in his system. Not when anger could take its place. "Your mother," he managed to say, struggling to keep his voice neutral. "What did she think about all of this?"

Jason picked up on his tone anyway. "Don't blame her. She was young, and after she lost her mom, I think she was pretty lost. It's not that she didn't care. I told her what was going on, and she would get upset and angry. The thing is, her way of dealing with feeling that way was to have a drink. So she might say she was leaving him, but then she'd need to work up her courage before he came home, which meant getting drunk..." Jason sighed. "People talk about alcohol poisoning, and they mean what it does to your liver or whatever. For some people though, it poisons the soul. Alcohol changed who she was. In a way it killed her years before she actually died."

"Sorry," Ben said, feeling bewildered. Jason was right. These things weren't easy to learn about, or accept, but Ben was determined to understand as much as he could. "When your mom died, is that when you went into foster care?"

"No. She was still alive then. I was hiding from Hank in the station wagon. I'd done something bad, and I knew I was going to get beat for it when he woke up. I was in the back under a blanket, and it was summer. The car got really hot, but I was too scared to move. I must have passed out because the next thing I know, I'm in the emergency room. That's when they found the bruises." Jason looked over at him, jaw clenching a few times. "She was a good person. Seriously! She worked hard to take care of me. My grandma did too. When you're a kid, you don't really understand how difficult it can be to make ends meet. My mom must have been really tired, but I know she had a good heart. I loved her."

"I'm sure she loved you too," Ben said, but only because it seemed the kindest response. He couldn't imagine standing by and letting anyone hurt the people he loved. Hell, he couldn't even tolerate seeing a stranger being abused. He always had to do something. Anything!

"So yeah," Jason said. "Lots of foster homes afterwards, me doing everything to sabotage my chances, thinking it would get me back to her. By the time she died, I guess that self-destructive behavior had become a habit. Uh, one I've broken now. I'm not planning on doing anything bad, I swear."

Ben shook his head. "You're not in a foster home. You're *home*. Simple as that."

Jason shot him a grateful expression. "So that's my big sad story. Sometimes I wish I could forget it all. I may have had a rough start, but all the crap I went through afterwards was my own fault. I was only making things hard for myself."

"I understand feeling that way," Ben said, "and I know how the past can trip you up. It's good you can't forget though. The hard times are what define us. The happy times also, but when the shit hits the fan, that's when we're tested. The decisions we make when facing those challenges reveal who we really are. That you've survived everything you have and still… I know we've only just met, but you're likeable. You're fun to be around. That you could go through so much and still turn out so cool—I think that makes you pretty awesome."

Jason considered these words. Then he laughed. "I don't know how you managed to put a positive spin on all of that, but I'm impressed."

Ben grinned. "Thanks. But I mean it."

"It wasn't all bad," Jason said. "Some of the families I stayed with were really nice, even if I didn't give them a chance. I definitely had some good times." His face grew red again, but for a very different reason.

"What was his name?" Ben asked knowingly.

Jason groaned. "That obvious?"

"Hey, I've got a lot of experience in such matters."

Jason stopped to look at the window display of a music store, a cardboard cutout of a rapper glaring back at him. "His name was Caesar. I was sixteen, he was a few years older. It might sound gross that he was my foster brother, but he never felt like family to me. He was a stranger, just another guy, except he listened to me. He cared."

"Caesar?" Ben repeated. "Sexy name."

Jason's expression became dreamy. "I thought so too. Trust me when I say it suited him. His parents treated him like royalty, but not the fairy-tale kind. He had benefits, sure, but also plenty of burdens. I was crazy about him. Caesar was my first everything. Well, maybe not my first crush. I had liked other guys before, but he was the only one who liked me back. He even said he loved me. After it was all over." Jason's brow furrowed. He looked away and noticed the food court. When he turned back again, his thoughts had apparently changed course.

"You're hungry already?" Ben asked. Then he laughed. "God, I miss having a metabolism like that."

Jason made a face. "You're skinny. I bet you don't have an ounce of fat on you."

That confirmed he hadn't caught them in the act last night. "I suppose a slice of pizza won't kill me."

Once they had their food and were seated, Jason kept talking between bites, still fixated on Caesar and everything that had gone wrong in that situation. His tone was anything but steady, implying those old feelings hadn't faded. Like most love stories, this one had ups and downs and one big tragedy at the end, but Ben was relieved to hear Jason talking about such ordinary problems. Suffering a broken heart as a teenager was normal. Nearly suffocating in an overheated station wagon was not. What Jason had been through hadn't stunted his emotions. Judging from his tale, when he felt for someone, he did so passionately. Ben could certainly relate to that.

"When it came down to it," Jason said, "he didn't choose me. That's what hurt the most."

Ben nodded in understanding. "If it's any consolation, he probably regrets that choice now."

"I don't know. Maybe." Jason's jaw clenched as he considered the leftover pizza crust on his tray. "I still haven't gotten over him. Isn't that sad?"

"Not at all. He's a part of you now. Just like you are for him. There's no sense in fighting that, but you do need to move on and make room in your heart for someone new. How long ago was this?"

"About three years."

"And since then? Have any guys come close to competing with Caesar?"

Jason seemed puzzled. "There haven't been any other guys."

"None?"

"Some unrequited crushes, but besides that, nada."

"Wow." Ben leaned back. "That's one hell of a dry spell!"

Jason bemoaned the difficulties of meeting someone. Ben gave him a pep talk, which wasn't hard because it boiled down to getting out there and trying over and over again. Persistence was the key. This led Jason to ask about Ben's convoluted love life. He did his best to summarize it, realizing it was like a layered cake: Tim was the bottom layer, and then came those nice spongy years with Jace. Another thin layer of Tim interrupted this and then yet more Jace before it was all topped off with hunky Latino frosting. Ben refrained from explaining it this way to Jason, thankfully. During this conversation, Jason clearly had his doubts. He didn't say so outright. He was too polite for that, but he didn't look quite convinced whenever Ben had something nice to say about Tim.

Par for the course. Most of Ben's friends and family had needed time to warm up to Tim. That Jason had fallen for Jace's charms certainly didn't help matters, but the solution was simple. They merely needed to spend more time around each other. But first...

"We haven't gotten much shopping done," Ben said.

"I guess not," Jason replied. "Does pizza count?"

"Nope. Time to get serious!"

The mall had been a failure, so they hit large retail outlets. Jason was still resistant even though he wasn't spending his own money. After enough encouragement, he finally bought the bare necessities and one impulse item: a stand to go with the ratty old guitar he'd brought with him. Those guitar lessons his mother had given him had stuck, his love for music anything but superficial. Jason expressed gratitude, promising more than once that he would get a job and pay it all back.

Ben didn't think this was an act. Jason was a good kid. A little too influenced by his emotions, but good nonetheless. They were both in high spirits at this point, so the time seemed right to try again. They drove to an older part of the city and parked beneath a tree bursting with green leaves. The gallery had been a lucky place for Ben. His life had changed for the better there, sparking a new beginning. Maybe some of that magic would rub off on Jason.

"Do you like art?" Ben asked as they paused out front.

"I guess so." Jason peered at the window display. "I don't get some of it."

"Me neither. Let's go inside."

Tim was seated at the desk in the large central room. He tore his eyes away from the computer screen and smiled at them both. A promising start. Jason darted into one of the side rooms, which wasn't ideal, but at least Ben could assess the vibe before taking any risks.

Tim walked around the desk to receive a kiss. "This is a nice surprise," he murmured.

"It's a rescue mission," Ben said. "We're heading home. Come with us."

Tim shook his head. "Someone has to be here. Some crazy rich couple might come through that door any second now. Wait, are you rich? If so, looking to buy?"

Ben ignored his humor. "What happened to the artists being here to represent their work?"

"They're college students," Tim replied. "They have to go to school."

"I know, but one of them is usually here. You don't normally put in this many hours."

"It's fine. So what have you been up to?"

"Jason and I went shopping."

"Have fun? Did you get anything for me?"

"Yes we did, and no, I didn't. Will you be home for dinner?"

Tim looked away, eyes on the street outside the window as if hoping a timely excuse would drive by. "I might have to stay late."

Ben lowered his voice to a whisper, but still squeezed some

anger out of it. "Are you kidding me? He's living under your roof. You can't keep avoiding him."

"I'm not."

"Then go talk to him!"

When Tim didn't budge, Ben pulled on his arm, yanking him in the right direction. Tim resisted, so Ben changed tactics, appearing hurt instead of frustrated. That did the trick. Tim took a deep breath, nodded, and walked over to where Jason had disappeared. Ben knew he should give them space, but his curiosity got the better of him. He tiptoed to the doorway leading to the west wing.

Jason and Tim were standing in front of a painting, their voices low. After a minute of this, Tim turned around, as if seeking help. Ben gave him a big thumbs-up and remained where he was, straining to hear. They were really talking now, probably about the paintings. They moved from one canvas to another, even making eye contact a few times, the scene resembling a father explaining the world to his son. Ben was tempted to snap a photo, certain this would be a defining moment in their relationship. Then it got loud.

"You think I'm a salesman?" Tim spun around, his expression wounded. "He thinks I'm a salesman!"

Ben laughed in relief. Just a silly misunderstanding. He hurried over to explain. "Tim doesn't get paid for being here. He helps run the foundation that opened this gallery. Tim's an artist. He had his first exhibition here."

Jason glowered at Ben, his cheeks red. "I think I need some fresh air," he said. Then he stomped off toward the exit.

Ben waited until Jason was around the corner before turning on Tim, noticing his scowl. "Don't make that face! How is he supposed to know anything about you when you keep avoiding him?"

"I'm not avoiding him!"

"Then you'll be home for dinner tonight."

"Yeah. Sure. He thought I was—"

"A salesman. I heard. He didn't realize that you're *the* Tim Wyman, internationally renowned artist. I can't believe he didn't ask for your autograph!"

Tim's shoulders sagged. "That's not what I expected. I was just surprised."

"If you want him to know who you are, you need to make an effort. Talk to him. Simple as that."

Tim looked skyward in exasperation. "Why do I suck so bad at this?"

"Because you're scared to let down your guard. So is he. You're both to blame, but one of you is a teenager in the middle of a crisis." Ben took his hand. "And one of you is an adult. Sometimes. On good days."

Tim glanced toward the front windows. Jason was leaning against the car, his head shaking occasionally. "It's too late. He hates me."

Ben rolled his eyes. "He doesn't hate you."

"He does. It's just a matter of time before he punches me. Jace put some sort of voodoo curse on me. I'm doomed."

Ben laughed. "Like all such things, it's all in your head. Try again, okay? For me?"

"I will," Tim said. "Tomorrow."

"Tonight. We're having steak. Be there." Ben turned to walk away.

Tim caught his arm. "Don't hate me. If I can't do this, please don't hold it against me. Not everyone can be like you. Or Eric. You guys are special, like angels or something."

Ben remembered feeling that way about Jace. How odd to think anyone saw him in a similar light. "I'm messed up," Ben said. "We all are. All I'm asking you to do is to let Jason discover that. You don't have to be perfect for him. You just have to be yourself."

Tim still didn't seem certain, but he nodded. He released Ben's arm, but Ben grabbed him, hugged him tight, and smiled when backing away. "You're the bomb. Show me that winner's smile."

Tim seemed puzzled by this, but forced a grin. When Ben pretended he was about to swoon, the grin broadened and brightened. There it was. A touch of swagger. They would be okay. A few more disasters like this, maybe, but they would get there eventually.

Dinner for two, and not in the romantic sense because Tim hadn't shown up. Ben tried to maintain his optimism, but he was only human. He didn't finish his steak and didn't argue when

Jason offered to do dishes. Instead he went to the living room and stared at the front door, willing it to open. When it didn't, he decided to sing. For him singing wasn't just a release. It could make things right. If not the whole world, then at least the one within himself. When Jason reappeared, Ben told him to grab his guitar, hoping he wouldn't pluck a few strings before mumbling how bad he sucked. Ben needed music, and he needed it now.

They debated which song to choose, trying to find common ground. This increased Ben's frustration. Were these just excuses to delay performing? They finally settled on a song, *Go Your Own Way* by Fleetwood Mac. The lyrics seemed particularly appropriate. Jason started playing, comfortable with the chords and proving himself instantly. The kid was good! Now he was the one looking expectant.

Time to sing.

As always, Ben put all of himself into his music. Jason responded. They found equal partners in each other, both rising to the occasion. They moved from song to song, neither needing to ask if they should continue. This felt good! Ben's emotions travelled a road that began with pent-up frustration and ended with longing hope. Why couldn't this new living arrangement work? Why did it have to be so hard? He loved Tim, and Ben was pretty sure they could both give Jason the sort of love he needed. Ben was only trying to do the right thing. At least he thought it was right. Maybe the universe was trying to show him otherwise.

Jason hit a wrong note. Ben turned his head and discovered the reason why. Tim, standing in the doorway, eyes shining like they always did when Ben sang. Except this time Tim wasn't looking at him. He was watching Jason, wearing the same smile he had at the gallery when they had parted. Tim nodded in approval as Jason played to the end of the song, Ben backing him up vocally. Then his eyes met Ben's and his faith was restored. They were doing the right thing. Jason belonged here. Maybe they weren't out of the woods yet, but at least now they were all walking the same path.

Jason shot to his feet. "My hand is cramping."

His body language was stiff as he disappeared up the stairs.

"Did I interrupt?" Tim asked.

"Not at all," Ben said reassuringly. Jason seemed intent on avoiding Tim, but hopefully that would pass.

"I can go," Tim said. "If you think it will help."

"You can stay here and eat dinner," Ben said warmly. He rose and led the way to the kitchen, deciding not to make Jason a topic. Perhaps Tim needed to see that their lives hadn't changed completely. They could still share blissfully selfish time together. "I made scalloped potatoes to go along with the steak. I'll heat some up for you."

Tim joined him at the stove, looking over Ben's shoulders. "Poor steak," he said, "I should have come home earlier."

"What's that supposed to mean?" Ben said incredulously.

"I didn't fall in love with you for your cooking." Tim laughed and leapt backwards when Ben tried to swat him. "You've improved, but you still don't know how to handle meat."

"I don't remember you ever complaining!"

"That's the bedroom. The kitchen is entirely different."

Ben crossed his arms over his chest. "Do you want leftovers or not?"

"I do," Tim said. "It looks delicious. I was only kidding."

Except when they were sitting at the table, Tim drowned his steak in barbeque sauce. Jason had done the same with ketchup. Ben had to admit the meat was a *little* dry, and he did prefer Tim's grilled steaks to his own. At least the potatoes were a hit, since Tim helped himself to seconds.

"So how was the rest of your day?" Ben asked, not mentioning their impromptu visit.

"Fine," Tim said. "Had an interesting conversation with one of the artists we're exhibiting. Oh, and I interviewed a new one. Get this, he only creates art on uh… disposable paper."

Ben scrunched up his face. "You mean like napkins and tissues?"

"Yeah, but bathroom stuff too. Including feminine products."

"Classy!"

"I gave him the brush-off and said we're all booked up for the semester. He left a sample though, which is good, because we were running low on toilet paper."

They laughed together. When Tim's phone rumbled, he leaned to one side to pull it from his pocket. He glanced at the screen, and his face lit up.

Ben had seen that expression before. "Your mother?"

"Yeah! I tried calling her earlier." Tim glanced at his plate and the wine Ben had poured for them both. "It can wait."

"No, go ahead!" Ben said. "I don't mind."

"You sure?"

After Ben nodded, Tim pushed the button to answer, wearing a grin as he talked to his mom. The conversation was fairly mundane, but he seemed happy. Too bad she didn't make time for him more often.

"Yeah," Tim was saying. "Can you mail it to me? No, they want the actual birth certificate. I don't think a copy would work. Yeah. That would be awesome. Thanks!" Tim shot Ben a wink. Then his face fell. "No, you don't need to bother him. Really. Oh, okay."

Tim's eyes unfocused, the corners of his mouth downturned as he waited in silence. A moment later, his cheerfulness sounded much more forced. "Dad! Hey! How about that Royals game, huh? Brutal, I know, but I'm sure they'll bounce back. Uh-huh. At least you didn't bet any money!" Tim's laugh was hollow. "Work is fine. We had a new exhibit a few weeks back and sold seven pieces. That's a lot for— No, the artists keep all the money. I know what commission is but— Uh huh. Yeah. I don't earn anything because this is a foundation and—" Tim sighed. "No, I don't get a salary."

The rest of the call was much quieter. Tim stared at the table, one hand covering his forehead, like he was in pain. He mostly just made noises in the affirmative, getting an earful until the very end when he cut the call short. "I gotta run. Love you guys. Bye." He hung up the phone and set it aside, seemingly unaware that Ben was still sitting there.

"That sounded rough," he tried gently.

Tim snapped back to the present. "Yeah. Dad thinks I'm gullible for not earning money at the gallery."

"It's a charitable foundation!"

"I tried telling him that, so then he started reading off the salaries of big charity CEOs. These guys are pulling in six figures a year, sometimes more, which seems fucked up because people gave that money thinking it would go to a good cause, not to make one person rich. Besides, the money I live off comes from Eric. That's already more than I deserve, so I'm not about to take money from the foundation created to honor him. Of course I can't tell Dad that, because he'd end up saying something bad about Eric and piss me off."

"I'm sorry."

Tim exhaled. "It's fine."

"How's your mom?" Ben asked, hoping to steer the conversation toward more cheerful horizons.

"Good," Tim said. "She's planning a trip to Mexico to see Nana, so she's excited."

"What was all that about a birth certificate?"

"Oh nothing. Just insurance stuff."

Ben blinked. "What sort of insurance? You said the house was already covered."

Tim licked his lips nervously. "Just in case."

"Life insurance?" Ben didn't mean to shout this, but he couldn't even consider the possibility. "Why are you worrying about things like that?"

"Nothing's going to happen," Tim said. "It's for my own peace of mind. I want to know that you're taken care of, no matter what."

"I don't need money! I need you to keep your promise!"

Tim looked away, expression weary. "Sorry."

Ben took a deep breath and exhaled. "No, I am. I just hate the idea."

"I know. I shouldn't have mentioned it."

Ben nibbled his bottom lip, then reached for the bottle. "More wine?"

Tim grimaced. "I think I'll go for a run."

"I didn't mean to sound angry."

"It's not you," Tim said. "I just feel pathetic. I'm supposed to be an adult now, but one call from my dad, and I feel like a fuck-up. Again. I just need to blow off some steam."

Ben moved the bottle aside. "Okay. But first..." He stood and offered his hand, pulling Tim to his feet. Ben dragged him to the living room, sat on the couch, and patted his lap. Some of the tension left Tim's face when he placed his head there, the rest of him stretching out on the couch.

Words had proven unreliable, so Ben simply stroked his hair, toyed with his ears, and ran a finger tip over his eyebrows, across his cheeks, or along his jaw. As he did this, he considered how on edge Tim had been, how worried he was about making mistakes or failing completely. He had felt that way most of his life, trying to please his parents and never—at least when it came to his father—finding success. Tim had escaped that life, and yet recently, he probably found himself under the same pressure again. Struggling to get along with Jace's family, or accept a teenager into their home, or any number of things to please Ben, all because of one constant fear.

"I'll never leave you," Ben said. "No matter what."

Tim rolled onto his back, looking up at him questioningly.

"I know I did once," Ben said. "And there were other times we couldn't be together, but all of that is past us now. You don't have to be perfect for me, and it's okay if you make mistakes. Lots of them. It won't make a difference because I'll still love you just as much. I'll never say goodbye. I don't care what happens. I won't. Ever."

Tim reached up to catch the tear running down Ben's cheek. Then he rolled over again, reaching behind Ben and squeezing him tight. Tim's face was buried in his stomach, so it was hard to tell, but Ben was pretty sure he heard a muffled response.

"I love you too."

Ben promised himself never to sleep again because he had missed... something. Somehow, in the middle of the night, everything had changed. Tim was at the breakfast table the next morning. So was Jason. Instead of glaring or looking anywhere but at each other, they seemed relaxed. Like they were old friends, and that any conflict had taken place ages ago. Ben made sure they were both fed, walking on eggshells and waiting for the next misunderstanding, but it didn't come. When he left for work, he imagined them getting into a brawl the second he drove away. When he returned later in the day, he didn't find any bruised faces or missing teeth. Tim was reorganizing the garage, the open doors revealing that his car was gone. *The* car. The Bentley whatever-it-was, which cost a small fortune and was treated not only like a baby, but the last in a royal bloodline.

"What happened to your car?" Ben asked.

"Jason has it," Tim said easily, shifting a cardboard box to a different stack. "He has a job interview."

"Okay." Ben stood and waited for a horror story or some complaint.

Tim simply kept working like nothing was amiss.

Ben went inside and considered having a stiff drink.

When Jason returned home, he was all grins. Ben asked if

he had gotten the job, but Jason refused to say. Only when Tim came back inside and was in the room with them did Jason share the good news. He had gotten the job, which was great, but the real news was how he waited to make sure Tim was included in this announcement. And Tim seemed genuinely happy for him. Ben covertly checked the date on his phone, wondering if he'd actually slept for days. How could so much progress have been made in one night?

Not wanting to jinx this positive turn of events, he waited until Jason went upstairs before he asked.

"Well?" he said, following Tim into the kitchen. "What happened?"

"Hm?" Tim said, wearing an all-too-innocent expression. "What do you mean?"

"You guys seem awfully chummy."

Tim started poking around in the refrigerator. "That's what you wanted, right?"

"Yeah! I just didn't think it would happen so fast. Did you guys talk or…"

"We shared a moment. I have a new theory too." Tim stood, bringing a carton of orange juice to his lips. He gulped a few times before continuing. "I think Jace sent him."

"Here we go," Ben said, shaking his head.

"Hey, I was raised Catholic. That kind of stuff is hard to shake. My mom used to make me pray to Saint Fiacre before I was allowed to mow the lawn. Otherwise she worried I'd cut off a leg or whatever."

"Did it work?"

Tim closed the refrigerator, revealing two whole legs. "Anyway, hear me out. I think Jace sent him for you so you'll never be lonely. If something ever happens to me—"

"Not this again," Ben said, his throat feeling tight.

Tim's smile was gentle. "I won't die first. I'm just saying that if I, uh, have to take a long business trip or whatever. Say I'm out of the country for a few weeks. You'll still have someone around. You won't be lonely. That's a good thing, right? Here's the twist. I think Jace teamed up with Eric."

Ben took in his earnest expression. "How so?"

"Eric knows that this is my chance to be a better man than my father." Tim jutted out his chin. "I'm not going to be distant or judgmental. Whenever Jason needs me, I'll be there. Chances are I'll still manage to screw it up, but not before I've tried my best."

Ben eyed him curiously. "Do you really believe Jace and Eric have a hand in this?"

Tim exhaled. "I don't know. Maybe it's just my way of making sense of the situation. All I know is that I like the idea."

Ben stepped forward, took the orange juice carton from Tim, and set it on the counter. Then he placed his head against Tim's chest. "I like the idea too."

"They're with us." Tim sounded certain. He wrapped his arms around Ben and squeezed. "One way or another, they always will be."

Ben was cleaning Jason's room without actually trying to do so. Over the last few months, he had worked hard to give Jason his independence, which meant allowing him to run his life as he saw fit. That was fine, but every time Ben walked past his room, it seemed to be more cluttered and disorganized. Ben wasn't a neat freak, but he liked things to be *somewhat* organized. With everyone out of the house today, he decided to wash all the sheets. Normally he didn't do Jason's laundry, but this was a good pretense to straighten things up while he was in there.

Once the washing machine was running, he returned with a trash bag. Then he wished for latex gloves. Had he been this bad as a teenager? Ben's mind flashed back to piles of dirty laundry, stacks of loose CDs, and empty cups from gas station sodas. Suddenly he felt like calling his mom to apologize. Then again, he was about to pay back his karmic debts. He began by throwing away obvious trash. That would reduce the mess and maybe inspire Jason to do the rest on his own. Or at the very least, it would make walking by his room a slightly less harrowing experience.

He was plucking empty cans of Mountain Dew off the dresser, tossing them into the trash bag, when he noticed his name in writing. *Ben*. He stopped, because the handwriting looked familiar. In fact, it resembled Jace's. Ben stared without touching the thin brown cardboard, which was almost entirely obscured by junk mail. He examined it long enough to be certain. Jace's loopy handwriting. Ben smiled, and still feeling puzzled, brushed at the envelopes and papers, revealing his last name. *Bentley*. He tugged at the cardboard, inching it to the side, revealing a dash. Then a hand-drawn heart followed by an exclamation point.

His breath was shuddering, his hand shaking when the junk mail shifted under its own weight, revealing one more name. *Jace.*

Like a letter to him after all this time. One last message. One final goodbye.

Ben ripped the cardboard free and accidentally flipped it over in the process. The tears on his cheeks were joined by puzzled laughter. The top of a cereal box. Lucky Charms. He couldn't remember the last time he had bought that brand of cereal. Not since moving to this house. The opposite side revealed a very mundane explanation to it all. Jace's name, then his old phone number. Beneath this were Ben's name, the playful heart, and his cell phone number. This is what Jace had given Jason all those years ago.

Ben laughed at himself, feeling silly. Then he set it down, letting his fingers trace the letters of Jace's name. "Thank you," he said out loud. "For everything. All the love… just everything."

He allowed himself to cry. Then he dried his eyes and got back to work. Ten minutes later, he heard the stairs creak. Tim was back from a jog, still panting, his hair damp. He paused in the doorway, puzzled until he saw what Ben was doing.

"Brave man," he said.

"Yeah," Ben replied. "Look what I found!" He returned to the dresser and held up the box top, but it was facing the wrong way, the names and numbers visible to Ben alone.

"Lucky Charms!" Tim said with a grin. "Those were Eric's favorite. Hey, I'm going to hop in the shower. Care to join me?"

Ben stared a moment in shock and nodded. "I'll be right there." When he was alone again, he addressed the room. "Thank you both! Just one more favor." He glanced toward the hallway, hearing the shower water begin to run. "No peeking, all right? Either of you!" Then Ben laughed, set the box top back where he'd found it, and went to join the man he loved.

Something Like Tonight

by Jay Bell

Austin, 2015

I've got nothing left to give. I've dug deep, just as I once did while tilling the soil, bringing fresh nutrients to the surface so new life could grow and thrive. The farm is long gone, as is my soul, pulled and stretched from so many directions that it was torn to pieces. I'd give anything to have those tattered remnants back, or to feel the dirt beneath my fingernails again, but some things can't be bought. Not once they've been sold.

Allison Cross looked up from the script, the breath catching in her throat. She almost expected, when gazing across the table, to see tears pouring down the face of the man seated there. Instead her husband seemed anxious as he rubbed his brown hair, a bad idea since he didn't have much left. Not on top, anyway. The sides were trimmed short to match the length of his beard. He was nothing like the men Allison had fawned over in her youth—ripping their images from magazines and taping them to her bedroom wall—but Brian Milton had different qualities that made her swoon, such as now, when he appeared so adorably vulnerable.

"What do you think?" Brian asked, his eyes darting to the script.

"You changed the ending," Allison said.

Brian nodded. "It's good to leave the audience crying. Isn't it? Or do you think it's *too* sad? I can change it back!"

"I like it," Allison said quickly. "I really do. It's just…" She scanned the final paragraph. "This is heavy stuff! Where are you drawing it from? Is this how you feel?"

Brian laughed. "No! Of course not. Are you saying that people won't be able to relate?"

"Not at all." Just the opposite, in fact. The plot might have been a little maudlin, but at times Allison felt equally drained, pulled in too many directions at once. She had never wondered if Brian felt the same. They were parents now, which ate up a lot of their time. In addition to raising a three-year-old child, they had their marriage to maintain, as well as their separate careers.

Her work as a therapist presented its own challenges, and Brian's job was equally demanding. Not only was he partial owner of a dinner theater, but also the director of each production and occasionally the writer of the season's featured play. Those were some daunting responsibilities. Aside from his hair jumping ship, he seemed to handle them well. Or so she had thought. "You would tell me if this is how you felt."

"Yes!" Brian insisted. "You know me. I'm an open book. Or an open script. Ha ha."

"Okay," Allison said, questioning her taste momentarily. Brian was a nice guy, but he wasn't exactly cool. In high school and college she had dated guys with their own bands, or pretty boys who preened themselves constantly, or athletes from just about every sports team on campus. Brian didn't have the body or the looks or the moves, but he was kind. Honest and trustworthy too, traits which were considerably rarer and worth more to her these days. "I think this play is going to click with a lot of people."

Brian smiled. "Really?"

"It'll be a hit. I promise." Allison glanced at her watch, then pushed away from the table. "I better get going. I have a full day of appointments."

"Don't be late getting home. The first read-through is tonight. I have to be there."

Allison raised an eyebrow. That's all it took.

Brian winced. "Sorry. I'm just nervous."

"And I reassured you. Now unless you want something to *really* worry about—"

Before she could finish her sentence, a pair of pint-sized feet came tromping across the kitchen floor. Then Davis plowed into her leg. He looked up at her, all gapped-tooth smile and dirty cheeks.

"Mama, guess what?"

"What?"

"Poop." This declaration was followed by a gurgling laugh.

Allison sniffed. Then she sighed. "Where is it?"

"Where's what?" Davis said, already on the verge of hysterics.

"The poop."

That set him off. When he was done chortling, he raised one of his feet. That didn't help Allison see, but she could guess.

"You stepped in dog poop again?"

Davis was too amused to answer, so she stooped to undo the Velcro strap on his shoe. "That's the third time this week. I swear you're doing this on purpose. If so, then kiddo, we need to have a serious talk!"

"I've got this," Brian said, hurrying around the table.

"You sure?" Allison asked as she stood.

"Absolutely. Go to work. We'll be fine."

She kissed him on the cheek. The man—despite all his imperfections—was a godsend. Deciding he deserved more than a simple peck, she went for his lips. Davis found this much less amusing and, after expressing his disgust, headed for the living room.

"Or you could cancel your first appointment," Brian said when they heard the television switch on. "You know how *Sesame Street* keeps him hypnotized."

"Rain check," Allison said. "I'm needed elsewhere, but feel free to make an appointment."

Brian perked up. "Now there's an idea. We've never done it in your office before. Oh! The consultation couch! We could—"

"Continue this some other time." Allison kissed him again, then headed for the garage. As soon as she was seated in the car, she allowed herself a blissful moment of silence. Then she pushed the button to open the garage door and braced herself for a day full of problems, none of them her own.

Patient Name: Kelly Phillips

Assessment: In his youth Kelly struggled with anger, particularly in romantic relationships, mostly due to not allowing others to accept fault. As a result of this, he would shoulder the blame himself, leading to feelings of resentment. While he seems to have mastered emotional control, he still makes the problems of others his own.

Recommendation: Kelly must learn to allow others to accept responsibility for their actions.

"I never thought I'd be on this couch again," Kelly said, bouncing up and down. "Is it the same one? I remember the fabric being darker."

"I had it reupholstered." Allison looked up from her notepad. "It's been a long time. Around five years, in fact."

Kelly went still. "That long?"

"Mm-hm." Allison consulted her notes. "Your last appointment was in twenty-ten. So how have you been? You said on the phone that your boyfriend is having issues."

"I'm fine," Kelly said after a pause. Clearly he wasn't ready to delve right in because he started making small talk. "We've been doing a lot of traveling. I loved it, for the most part, but I haven't settled down since I quit modeling. I'm used to moving every year. The only difference this time was I had fewer boxes to pack."

"How so?"

"Well, we've been touring around in an RV. That's been our home, aside from the occasional hotel when I need a breather. Sometimes we return here to Austin. We have a house, which is excessive because we hardly ever see it. This time we came back to discover that the kid we paid to mow the lawn had graduated and moved away. We're talking weeds up to my waist, and you don't want to know how many mice this attracted. The neighborhood association was *not* pleased. The cat next door seemed to like it though."

Allison nodded. "It's your hour," she said. "If this is how you want to spend it, that's fine, although you might have noticed my rate has gone up."

"Right," Kelly said. "Okay. I guess I'm out of practice, but here goes." He took a deep breath. "I'm in love with a violent man."

Allison's stomach sank. She dealt with such issues every day, but it never got easier. Especially when she knew the patient so well. She had always liked Kelly and still did. "You need to draw a line. Right away. You're not going to see him again until he gets help, you hear me?"

Kelly's jaw dropped. Then realization dawned. "Oh! Sorry. He doesn't hit me. Are you kidding? If he ever did that I'd smother him with a pillow while he's sleeping."

She breathed out in relief. "Okay, let's start with the basics. You're still with…"

"Nathaniel," Kelly said. "Yes. He's never laid a hand on me. Technically, I guess he has. Plenty of times, but not in a way I didn't appreciate."

"Again," Allison said. "It's your hour. I certainly don't mind hearing details, but… you know."

"Right." Kelly's brow furrowed with determination. "I've got this theory I'd like to run by you. Nathaniel and I have really gotten to know each other, which is wonderful, but I've noticed a pattern. He grew up in a violent household. His parents are good people, but his brother abused him. Physically mostly, but some of it was psychological. One day Nathaniel snapped and fought back. It sounded pretty bad. Then there was the time he caught his boyfriend—well, the details don't matter. Nathaniel got angry enough to start choking the poor guy. This was years and years ago, but that's still bad no matter what age you are. I don't know if you remember, but the event that led Nathaniel and me to break up the first time was when a guy at a party kissed me. Totally against my will, you understand. Even though I can take care of myself, Nathaniel decked the guy and would have done worse if I and some others hadn't intervened."

Allison scribbled down the key facts in abbreviated form. She would write them out in more detail later. "Have you ever worried that he might lash out at you physically?"

"No," Kelly said. "He loves me too much. I've never felt threatened when I'm with him. I trust Nathaniel with my life. I just don't want him to get in trouble. There was an incident last month."

"Tell me about it."

Kelly took a deep breath and exhaled. "We had left the RV at an overnight park and walked to a local bar, so please keep in mind that alcohol was involved. That's usually not a problem. We had a good time, kicked back a few beers. When we left and were walking across the parking lot, we saw a group of younger guys. Old enough to drink, I guess, but just barely. One of them said to me—I think he was trying to be cool, you know? Or maybe he was just stupid, because he gives me an upward nod and says, 'What up, nigger?'"

Allison grimaced. "Was this a white guy?"

Kelly nodded. "I just rolled my eyes, but Nathaniel flipped out. Before I knew what was happening, Nathaniel had swung, the jerk who had used the N-word went down with a single punch, and then Nathaniel started chasing after his friends."

Allison's lips twitched as she held back a smile. "That's terrible," she managed to say.

Kelly wasn't fooled. "It's totally hot and you know it. But I love Nathaniel enough that I don't want to see him thrown in jail or worse. Any of these guys could have been carrying a gun. While I've never been fond of that word, it's not worth getting killed over."

"I agree."

"We were both taken off guard. This wasn't a small town. We were on the outskirts of a big city. I know racism is everywhere, but like I said, this could have been social ineptitude instead."

"Lesson learned either way," Allison said. Then she cleared her throat. "But you're right. Both of your lives could have been put in danger by his reaction."

"I'm worried about him. Considering the environment he grew up in, this isn't completely unexpected, right?"

"Not at all, but it also doesn't justify his actions."

"You helped me to become less reactionary," Kelly said, "but this is different. I've always had a bad temper and a big mouth, but my first instinct was never to attack physically. I'm not sure how to help Nathaniel, but I know you can."

Allison nodded. "I'd be happy to."

Kelly flashed a smile. "I knew it. So what do we do?"

"Nathaniel needs to make an appointment."

Kelly's face fell.

"It's okay," Allison said. "I won't bill you for today. You're referring someone to me, which is fine. Give him my contact information, and I'll get him scheduled."

Kelly didn't seem any happier. "He doesn't know I'm here."

"I thought you were open with each other."

"We are! But he's stubborn, and I know he'll hate the idea, so I figured you could share whatever advice you have and I'll pass it on to him."

Allison shook her head. "If only it were that easy. Think of the therapy sessions we've had together, and then imagine how effective they would have been with a mediator between us."

Kelly's shoulders slumped. "You're right."

"And you're still trying to face consequences on your own."

"So help me face this one. What should I do?"

Allison tapped her pad of paper as she thought. "Nathaniel loves you, right?"

Kelly grinned. "Yes."

"Then he'll do this for you."

The grin faltered. "He would, but I'm not sure he'll actually listen when he's here. He'll go through the motions to please me—"

"Then bring him with you. Sit on that couch together, look him in the eye, and tell him what you've told me: You appreciate him punching stupid people, but you'd rather he make being with you a priority, which he can't do from behind bars."

Kelly mulled this over. Then he nodded. "That might work. Thanks."

"My pleasure." She checked her watch. "You still have time left, but it's the end of the day and I have a few things to take care of. Do you mind?"

"Not at all!" Kelly hopped to his feet, his features more relaxed than they had been when he arrived.

She walked him to the front of the office, scheduled another appointment, and offered her hand. Kelly ignored it and gave her a hug. This job often left her stressed, but at moments like these, the burden was easier to bear.

Patient Name: Brian Milton

Assessment: Brian is a recovering alcoholic who I first met during my internship at a rehab clinic. He has remained sober for more than ten years—a testament to his willpower and determination. These strengths are useful to him in business, although his hidden vulnerability is often expressed through the artistic side of his work. Or at the dinner table, when he gets caught in a cycle of self-doubt instead of focusing on the food.

Recommendation: Brian needs to take credit for his achievements and allow them to reinforce his self-esteem. He also needs to realize that he didn't land such a sexy, smart, and talented wife by pure chance.

Allison shook her head, trying to clear it. At times she struggled to transition back to her personal life. Brian was definitely *not* one of her patients, but occasionally she still had to rely on her training, even at home. Currently her husband was paler than normal, meeting her at the door with words she had already anticipated during the drive home.

"You're late!"

"I know."

"You said you wouldn't be!"

"I know. Someone flipped their car on the highway. You didn't get my text?"

Brian blinked a few times, then hurried toward the kitchen, no doubt to check his phone. Allison didn't take this personally. Brian was the sort of person who—when standing directly in the heat of the sun—needed to check a weather app to find out if the day was hot or not.

She found him at the kitchen counter, holding the phone, his expression concerned. "You're okay?"

"I'm fine. How about you?"

Brian took a deep breath. "I'm okay. I wasn't, but I am now. I reread the script, and you're right. The ending sucked."

"I never said that!"

"I could tell from your face. I added a few paragraphs, and I think we're back on track. I'm going to leave the audience smiling. Speaking of which, I need to get to rehearsal. Dinner is on the stove. Davis already ate. He's in his room building a Duplo castle. That's what he calls it, anyway. It's really just a tower. I promised him I'd help when it gets too high. Um…"

"I'll take care of it," Allison said, forcing down a smile.

"Okay. I think that's everything!"

Brian leaned in to give her a kiss, then grabbed his script from the table and headed for the door leading to the garage.

"Darling," Allison said gently.

Brian paused. "Yes?"

She pointed to his feet, which were still bare. "You might want to cover those hairy things. Clean socks are in the dresser."

Brian groaned. "I'm definitely going to be late."

"You're the boss. You're allowed to keep everybody else waiting. But first…"

"Socks and shoes, got it." Brian started to leave the room, then turned back to thrust a heavily rumpled script into her hands. "Could you read through the changes real quick? Last page. Let me know what you think."

Allison maintained her pleasant expression until he was out of sight. Then she rolled her eyes. She liked his plays, but right now she needed to check on Davis and then heat up and eat her dinner. Still, reading a few paragraphs wouldn't take long. She sat at the table, opening the script to the last page. She ignored the messy handwriting while she reread the original ending that had struck a little too close to home. Then she moved on to the new material.

"What do you think?" Brian asked when he reappeared.

Allison chose her words carefully. "The protagonist, who is both spiritually and financially broke, decides to visit the circus. He can't afford tickets to the show, so he sneaks into one of the trailers, remembers his childhood love of clowns, and puts on a red nose."

"Because he decides *to be* a clown, which makes him happy again."

"Which is demonstrated by him staring into the mirror and laughing like a maniac."

Brian frowned. "It'll be more subtle than that."

"You were worried about relatability? Not many people feel like breaking into a clown's trailer to steal a nose. Seriously, honey. Your original ending was good! You don't need to cheapen it like this."

"We're a dinner theater. We can't leave people too depressed to order dessert or have another drink."

"Because sad people *never* pig out or get drunk." Allison glanced at the script again. "Maybe you could end with a song. Not a happy little tune exactly, but one about looking back to the potential of youth and wishing for the chance to do it all over again. You know how the audience reacts when Ben sings. Depressing or not, you'll leave them wanting more."

Brian perked up. "We can make it a cautionary tale. The audience will feel relieved they haven't ruined their own lives yet. And with Ben singing..." He grinned madly. "You're a genius! I love you!"

"I love you too," Allison said.

Brian kissed her, grabbed the script, and disappeared out the door leading to the garage. Once she heard his car back out, Allison allowed herself thirty seconds to sit and breathe. Then she rose to go find her son.

Patient Name: Davis Milton-Cross

Assessment: Davis can be manipulative, especially on the playground when bigger kids give him a hard time. He's disturbingly good at falling to the ground and summoning tears, only stopping when the offending child is punished by his or her parent. When not incriminating others, Davis enjoys anything disgusting—boogers, slugs, and even old gum, which he calls "chewy putty." This results in constantly sticky hands, no matter how often his mother washes them.

Recommendation: None. He's perfect. Although maybe a little sister would help deplete some of that excess energy and inspire him to become a role model. Ah, who am I kidding? A sibling would only double my trouble.

"I don't like it. I don't like it. I don't like it."

Allison stifled a yawn and kept hitting the button on the remote control. The picture on the television changed every few seconds. The little man sitting next to her on the couch—back straight, legs crossed beneath him, eyes alert—remained undeviating.

"I don't like it. I don't like it. I don't—"

"Davis!" Allison said. "Choose something!"

"I don't like it," Davis said matter-of-factly.

She could still remember how excited she was when he had first started talking. Just a few words initially, followed by little sentences. If only she'd known how Davis would eventually ramble on and on, never worried about being repetitive or infuriating. Not that she could stay mad at him for long. Allison glanced over at her son. His skin was a shade somewhere between her own and Brian's. Cinnamon, as Tim's grandmother had described it once. That went nicely with his dark brown hair that had just a hint of crimson, like Brian's beard when he grew it out. Davis' green eyes were from his father as well, but the wide smile had been passed down from Allison's mother, to her, and now to him.

Davis glanced over, seemingly puzzled. "Why'd you stop?"

"Because we've been through every channel three different times. I'm done. *You're* done. It's time for bed."

Davis rolled backward, arms and legs flopping loose in preparation for a tantrum. "Nuh-uh! TV! You said!"

"I said you could watch one show. It's not my fault you can't decide." Allison tried to sound stern, but ended up yawning around most of these words. Why was he resisting bedtime? She'd be happy to switch places with him. Let him do the dishes and straighten up the house. The Duplo tower had been dragged out here to the living room, built even higher, and then destroyed. A bath had followed, most of the floor getting soaked in the process. Davis had thrown a fit during most of it. This had resulted in her bargaining with him. An extra TV show before bed if he stopped fighting her. Now she was beginning to regret that decision.

"You said! You said!"

"Fine! Go choose one of your DVDs."

Davis grinned, slid off the couch, and ran to the shelf where his DVDs were kept. Allison zoned out until he returned. When she saw what he had chosen, she laughed.

"This is a big DVD, Mama!"

"It's a VHS tape," she said, taking it from him. "Choose something else. We can't play this one."

"Why not?"

"Because we don't have a VCR hooked up. Go get something else."

Davis went to do so, leaving her with the tape. The case was generic—the blank kind for home recording. She checked the label on the spine and recognized her own handwriting, although her penmanship had been less disciplined back then. *Home Movies: Volume One*. This was surrounded by drawings of flowers and a few hearts. In purple ink, naturally. She chuckled to herself, then groaned when Davis thrust another VHS tape into her lap. *Home Movies: Part Two*. The naming scheme wasn't consistent, but at least she had remembered the hearts and flowers, this time in cyan ink.

"That one," Davis prompted.

Allison was about to give him the same explanation. Then she remembered a large plastic container in the garage, full of random cables, remotes, and—if she wasn't mistaken—a VHS player. She couldn't recall the last time she had watched these movies. She'd been meaning to have them digitized, but the effort hardly seemed worth it. Then again, why not double-check the content?

Fifteen minutes later she was seated on the living room floor, the VCR set before her, wires snaking across the carpet and disappearing behind the television. Davis was on his knees next to her, eyes lit up like they were about to play a video game. When the machine sputtered and droned, a fuzzy picture flickering to life on the TV, he didn't look so impressed.

"Who's that?"

Allison stared. On the screen was a little girl, her bashful smile a few teeth short of a full set. Each tiny hand was filled with white cotton, grasping the dress and spreading it wide as she performed a wobbly curtsy.

"Mama, who is that?"

Allison blinked. "That's me! Gosh, I must be... six years old?"

Davis looked between the screen and her a few times. "Nuh-uh!"

"That's me!" she insisted. "I wasn't always this old, you know."

"You were a little girl," Davis said. Then he laughed, as if this were something she should be embarrassed about.

Allison watched herself shake her head and nod a few times, answering questions they couldn't hear. "I wonder who's filming?" She leaned back and grabbed the remote from the coffee table. Then she pressed one of the buttons; green bars increased in number on the screen. A new voice filled the room. At first she thought it was her own, sounding like the patient notes she sometimes recorded on audio to play back later. Not the voice of a little girl. It belonged to a grown woman, one so special that Allison still dreamed of her.

"And do you remember why you wanted this dress?" the voice asked.

Little Allison nodded. "Because the photo of you."

"That's right," the voice responded. "You wanted the same dress as your mother. Isn't *that* sweet? Not every little girl wants to dress like her mama, but just like I tell everyone at work, you're my best friend."

Little Allison smiled broadly, radiating with pride.

That dress! Allison had found a black and white photograph of her mother as a child, sitting on a swing. In it she was wearing a simple white dress, the design not really noteworthy, but the image had been so romantic that Allison became enamored with it. When she had asked for the same dress, her mother had made one exactly like it from scratch. Not just that, but she had adapted the design for herself too, so that they could both be wearing the same outfit. Oh how Allison had loved that! How proud her father had looked when—

"Let's go show Daddy."

Little Allison nodded. "Okay."

"This is boring," Davis said.

"Hush." Allison watched herself run down a hallway and

push open a door. The camera followed, rising to focus on a man seated at a desk. He took off his reading glasses, revealing weary eyes, but they lit up when he watched his daughter twirl.

"Who's that guy?" Davis asked.

"My father." Allison said, throat constricting.

Davis scrunched up his face. "You have a dad?"

"Of course!"

"How come you don't live with him?"

Allison reached over to tickle his stomach. "Then where would you live?" She was avoiding the question, but luckily Davis's thoughts were traveling in a different direction. "Does Dad have a dad?"

"Yes. That's who Grandpa Joseph is. He's your father's father."

"I knew that," Davis said, feigning bored disinterest.

Or maybe he wasn't pretending, because the man on the screen was still making a big deal out of the dress. Little Allison had climbed onto his lap, and he was examining the hem. Then Charles Cross smiled directly at the camera, pure adoration in his eyes, before he returned his attention to his daughter.

"You're my pride, Alli," he said. "You're my joy."

Allison swallowed against the lump in her throat and grabbed the remote. "I have a mother too." She hit the fast-forward button. The machine rumbled with effort. Little Allison hopped with alarming speed to the carpet and performed a frantic dance, causing Davis to howl with laughter. The images gave way to static and were replaced by a cereal commercial. Halfway through it the image jerked suddenly. Little Allison was back, prancing around the living room and singing. They only watched a minute of this before zooming forward again.

Allison could remember gathering all the home movie cassettes and hooking two VCRs together to make this compilation. A Mother's Day present, if she remembered right, which would explain the hearts and flowers. Time skipped ahead a few years. Allison was joined by another little girl— Karen Bentley—as they filmed silly sketches together. Allison remembered these well enough to know she wasn't eager to rewatch them. Instead she kept zooming ahead, searching for more footage of her parents. She found a segment of her father hosing off the car in the driveway, her voice behind the camera now. He had seemed so old to her back then, but now she was the same age. Pushing forty.

"Make them go fast again," Davis said.

Allison complied, frustrated that she couldn't find footage of her mother.

The tape came to an end, the static not relenting this time.

"Maybe on the second volume," she said, ejecting the tape to replace it with the other.

After it had finished rewinding, she hit play.

"Ready?" asked a fifteen-year-old girl.

"Ready to rock!" declared a skinny guy at her side. Ben Bentley.

They were both wearing sunglasses and holding hairbrushes like they were microphones.

"Give me a beat!" Allison demanded.

"Deeeee Jaaaaay!" Ben cried. Then he reached over and pushed a button on a boombox.

Allison leaned over and jabbed at the VCR, ejecting the tape.

"Hey!" Davis complained. "Why'd you do that?"

"You've watched enough TV. It's time for bed." Not to mention that music always made Davis hyper. The last thing she needed was him bouncing around the room and getting worked up again. Besides, her mother wouldn't be making an appearance on this tape. By the time Allison was a teenager, she was already gone. All in the blink of an eye. One day there, and the next—

"Don't wanna," Davis sulked.

Allison glanced over at him, reminded of how precious every second could be. "Want to look at some old photos with me?"

"Photos?"

"It's either that or you go to bed."

"Okay!"

Anything was better than bed, apparently. Allison grabbed a couple photo albums from the shelf and sat on the couch. Davis settled into the crook of her arm. He helped her turn pages, playing a game of "Who's that?" and pointing to each picture, even if he knew the answer. The content of the albums was more familiar to Allison, images she had looked at many times over the years. She lingered on the photos of her mother, feeling proud when explaining to Davis what kind of person she had been, but also a sense of loss because he would never truly know his grandmother.

"My mother, Tonya, she had a terrible sense of humor," Allison said. "I mean lowbrow. It used to drive my father crazy. She had a whoopee cushion, and as far as I know, she bought it herself and would always try to get one of us at the kitchen table. My mother would have loved you, because to her, nothing was funnier than a fart."

The word alone was enough to make Davis laugh, which was good, because the rest of the conversation was probably lost on him.

"She was every bit a lady though. My parents used to host parties, mostly coworkers and such. My father wasn't great at socializing. He could be awkward, but my mother was elegant. I remember her gliding through the room, making people laugh, remembering everyone's names, even if they were my father's coworkers instead of her own. I wanted to be like her. What about you? Do you want to be like your daddy?"

When no response came, she glanced down to see that Davis had dozed off. She was too relieved to feel slighted. She stared at the open page, at a photo of her parents when they had gone on a cruise, and another of her mother kissing her cheek—or more likely a zerbert since Allison's nose was crinkled and her eyes wet with tears. Even when being silly, Tonya still appeared elegant. Allison had assumed that her own elegance would come with age, but it never did. Most of the time she still felt like that little girl, so eager to be the lady her mother was, but falling short.

Allison let her gaze linger on the images a while longer. Then she stood, picked up Davis and carried him to his bed. After making sure he was tucked in, she kissed his forehead and left the room. She stopped by the messy bathroom and picked up the soaked towels. After dropping them in the hamper, she surveyed the living room, decided she didn't care about the mess, and sat on the couch, determined to bask in silence until Brian came home from work.

Patient Name: Benjamin Bentley
Assessment: Ben is awesome, clearly, or he wouldn't have the honor of being my best friend for over twenty years. That's not to say he doesn't have his faults, most of them matters of the heart. Ben loves with all of his being, which presents a problem when he loves the wrong guy, or he loves more than one person, or he has to deal with relationships reaching their natural conclusion.

Recommendation: Ben could use regular therapy sessions to help strengthen his coping abilities and to self-evaluate his decision-making process. Or he could just keep hanging out with me, because let's face it, I've been his own personal therapist since we were thirteen years old.

Five minutes of glorious solitude, staring with unfocused eyes at a dead television screen that seriously needed to be dusted. Then the doorbell rang. Allison tensed, her first thought of Davis and the difficult process of getting him calm again once his sleep was interrupted.

When she heard no sign of him stirring, she hurried to the door before the moron standing on her porch could ring the bell again. As she peered through the peephole, some of her anger ebbed away because on the other side of the front door was *her* moron. The two pints of ice cream he was holding didn't hurt either.

"Ben," she said in a hushed voice after opening the door.

Her best friend picked up on this immediately. "Davis is sleeping?"

She nodded. "Yes. We don't have to whisper. Just keep it down." Her eyes darted down to the ice cream. "Is that Karamel Sutra?"

"They were sold out," Ben replied. "I got you Salted Caramel Core. Mine's called Blondie Ambition. I've never tried it before."

"You're adorable," Allison said. "Get in here."

They went into the kitchen for spoons and reconvened to the living room. Ben paused before he sat, surveying the chaos: Building blocks, illustrated children's books, and an entire pack of crayons were spread out over the floor in one big rainbow mess.

"Wow," he said. "Uh…"

"Feel free to pick up," Allison said with a sigh. "Or hire me a maid."

"Now I know what to get you for your birthday." Ben wisely turned his attention away and sat on the couch beside her. Only a house fire would get Allison to move from her position.

"Dig in!" Ben said, his smile a little forced.

Allison eyed him suspiciously. He looked good. His hair was longer than it had been for quite some time, reminding her of their youth. The tint was lighter too, no doubt due to the summer sun. He never seemed to put on weight no matter how many ice cream sessions they shared, and she had witnessed him get ID'ed for trying to buy alcohol just a few months ago. She could only imagine his assessment of her appearance. Fat chance that he thought she looked young for her age. She didn't stew on this, returning her attention to that smile. She took a bite of ice cream and nearly spit it out again.

"What are you doing here? You're missing rehearsal!"

Ben swiftly scooped ice cream into his mouth, then shrugged helplessly as if unable to speak.

"It's the first night of rehearsals," she stressed, "and this is the first play Brian has written in years. It's important to him!"

"I know," Ben said after swallowing. "That's why I'm here. Hey, what do you think of the new flavor? Better than your usual?"

Allison narrowed her eyes, then set the pint on the coffee table. "You've heard of dirty money? I've got a feeling this is dirty ice cream. I'm not eating one more bite until I know what this is about."

Ben sighed, setting his own aside. "I'm not sure I want to do this anymore."

"Acting?"

"That's part of the problem. Last week I was on stage, and the audience isn't exactly young. We get a mix, but most people are older, so I was facing them and trying to imagine being their age. Twenty or thirty years from now, do I really still want to be in a theater playing make believe? I feel like a liar. I don't know anything about being a corrupt banker or a mechanic with a heart of gold. It'll get worse when I'm older because all the roles will be politicians or grandpas or… I don't know."

"Wouldn't that keep the job interesting for you?" Allison countered. "Most actors age into different roles. It's perfectly normal."

"I don't like being reminded of my age when I'm *not* on stage. And I'm not an actor. That's the ridiculous part."

"Could have fooled me."

"Seriously? There's more to acting than standing up there and reading lines. What sort of professional training do I have?"

"Ninth grade drama class," Allison said. "Remember Mrs. Perlstein?"

Ben snorted. "Oh my gosh. We got in so much trouble in that class!"

"I don't think I've ever laughed so hard!"

"Me neither, but seriously, I never wanted to be an actor. You only talked me into this gig because I wanted an excuse to sing."

"Brian is adding another song to the new play if that's what you're worried about."

Ben shook his head. "It's not. Maybe I'm tired of doing something that I suck at. Don't say something nice either! You and I both know that I'll never be a great actor. I don't even have a convincing poker face."

"You have a beautiful voice. It would be a shame if people no longer got to hear it."

"Your voice is just as good, but you're not singing to your patients."

"That's what you think."

Ben locked eyes with her, his expression pleading. "You know what I mean. You have a job you can feel proud of. You're helping people. Being an entertainer—"

"Helps people too. Just think how often music got you and me through hard times. I don't mean just singing. Remember all those days we were down and needed to feel like we weren't alone, so we listened to sad songs and moped? Or when we got sick of being miserable, put on dance music and shook our butts? Or what about that actor when you were younger? You said he helped you accept yourself."

"Scott Thompson," Ben said with a smile. "He was openly gay before any of the big celebrities were. He seemed so shameless about it. Hell, he even incorporated it into his act. I made it my goal to be like him."

"And those were just comedy skits," Allison said. "You might assume they don't help people, but they did more than just make you laugh, am I right?"

"As usual," Ben said. "Still, I don't feel like performing on stage is my calling, and as much as I like singing, I'm not sure that's it either. My work at the hospital—speech therapy—*that* I feel good about. I asked them for extra hours."

"And?"

Ben exhaled. "Something about money. It's not like I was asking for more, but I guess the hospital budget would have to go under review and blah blah blah. I'm thinking about going back to college."

Allison widened her eyes. "Seriously? You were desperate to

graduate so it would finally be over. Now you want to go back?"

"I know, but I thought maybe I could increase my skill set and uh, help people. I guess. Somehow."

"Sounds like you've got this all figured out," Allison teased. She reached for his pint of ice cream and handed it back to him, then grabbed her own. "You know what's really going on, don't you?"

"What?" Ben noticed her expression and grimaced. "Don't say it!"

"Mid-life crisis!"

"Ugh." Ben sucked on a spoonful of ice cream and thought about it. Then he reached a conclusion. "Ugh."

"Public speaking obviously isn't in your future. Hey, I know what will cheer you up."

She reached for the remotes and turned on the television. Then, with the tip of her toes, she pushed the tape back in the player, motors whirring as it rewound.

"You have a VCR?" Ben said disbelievingly.

"Watch," Allison replied.

Soon they were staring at much younger versions of themselves.

"Give me a beat!"

"Deeeee Jaaaaay!"

"Oh, God," Ben said with a chuckle. "I'd forgotten all about this. What song did we—"

His question was interrupted by music. The song had no longer been fresh at the time, and it certainly wasn't intended to be performed by two fifteen-year-olds who kept bouncing around each other.

"Poison!" younger Ben declared, his voice wheedling. "That boy is pooooi-sooon!"

"You changed the lyrics," Allison said, clutching her stomach. "You were so gay, even back then! And why are you taking all the high notes?"

"Why are you taking all the low ones?" Ben asked, wiping tears of laughter from his eyes.

Both stopped laughing when, halfway through the song, they starting rapping together in perfect unison.

"Burn this tape," Ben said. "I'll pay you. Name your price. Just make sure you destroy it."

"It's too funny to destroy," Allison said, lowering the volume, "but I'll put it in a safe deposit box in Switzerland where no one will ever find it."

"Must have been summer," Ben said nodding at the television.

"Why do you say that?"

"Because we're at your house. We never would have risked making this if there was any chance of your father coming home."

Allison frowned, remembering how much had changed between the innocent footage she had shown Davis earlier and what had come later. She pushed a button on the remote and the image froze, younger Ben and Allison singing into each other's hairbrush microphones.

"We need to digitize this," Ben said. "As embarrassing as it is, I love that you still have it."

"As do I. You were always a performer. If not this, then the talent shows at school, or putting on a brave face in front of all the homophobic bullies."

"I never wanted to do it for a living though," Ben said. He sighed. "You ever miss those days? We were so innocent back then. I remember being desperate to find a guy who could love me. Just the idea conjured up some serious angst. Almost beautiful, in its own way. I had no idea what was ahead of me, that love and loss go hand in hand. I hadn't experienced anything like that yet."

Allison stabbed at her ice cream. "I had."

"Sorry, I wasn't—"

"It's fine," Allison said reassuringly. "It's easy to forget. You never met her, did you?"

"Your mother? I did. Remember when Karen was forced to take me with her on play dates? In retrospect, I think my parents wanted privacy so they could... Yuck. Anyway, you guys would force me to sit in the corner, and if I was lucky, I might get a Barbie horse to play with."

Allison laughed shamelessly. "That's right!"

"More than once I snuck away and wandered around the house. The two of you never paid attention to me anyway, and sometimes your mom would give me cookies or some other treat. She would sit at the table and talk to me like we were friends."

Allison's throat felt tight. "I'm so glad you got to meet her."

"She was a good woman. You remind me of her a lot."

"Stop," Allison said, but mostly because she didn't want to cry. She mustered up some attitude in the hope of preventing this. "Your flattery isn't going to get you out of trouble. You're letting my husband down."

"I know," Ben said, slumping into the couch. "There's more happening than I've let on. I don't think Tim loves me anymore."

"What?" Allison cried. "Why do you say that?"

"Because I told him that I'm moving to Thailand and he didn't even get upset."

Allison studied his face to make sure he was serious. When certain he was, she laughed. "Why are you moving to Thailand?"

"A school there is looking for English-speaking language therapists. It seems like a good opportunity."

"And naturally you couldn't find anything closer to home."

Ben shrugged moodily.

"And Tim didn't fall to his knees and start wailing, so clearly he doesn't love you anymore."

"Basically."

Allison rolled her eyes. "Maybe your loving husband, who isn't exactly tied down to Austin by his work, just assumed that he'd be moving with you."

"He runs the gallery," Ben said. "And the Eric Conroy Foundation. That means too much to him to give up. People are counting on him to be here. I told him so."

"I bet you did. And how did he react?"

Ben glowered. "He said he waited years and years to be with me, and that if he had to do so again, he would."

"That bastard," Allison deadpanned. Then, after a dreamy sigh, she added, "Who would have thought that selfish Tim Wyman would grow up to be so damn romantic."

Ben seemed somewhat appeased by this. "It was pretty sweet. Still, he could have squeezed out a few tears for me."

"You're sadistic. I'm sure he's done enough crying over you, and for once, he's not the problem. You are."

"I am?"

"Yes! You obviously don't know what you want for your future, and you're taking it out on your husband. And *my* husband, which doesn't seem fair. You want my advice? Stay the course while you figure it all out, and stop letting your crisis affect the people who love you."

Ben thought this over. Then he sat up, pulled out his phone, and checked the time. "I could still make the last hour of rehearsal."

"You'll be preventing a heart attack if you do."

"Okay." Ben set his ice cream on the coffee table, kissed her on the cheek with cold lips, and stood. "Thanks. And I'm sorry. You're the best!"

"I know," Allison sighed. "Show yourself out, okay?"

"Yeah. I'll call you tomorrow. Bye!"

Allison listened to the front door slam, took a deep breath, and closed her eyes. They shot open a moment later.

"I can't sleep," Davis said from somewhere close to her elbow. "I heard thunder. Yay! Ice cream!"

Allison tried to muster up the energy to be a parent and failed. "Help yourself," she said. Then she unpaused the video and dug into her own ice cream, joining her son in a sugar high that she hoped would end with her slipping into a coma. At least then she would get some rest.

Son put to bed, living room picked up, and dishes placed in the machine. Allison was wiping down the counters when she heard the front door open. Brian swept into the room, buzzed and excited.

"Honey!" he declared, his voice theatrical. This also meant it was loud. "Darling!"

Allison tensed. "I finally got Davis to bed."

"Sorry," Brian said in a softer voice, but he was still grinning. "Rehearsal went well?"

"It went great!" Brian took the washrag from her hand and continued wiping the counters. "It started with disaster. Ben was running late and I couldn't get a hold of him. Someone offered to fill in, but it wasn't the same. When Ben finally did show up—well, I haven't seen him this enthusiastic for a long time. I don't want to jinx it, but this production might be our best one yet!"

"That's great," Allison said, trying to share his enthusiasm.

Brian wasn't fooled. "Uh oh. I've seen that face before! Did Davis run you ragged?"

Allison exhaled. "It's been a long day."

"Come along. I know exactly what you need." Brian tossed the rag in the sink and offered a hand. "To the bedroom!"

Allison didn't budge. "I love you, but I'm not in the mood right now."

"You don't know what I have in mind."

"I can guess."

"Come find out."

Allison accepted his hand and allowed herself to be led down the hallway to the back of the house. Brian had made the beds in the morning, thankfully. Allison loved her bedroom. Chocolate and burgundy were the primary colors, the heavy curtains keeping the room as dark as it was earthy. Brian switched on the low lighting and guided her toward the bed.

"Shouldn't we get undressed?" she asked.

"I'll take care of that. Get into bed." Brian fluffed some pillows, angling them to support her back. She wasn't sure what position he had in mind, or why he was so concerned about getting her socks off but—

Heaven!

Brian sat on the end of bed, gently massaging her feet, sending pleasure through her entire body. Allison let out a moan of appreciation. "This is what you had in mind?"

Her husband smiled bashfully. "My thoughts might have been less innocent at first, but ultimately I only wanted to make you happy. How am I doing?"

"I mentioned that I love you, right?"

Brian chuckled. "So tell me about your day. What went wrong?"

"Just a bunch of little things that added up. I don't really have problems of my own, but somehow, everyone else's problems become mine."

"I guess that's an occupational hazard. My little anxiety attack earlier probably didn't help. Sorry about that."

"That's also in the job description," Allison said. "Or part of our vows. I *want* you to tell me when you're upset. I hate the idea of you holding back. That wouldn't be healthy."

"No, but everyone deserves a break occasionally. Tell you what... tomorrow we'll have a picnic. I'll whip up a potato salad in the morning, you make your deviled eggs, then we'll load Davis into the car and—" Brian stopped kneading the balls of her feet, his face shocked: His wife was weeping.

Allison sniffed, also surprised by the tears. Then she started crying so hard her sobs shook her body. She couldn't help it. She felt overwhelmed by emotions she could barely comprehend. Allison called on her training, forcing herself to analyze why she was having a breakdown.

Brian moved higher up on the bed, putting an arm around her shoulders. "Are you okay? Was it something I said? What aren't you telling me?"

"I'm just tired." That summed it up nicely. "The idea of getting up in the morning, having to cook anything—"

"Forget the deviled eggs!" Brian said. "I can live without them!"

"It's not just that. We'd have to get Davis dressed and in the car, then keep an eye on him as he goes nuts in the park. You know he won't just sit on the blanket. You and I will barely have time to talk, because he'll be running around, making trouble, and I don't know what I'd talk about except what my patients are going through because I haven't got a life of my own!" Allison sniffed, then tasted guilt. "I love our son! I really do. I'm just… I'm a horrible mother for saying these things!"

"You're a wonderful mother," Brian said, "but you're also a human being." He took a deep breath and moved his arm away. "You need time to yourself. I get my share at the theater. When I'm in my office, I'm usually alone. At your office, you've always got someone there who needs your help. Then you come home and I suppose that doesn't really change. Anyone would find that stressful."

"I'm fine," Allison said dismissively. "I just needed to get it out of my system. I was looking at old photos of my parents tonight, which brought back a bunch of good and bad memories. Sometimes I wish I could go back in time, be a child again and be shielded from the world's problems by two giants who seemed so invincible."

"I'm sorry," Brian said. "I don't know that kind of loss. I can't even imagine how that must feel. You know my parents consider you their daughter, right?"

"Yes," Allison said. "And I'm grateful. Sorry I'm being so dramatic. I'm okay."

"You're not okay!" Brian said, his voice terse. "Stop saying that! You need to take care of yourself just as much as you take care of, well, *everyone*! If you miss your parents, why don't you take a trip back to your hometown? Get yourself a hotel room, enjoy some downtime, and maybe chase down a few memories."

Allison was about to shake her head, but then she thought of room service and a maid. She and Brian had a beautiful home, but suddenly a generic hotel sounded like paradise.

"Sounds good, doesn't it?" Brian said, reading her expression. "I'll take care of everything while you're gone. I can handle it. I'll even make the reservations."

"Nothing fancy," Allison said quickly. "No bed and breakfast where they feel the need to pamper me. Just a completely anonymous room with an ice machine down the hall."

"How many nights?" Brian asked. "Three? Seven? Fourteen? Are you ever coming back? No, I've changed my mind. You can't go."

But he was smiling. Allison found, much to her relief, that she was too.

The Woodlands, Texas. Allison rarely found reason to return there. Once her parents had died, her last ties with the area had been severed. At the time she had already relocated to Austin for college, and aside from distant relatives in Colorado, she was alone in the world. Except for Ben, who had switched schools just to be near her again. They had lived together for years afterwards, his presence saving her from going off the deep end. Ben had become her family, which is perhaps why she started there, with his childhood home. After checking into the hotel, Allison drove to a neighborhood that wasn't as polished as she remembered. The trees seemed wilder and the driveways more cracked, but most of the houses were still well maintained, despite their age.

The home of the Bentleys was next to the entrance of a subdivision, surrounded on three sides by roads. More than the usual number of trees had been left on its lot to compensate, shielding the house with green leaves and towering trunks. None of the other houses on the street were quite so hidden away, not unlike Ben's current choice of home, which wasn't the easiest to find either. Allison parked her car out front, tempted to ring the bell and surprise Mr. and Mrs. Bentley, but instead she walked down the street, following a familiar route to one of the many bike paths that linked each neighborhood. Her childhood home wasn't far away.

When Allison reached the house, she felt a slight sense of disappointment when it wasn't quite as she remembered. Had the front door been painted? Surely it used to be red, not blue. The shutters on the side of each window—purely decorative—had been removed. Unlike at the Bentley house, the front yard of her childhood home was a long stretch of green grass without trees. What struck her was the dwelling's sheer size, a row of six windows on the second floor reminding her of how many rooms the house had. She now realized that couples bought homes of that size when expecting more than one child. At the time her parents must have made optimistic plans that never came to pass. But why? Allison had been nine years old when her mother died; surely within those years her parents had plenty of time to make more children.

She thought then of the hospital visits, infrequent at the beginning and occurring more often toward the end. Nephritis. The word hadn't meant much to Allison when she was a child. She had researched it of course, but the illness was difficult for her to comprehend. Had it been cancer, a heart attack, or even a car wreck—these were causes of death that television had exposed her to. She would have been able to grasp these easier than a confusing disease that affects the kidneys. She had attempted to learn more after her mother died, doing the same research every year as she neared adulthood, wanting to better understand what had stolen Tonya away and wishing she had someone convenient to blame. A doctor who hadn't made the right diagnosis, or a greedy insurance company that refused to pay for a life-saving treatment. No such villains were to be found, no matter how hard she searched. She couldn't even blame her mother, who didn't smoke or drink too much, and who always preferred a salad to a burger. Tonya had been unlucky and nothing more, her body turning against her.

Nothing had prepared Allison to deal with this death. She didn't recall any gentle conversations about mortality. Her mother had simply gotten sick and never gotten better. Nor had she been prepared for the aftermath, because two people had died that day, even though one of them had gone on living. Allison moved toward the driveway, looking up its length at the detached two-car garage where her father had spent so much time tinkering. He had been an engineer by trade, which mostly took place in an office and involved computer work, but at home his curiosity was satisfied with his hands. Allison remembered him taking apart everything from hairdryers to kitchen appliances, and only rarely was he unable to put them together again. She remembered watching him, chatting nonstop while he worked, or sometimes sitting in the corner of the garage with her dolls.

The same garage that was currently open. A car was parked there and nobody was in sight. Allison walked up the driveway, wanting to get a closer look. She also remembered standing against the wall, her father measuring her height and whistling under his breath, as if he couldn't believe how tall she had grown. She still knew exactly where those marks used to be. Probably. Wanting to prove herself right, she ducked into the garage, feeling like a burglar as she frantically searched. The workbench was no longer there, storage shelves installed in their place. Did they cover the marks? Or were those farther down? She moved deeper into the garage, tripping over a board. In an effort to keep from falling, she reached out for the shelf, accidentally knocking off a cardboard box in the process.

Allison winced, both at her stubbed toe and at the noise. She crouched to pick up the box, intending to reshelve it and make a hasty retreat. Her hands were on each side of the cardboard container when she froze, a memory coming to her. She had just learned to drive and was parking the car in the garage. One of her favorite cassettes was playing on the stereo, the upbeat rhythm making her dance in her seat. She had been a little too caught up in the music because the front bumper grazed her father's work bench, the collision knocking a coffee mug off the edge. This particular coffee mug held random nails and screws, many of them tiny. Allison had the sense to stop before a tire got punctured, but her father had heard the noise. That was the first time he hit her. Not a spanking. Nothing like that. He had slapped her across the face with the palm of his hand, hard enough to make her see stars.

That he was angry at her wasn't a surprise. Since his wife had died, Charles Cross had withdrawn into himself, coming back out as a different person when drunk. She could understand though. Allison had been angry and hurt too, but she couldn't suppress it like he did, or try to kill the pain by drinking. So when her father yelled and acted irrational, she forgave him because she had lost a mother, and he had lost a wife. They had that in common, but never before had her father hurt her so intentionally. The worst part had been the absence of regret, of any sign that he was ashamed about what he had done. Instead he had stood there and held a box while Allison got down on her hands and knees to find every shard of mug and each nail and screw that it had once contained. She placed each in the box, trying to hold back the tears, trying to banish the hurt confusion. The next day, when he was sober again—that's when Charles expressed his regret. That's when he begged her forgiveness.

She should have hated him, but just like the times he was so inebriated she had to help him into bed or the dinners at the kitchen table where he refused to speak a word, Allison understood the cause. She hadn't done anything wrong. Neither had he. All of this was happening because Mom had died.

"What are you doing here?"

Allison spun around, expecting to see a tall foreboding silhouette. She did indeed find a shadow standing against the daylight, but it was much too short. Instead of an imposing physique, she saw narrow shoulders and a slightly paunched belly. The man's features were Asian, his expression more concerned than angry. Allison sought an acceptable excuse, but none were as water-tight as the truth.

"Sorry," she said. "I used to live here when I was a little girl. My curiosity got the better of me. As did my clumsiness."

The man smiled, as if what she had said made perfect sense. "When I went back to China last year with my wife, I found out my childhood home had been bulldozed. A big apartment building, brand new, has taken its place, but I still recognized the old tree that used to be outside my window. Now it stands beside a new home, a stranger looking out the window instead of me. The person living in the apartment let me inside, and even though nothing was the same, it still felt good to be home. Would you like to come inside?"

Allison laughed. "Anyone else would have called the police by now."

"No way," the man said, shaking his head. "What do I care if you want to steal my—" He peered at the box. "—old love letters from college. Those are priceless! Help! Police!"

He spoke this rather than shouted it, laughing soon after.

Allison put the box back on the shelf, hefting it before she did. "If these really are love letters, then your wife must be crazy about you."

"Those are the letters I wrote *her*. She can't love me too much or they wouldn't be out here in the garage. Why don't you come inside and meet my wife?"

Allison shook her head. Just being in the garage had been a seriously stressful experience. She didn't want to have another breakdown while two kind people were playing host. "No, thank you. Really. How long have you lived here?"

"Six months. My wife thought it was too big, but I want a family. Now guess what?"

"What?"

"She's having twins!"

"That's wonderful!" Allison said. "I have a little boy at home."

"Just one? You should have more. A big family is never lonely. You really grew up in this house? Were you born here?"

"Yes. I mean, I was born in a nearby hospital, but this is where I was raised."

The man perked up. "You must be Alli!"

Her jaw dropped. Only her parents ever called her that. "How did you know?"

"Over here." The man moved past her, shoving aside a stack of boxes near the shelves. In the gloom they couldn't see much, so he hit a light switch. A fluorescent tube flickered on above. That's when she saw the faint pencil marks, some smudged and dirty toward the bottom, but higher up...

¯¯¯
   Alli 3'7"

¯¯¯
Alli 4'8"

¯¯
Alli 5'2"

She saw more than a dozen such markings, the year accompanying some of them, all but one in her father's handwriting. Allison cupped a hand over her mouth, torn between wanting to laugh and cry. She chose the former. "This is what I was looking for!"

"I thought maybe you were a boy. Very tall."

"I'm not exactly short."

The man assessed her. "How tall are you now? No, wait."

Before she could protest, he moved deeper into the garage and returned with a measuring tape and pencil. "Okay, Alli. Let's get this updated. Better now than later. When you get to be my age, you'll find yourself shrinking."

Her face was burning as she pressed her back against the wall, and she felt mortified when the man had to stand on a stool to get high enough to make a mark just above her head. The results weren't so bad though.

"Five ten," the man said. "Very nice size. I hope my girls are that big. I don't want them to be short like me."

"They might feel differently," Allison said.

"You know what? I'll measure them right here. I'll tell them if they eat their vegetables, they can grow up tall like Alli."

Allison laughed. "I'd like that. And here." She dug in her purse for a business card and handed it to him. "Let me know if you're having a baby shower, or at the very least, send me a photo when the twins are born. I'd like to see who will be growing up in my old house." She would also make sure to send a present, but she'd let that be a surprise.

"I will. Come inside. You really should meet my wife."

"I have an appointment to keep," she lied, still feeling too emotional for such a thing, "but thank you."

The man walked her down the driveway, and she felt slightly ridiculous not having a car to get into, but like everything, he seemed to take this in stride. "Did you have a good childhood?" he asked before they parted. "Was it a happy home?"

Allison glanced once more at the house, choosing to remember when it was filled with sunlight, two people in love, their daughter, and a future full of potential. "Yes," she said. "It was heaven."

Patient Name: Unknown. Let's call him Cherry Soda.

Assessment: Cherry Soda seems eager to please. When not sucking on his straw and looking starry-eyed at the guy sharing his booth, he's telling jokes, making funny faces, and doing anything humanly possible to keep the conversation going. He might want to rethink his choice of companion though, because the guy sitting across from him—let's call him Mr. Paranoid— keeps whipping his head around every time the diner door opens. Cherry Soda doesn't seem to mind. He just uses these opportunities to stare.

Recommendation: Cherry Soda might want to work on developing a poker face, because anyone can see how enamored he is with his friend. Judging from Mr. Paranoid's behavior, this will soon complicate their young lives.

Allison tore her eyes away from the two teenagers and focused on her coffee. She had her own issues to deal with. Visiting her childhood home might have opened old wounds, but her profession qualified her to analyze and overcome them. She imagined a client telling her the same story: A young girl feels forced to take care of her father, then finds herself doing the same for all the men in her life. Ben, Brian, Davis...Hell, even most of her clients were male. She assumed some people preferred to confide in someone of the opposite sex, but what if there was more to it? Maybe she gave off some weird vibe that signaled to men that she was willing to do anything to ensure their happiness. Maybe her upbringing was to blame. But was that unhealthy? Helping people wasn't a bad thing. Was it? Normally she felt good about her work, but something must be wrong or she wouldn't have had a meltdown the other night.

"You worry too much!"

Allison's eyes darted back to the couple in the booth directly ahead of her. Cherry Soda's nose was crinkled, his eyes shining. Mr. Paranoid's shoulders slumped as he mumbled an apology. She was getting a serious Ben and Tim vibe from them, but after all these years surely this young couple had a better chance of making it work. The national opinion had finally shifted, the ignorant and hateful now in the minority. Then again, she knew how vocal the haters could be, no matter how outnumbered.

Allison took out her notepad and pen, resisting the urge to start a file on the young couple. Instead she considered her own life. She listed all the people she took care of and decided to see how mutually beneficial each relationship was. She dismissed her clients immediately. They gave her money and a sense of purpose. She gave them help. Perfect. Her relationship with her father hadn't been so healthy. No need to test the validity of that statement. She wrote down his name anyway—Charles—just in case a pattern developed. People often married partners similar to their parents, which brought her to Brian.

Allison had many female clients who complained about their

husbands and their lack of willingness to help around the house. Brian had the opposite problem. He was so willing to help that he had been taken advantage of in previous relationships. Allison had to watch herself to make sure *she* didn't take advantage of *him*. Occasionally he could be too self-centered when it came to his work, but a gentle reminder always set him straight. Was he at all like her father? Both men had a history of alcoholism, certainly, but Brian didn't have an angry bone in his body. When a critic had written a scathing review of his first play, Brian had stomped off down the hall to the bathroom. When Allison followed, she found him sitting on the toilet and sobbing. Brian didn't get angry. He got sad. That often forced her to be the disciplinarian of their child.

Davis. On paper he was as selfish as could be. He wanted immediate attention. It didn't matter if she was speaking with someone else. A barrage of "Mama, Mama, Mama," would soon end any adult conversation. Davis didn't care if she was tired or unwilling to play or had reasons for each and every rule. He wanted what he wanted and fought to get it. That was typical for a child of his age though. Allison would teach him to be more considerate, but even now, the satisfaction she got from being a mother was more fulfilling than she had ever imagined. There wasn't an adequate word to describe the feeling. Love was too simple a term.

Her immediate family relationships seemed healthy enough. What about her best friend? Did Ben ask too much without giving in return? He had forgotten to pay back a borrowed mortgage payment, but that was shortly after Jace died, and Allison hadn't needed the money. Chances were that he had forgotten in his grief. Ben often paid for their nights out together, so he wasn't a moocher. Just an old friend who sometimes bared his soul and was totally open to her doing the same.

"Shit!" hissed Mr. Paranoid, who slid down into his booth in an effort not to be seen.

Allison looked instinctively to the door where three teenage boys were entering the restaurant. They were nudging each other and laughing, one of them making a lewd face at the woman offering to seat them. Mr. Paranoid decided on a new strategy. Instead of trying to hide, he shot to his feet and put as much distance between his friend and the booth as possible.

Cherry Soda looked confused as he turned around to see what had happened. He didn't seem surprised though. His eyes met Allison's briefly when he turned to face forward again, and she recognized the despondent acceptance in them.

Mr. Paranoid greeted his friends, and as luck would have it, the restaurant hostess walked the party right by the booth he had so recently fled. One of the guys noticed the lonely figure sitting there.

"Hey, it's Dipshit Danny!" he said. The others laughed, including Mr. Paranoid. "Where's your boyfriend?"

"I don't have one," Danny shot back. "I just broke up with him."

The forced grin slid off Mr. Paranoid's face, the hurt transparent. He clearly had feelings for Danny, but was too frightened to make them a priority.

"I'm sure you'll find someone new," one of the other guys said. "Especially if you hang out in the bathroom long enough."

"I'll say hello to your dad while I'm in there," Danny muttered under his breath.

His comeback went unheard. The group of teens was ushered to the back of the restaurant, away from the other patrons. That left Danny holding on to his drink with both hands, although he was no longer sipping on the cheerful red straw. Instead he was staring at the plate of nachos that Mr. Paranoid had abandoned.

Allison resisted a sigh. No rest for the weary. She couldn't let him just sit there, especially when she was so familiar with this sort of situation. She'd seen Ben go through it more than once and had consoled him on each occasion. Time to share the benefit of her expertise.

She was about to stand when someone got there first. Her back was to Allison, a narrow figure and long brown hair obscuring her view as the woman slid into the booth. Allison shifted to the right so she could still see Danny who, past his initial surprise, didn't seem cheered up by this gesture. She strained to tune in on the conversation, hearing encouraging words and an offer of help. The woman even offered a business card, which had Allison itching to get out one of her own. After more murmured words, Danny nodded. Then he got up and left the restaurant.

Allison watched him through the window, saw him look back

at the restaurant with a defiant glare. He'd be okay. Eventually. She noticed that the woman remained seated, signaling to the waitress that she would like to pay. For the drinks and nachos, if Allison wasn't mistaken. That was a nice touch. Otherwise poor Danny would have had to pay for the guy who had just ditched him.

Once the transaction was completed, the woman stood, glancing at the back of the restaurant where the group of teenagers was still acting up. Allison got a decent look at her for the first time. That face! It was familiar. *Weirdly* familiar!

"Excuse me," she said as the woman began to walk away.

The woman looked over her shoulder, did a double take, and turned around. They stared at each other a moment, minds working to summon the right names because they knew each other. Oddly enough, the first name that came to Allison was Jace. That led her one step further, to his sister.

"Michelle," she said.

"Allison! My gosh!" Michelle took a few steps closer. "I haven't seen you since…"

"Ben and Tim's wedding."

"Wow. Why does that seem so long ago?"

"Time flies," Allison said.

They shared a chuckle. Then Michelle looked at the mostly empty table. "Are you by yourself?"

"Yup. Care to join me?"

"I'd love to." Michelle took a seat.

An awkward moment followed. Allison realized that all they had in common was knowing the same people, although perhaps that wasn't entirely true.

"Thanks for stepping in like you did. He seemed like a nice guy."

"Danny?" Michelle asked. "That was painful to watch."

"It was good of you to intervene."

Michelle shook her head, refusing to take credit. "Just a habit from work."

This triggered another memory. "You deal with foster kids, right?"

"I'm a caseworker for Child Protective Services, so it isn't just foster care, but that might be my favorite aspect. Successfully finding a new home for a child after they've gone through so much… It keeps me going."

"Still," Allison said, recognizing a kindred spirit, "a job like that must take its toll on you."

"Absolutely. You're a therapist, if I'm not mistaken. Don't you find it difficult at times?"

"That's what I'm trying to figure out," Allison admitted.

Michelle noticed the pad of paper on the table, cocking her head in an effort to read it. "What's this? A list of ex-boyfriends you plan to get revenge on?"

Allison smiled. "Nothing quite so exciting. Just trying to figure out if the men in my life are to blame for making me crazy."

Michelle's eyes lit up, as if she understood perfectly. "House full of men? Since my daughter moved out, it's just me and three boys. One of whom I'm married to, and I promise I'm using the right term when I say 'boy.' He uses his sons as an excuse not to grow up." Her words were condemning, but her tone was full of affection.

"Two sons? I can barely handle one."

"I never claimed I could handle mine," Michelle said. "So what's your conclusion?"

"The list?" Allison asked, glancing down at it. "They're fine. Healthy relationships all around, which doesn't help explain why I had—not a nervous breakdown, exactly. More like, for the first time in nearly forty years, I finally ran out of steam. And patience."

"Which is amazing, considering your line of work. Dealing with other people's problems all day can be draining, I know."

"How do you cope?"

"Occasional bouts of selfishness," Michelle said, leaning back. "Every once in a while, I do what's best for me and me alone. Like now. Greg wanted to take the kids to Missouri to see his parents, and while my own parents would love to see me, I know that I'm reaching my breaking point. So I stayed here."

"My son is still young. He's only three."

Michelle nodded her understanding. "That makes it harder. I've got teenagers now, but you still need to think of what's best for your son. You can't take care of him properly if you don't also take care of yourself. Try putting your own name on that list."

Allison glanced down. "What?"

"You have a relationship with yourself. Is it healthy? Are you getting anything in return for all that you give?"

She almost laughed at the idea, but when she considered it, she knew Michelle was right. That she was helping others wasn't the problem. That she wasn't helping herself was. "What's the solution?"

"Ask yourself that. What do you want most right now?"

"To be young again," Allison said instantly. "Just for one night. I want to make stupid mistakes, be irresponsible, and not think about anyone but myself."

Michelle grinned. "Sounds like a plan. Want company?"

"That depends," Allison said, smiling back. "I'm thinking of bar-hopping. I don't usually drink when I'm at home. It wouldn't be fair to my husband because—"

"Ah ah ah!" Michelle said. "There you go again. Thinking about others. I can see that you'll need me to keep you on the right track. Bar-hopping it is. Or how about a bender? On the beach! Let's drive to Galveston."

Allison paused. She barely knew the person sitting across from her, didn't know how she would get back to her hotel if they started drinking so far away, and worried that it was still too early in the day to even think about getting drunk.

"A bender on the beach?" Allison considered the alternative, which probably involved a hurried drink at a bar, then hours spent sitting in her hotel room, worrying about Brian and Davis. "That sounds... perfect!"

Allison sat in the passenger seat of a car whizzing down the Interstate, driven by a woman she barely knew, and yet their conversation came easy. First they shared memories of Jace. Then they talked about their children, before comparing notes on their husbands. In the middle of this, Michelle made a face.

"What?" Allison asked.

"This is exactly what I mean. We're supposed to have a girls' night out, and what are we doing?"

"Getting to know each other?"

"Mm-mm," Michelle replied with a shake of her head. "Have you ever heard of the Bechdel test?"

"No, but I'm going to pretend I have, just so you don't think less of me."

Michelle laughed. "The Bechdel test shows just how skewed modern movies are toward men. Most leading roles are male.

Think of a spy movie and you'll probably picture a guy in a tuxedo. Or how about superheroes?"

"Wonder Woman," Allison interjected.

"Yeah, but where's her movie trilogy? And even if she gets one, think how many more Superman and Batman movies there are in comparison. A lot of this depends on the genre. Most of the good movies, like dramas, will have more female leads than action flicks do. The real problem, no matter what the plot, is that women represent half the population, but rarely represent half the cast. Think about it."

Allison did. Many of the movies she enjoyed were balanced, but others only had a token female who was usually the main character's love interest. Still, she couldn't say it ever bothered her before. "You want my honest opinion? The kind of movies that are full of guys would be just as dumb if women played half the roles."

"True," Michelle said, "and you won't catch me complaining about seeing Daniel Craig squeezed into a tuxedo. But it would still be nice if there was a greater balance. Strong female characters exist, but rarely are they as developed as their male counterparts."

"Where are you going with this?"

"The Bechdel test tries to determine just how balanced a movie is. Three simple rules: The movie has to have at least two women in it. They have to actually talk to each other. What they discuss has to be about something other than a man."

"Is that so rare?"

"You'd be surprised."

She considered a few movies before moving on to something much closer to home. "I'm not sure my own life would pass the Bechdel test."

"Exactly!" Michelle gripped the steering wheel tighter. "I totally feel that way sometimes. Between my career and my family, I let my social life suffer. When I *do* actually hang out with someone else, I might as well still be at home because all I talk about are my husband and kids."

"That's not a bad thing."

"No, of course not. We love them. I'm sure they talk about us just as often. Well, maybe the kids don't, but you know. My point is that the Bechdel test might be the perfect thing to keep us in line. For the rest of the night, we'll follow it. We'll set the men aside and focus on us."

Allison nodded slowly. "Okay. Let's try it."

Silence followed this statement. Then they both laughed.

"No pressure," Michelle said. "Just talk normally and if one of us strays, the other will point it out."

"Okay. Hey, Galveston city limits! Do you know where we're going?"

"To the beach!"

Except that wasn't their first stop. They parked at a convenience store and went inside for what Michelle called snacks. They came out with three bottles of wine.

"Think that'll be enough?" Allison asked on the way back to the car.

Michelle paused. "I can run in for more."

"It was a joke! What about a corkscrew?"

"There's a Swiss army knife in the glove box. A present from… uh… Well, it was a gift."

"Almost slipped there!" Allison said, wagging a finger.

They drove along the coast, searching for parking. They ended up on the north end of the island, the city behind them. They couldn't see much except sand, struggling plants, and the Gulf of Mexico. They reached the end of the road, hesitating at a stop sign.

"I'm pretty sure the east beach is to the right," Allison said.

"Yeah, but we're going to be drinking in public. That's illegal, and besides, I really don't want to watch a bunch of tourists building sandcastles for their children. It'll totally kill the 'girls gone wild' vibe I'm aiming for."

"There's a place to park straight ahead."

Michelle peered at it. Then she hit the turn signal and went left, which was alarming because Allison couldn't see a road there at all. Just a glorified dirt path.

"I don't think—"

"I saw tire tracks," Michelle said. "What's that ahead? Maybe someone lives out here."

The land was cleared and fenced, but the large square building was devoid of any personal touch, suggesting it was an electrical station or some other utilitarian structure. Regardless, Michelle pulled the car next to the gated fence and parked.

"If anyone notices," she explained, "they'll think we're inside reading meters or whatever."

"Sounds like a plan. I wish the beach was closer. I can't even see it."

"Which means we'll have privacy. No one else is dumb enough to park way out here."

They grabbed the wine from the back seat, hid their phones and purses from sight, and locked the car before starting to hike. Despite Allison's concerns, they only had to cross a field and walk a path between a brief burst of trees to arrive at sand, waves, and best of all, seclusion.

"Too bad we don't have a blanket," Michelle said.

"No need," Allison said, getting into the spirit. She plopped down on the beach with a smile. "Nature provides all the comfort we need."

"An indoor toilet would be nice," Michelle murmured. "Why didn't I go at the store?"

"Girls gone wild," Allison said. "The bushes over there look cozy."

"That's brush," Michelle said, "and it's about ankle-high."

"I won't peek."

"Be right back," Michelle said before hurrying off toward the trees they had walked past.

Allison used the time alone to survey the horizon. Galveston was by no means a tropical paradise. Shipping containers drifted in the distance; a number of buoys floating in the water to keep them from coming too close. An artificial wall of rocks separated a narrow strip of the gulf from the shore. She ignored this breakwater, staring past it at the distant point where sky met sea.

When Michelle returned, she sat down next to Allison and did the same, soaking it all up in silence. Then she pulled out two bottles of wine and worked on getting the corks loose.

"We can't clink glasses," she said, tongue sticking out in effort, "but if we each have our own... there!"

Allison accepted one of the bottles, its surface cool and wet with condensation. "What are we drinking to?"

"To us!" Michelle said with a grin.

They knocked the necks of the bottles together. Allison took a sip. White wine. A pinot blanc, if she wasn't mistaken. She was no expert and usually preferred a wine with more kick, but the fruity flavor was perfect for such a warm afternoon.

"You're doing it wrong," Michelle said. "See the very top of the label? That's the starting line. You don't begin with just a sip. You drink down to that point."

Allison raised her eyebrows. "Is that what connoisseurs do?"

"No, they swish and spit or something stupid like that. People who want to have fun respect the starting line. Afterwards, the goal is to reach the finish line." She tapped the bottom of the label on her own bottle.

"What about the wine below that?"

"Oh, you drink that too. When runners reach the finish line, it's not like they stop dead. They always jog a little farther, right?"

Allison laughed. "Are you always like this?"

Michelle refused to answer until Allison drank to the starting line. "No, this isn't really my style. I'm usually Little Miss Responsible, always trying to get people on the right track. I was never very fond of rules when growing up though, which is handy because a lot of the kids I work with aren't either. When they test the limits, I don't automatically discipline them. Despite being twice—sometimes triple—their age, I like to think I still understand where they're coming from."

"I love the work you do," Allison said. "I've seen firsthand how it can transform a life. When you asked Ben and Tim to—"

"Bechdel!" Michelle declared. "Take another swig. That's your penalty."

Allison smiled and accepted her punishment. "I'll just say that you improved three lives at once. Very impressive."

"Well, thanks. I wish they could all be success stories, but when they do work out, it sure feels good."

"I bet," Allison said. "What made you want to be a social worker in the first place?"

"Geez, that's a tough one." Michelle brought the bottle to her lips as if it would help her answer, but she remained deep in thought.

Allison could relate to her confusion. "I've been asking myself the same question lately, and it seems like it has everything to do with how I was raised. I was in a position where I was forced to help one of my parents, and I'm wondering if it just became a habit."

Michelle snorted. "My parents raised me not to swear and

not to drink, but this wine is fucking delicious." She laughed at her own joke. "Seriously, think about all the ideals our parents tried to instill in us and ask yourself how many of them stuck."

"True. I got in my fair share of trouble. But some of those ideals stay with us, don't they?"

Michelle grunted. "They do. My parents were always helping people, when they could. They didn't volunteer at soup kitchens or anything like that, but when they met someone who needed help, they never hesitated. It's funny though, because I can remember a time in college when my philosophy shifted. I thought helping people was fine up to a certain point. Past that, I felt they need to pull themselves out of the muck."

Allison nodded. "Some people will only learn to help themselves when everyone else stops enabling them to be so helpless."

"Right, but it doesn't always play out like that. Remember learning to ride a bike? Our parents had to let go so we could learn to balance on our own, but some people—" Michelle took a swig of wine. "Some people crash and never get up again."

"Who are we talking about here?"

"Bechdel," Michelle said, her smile forced. "I'm happy to hide behind that excuse because talking about it and drinking isn't the best combination. It was a turning point in my life. When I realized how some people self-destruct, I decided I'd rather err on the side of caution. I'd rather do everything in my power to help than let anyone struggle on their own. So that's why. I joined Child Protective Services because I thought it would allow me to change the world."

"From what I've heard, it has. For the better."

Michelle shot her a grateful expression and raised her drink. Then they clinked bottles again, continuing their race to the finish line.

"My daughter is *the best*," Michelle said, gesturing grandly. "Emma is like... She's smart, she's strong, she knows exactly what she wants and she's clever enough to get it. I don't worry about her anymore. Maybe at first, but I swear she's got the whole world figured out. Future president. You wait and see! You want a best friend for life? Have a daughter. Nothing better."

Allison grinned. She'd been grinning for the last ten minutes.

In front of them, sticking out of the sand, were two empty bottles. The sun had gone down, the third bottle had been opened, and they were passing it back and forth while chatting about whatever came to mind.

"I'd love a little girl," she responded, "but it's a gamble right? You never know what you're going to get, so I was thinking… a dog maybe? A female one."

"Bitch!" Michelle shouted before cackling madly. "No, you're right. You might keep trying and end up with tons of little Brians instead."

"Bechdel!" Allison declared.

"Oh god!" Michelle took another drink. "You want a girl? Adopt. I will hook you up! Let's head to my office, look through some files."

"You go get them, I'll wait here." She dragged the back of her arm across her forehead. "Damn it's humid tonight!"

"You know what would be good? Ice cream! Or some popsicles. Or even just a bag of ice."

Allison eyed the water ahead of them longingly. Then, feeling inspired, she got to her feet. Michelle wasn't the only one who could suggest crazy ideas. "Girls gone wild," she said, walking across the sand. When she reached the water's edge she pulled off her shirt.

Michelle was soon at her side, already tugging at her own clothing. "You. Are. Brilliant!"

A few minutes later they were completely naked, their clothes in two separate bundles on the sand. They took each other's hands, ran forward, and screamed with delight as they splashed into the cool water. They were up to their waists when they reached the stone breakwater wall. They clambered onto it, Michelle stretching out briefly like she was modeling for a nude drawing class.

"I'm a mermaid," she declared. "The news tomorrow will have sailors reporting what they saw. Maybe a few crashed ships as well."

"You're thinking of sirens," Allison said, dipping a toe into the water beyond. "This looks deep enough that we could really swim."

Michelle hissed in pain. "Ouch! I don't know how mermaids do it. These rocks are killing my butt!"

"Are you a good swimmer?" Allison asked, her attention still on the water.

"Sure. You?"

"I guess so." Part of her was aware of the danger, that anything could lurk beneath the dark surface, but she glanced out at one of the buoys, now an eerie light. "That's our goal," she said, pointing to it.

"Oh buoy!" Michelle said. Then she hastily apologized.

"Ready?" Allison asked. Instead of waiting for an answer, she climbed down off the rocks, the stones beneath her feet slick with algae, waves crashing against them. She tried not to think of rusty metal edges or washed-up syringes as she worked her way into the water and felt more at ease when she was deep enough to wade.

"Wave pool!" Michelle said from not far behind her.

The surf was minimal at the moment, but the ocean swell was enough to lift them up and down in a gentle bobbing motion that only added to Allison's feeling of intoxication. "I hope you don't get seasick!"

"I'm all right," Michelle said, long hair plastered to the back of her head. "Which buoy are we heading for?"

"That one," Allison said, nodding in the right direction. She had imagined them cutting through the water with powerful strokes, but the reality was a lot less impressive. They slowly doggy paddled or attempted a halfhearted breaststroke in an effort to reach their goal, but their progress was slow. They kept stopping to laugh together or to shriek when they felt things brush against them in the water. Once they spooked each other by accidentally touching, the resulting laughter slowing them down even more.

When they reached the buoy, Allison was exhausted. She had thought they could climb up on it and take a break, but the red and white platform—which resembled a life preserver—was much larger up close and slimy with some sort of plant growth.

"You climb up first," Allison said, unwilling to touch it.

The face Michelle made said she felt the same. "Maybe we should head back. I remember reading about a tourist who got caught in the undertow and died."

Allison's mouth dropped open, aghast. "When was this?"

"I don't know," Michelle said. She glanced down at the water, as if expecting to see a water-logged body there. "Uhhhh. I'm freaking out a little."

"It's your own fault," Allison said, swimming closer and taking her hand. Her mind raced, trying to remember what she knew about tides and currents. "The undertow is beneath us, right? It's lower down."

"Down under," Michelle said in an Australian accent. "I guess so."

"Okay, so we float on the surface. That should keep us safe."

"Float? On our backs? Everyone will be able to see our buoys."

"You were just playing mermaid a second ago. Besides, there's no one here. Come on." Allison led by example, relaxing and letting her body float to the surface. She kept hold of Michelle's hand and began kicking gently. This did leave her feeling exposed and a little chilly on certain parts, but she felt safer. They had to keep craning their heads to make sure they were headed in the right direction, which made the swim back even more time-consuming than the first had been, but they were nearing the shore.

"Where's the wall?" Michelle asked.

"Oh. Um…" Allison allowed her body to go vertical. She could see the beach, but no wall. "Maybe we've drifted farther down the shore. I remember that happening when I was a girl. I don't know how far the breakwater runs…"

"Or maybe the tide has come in," Michelle suggested.

They were both right. Eventually they felt rocks brushing their backsides and stopped to find themselves on the now-submerged wall. From there they felt safe enough to wade normally back to the beach, but their possessions were nowhere in sight.

"This way?" Michelle guessed, trying to cover herself. "Shit! What if someone is out here walking their dog or whatever?"

They ran, streaking down the beach and searching for signs of where they had been. Michelle was the first to skid to a stop. "My bra! I never thought I'd be so glad to see it."

Allison halted next to her, trying not to laugh since catching her breath was already difficult. Her grin faded. "Where are my things?"

"Oh. Oh! Oooooh."

She didn't like the sound of that. Michelle had put her

shoes on top of her clothing so everything she had worn was still anchored on the sand, but the water was already lapping dangerously close. If Allison had placed hers even the slightest bit closer to the water... She looked at the Gulf and thought she saw a pair of panties cresting on a wave before being lost to sight. "You've got to be kidding me!"

Michelle tittered before getting herself under control. "Sorry. Um... Maybe you could borrow something from me?" She held up a bra that Allison only wished she could fill.

"Maybe if we go back out there, we could find my stuff."

"We barely made it back alive!" Michelle said. Then she pointed. "Hey look! There's one of your sandals."

The footwear was half-buried in sand, but it was better than nothing. Allison raced to get it, finding the other not far away. Everything else had been claimed by the sea.

"I think I've got it," Michelle said, pulling on her underwear. "I'll wear this and my bra, you take my shorts and blouse."

"Are you sure?" Allison asked.

"Yeah! It's not so different from a bikini. We only need to make it back to the car. From there we'll go straight to your hotel room. You can get dressed and give me my clothes back."

"Thank you!" she said, hurrying to pick up the shorts. Now that they were out of the water and the sun had gone down, she was feeling chilly. Michelle must have felt cold too, because once they were both dressed—or half-dressed—she grabbed the last remaining bottle and took a swig. Then she offered it to Allison, who eagerly did the same.

"Crap." she said.

Michelle blinked. "What?"

"We can't drive."

Michelle snorted. "Oh, right. On the way down, I already thought of that. I figured we'd call a taxi and get a room down here, but uh, maybe we could sleep in the car."

"Let's just get back there," Allison said. "Then we can decide."

"Agreed."

They began the walk back, feeling somewhat defeated. More wine helped lift their spirits. Abstaining now wouldn't make them sober enough to drive. Not in the short time it would take to reach the car, which must have been farther away than Allison remembered because when they broke through the trees and reached the dirt road, the vehicle was nowhere in sight.

"No!" Michelle said, racing forward. "Someone stole the car!"

Allison hurried to keep up. They reached the fenced area, lights illuminating the silent building within. The car was definitely gone.

"What sort of car thief would come all the way out here?"

"Maybe it was towed," Allison said, pointing to a sign that threatened exactly that.

Michelle amended her statement. "Okay, what sort of meter maid would come all the way out here?"

"Meter maid," Allison repeated, laughing at the archaic term. Then she squinted, reading faded words on the building. "The Galveston Beach Patrol. Maybe they keep equipment in there or something."

Michelle marched to the gate, grabbed the chain link material, and started shaking it. "Hello! Beach patrol! I want my fucking car back! HEY!"

They waited for a response but were rewarded only with silence.

Michelle swore.

"Sorry," Allison replied. "We're lucky they didn't find us."

"Not much of a silver lining," Michelle said, looking dejected. "What are we going to do? Our phones were in there. Our purses!"

"How much wine have we got left?"

Michelle held up the bottle. They were near the finish line. "Well, we're already in this deep."

They took turns swigging until it was gone. Then Michelle tossed the empty bottle over the gate, where it shattered loudly. A ridiculous moment followed where they hoped this would attract attention, and thus help, but no. They were all alone.

"Let's walk back to the main road," Allison suggested. "We can flag down a police officer and have him take us to your car."

"They're totally going to arrest us. We're drunk, I'm nearly nude, and that blouse looks terrible on you. Never wear peach again. You hear me?"

"Loud and clear," Allison said. "Come on."

They trudged down the road, feeling apprehension as they neared the street lights. Michelle had a nice body and was literally in her underwear. Allison prayed that the first car they saw wasn't full of ornery frat boys. The main road was silent when they reached it, the parking area to the left empty except for a semi-truck with its engine shut off, but she could hear the generator rumbling. That meant it was producing electricity for someone inside.

"Hey," Allison whispered, nudging Michelle and pointing at the truck. "Maybe they'll give us a ride."

"We don't know who's in there!"

"No, but it's better than the police. At the very least they can call someone to help us."

Michelle peered at the truck suspiciously. Then she shivered and nodded.

They approached the cab cautiously. All the windows were covered, the curtains pulled shut, light bleeding through around the edges. From the ground, the door was so high they were forced to crane their necks upward.

"What do you think's going on in there?" Michelle whispered.

"Only one way to find out."

Allison knocked. One of the curtains was swept aside, a silhouette lit from behind. A man, that was for sure. The door swung open. A big man! His shoulders were rounded, the muscles of his arms tight. Rugged or rough, Allison couldn't decide which word fit him better. His blond hair was buzzed, his brow furrowed, and his eyes burned with an intensity that made them appear crazy. Even in the limited light she could see the nasty scar cutting a diagonal line across his neck to his jaw.

"Bechdel!" Michelle said, pulling on Allison's arm. "This totally goes against the rules. Let's get out of here!"

Allison felt like retreating too, but she caught the flicker of hurt on the man's features. The words he spoke were hardly threatening either. "What happened? Are you okay?"

"We, uh…" Allison sighed. Where to begin? "Our car got towed," she said, deciding to keep it simple.

The man looked them both up and down, eyes remaining on Michelle. "You shouldn't be running around half-naked. It isn't safe."

Was that genuine concern or a veiled sexual threat? "Maybe you could call the police for us," she tried.

"Yeah, okay. No problem. Your friend looks cold. Wanna come inside?"

"No!" Michelle said.

Again the flicker of hurt. "Okay. Just a second."

The man retreated into his cab. They heard him rustling around. Then the door opened wider and he hopped out. He had a phone in one hand, a blanket draped over his arm. "Here," he said, offering it.

Allison took it gratefully, wrapping Michelle in it before turning her attention back to the man.

"Calling nine one one seems a little weird," he said. "This isn't an emergency. Is it?"

"No. Just the normal police number or the tow truck place."

"Tow truck place?"

"Lock up?" Allison said, her thoughts anything but clear. "Jail for cars. You know what I mean?"

"The impound lot?"

"Yeah."

The man studied her. "Are you drunk?"

"I'm not!" Michelle declared.

Allison put on a sheepish expression instead of admitting the truth.

The man shrugged. "Who am I to judge? Sometimes the tow truck companies leave a sign, like a piece of paper with a number on it to call. See anything like that?"

"No."

"Then maybe your car was stolen."

"Better call nine one one!" Michelle said.

The man looked down at his phone and thought for a moment before addressing Allison again. "I could call the cops, but you're drunk, and I'm not sure how well that will go down. I can give you a ride home instead and you can sleep it off, deal with all this in the morning."

Allison sighed. If only it were that easy! "We're not from around here. My hotel room is on the other side of Houston, and our money and credit cards are wherever the car has been taken."

"Oh." The man rubbed his palm across the bristles of his hair. Then he exhaled. "There's a hotel just down the road. Why don't I give you a lift there and—"

"We don't have—" Allison tried to interject.

"—and I'll pay for it," the man said. "That way we don't have to get the police involved."

"Had trouble with them before?" Michelle asked, eyes narrowed like she was close to cracking the case.

"Yeah, but I didn't do anything that I'm ashamed of. Anyway, up to you."

Allison glanced at Michelle, who suddenly seemed a lot less interested. She yawned and shrugged her agreement. They were both too tired and tipsy to deal with the authorities. Or paperwork. A hotel room would be much better than a jail cell.

"Up to you," the man repeated.

They accepted and climbed into the cab. When Michelle saw the bed behind the seats, she abandoned caution completely and climbed into it. That seemed excessively dangerous. Then Allison noticed the photo taped to the dashboard. A younger guy with curly brown hair and sun on his face. He didn't look related to the driver. Probably not a brother, and as much as she loved Ben, she had never been tempted to tape his photo to the dashboard.

"Seatbelts," the man said. He looked over his shoulder to where Michelle had passed out on the mattress. "Eh. I'll drive safe."

The engine came to life with an impressive rumble. The man focused on backing out and getting the truck turned toward the road. If he had ill intent, he seemed blasé about the situation. She was pretty sure they were safe.

"I'm Allison," she offered.

"Connor," the man replied. "Is this part of a bachelorette party or something?"

"No, we're just blowing off steam. We're both married. What about you?"

The man grinned, eyes darting to the photo. "Not yet."

"What's his name?"

"Oh! Busted!" He laughed without shame. "David. He's... he's awesome."

Allison grinned. "I bet he is. Sorry about all of this. Normally I'm a lot more respectable." Now it was her turn to laugh. "That sounds ridiculous. I just mean I don't usually get drunk in public and lose my clothes. What I'm wearing belongs to her. Otherwise I'd be naked."

"She must be a good friend," Connor said.

"She is," Allison said, surprised by the implication. She hadn't had time to consider it all, but she had made a new friend. "If the roles were reversed, I'm not sure I'd have been willing to run around in my bra and panties for her."

"Wait, you guys were skinny-dipping?"

Allison sighed. "This is so humiliating."

Connor chuckled. "I think it's funny. And hey, I've done worse things out in nature. I was just smart enough not to get caught."

"Yeah yeah, rub it in," Allison said, shaking her head ruefully.

The semi-truck slowed, then pulled over to the side of the road. An illuminated sign for a hotel was just outside the passenger window. "Wait here," Connor said, turning on the hazard lights before hopping out. He left the truck running, the keys in the ignition. Talk about trust! Allison repaid this by not stealing his truck and driving off into the night. She waited, and before long, Connor returned to the driver's seat and offered her a key.

"Room one oh four," he said.

"Is this on your credit card?" Allison asked.

"Yeah."

"Wow. Knight in shining armor. I'll pay you back for everything, I swear. Do you have a business card?"

He laughed. "I'm not that grown-up."

"Pen and paper? Write down your contact info. I mean it. You shouldn't have to pay for our dumb mistake. Please."

Connor relented. He produced a pen and a scrap of paper and wrote down the information.

"Give me his email address too," Allison said, pointing to the photo on the dashboard.

"Huh? Why?"

"Because I want to tell David what an amazing boyfriend he has. Once I have, he'll be begging you to marry him."

Connor grinned. Once he had complied, Allison folded the paper and pocketed it. Then she reached back to rouse Michelle.

The lump on the mattress barely moved, but it did speak. "Are we home yet?"

"Need help getting her to the room?" Connor asked.

"I'll manage," Allison said. "I'm not letting you get your truck towed. The night's disasters stop here."

"I'd like to see them try to tow this baby," Connor said with pride, "but if you really think you'll be okay…"

"We will, thanks to you. Best of luck with you and your man!"

Connor nodded. "Thanks."

He was nice enough to let them keep the blanket, so Michelle wouldn't have to stumble through the lobby in her underwear. Allison would mail it back to him too, with money and exotic fruits and maybe a few bags filled with diamonds. The man could have everything she owned because right now nothing sounded more valuable than a nice cozy bed. Once she had unlocked and opened the room door, she didn't bother with the lights. She made sure Michelle made it to the bed before tumbling in herself. Oh yes, she would pay Connor back, and judging from how the room was spinning, she would also have absolute hell to pay in the morning.

Hot, sweaty, itchy, aching. These four words could be assigned to pretty much every part of Allison's body, in different combinations. She rose, head throbbing, and dragged herself to the bathroom. She used the toilet, drank from the sink, then paused to look in the mirror, seeing someone who looked like she needed help.

Patient Name: Allison Cross

Assessment: Allison has her life together. Usually. She's reliable, has a steady head, and has never been short on perspective. Perhaps that is why so many people turn to her for help. She even made a career of it. And yet, maybe she's been relying a little too much on the tools of her trade, treating the problems of the world like individual cases that she can analyze and solve. Few things in life can be so easily compartmentalized.

Recommendation: Allison needs to stop worrying so much. Not everyone needs to be fixed, including herself. She could also use some coffee. The sooner the better.

Allison left the bathroom and started fumbling with the coffee maker. Once it had started brewing, she put the air conditioner on a lower setting and returned to bed. This woke Michelle, who rolled over onto her back and groaned.

"I'm dying!" she rasped.

"You're not dying."

"I wish I was."

Allison sighed. "Yeah, me too."

They listened to the drip drip drip of coffee being born.

"I don't get like this often," Michelle said. "It's really rare, I swear, but when I do, Greg always gets up early. Even if he drank just as much as I did, he gets up and goes out for donuts. He knows they're the only thing that make me feel better."

"Good man," Allison said with a yawn.

Michelle thwacked her with a hand. "Wanna be my man? Go get me some donuts."

"Not a chance. Besides, we don't have any money. Remember?"

"Go steal some."

"Money?"

"Donuts."

Allison shoved her playfully. "You're a bad influence! I never should have listened to you. What a night!"

"You loved it."

Allison considered it all. "I did. But now I'm really looking forward to my completely normal and boring life again."

"Mission successful," Michelle said. "On Monday, when we're juggling family and careers, we'll do so with grins plastered on our faces. And when it gets to be too much again?"

Allison laughed. "I'll call you."

"Awesome." Michelle rose and went to the coffee machine, which had grown silent. She poured two cups.

Allison sat up so she could accept one. "I wish I could chug it."

"Me too." Michelle sat on the edge of the bed. "It's good. Who you are, I mean. All that stuff we talked about last night about why we both feel driven to help people—none of that really matters. You think super models look in the mirror and agonize over being so hot? Wanting to help people is a good thing, even if it's a royal pain in the ass sometimes. That guy last night? Who knows why he felt compelled to help us. All that matters is he did. We'd probably be in worse shape if he hadn't. Who knows what would have happened!"

"No kidding."

Michelle blew on the surface of her coffee, then took a tentative sip. "My mom once said, out of the blue, that she's proud of me. I asked her why and she said 'Because I can be.' Enigmatic, right? But I sort of get it now. The reasons don't matter as much as the results."

Allison considered this and smiled. "I like that."

"Thanks. Now for the bad news. I'm going to need my clothes back when I go get my car from wherever it is, and I really don't see myself driving you back to your hotel in my bra and panties. So basically I hope the maids don't barge their way in, because you're going to be naked and trapped in this room for a while."

Allison looked over at her. "Never speak a word of this to anyone."

"No need to tell me! If anyone ever finds out, we'll join a convent or something. Deal?"

"Sister Allison?" she asked.

"Sister Michelle," came the somber response. "Nuns gone wild!"

"Look who's home!"

Allison stood in the entryway to the living room and surveyed the scene. Brian was poised on the couch. His posture was upright, he was wearing one of his nicer shirts, and his hair had been freshly cut. Davis, seated next to him, was a miniature version of his father. He was squirming with excitement, demonstrating rare restraint. That meant Brian had bribed him because her husband wasn't the best disciplinarian. He was a good man though, Allison having already seen that the house interior was pristine, freshly cleaned. None of this was necessary. Messy, exhausting, and taxing—she loved them just the way they were.

"You guys are adorable. Come here."

Davis launched off the couch; Allison crouched to hug him. When she stood again, Brian was close, cheeks rosy as he smiled at her. "How was it?"

"Quiet," Allison said, referring to the drive home. Not the most honest way of describing her weekend, but she had a vow of silence to keep.

"I see you did some shopping. Is that a new outfit?"

"Yes," Allison said. Michelle had bought it for her before returning to the hotel room, proudly brandishing their purses and phones, having rescued them and the car from the clutches of a cruel towing company. Or in less dramatic terms, she had paid the fines. Allison promised to chip in for half of that, as well as reimbursing the full amount for the clothes. The new outfit had spared her a car ride to The Woodlands wearing nothing but a blanket. Michelle had good taste, but when added to what she still owed Connor, Allison was discovering how expensive traveling could be.

"Did you get me something?" Davis asked.

"Of course, but you have to find it."

She relinquished control of the luggage to him and stepped forward to kiss her husband. "Thank you," she said. "Time off was exactly what I needed."

"I'm so relieved," Brian said, getting emotional. He'd be in tears if she wasn't careful.

"You should try it sometime," Allison said. "Maybe take a trip to your hometown, get drunk, go skinny-dipping. The usual."

"You're funny," Brian said, kissing her again. "Did you get me something?"

"Later," she promised. "The house looks nice."

"All for you. I wasn't sure if you wanted me to put the VCR away, so I left it out. I'm surprised we still have one. Why did you hook it up?"

"I'll show you," Allison said. She switched tapes before turning it on, not quite ready to see her and Ben rapping again. Soon they were sitting on the couch together, Davis tearing into his new toy. The television screen revealed a little girl, twirling in her brand-new dress. She was sure Brian had seen these videos years ago, but he seemed fascinated anyway.

"You look so proud," he said. "Your mother must have been too."

"She was," Allison murmured. "And my father." *You're my pride, Alli. You're my joy.* As a child, Allison had taken those words to heart, like her father's happiness relied on her. She supposed that, as she got older, it really did. Once her mother was gone, Allison had been the only one there to pull him back from the brink. When she was frustrated with her father and on the verge of giving up, she would think back to her mother and try to keep a promise that had never been made.

Maybe that was the beginning of it all. Michelle was right. The results mattered more than the reason, but now Allison felt less like a foolish girl who had made bad decisions. She had remained strong, for both her parents really, and that was something she didn't regret.

She reached over and took Brian's hand. "It's good to be home again."

Her husband squeezed in response. "I feel the same way. Without you here, it didn't feel right."

Allison leaned against him. "Still up for that picnic?"

"Picnic!" Davis said, dive-bombing onto their laps. "Right now? Mom! Can we go now?"

"We talked about this," Brian said, doing his best to sound stern. "Give your mother a break."

"But I wanna go on a picnic!" Davis whined.

"Don't make me send you to your room!" Brian scolded.

Allison pinched the bridge of her nose, but a familiar voice caught her attention. "You're my best friend," her mother said, a little girl beaming at her in response.

Allison studied the screen a moment. Then she grabbed Davis and started tickling him. He squealed until he couldn't take anymore and ran from the room. Brian didn't hide his puzzlement.

"I was trying to be strict."

"You're perfect the way you are," she said, moving in for a kiss. "You're exactly the sort of man I want raising our child."

When she pulled away again, Brian's confused expression was replaced by one more amorous. "You know," he said. "Technically your weekend break isn't over. There's still tonight. We could hire a babysitter and see what the evening brings."

Allison smiled in response. "Or we could have that picnic, let Davis exhaust himself, and once we're back here and he's in bed..."

"Yes?" Brian said eagerly, leaning forward. "What then?"

"I'll let you rub my feet again."

"Oh."

"And then we'll trade places."

"I don't really like having my feet rubbed," Brian said, starting to look pouty.

"Then I'll find something else of yours to rub."

Brian hopped to his feet. "Davis? Get in the car, son! We're having a picnic!"

"Yaaaaaaay!" Davis said, returning to run a lap around the living room.

Allison laughed, then looked back to the screen and saw her

father gazing at her in pride. No adult is perfect, and no first-time parent is prepared to raise a child, no matter how much they think they are. Her mother and father had given her life and given her love. They had taught her right and wrong, often when not meaning to. She would take the best from each experience, no matter how dark, and use it to give her own child the best life possible. And she would never take this little family of hers for granted. A hyperactive son and a man who was stronger than he realized because only the weak strike a child unnecessarily. She would always love them both with all of her heart. They were her pride. They were her joy.

———————

Note

The following story takes place after the events of *Hell's Pawn*. What do you mean, you've never read that book? I know, I know... the premise is kind of bizarre. Sort of like that weird guy at the diner, the one who's always sitting in the corner booth alone, drinking a never-ending cup of coffee and muttering to himself under his breath. He's strange, and our first instinct is to avoid him, but if we muster up the courage to sit down with him and get past the awkward introduction, we'd probably be in for an interesting conversation. That's *Hell's Pawn*. It's my slightly crazy book that doesn't quite fit in with the others, but it *does* have some connections, as you're about to see...

Something Like Eternity

by Jay Bell

The Astral Wilds, ???

There's a place beyond truth and fiction, where right and wrong cease to have meaning. A world where the untamed dreams of the mind are no longer restrained by the physical. No more boundaries. No limits. Endless potential to create palaces and pyramids, castles and citadels. Or a simple clearing. A circle of trees. That's where you'll find me. Just as you always did before, no matter how dark the shadows. You will find me.

Victor rubbed his hands together, then stretched out his arms, palms open to the fire. From between his fingers he stared at the orange glow, basking in the warmth as it spread through him. Strange, considering he no longer had a body, and yet he felt more now than he ever had while living. Tactile sensations were more intense—the hard ground that made his butt numb, or the sting when a shifting breeze blew smoke into his eyes. He felt leaves crunching beneath his hand as he pushed himself up, even noticed the shifting weight of his clothes as he stood. Victor felt so much, but lately he found one sensation impossible to ignore. A pulling. A need. Something inside him that he was tempted to label as instinct or urge, but these words weren't sufficient. He was being drawn away from the clearing that had so long been his sanctuary.

Victor walked to the trees, which unlike their counterparts back in Warrensburg, Missouri, were only a few rows deep. Past them the ground ended suddenly, as did his forest, leaving a sky painted by van Gogh. Stars were no longer distant pinpricks. Instead he saw great fiery balls pulsing with light. Swirls of multicolored energy wafted between them on invisible currents, flowing like rivers out into the astral wilds. Victor had wandered those wilds when first arriving here. Finally free from the mortal coil, he had walked constantly, never tiring as he passed through realm after realm, each a different fairy tale. Or faith. None had been right for him—much to his relief—so he continued to wander. Then he had discovered a new world, a blue sphere shining like a beacon in the darkness. But when he got close,

Victor discovered a nightmare, a realm of rules and stagnation. He was tempted to call it Hell, except he had already visited there and found it highly enjoyable. This place though—a land of bland limitations—was insufferable. A literal purgatory. Victor had been eager to leave, but was unable to do so. Purgatory had become his prison.

He didn't remember much past a certain point. His thoughts had gone silent, his body numb. And then... nothing. When he awoke, the blue world was falling to pieces around him, crumbling and fading from existence. Victor found himself surrounded not just by other liberated souls, but demons, angels, and any number of extraordinary creatures who had come to their rescue. Victor hadn't stuck around long after that. He had started walking again, putting these incomprehensible events behind him. That's when he had come here, to his clearing, where he could be alone and rest. Of course it hadn't always been a solitary place. Occasionally in his youth, the leaves would rustle as footsteps neared and from out of the trees would appear eyes filled with transparent longing.

Victor smiled at the memory, the need inside him increasing. Much more than nostalgia-fueled desire. He glanced back at the clearing, at the long fire that a Boy Scout had once taught him how to build. Then he looked skyward and decided to set out into the wilds once more.

Few things about his new life—if it could be called that—made sense. He had a body, despite not needing one, and for the most part he moved around and behaved just as he always had in life. One of the first creatures Victor had met after dying, an anthropomorphic coyote of all things, assured him that physics were a bad habit left over from the living world. Some chose to break those habits and discover new possibilities, while others sustained them like a proud tradition. Victor delighted in not subscribing to either mindset, and as the ground beneath his feet ended and he stepped out into nothingness, he felt no fear. Just a mysterious urge that he was no closer to understanding. Rather than struggle to decipher it further, Victor decided that what he really wanted was a drink.

Instinct was his guide, as it so often was these days. He strolled through an environment of vibrating light and emotional sound—the astral wilds, they were called. He had never been told this. He simply knew. Similarly, when needing a place of his own, he had known to focus on memories of the clearing with its little shelter in order to recreate it in this world. Like a stage magician who didn't know the secret to his own tricks, Victor could conjure up whatever he desired. Places and things, anyway. People didn't appear, no matter how hard he wished them to. He found little ways of comforting himself regardless. Old habits, as Coyote had said. Victor pulled a cigarette from the air, embers already glowing red at one end, and smoked as he continued to stroll.

Time held little meaning here, but eventually the astral wilds gave way to form. A huge land mass appeared, solid and reassuring. He approached this feeling like a ship nearing the coast. Indeed, when his feet touched down on a pier and he glanced back, all he could see was ocean. Ahead of him was an unfamiliar city. This wasn't one of his inventions. It belonged to others, a community of creators numbering in the thousands, if not millions. This was a proper realm, the sort of place he had explored freely before—well, *whatever* had happened.

Victor headed for the action, passing on his right a train station and a long stretch of pavement filled with pedestrians, street cars, buses, and bicycles. After being alone for so long, he basked in the noisy chaos, feasting on the overwhelming buffet of sights and sounds. He skirted the crowds, eyeing with equal wonder normal people and the bizarre creatures interspersed among them. Victor had spent most of his life in a small town, but the few times he visited cities, he always found the variety of humanity there appealing. Here it was even more pronounced. What city on Earth could offer a gorgon walking hand-in-hand with a stone golem?

As delightful as the sights were, Victor wasn't satisfied. He crossed a street, dodging traffic and wondering what would happen if he were hit. He couldn't get any deader. Could he? Another mystery for another day. Instead he turned his attention to the neighborhood he had entered. Old buildings loomed tall overhead, narrow alleyways cutting paths between them. Many of these shops specialized in sex toys or drug paraphernalia.

Amsterdam. Or an afterlife version of it. He grinned, picked up the pace, and made a beeline for a corner bar named *The Inferno*. He pushed against the door, stepping aside as two red-skinned demons stumbled out. Victor stared after them a moment, then entered. The bar was dark despite the yellow-tinted windows that offered an unobscured view of the world outside. The demons had been the last patrons, the establishment empty and quiet now. Victor walked along the row of stools until he stood in front of the bartender. Then he took a seat and cleared his throat.

The bartender spun around. He had spiky hair the same dark shade as the stubble on his chin, eyes that appeared crazed from one too many benders, and thick eyebrows. One of these shot up. "We're closed," he said in a heavy Irish accent.

"Why?" Victor asked.

"What do you mean, *why*?"

Victor drummed his fingers on the counter. "It's not like any of us need to sleep. We don't get tired. Without the need for rest, day and night cease to have meaning, not that they had any before. We only agreed as a society to sleep during the night because it's the least convenient for visibility. Candles were expensive, and before the invention of electric lights, more people were biphasic sleepers. We'd go to sleep soon after it became dark, but nights are long, and we'd often wake up in the middle of it to socialize or get little jobs done. So basically it's only natural that we have a night life."

The bartender's eyebrow remained raised a moment longer. Then it shot down. "We're closed because I say we are, and mate, the more I listen to you talk, the more exhausted I get."

"Sorry. It's been a while since I had anyone to talk to."

"Well maybe you should get a pet. One without ears, so the poor thing won't have to suffer."

"Just a beer," Victor pressed. "Then you can go pretend to sleep."

The bartender eyed him. "You don't know where you are, do you?"

Victor shrugged. "Enlighten me."

The bartender put his hands on the counter and leaned forward with a menacing smile. "The people of this realm *can* sleep, and they do, because laziness is a sin. As for prowling around at night instead of being safely tucked in bed, you might want to rethink your strategy, because you're in Hell now!"

"Ah, okay."

The bartender frowned. "That usually gets more of a reaction."

"The demons I bumped into on the way in were my first clue. Besides, I've been to Hell before. First place I arrived except a different part, I guess, because it looked more like Vegas."

"Gambling," the bartender said with a snort. "What a bore." Then he looked hopeful. "Unless they have horses. See any racetracks while you were there?"

"Afraid not," Victor said. "I didn't stick around long. Not my scene. I never had any money to throw around. Not while living."

"You and me both, brother." The bartender hesitated. "I suppose, after a hard day's labor, that I've earned a drink. You can join me if you want. Then you need to piss off, because I've got better things to be takin' up my time."

"Sounds good. My name's Victor."

The bartender's focus remained on the tap as he filled a mug. "Dante," he replied. "And before you ask, yes, I'm *the* Dante."

"From the poem?"

Dante's head shot up. "No, not from the bloody poem! You're pulling my leg, right?"

Victor hesitated, worried about wearing out his welcome before he could drink the liquid temptation that had been set on the bar. "Like I said, I'm new here."

"You must be." Dante filled another mug for himself. "Speaking of money, how do you intend on paying for this?"

"Oh." A little desire was all it took. A crumpled twenty-dollar bill appeared in his hand, which he held out. "Keep the change."

Dante laughed and shook his head. "Nice try. That's not how it works. Cruddy pieces of paper aren't worth anything here. You've got to give up something meaningful. How about that tattoo?"

Victor glanced down at his left arm where a fox ran along a black line, the words *No Limits* written beneath it. That truly did have value, not just because it represented his philosophy, but because of the person who had loved him enough to pay for the ink work. He shook his head. "I can't exactly peel it off."

Dante leered. "Have you tried?"

Victor reached for it out of curiosity, finger rubbing at the fox's tail. Sure enough, the tip lifted away from his skin, as if it were only a sticker.

"Sweet Mary, you are new!" Dante said with a laugh. "Leave it there. Even I can see it's worth a fortune."

Victor glanced up. "Really?"

"Yeah. Hold on to that. It's your retirement fund."

Victor looked down at the tattoo again and scratched at it, but it didn't budge, having become part of his skin once more. "You're messing with me, aren't you?"

"A little," Dante said, still looking him over. "What else you got?"

Victor patted his pockets. "Nothing. Wait a minute, this is stupid! I can make my own beer, just like I do this." He conjured up another cigarette.

Dante peered at it critically. "Not bad, but that's not why people come to this bar. Here." From under the counter, he produced a small box and opened the lid. Inside were row after row of pristine cigarettes, the paper crimson, a thin gold line separating the black filter. "Try one."

Victor accepted the offer, setting aside his own. Once in his mouth, the cigarette sparked and lit automatically. He inhaled, and in an instant was transported back to the very first cigarette he'd ever smoked. His cousin had given it to him, and while most people talked about choking and retching during their first attempt, Victor remembered it as perfection. Smooth smoke had slipped down his throat, his head becoming dizzy soon after, the tips of his fingers tingling. The absolute best. Until now.

"Pure craftsmanship," Dante explained. "There's an art to creation. You can make your own beer, sure, but will it make you feel as good as that cigarette does?"

Victor thought of a hot summer day and the first time he'd cracked open a can. The memory made his mouth water until he remembered his predicament. "Like I said, I was poor while living. Being dead hasn't changed that."

Dante seemed to weigh the honesty of this statement. Then he waved a hand dismissively. "It's not like I have any use for money. People never let me pay for anything. Not since—" He puffed up his chest. "—all that business with Purgatory. Ring a bell?"

The blue sphere. Cold unconsciousness. Enforced sleep. "I was trapped there."

"Exactly," Dante said. "Then I saved the day, united the realms, and changed all of existence for the better. I'm basically history's greatest hero."

"You did all that on your own?" Victor asked. "I'm pretty sure I saw an army there."

Dante blanched. "I might have had *some* help. Just a wee little bit. Never mind that. Drink up. It's on the house."

They clinked mugs. Victor brought the beer to his lips. After a moment of bliss, followed by a satisfied gasp, he said, "Nectar of the gods."

"Most of them prefer wine," Dante said, "but I catch your meaning. My best mate always called it angel's piss. Don't make a face, he was only being colorful. Although if you're into that sort of thing, I know a demon or two willing to accommodate you."

Victor laughed. "I'll take a rain check on the golden shower."

Dante shrugged. "So what brings you to Hell? What great sins did you commit in life? Anything juicy?"

Victor shook his head. "I never believed in sin."

"Then you must have a vice you intend to keep indulging. What was it? Sex? Drugs? Booze? You didn't seem *that* desperate for a beer."

"Decadence was never my style. Nor was dependence." Victor stubbed out the cigarette in an ashtray. "Aside from tobacco."

Dante took a long swig and considered him. "Listen, you can tell me anything. No need to hold back. A bartender is just an underpaid therapist with a stool instead of a couch. I've heard it all before. People either end up in Hell because they feel guilty or because they fit right in."

Victor mulled this over. "I killed myself. Could that be why?"

"Nah," Dante said. "No chance. You can't be punished for stealing what belongs to you, any more than you can be put on trial for murdering yourself. When you see someone falling, you don't step aside. Not when you can catch them."

"Spoken like a true hero."

"I didn't mean *me*. God, on the other hand… I've been to Heaven. They have a nice fluffy cloud for suicide cases to land on."

"Never been there," Victor said.

Dante narrowed his eyes. "Some blokes just love to be contrary. I bet you're one of them. Always the exception to the rule, eh?"

"Guilty as charged."

"Huh. Well you must be here for a reason. You said Hell was where you first arrived?"

Victor nodded. "Just outside of it, but yeah."

"You can go anywhere these days," Dante said, "but that first destination is telling. If you didn't come here to indulge, then guilt is the most likely culprit."

"My conscience is clear," Victor said, but the words felt hollow.

Dante didn't believe them either. "Right. And what about the people you left behind? I'm sure they suffered, whether you meant for them to or not. I'm not trying to bring you down. I hate a weepy drunk, but you can't tell me your conscience is clear. I haven't been able to say that since…" Dante blinked. "Quite a few lives back, actually."

The people he had left behind. Victor swallowed. He'd felt so alone in the end. He'd *been* so alone. But not completely.

"Is that yours?"

Dante pointed to the end of the bar where a gray cat was sitting on the surface, calmly watching them both. Victor stared. It took him a moment to recognize the animal. He had put on a healthy amount of weight, and his fur was glossier.

"Samson?"

The cat blinked slowly, remaining where he was.

"That's the reason?" Dante asked, spluttering laughter. "You left your cat behind, and *that's* why you think you belong in Hell?"

"He was my mother's cat," Victor said. "I got him for her. She had Alzheimer's, and I hoped it would give her something to focus on. Help keep her sharp. I couldn't always be there and…" He tore his eyes away to look at Dante. "Is this judgment? Is that what's really going on here? Are you God?"

"I'm just a bartender, mate. Like I said, you're either here because you belong, or because you're trying to work off your guilt. Either way, I'd say you've got unresolved issues."

The restless longing. Victor still felt it pulling on him, even now. "I have this nagging feeling," he said. "Like I have an appointment I need to keep, but I don't know where or with who."

"The calling," Dante said, nodding in understanding. "It drove me crazy until I ended up here. Then I felt like I'd finally come home."

"That's not how I feel, so where am I supposed to go?"

Samson strolled down the bar, ignoring Victor. Then he hopped on a stool and to the floor. He looked back once before sauntering to the door with the casual confidence of all cats.

"I once knew a dog who did the same trick," Dante said. "You'd ask him to find something, and he'd be off like a shot. Better finish that drink because you, my friend, have a date with destiny. She's a beauty, but man oh man, can she be a bitch at times!"

Victor followed Samson out of the city and into the countryside. Aside from occasionally glancing back to make sure he was still there, the cat didn't seem terribly interested in him. This caused a pang of guilt, which made him wonder if Dante wasn't right. Maybe he did have unresolved issues. They were walking across a farm, the stars twinkling above. Victor tried to avoid stepping on the young crops, but his thoughts were too distracting. He stumbled over a row of tilled dirt just as he spoke aloud.

"I'm sorry."

Samson stopped, turned around, and sat.

Victor approached and knelt. "I wasn't thinking of you when I decided to call it quits. My mind was all messed up. At times I wasn't even sure if you were real. I should have found you a new home. Instead you were trapped indoors with me. Jesus, I can't believe I didn't set you free! Me, of all people! I guess that shows how far gone I was."

Samson blinked slowly.

"I hope you were okay," Victor continued. "I hope you didn't starve to death inside that house or have to... ugh. Actually, if you were hungry, I hope you did eat me. At least then I would have been useful to you. Really though, I like to imagine some nice police officer found you and took you to an awesome farm like this one, where you had a long life hunting mice. Is that where we are? Is this feline Heaven? I don't think we're in Hell anymore."

Samson continued to stare.

Victor reached out and stroked the top of the cat's head. "I hope you were loved. I'm sorry that I let you down."

Samson purred a moment, then turned to continue leading the way. A breeze swept across the farm, blowing in a low fog, which obscured the ground. Victor could no longer see his own feet. He peered ahead, trying to keep tabs on the cat, but only the tips of two gray ears and a tail were visible.

"Wait up!" Victor said, hurrying forward.

He picked up Samson and pressed on, the fog thickening and billowing around his ankles, making him feel like he was wading through shallow water. He pulled one foot free. When he set it down again, it met resistance. Victor stared. One foot remained hidden. The other was standing *on* the fog, which sure had gotten fluffy and white. Victor lifted the other foot so both were now standing on what he realized were clouds.

"You've got to be kidding me," he said, spinning in a circle. The world had become black sky above and clouds below, like a child's drawing of Heaven, albeit at night. Despite all the wandering Victor had done, he'd never been here before. And yet the calling, that feeling of needing to be somewhere else, hadn't gone away. This wasn't his home either, so… "What are we doing here?"

Samson hopped down and raced across the clouds. Victor almost chased after him. Then he noticed another figure, one who crouched so the cat could leap into his arms and climb onto his shoulders. The newcomer stood. He was handsome and dressed head to foot in an airline pilot's uniform, hat and all. Eyes sparkled over high cheek bones, the smile bright and careless, like a child's. He was definitely a man though—older than Victor remembered him ever being, and what memories those were!

Evenings spent at a gas station, whiling away the hours beneath fluorescent lights or out front so he could smoke a cigarette. Nights in a middle-class house much bigger than his own, a warm body pressed against him in the queen-sized bed. Or early mornings, the sun still young, Victor sitting next to the smoldering embers of a fire. On the best of these dawns, he would watch a figure slumbering in the sleeping bag, sometimes brushing the hair from his cheek, just to see him better.

"Jace," he said aloud.

Then they were moving toward each other. Jace opened his arms, but Victor opened his wider, winning the right to hug Jace to him and hold on tight. Emotions in the living world remained trapped inside physical bodies, but here there were no such limitations. The love he and Jace felt for each other intermingled and exploded outward. When Victor pulled away, the midnight sky had turned blue, the warmth of the sun now on his back. As for the man in his arms, he looked much younger, his clothing casual, his brownish-blond hair nearly touching his shoulders.

"There's my lion," Victor whispered. "I always knew I'd see

you again. I just didn't expect it to be so soon."

Their foreheads touched, then Jace's nose brushed his, their lips close. They didn't kiss though. Instead Jace spoke.

"We could have seen each other sooner if you weren't hiding away."

"Hiding away?"

"Yes, but it's okay. I like your choice of sanctuary."

Victor experienced a moment of disorientation and heard the crackle of a fire. He stepped back and found himself in his clearing again. A gathering of trees, a rustic shelter, and plumes of white smoke floating away into the blue sky. Jace appeared older again, the uniform having returned. He watched Victor with a hint of amusement in his eyes.

"You're just full of tricks," Victor said. "How did you do that? Weren't we in Heaven? And where did Samson go?"

Jace's expression remained neutral. Then he grinned and did a fist pump. "Yes! Oh my gosh. You have *no idea* how good it feels to not be the one asking questions! The whole time we were together was like trying to solve a mystery. Jace Holden, junior detective. Now the tables have turned!"

Victor snorted. "You don't have to gloat. Or strut around like that."

"So awesome," Jace was singing to himself while doing a little jig. "I'm so deep and mysterious, just like you used to be. But now you're not, because I am! Uh-huh, uh-huh!"

Victor watched him, shaking his head in amusement. "I'm happy to see you too. I just didn't expect you to be so young."

Jace stopped goofing around. "This is older than you last saw me. Aren't you going to give me shit about the uniform? Go on, accuse me of being a conformist, or limiting what else I could have been."

Victor shook his head. "You look handsome. Although…"

Jace blinked. "What?"

"Lose the hat."

"You think so?"

"Yeah."

Jace removed the hat and placed it on Victor's head. "There. Better?"

Victor took it off, a pang of sorrow hitting him as a cloud blocked the sun. "What are you doing here?"

"This is our special place. I thought you would—"

"*Here*. In the afterlife. I won't pretend to know how time works, or if it even exists here, but I hope you lived a long life." Victor looked him over again. "This can't be how old you were when you died. What are you, thirty?"

"A little older than that." Jace's expression grew somber. "And you're not one to talk. You were twenty-three. A baby."

"I don't care about that. What happened?"

"I spent more than a decade asking myself the same thing. You didn't even leave a note."

"Who was left to read it?"

"Me!" Jace said, thumping his chest. "You really thought I wouldn't find out? Did you think I wouldn't care?"

"I never asked you to," Victor said gently.

Jace stared at him incredulously. Then he spun around. "Ugh! You never change." He walked to the edge of the clearing, shook his head, then marched back. "I cared! Even if you didn't want me to! I never stopped!"

Thunder rumbled in the distance. They stood facing each other, a mixture of accusation and betrayal on Jace's face, but Victor didn't need to see it. He could feel Jace's pain almost as if it were his own.

"What I did was selfish," Victor said. "I wasn't thinking of anyone else. I admit it."

Jace stared at him a moment, his anger ebbing away. Then he exhaled and pinched the bridge of his nose. "This isn't who I am. Maybe when I was younger..." He let his hand drop. "I'm not so reactionary anymore. Believe it or not, I have a reputation for being calm and collected. I'm cool."

Victor smirked. "Sounds like you stole my act."

"Maybe I did. Still, we need to talk. I have questions. That's why I brought us here." Jace gestured to the campfire. "This was always my favorite place for us. I was happy when I saw that you recreated it."

"You knew I was here?"

Jace nodded.

"How?"

"I have my ways."

Victor looked him over again. "You must have died recently or I would have seen you sooner."

Jace shook his head. "I was waiting until I felt you were ready. When I saw that you had ventured out, I sent the cat."

Victor swallowed, feeling guilty.

Jace noticed. "Samson had a beautiful life. I adored him and spoiled him rotten. When I couldn't be there anymore, one of the bravest hearts I've ever known took over."

"What happened?" Victor repeated.

"I don't mean to sound petty, but I've waited a long time for answers. Please don't make me wait any longer."

Victor exhaled. "Fair enough, but not here. If we're going to get gruesome, I don't want it to tarnish this place. Follow me. I promise the walk isn't as far as it once was."

He led the way through the trees. Before long they were standing in front of a lake.

"Wow," Jace said. "The clearing I expected, but this?"

Victor smiled. "It's where you taught me that I don't like to fish. I also remember swimming together. And what happened afterwards."

Jace glanced around. "Just tell me the rest of Warrensburg isn't here too. I'm not sure I can cope with it existing in the afterlife. Some places should stay dead."

"I disagree." But there was no sign of middle-class houses in the distance, or the road on the far side of the lake. Victor had craved privacy, so such things hadn't manifested. They walked to the end of a rickety old dock and sat side by side with their legs dangling off the edge.

"Okay," Jace said, his voice sounding weak. "Tell me everything."

Victor gazed out over the water. "I used to imagine that when we die, all the impossible questions would be answered. Every mystery would be solved. That's obviously not the case, but the idea had appeal, especially after years of not knowing what to do with myself. My life became one big question I couldn't find the answer to."

Jace leaned forward, trying to make eye contact. "Is that why you did it?"

"No." He struggled to find the right words. Even though emotions were tangible here, Jace would need more than just this feeling of despair. Victor thought back to a hollow home, the rooms dark, silent, and choked with cigarette smoke. The colorful memories of childhood bleached white by the bleak realities of adulthood. His mother, her Alzheimer's, the way she slowly forgot who he was, and how he felt he couldn't turn his back on her. The confusion and fear on her face every time he reached out to touch her. He had given up on hugs, but at times he saw her hands, the same ones that had cared for him over two decades, and he couldn't help himself. He wanted to feel that comfort one more time, but she never placed those hands on his cheeks anymore. Her eyes had never again sparkled with perfect love for him.

"I know you stayed in that town for your mom," Jace said, "but the last time we met, you weren't even visiting her anymore. So we could have—"

"I felt trapped," Victor said, taking a deep shuddering breath. "I thought of running to you or to anywhere at all, but if I had, that would have meant giving up. She never would have done that to me. I wouldn't have been able to live with myself, but the fucked up thing is that I wasn't living at all. All I could do was work that gas station job and try to keep up with the bills, but I was never good at that sort of thing. I felt like a hamster trapped in a wheel. I could either keep running in place, or I could stop playing the game."

"You had options," Jace said, voice terse. "You could have lived with my parents or found some woods next to the nursing home to camp out in. *Anything* would have been better. I would have paid every bill or found ways to—"

"Jace," Victor interrupted softly. "The decision I made wasn't rational. Explaining it to you feels hopeless because logic wasn't involved. I felt trapped. Not just by my situation, but in my own head. There were voices, thoughts that didn't feel like my own. They sure as hell didn't make sense. I'm not sure what was wrong with me, but I worried that eventually I'd stop noticing that those voices didn't belong to me. The line was becoming so blurred that sometimes I couldn't tell the difference. My greatest fear became losing touch with who I really was. I didn't want to fade away and be replaced by someone different. I'd already seen that happen to my mother. I wasn't going to let it happen to me."

"I wish I had been there." Jace's cheeks were flushed, his eyes wet. "If you had to die, I hate that you did so alone."

"What, you wanted to hold the shotgun for me?"

Jace glared. "I would have held you! Stop being a jerk."

"Sorry. I know you wanted to be there for me but—" Victor swallowed. "We all die alone."

"I didn't."

Jace's hand was splayed out on the dock, so Victor placed his own over it. "I'm fine now. We both are. Why are you upset when we've finally awakened from the dream?"

"Because I wanted more for you," Jace said, still sounding angry. "A better life. A happier ending to your story."

"Maybe this is it."

"You could have tried," Jace pressed. "Before you gave up, you could have reached out to me or tried living with the guilt rather than... You have no idea how much damage you did, how many people were devastated when you died. Greg, Michelle, Bernard, we all cared about you. Maybe you didn't realize it, but we did."

Victor took a deep breath. "I can apologize, if that's what you need. I don't feel I should have to, because as I said, I wasn't myself. You don't understand what it's like to have your mind turn against you. I did the only thing I felt capable of. I won't pretend I wasn't aware of other options, but I truly didn't feel I could live with any of them."

"Does that really make it acceptable?"

Victor glanced over at Jace. He had never been judgmental, but at times he struggled to understand. Right now he was radiating with emotion. They both were, but the guilt and uncertainty in the air didn't belong to Victor. "What's this really about?"

Jace's eyes darted to meet his. Then he sighed. "You always could see right through me."

"How did you die?" Victor pressed. "What happened to you?"

"Brain aneurysm. I survived the first one, and you're wrong, because I do know what it's like to have your mind turn against you. That first aneurysm left me changed. I was irritable, I had constant memory loss, and at times I couldn't do anything but sit in a dark quiet room. So when the second aneurysm came along, I made a choice. Like you, I could have done more. I could have tried. Instead I allowed myself to be selfish, and those same people you hurt—" Jace's voice squeaked to a halt. "Sorry," he said, clenching his jaw. "I just hate the thought of what I put them through."

"Death always hurts those who are left behind," Victor said, "even when the causes are natural. Do you love me any less for what I did?"

"No," Jace said.

"Then don't think any of those people love you less. Or that they blame you for trying to do what was best for you. Stop being angry at yourself." Victor nudged him playfully. "And while you're at it, stop being angry at me."

Jace breathed out. "I'm not angry at you. I just wish I could have chosen a better ending. For both of us."

"Our story isn't over yet. Or hadn't you noticed?"

Jace's eyes met his, the sorrow there alleviated somewhat. He arched his hand, allowing their fingers to intermingle. Victor felt something hard pressing against a knuckle. He looked down to see a golden band.

"Is that what I think it is?"

Jace followed his gaze. "Ah."

"Ah?"

"Uh…"

Victor laughed. "You're a married man."

"Yeah," Jace said sheepishly.

"I shouldn't be surprised. You and your traditional values. Better be careful. What would your husband say if he saw you holding hands with your dead boyfriend?"

Jace pulled away as if he'd been caught but then smiled in amusement. "Actually, I've been trying to figure that out. It's complicated."

Victor chuckled. "Some things never change."

"They certainly don't." Jace looked around and sighed. "I always felt that way when returning to Warrensburg. This place you've created is a little too real. I practically expect Bernard to call and say I'm late for work."

"The gas station," Victor said, shaking his head ruefully. "I'll never forget having to wipe out that microwave. Disgusting. I'd like to think it's in Hell somewhere."

"Maybe, like our surroundings, it also transitioned to the afterlife."

"A demonic microwave," Victor said musingly, "stalking me all this time."

After a moment of silence, they both glanced toward the trees, as if expecting the microwave oven to appear there. When it didn't, they both laughed.

"Have you seen Bernard around?" Victor asked. "He wasn't exactly young."

"He still isn't."

"You mean he's alive?"

"Yup! See for yourself." One of Jace's feet tapped the lake's surface. The reflection there disappeared in a series of ripples. When the water calmed again, they were looking at the convenience store. Bernard was older. He'd lost weight and seemed more stooped, but his eyes were still vibrant. Currently he was showing a young woman how to run the register.

"How did you do that?" Victor asked in wonder.

"That's nothing. Watch this."

Jace grabbed his hand, then scooted forward.

"What are you doing?" Victor asked, resisting him.

"It's a leap of faith," Jace said with a wild grin. "Come on. Take the plunge!"

He hopped forward and slipped off the dock. Victor was dragged along with him. He closed his eyes instinctively but heard no splash. The sensation of falling had already ceased. When Victor opened his eyes, he was standing in Bernie's Stop and Shop, except this was *real*, not some nostalgic recreation in the afterlife. He didn't know how he knew, but he could feel the difference.

"Take your time and count the money back to the customer," Bernard was saying. "That's for your benefit as much as theirs, since it allows you to catch any mistakes."

"Holy shit," Victor said in hushed tones. "This is crazy!"

Standing next to him, attention on their former boss, Jace laughed. "You don't have to whisper. They can't hear or see us."

Victor glanced around, taking in details both familiar and strange. Wasabi-ginger flavored potato chips? Too bad those didn't exist when he was still alive. "Is this now?" Victor asked. Then he shook his head. "I mean, are you showing me a memory, or is this happening in the living world right at this moment?"

"This is the present," Jace said. "For them, anyway. Space *is* time, and we have neither. What we do have is order and chaos. Apparently. An Incan priest tried to explain it to me once. Only time I've ever gotten a headache in the afterlife."

"But this is real," Victor stressed, watching as Bernie walked past him to one of the freezers. "This is the living world."

"Yes," Jace said.

"Wow. Nice trick." He moved toward the counter where the young woman was jabbing at the cash register buttons and looking anything but certain. Then he noticed the cigarette display behind her. "Can we—"

"No," Jace said instantly.

Victor chuckled. "How are you doing this? I have to walk anywhere I want to go—not that I mind—but you have us zipping from Heaven to my own little paradise and now here."

"It comes with the territory," Jace said, trying to look modest.

"Meaning what?" Victor eyed him and laughed. "Wait, don't tell me. You're some kind of angel."

Jace's cheeks flushed. "The proper term is guardian."

"As in guardian angel? Do you have wings? Is that what the pilot uniform is all about? Have you got your own angel airplane hidden away somewhere? An invisible jet! Are you Wonder Woman?"

"No!" Jace said, his face red now. Then he laughed. "Angels are something completely different. I've seen them before. They're magnificent and kind of frightening. I just keep watch over certain people."

A familiar ding caught their attention. "Like Bernard?" Victor asked, strolling toward the microwave. "Look at that! He totally overcooked his burrito. Bean and cheese explosion."

Bernard glanced around, as if making sure he hadn't been seen, then went to the back office with his food. "Might want to wipe out the microwave," he said on his way. "Someone made a mess."

Jace *tsked* and shook his head. "And you think you know someone."

Victor snorted. "No kidding. So anyway, back to you being an angel."

Jace almost took the bait, but he caught himself. "Anyone can be a guardian. It just takes training and an emotional connection. You get to watch the people you love, and occasionally, you can try to help them out."

"Help how?" Victor asked.

"You can't communicate with people directly, or control them, but you can sort of whisper in their ear and hope they take the hint."

"Okay. What sort of stuff have you done?"

Jace squinted while searching for a good example. "One time there was this guy who went to buy donuts in the morning. On his way home, I made sure he drove fast. *Really* fast. He did the rest."

"Wow," Victor deadpanned.

Jace's features remained serious. "If he had gotten home a minute later than he did, things would have turned out differently. Of course *he* ended up getting shot instead… Um."

"First day on the job?" Victor teased. "So this person you watch over. Is it the guy you married?"

Jace's grin was sheepish. "Yeah."

"Care to introduce us?"

"Maybe some other time."

"In case you're forgetting," Victor said, "I'm not the jealous type. I wanna meet the man smart enough to put a ring on your finger."

Jace squirmed. "It's complicated."

"Only because you make it so." Victor offered his hand. "Come on, angel. Time to spread those wings and fly."

"I was a flight attendant," Jace was saying, sounding defensive.

"Uh-huh." Victor ignored him as he walked through the living room. The house was large and spacious, the rooms nicely furnished. Cozy. The sort of environment comfortable enough to while away an entire day on the couch. In other words, not his sort of place at all.

"The pilot thing is just a joke," Jace continued. "I gave myself a promotion. No more serving drinks to thankless customers."

"Sure," Victor said. He noticed a guitar magazine on the coffee table and tried to open it, but his hand went straight through the cover.

"I'm definitely not an angel."

Victor turned to face him. "I'm pretty sure we did enough in our youth to forever disqualify you from being one. Remember that night we drank too much whisky and blacked out? Well, *you* blacked out. I was up all night because you kept wanting to…"

"What?" Jace said, his full attention on Victor.

He shook his head. "I can't even bring myself to say it. It's too shameful. Or should I say shameless?"

"Oh come on! Tell me!"

Before Victor could respond, they heard a voice from the

next room. "Over my dead body! I mean it! You'll have to kill me before I sell the farm!"

Victor raised his eyebrows and looked at Jace. "Sounds like trouble. Time to spring into action, Charlie's Angel."

They hurried into a kitchen. The floor was blue tile, the furnishings rustic. At the far end of a long kitchen table sat a solitary figure. He was slender and not very tall. His brown hair was mussed and sticking through the fingers pressed against each side of his head as he stared down at a piece of paper. Then he dropped his hands, and louder than before said, "You'll have to kill me before I'll sell the farm!"

Jace was already at his side, peering over his shoulder. "New script."

"He writes?" Victor asked.

"Acts."

The person at the table scoffed. "How can he sell the farm if he gets killed?"

"Dead people can do all sorts of things," Victor replied. Then he looked at Jace. "Is he always this judgmental?"

"He's the sweetest guy imaginable," Jace said. Then he reconsidered. "Except when he's not, but I like that part of him too. Victor, meet Ben. Ben, this is Victor."

"Hey, how's it going," Victor tried. Then he winced. "Silent treatment, huh? No need to be like that. I'm not trying to make trouble. We're just catching up on old times."

"Potatoes are worth more to me than oil," Ben declared. "That black sludge won't fill the hungry bellies of my brothers and sisters!" Then, in a less theatrical voice he added, "No, but you can sell the oil, and the farm, and buy them burgers for the rest of their lives. Hell, you could use the money to buy a different farm!"

Victor grinned. "I like him!"

"Thanks," Jace said. "We owe much of our success to you."

"How so?"

"You taught me a lot about love. Some lessons I wasn't willing to learn at the time, but—"

The sound of the front door opening caused three heads to whip around. Seconds later, the sound of skittering claws on the kitchen floor accompanied the arrival of a bulldog, hind quarters wagging in excitement as it approached. The dog wore a large red flower on its collar, which apparently wasn't the norm, judging from the way Ben reacted.

He pushed away from the kitchen table and leaned over. "Chinchilla! Look at you! You're such a pretty girl!"

"Isn't she adorable?"

Victor turned at the sound of a new voice. The guy had bronze skin, jet black hair, and a toned build. He was carrying two plastic bags, eyes shining as he watched Ben interact with the dog. "That new pet store is amazing! You don't want to know how much money I blew through."

"Who's this?" Victor asked.

"Tim," Jace said, grabbing Victor's arm and pulling. "They're roommates. Let's go."

"We just got here," Victor said, yanking away. "What's the rush?"

"Miss me, babe?" Tim said, helping Ben to his feet and placing a hand on his cheek. Then they kissed. No casual peck on the lips either! It went on long enough that Victor found plenty of silence to fill.

"Roommates, huh? Funny way of paying rent."

Jace crossed his arms over his chest. "Too much tongue, as usual," he complained. "Ben appreciates subtlety, you know."

"So…" Victor said. Then he laughed, because he couldn't help himself.

Jace glanced over at him and glared. "It's—"

"Complicated? I can see that. So what's really going on?"

Jace watched as the kiss ended and Tim sat next to Ben at the table. They started digging through the plastic bags, Tim showing off the things he had bought, Chinchilla hopping around and harrumphing because she wanted to see.

"They were high school sweethearts," Jace said, leading the way to the living room. On a narrow strip of wall between two tall windows hung a vertical series of photographs. "They met again in college, but by then Ben and I were already together. I could explain but it's com—"

"Stop saying that."

Jace paused. "Convoluted," he said a moment later, looking pleased with himself. "They never stopped loving each other, and it wasn't until I died that they were finally able to be together again."

Victor leaned forward to examine the photos. In one Ben and Tim were both dressed in tuxedos, a heavy-set man standing between them with his arms around their waists. In another they rode a rollercoaster, their terrified expressions just barely recognizable in the blurry image. They were in swimsuits in the next, joined by a teenager with messy hair. Above all of these was a photo of a more professional caliber.

"They're married?" Victor asked.

"Yes."

He looked at Jace to gauge his opinion of this.

"I'm fine," Jace explained. "Tim's a good guy. He wasn't always, but he worked hard to become one."

"Then why were you so eager to hightail it out of here?"

Jace shrugged a little too casually. "No reason."

Victor looked back at the wedding photo, the pieces falling into place. He tried to keep his expression neutral when he turned around again. "You know, nobody lives forever. Someday you and Ben are going to be together again."

Jace smiled. "I look forward to it. Not that I want him to die soon! I can wait! But I look forward to our reunion."

"That will be a special day," Victor said, still trying to force down a smile. "It occurs to me that he might not be alone. If Tim dies first, you might even be waiting together."

Jace sighed and shook his head. "I knew I shouldn't have brought you here."

"I'm just trying to imagine you, the guy who always preached good old-fashioned commitment, sharing a husband with Mr. Push-ups in there."

"You're such a jerk," Jace said, still shaking his head.

"This must be a fairly common problem in the afterlife. Makes me feel like one of us was right this whole time."

Jace snorted. *"People don't stop wanting other people?"*

"Wise words," Victor said innocently.

"I hate you," Jace replied.

"You love me. Admit it."

Jace grew solemn. "I'm more okay with the situation than you might imagine. Ben was on his own for years after I died. I watched him and took no satisfaction in his loneliness. I kept whispering in his ear, urging him to go out and find someone. I worried he would spend the rest of his life alone, just to honor my memory. I hated the idea. I tried my best to get him to move on, but he'd get that stubborn look on his face, like he knew better. If it wasn't for Allison, his best friend… And if it wasn't for Tim, he might still be alone, but luckily that love was already there. The roots had settled in long ago, enough that Ben couldn't fight it. I'm happy they're together, and yes, when they pass from this world, I will welcome them both with open arms."

Victor considered him. "You're all grown up now."

"I *am* ten years older than you. Funny how that changed."

"Then you'll forgive my juvenile sensibilities. I died young. Keep that in mind for what I'm about to say."

"Here we go," Jace said wearily.

"I'm just trying to picture how the dynamics will work. Are we talking threesomes, or is it more of a joint custody situation? Will you only get Ben on the weekends?"

Jace thought about it, laughed, and spread his hands wide. "You know what? I have no idea. You're not seeing the entire picture, because there's more than just Ben and Tim to consider. There's this other guy from my past, and I never got to tell him the truth when we were living, but I'm saying it now. Victor Hemingway, I love you."

"I know. I've always known."

Jace paused. "That's it?"

Victor shrugged. "What? If you need me to say it, I will, but personally I think what we've been through together holds more value than three disposable words. Especially when you consider how commercialized that phrase has become, or how casually people throw it around."

Jace scowled. "This is exactly why I never told you! I knew it would turn into some big philosophical discussion and not… Never mind."

Victor allowed himself a smile. "I forgot what a romantic you are. And I *have* spoken those words to you before. Don't you remember?"

Jace's expression lost some of its anger, although his cheeks remained red. "I do. Er, I mean—"

"That's right," Victor said, moving closer to him. "I said them in a church. I meant them then, and I mean them now. I love you, and I'm hoping this isn't just a short reunion."

Jace seemed appeased by this. In fact, he was fighting down

a grin. "If Ben gets to have his high school sweetheart, why can't I have mine?"

"Only seems fair." Victor cocked his head. "I imagine Ben and Tim will need privacy occasionally. In such situations, I'd be more than willing to let you sleep in my clearing."

"Or," Jace said, reducing the distance between them to mere inches. "You can hop into bed with all three of us."

"Oh yeah?"

"Yeah. You can keep Mr. Push-ups busy for me."

"Is that all you need me for?"

Jace nodded. "Yup. You're a decoy. I have to warn you though, he's a top, and boy does he have stamina!"

Victor shrugged. "No limits."

Jace's face registered surprise. "Wait, does that mean we could have…"

"Gee, looks like you need me for something after all."

Their lips neared, but before they could touch, a squeaking dog toy was thrown directly through Jace's head. A moment later, Chinchilla and Tim ran straight through both of them.

"That was weird," Victor said.

"Maybe we should go somewhere more private." Jace said, taking a step back.

Victor nodded. "Hey, can you travel anywhere you want?"

"Kind of. It's mostly limited to where I have emotional connections, but if Ben takes a trip to Hawaii or whatever, I get to tag along."

"Huh."

"How come?"

Victor shook his head, a longing filling his chest. "Have you ever heard of a calling?"

Jace nodded. "There's somewhere you feel like you need to be."

"Yeah."

Jace pointed toward the front of the house. "The restroom is right over there."

"Funny."

"I thought so. But yes, I know what you mean. I might be able to help you."

"Really?"

Jace shrugged and offered his hand. "It's worth a try."

Victor started to reach for him, then turned back toward the kitchen instead.

"Where are you going?"

"To say goodbye to your lovely husband," Victor said. He found Ben still sitting at the table, grumbling over his script. "So how's this whispering thing work?" he asked, leaning over him. From the corner of his eye he could see a panicked Jace motioning for him to stop. Victor had never cared for rules. He leaned close to Ben's ear.

"Good news, kiddo. Jace says there's enough room in Heaven for you *and* Tim. Try to picture that for a moment."

Ben stopped murmuring his lines and glanced out the kitchen window. A smile tugged at the corner of his mouth. Then he shook his head and resumed rehearsing.

Victor stood upright and found Jace still appearing concerned.

"What did you say?"

"Just told him to break a leg. You ever go to his performances?"

Jace looked proud. "I haven't missed one yet."

They returned to the clearing before beginning their experiment so Jace could be free of distractions. Night had fallen again. The fire roared and a breeze shivered the leaves above. All a manifestation of Victor's nervousness. He couldn't be certain what his calling was, and in truth he wasn't concerned. Concepts such as destiny weren't for him. Right now all Victor cared about was getting what he wanted. He'd never been a greedy person, or expected anyone to grant his wishes, but just this once…

"The key," Jace was saying, stooping to catch Victor's eye, "is focusing on the feeling inside you. Emotions are like a beacon, a radio signal that can broadcast or receive. When I want to go to Ben, I focus on how I feel about him. Or when he needs me most, I feel an echo of his longing."

Victor's mouth went dry. "So it's definitely a person we're travelling to?"

"Not necessarily. It might be a place. You've never been drawn to just one realm—"

"I might have an affinity for Hell."

"But you've been there, right? And did you still feel the calling?"

"Definitely."

Jace took a deep breath. "Then it could be anything. Or anywhere. Let's find out. Close your eyes and focus."

Victor did as instructed. He didn't have to search inside himself for long. The calling wasn't far beneath the surface. It responded to the attention he gave it, the sensation intensifying.

"Good," Jace said.

Victor felt arms embrace him. Any second now, Jace would work his magic, and they could end up just about anywhere. Victor wouldn't leave it to chance though. He knew what he really wanted, so he quickly changed tactics, focusing on that instead. His thoughts became singular. One person, one place.

"Wow," Jace said. "That's intense! Okay. Ready, set..."

They were falling. The sensation wasn't gentle or graceful. The world had been pulled from beneath their feet. They plummeted, the motion sickening. Travelling hadn't felt like this before. This was bad. Victor knew it instinctively, but he didn't care. Instead he focused on his desire.

They hit bottom, their bodies crumpling on the ground. Jace's arms lost their grip on him. When Victor opened his eyes, his surroundings were a blur, but he was in the right place. A nursing home. Pale laminate floors, a scattering of couches and chairs, a television broadcasting an old episode of *Columbo*, the volume loud. Victor got to his feet and turned, searching the room.

"This is wrong," Jace said, his voice distorted and choppy. "We've got to leave."

Victor ignored him, still checking each occupant. Old women and men, mostly stationary, but he could see their souls overlapping them, like ghosts sitting on their laps. None of them were who he was searching for.

"Victor! We must go!"

Jace reached for him. Victor took a few steps backward and then broke into a run. Nothing would stop him. Not when he was this close. He raced past a counter tended by two nurses, recognizing them both. Down a hall and to the right. The door was closed, but that presented no obstacle. Victor passed straight through it, spotting the name on the door as he went.

Rachel Hemingway

His mother. He found her standing at a window, her back to him, but he didn't care. He called out, overjoyed to see her after all this time.

"Mom!"

The body at the window remained stationary, but the light within it turned to consider him. "Victor? Where are you?"

She said his name! She recognized him!

He was about step forward when arms grabbed him from behind.

"We've got to go," Jace said.

"No!" Victor snarled, struggling to break free. "She remembers me!"

"This isn't the right place," Jace said. "We're not meant to be here!"

"Then go," Victor shouted. "Leave me here! She remembers me. We can finally go home!"

The world around them shifted again but remained blurry. The light had dimmed, as if the sun had set, but this darkness was artificial. The curtains had been pulled over each window, the house silent and gray. His home, but not how he chose to remember it. This was just the husk, what was left behind after his mother had been taken away.

The arms constraining him let go, freeing Victor. "Why did you bring me here?" he said, turning around. "Or is this my fault? I wanted to go home, but not without her."

Jace's only response was a shocked expression, his mouth hanging open as he stared at one corner of the living room. Victor followed his gaze and saw himself sitting on the floor, back to the wall. His hair was long and dirty, his features gaunt as he stared down the barrel of a shotgun. His expression was vacant, then slightly hopeful as he reached for the trigger.

"Don't look," Victor said, turning again to cover Jace's eyes. "Please don't look."

He glanced back over his shoulder, saw himself touch his lips to the end of the barrel. The kiss of death, he remembered thinking. All of this had happened before. Somehow they were in the past.

"Get us out of here," Victor said. "Jace! Anywhere but here! *Now!*"

Jace grabbed him suddenly, clutching Victor to his chest. The echo of an explosion followed, but from a distance. They were moving, surrounded by streaking lights. Victor squinted against them, waiting for them to cease, but they didn't seem any closer to a destination. Jace was still clutching him, his body shaking as he cried.

"It's okay," Victor said, trying to pull away but unable. "We're all right now. It's over."

Jace clung to him tighter. "I imagined it. So many times! I knew it must have been bad, but actually seeing you…"

"It's fine," Victor tried again, hoping that Jace hadn't witnessed the very end. The shotgun had sounded far away, so it seemed unlikely. Even Victor hadn't seen the aftermath of his decision. He pitied whoever had found him.

Jace was still trembling, his muttering incomprehensible. All Victor could decipher was one question. "Did it hurt?"

"No," Victor swallowed. "I don't remember it happening. I'm afraid it hurt you more than it did me. I'm sorry."

Jace's grip on him tightened.

"It's over now," Victor said. "Let's go home."

He focused on the clearing, hoping that would be enough. A moment later he heard the crackle of fire, the buzzing of insects in the distance. Victor slowly disentangled himself, surprised to see Jace young again, his hair grown out, his expression vulnerable.

"We're okay," Victor repeated. "It was just a bad dream."

Jace shook his head. "It really happened. What we just saw, that was the past."

"And I'd like to leave it there," Victor said gently. "We both went through hard times. Life isn't easy, but there's a safety net. That's where we are. We're safe now. Here we always will be."

"I know." Jace exhaled and shook his head. "I probably know that better than you. It's just being back there caught me off guard. I don't understand what happened. I guess I messed up somehow when—"

"I cheated," Victor admitted. "I wasn't focusing on my calling. I was trying to see my mom again. Somehow that translated into time travel, which you definitely didn't tell me was possible."

"It's not recommended." Jace took a deep breath and collected himself. "Same thing happened to me the first time I tried finding Ben."

"Where did you end up?"

"On an airplane, watching him sleep. Watching myself watch him sleep, actually."

Victor smiled. "Sounds nicer than what we just experienced."

"It was, until I started wondering how a ghost could stand in a plane moving five hundred miles per hour. That little doubt was enough to send it flying on without me. I forgot to doubt gravity though, which meant I started plummeting through the sky."

"So much for beginner's luck."

"No kidding." Jace ran a hand through his hair, then considered him. "You should have told me you wanted to see your mother."

Victor shrugged. "Sorry."

"I've got some—" Jace blinked. "I don't think people say this often, but here goes." He cleared his throat. "I've got some good news. Your mom is dead."

"She's here?" Victor said carefully. "In the afterlife?"

Jace nodded. "Her passing was a lot more peaceful than either of ours."

"You've seen her?" Victor pressed.

"Of course." Jace said. "I checked in on her."

"Where is she?"

Jace smiled. "Where do you think she would end up?"

Victor matched his expression. "In Heaven."

"Exactly."

"Take me to her."

"Okay," Jace said. "I'll need your help. Heaven is a big place."

"You found her once before."

"And it took effort," Jace said. "Your connection to her is much stronger. We'll try again, but this time don't focus on the nursing home or the past. Concentrate on your feelings for her. Follow that love like it's a trail."

Victor eyed him suspiciously. "You just want to hug me again. That's what this is about. I bet you can find her perfectly well without my help."

Jace chuckled, eyes shining with youth. "For the record, this little trick works just as well if you're holding me. Maybe it even works better."

"I see," Victor said. He walked close to Jace, brushed the hair from his forehead, and sighed. "Now stop being adorable or we'll end up right back here."

"I'll try."

"Good." Victor took Jace into his arms and closed his eyes again. This didn't make it easy to concentrate on someone else, but he started by remembering how safe he had always felt in his mother's presence. All the home-cooked meals she had made for him, and the innocent days spent at the kitchen table when she taught him how to count and read. He thought too of the darker times when he had come home from school angry or crying, and how she always chased those bad feelings away.

He felt a gentle twist that lasted mere seconds. When Victor opened his eyes, he was home. They were standing outside the same house they had recently escaped, but this time he wasn't afraid. The curtains were open, the windows raised to let in the cool spring air. The world wasn't blurred by stagnant time. The details were crisp and clean, even more so than in life.

Jace stepped back. "Warrensburg again," he said, shaking his head, but his voice was warm. "Actually, this might be the most beautiful part of it."

Victor grinned and nodded. "Come inside with me."

Jace shook his head. "This is your moment. We'll see each other again."

Victor stared. "You're leaving?"

"Are you finally going to ask me to stay?"

"Yes," Victor said. "Stay here. Don't leave Warrensburg."

Jace tucked his hair behind one ear. "I'll be back. Or you'll find me. We have time. Death can't divide us anymore, but right now, it's time for a different sort of reunion."

Victor turned toward the door, his longing irresistible. He glanced back at Jace, but he was no longer on the porch. Instead he was walking down the street, his silhouette already distant, a pilot's uniform framing his figure. Next to him walked a little cat. Jace took off his hat, and without turning around, waved it in the air as a parting gesture.

Victor was tempted to say goodbye, but he knew he no longer needed to. He faced the door, placed his hand on the knob, and turned it. When the door swung open, he found the house flooded with sunlight. The scent of freshly washed laundry, the sound of country music on the radio. He ran through the living room, which took longer than he expected because his legs were short now. His knees were scuffed from climbing the tree out front, one of his shoes untied. Mom would take care of that. He ran through the kitchen and slammed against the back door to open it. His mother was in the backyard, a silly hat on her head as she watered her tomatoes.

She turned when she heard him and dropped the watering can, smiling at the same time she started crying. "Victor!" she said. "Where have you been?"

"I'm sorry," he said, running to her. She dropped to her knees to take him into her arms. "I'm here now, Momma. I'm home."

"This is ridiculous," Victor said, eying the spread before him.

A roasted turkey, a baked ham, sweet potatoes, normal potatoes, and scalloped potatoes. Green peas and diced carrots slathered in butter, wheat rolls, three kinds of gravy, and—he counted under his breath—*five* different pies!

"This is the sort of Thanksgiving I always dreamed of giving you," Rachel said. "Oh! I almost forgot!"

The last empty space on the table was filled by a bowl of fruit salad, which appeared out of thin air. Victor chuckled. He'd been pulling cigarettes out of the ether, but his mother, *she* chose to cook. "From what I remember, this is pretty much what every Thanksgiving was like. We had to take food to the neighbors one year because we had too much."

Rachel's cheeks grew rosy. "Money was tight. I always had to be careful when grocery shopping, but Thanksgiving was the one day out of the year I let myself splurge."

"Not counting Christmas," Victor said, reaching across the table for the sweet potatoes. He was back to his usual self now. He had only remained a small boy when hugging his mom and crying happy tears. Good thing Jace had missed that. Victor wasn't ashamed exactly, but he knew Jace looked up to him, and that little outburst hadn't exactly been cool. Too bad Jace was missing this feast though. "So what are we eating exactly? I know what it looks like, but what is it made of?"

Rachel half-stood to load up his plate while he ate. "I attended a lecture about that once. Something about the light of the universe. I was bored to tears, to be honest. All I know is—do you remember my favorite cake?"

"German chocolate," Victor said automatically. "You had it every birthday."

"When I first got here, I ate it every single meal. I mean a whole cake, not just a slice." She laughed happily. "Hasn't affected my figure one bit!"

No, it hadn't. His mother looked great. She had dark hair like his, but now it was more silky than frazzled. The worry lines had gone from her face too. Victor was reminded of an old photo from the seventies that showed her posing in front of her first car, hands on her hips and a goofy expression on her face. He'd always liked that photo because in it she seemed so energetic. The woman he had known in life had been perpetually tired, even though she tried not to show it. Now she looked years younger. Full of life.

"You're beautiful," he said.

"Oh stop it," Rachel responded, clearly flattered. "I'm so happy to have you here. They kept telling me I was in Heaven, but I disagreed. Only now that you're here do I think they're right."

"I'm surprised you weren't the one to come find me."

His mother shook a spoon at him. "Don't think I didn't try! There was all this business with Purgatory and they wouldn't let us leave the realm. Ever try sneaking past an angel? I have! I worried myself sick, and when that silliness finally came to an end... I knew you were safe, and I've always known what it meant when you wandered off into the woods. I might not have liked it, but it's your way of working through your issues."

"You know me too well."

"I'm your mother." Rachel's lips became a line, but then they quivered. "I'm just sorry I couldn't always be there for you."

Victor took in the sorrow on her face and instantly wanted to banish it. "Don't feel guilty! You're right. I needed alone time. I'm not hurt that you didn't come find me."

Rachel shook her head. "That's not what I meant! I should have been there for you when we were still living. If I had, maybe I could've prevented what happened. I wouldn't have let you take your own life."

Victor's stomach sank. "You know about that."

Rachel locked eyes with him. "A part of me was always with you. *Always.* I might have been trapped in my own mind, but a mother's love goes beyond the physical."

"Then you know what it's like," Victor said. "You weren't in control of your own thoughts. I wasn't either. I don't know if that's possible to explain to most people, but—"

"—I understand." Rachel sighed. "It's just so hard for me to think about the pain you must have gone through, and I hate that I couldn't do anything to prevent it."

"And I hated that I couldn't help you," Victor said. "That's love. It doesn't always feel good, but I wouldn't trade it for the world. Besides, look at us now. We're together again. I dreamed of days like this, sitting across the table from you. Forget eating! I just wanted to spend time with you again. To talk. This really is Heaven."

His mother beamed at him. "You always wrote the best letters to me on Mother's Day."

"I'm charming," Victor said with a shrug. "I can't help myself. It comes naturally. Seriously though, before I take a bite of this drumstick, what's it made of? We're not eating the souls of dead turkeys, are we?"

Rachel tittered. The rest of their meal felt more festive. They ate until the table was nearly cleared, never feeling full, able to savor each bite like it was the first. They talked and laughed together, and when they were finally finished, Victor felt content. Mostly. To his surprise, a longing remained inside of him. The calling.

"There's something I'm missing," he murmured.

"Ice cream?" his mother suggested.

"No! Isn't gluttony a sin? We're going to end up in Hell if we eat any more."

"This is the best part. Watch." Rachel clapped her hands and everything from the table vanished. "No more dishes. Ever! When I first got here I created a dishwasher, but when I realized I could... Are you okay, honey?"

Victor looked up. "Sorry. It's just this feeling I've been chasing down. A calling. Have you heard of those?"

"Yes. There's somewhere you need to be. Or someone who needs you."

"Exactly! I thought it was you, and I think that's right, but not entirely. I don't get it, because who else is there? I already saw Jace. There are other people I liked or loved in life, but who is more important than you?"

His mother stood up from the table. Her features were determined, the emotion radiating from her difficult to interpret. Pride? Excitement? "I think we should find out," she said. "Together."

She offered her hand, head held high. Not knowing what to expect, Victor stood and walked around the table to join her. "You know something I don't," he said.

"Then let's change that."

He searched her eyes a moment, then took her hand.

"Do you know what to do?" she asked.

He nodded. "Focus on the feeling."

Except he barely needed to. If he had a compass, his mother had the map. The room spun once, transformed in an instant. Once again they were in the living world, the environment feeling more solid and yet less vibrant then the one they had left behind. The calling exploded inside him, the sensation overwhelming, but it soon stopped completely. This is where he was meant to be. Their final destination. A simple apartment living room, an open kitchen on one end, at the other a sliding glass door and a balcony overlooking green grass. Victor didn't recognize any of it, but the occupant of the room—a woman with blonde hair, an elegant fashion sense, and a wicked smile when she chose to display it—*she* was definitely familiar!

"Star?" he asked disbelievingly. Victor laughed, happy to see her again, but he still felt baffled. He loved her. She had always been a wonderful friend and at times much more than that. But they had gone their separate ways long ago. He had never thought she would have need of him. Currently she was standing, fiddling in her purse until she found car keys. Then Star adjusted the strap on one shoulder and addressed a seated figure.

"I'm happy we got to spend time together. You didn't have to sleep on the couch. I could have gotten a hotel."

"I always sleep on the couch." The voice was deep and mumbled. The man it belonged to had a strong brow, his build impressive as he stood. And recognizable. Victor thought instantly of Star's father, who shared this person's height. How many times had he towered over Victor, his mouth downturned in disapproval? Star had only fueled the fire, trying hard to upset her father and using Victor as a pawn to do so. Not that he'd minded. Mr. Denton was part of the establishment that Victor had been so eager to thwart. Or so it had seemed. They were young then. Teenagers. Years later, toward the very end, Victor had run into Mr. Denton on the street. No doubt Victor had appeared haggard and unkempt, but instead of disapproval, Mr. Denton had only expressed concern, asking if Victor needed anything. A good man, more likely than not. As for the man standing before him now with the same broad shoulders, he was familiar in other ways too, such as the blond hair.

Victor stared. He had it figured out. "Nate?" he asked. "Star's little brother? Boy did he grow up huge! I don't think you ever met him when he was little, did you?"

He spun around to see his mother's reaction. Her eyes were wet with emotion. But why?

"Honey, I'll always be there for you." These words sounded like something his mother would say, but they were spoken by Star. "I hate that we have to move. It's a miracle we stayed so long in the same place, but Illinois isn't so far away—"

"It's across the country!" Nate said incredulously.

"—and the company promises it's just for a year to get that division up to snuff again. I've already told your father that I want to move back to Houston. Or maybe even Austin. I want to be close to my grandson."

"Grandson?" Victor said. But even weirder was how she referred to Nate's father like they didn't share the same one.

"And I want to be close to my baby," she continued, reaching up to place a hand on Nate's cheek. "This is temporary. I promise."

Victor stared, trying to put the pieces together. He wasn't seeing a brother and sister parting ways. This was more like...

"*I have a little brother now,*" Star had once told him. Victor had just gotten out of that nightmarish military academy, and concentrating on anything but the mess inside his own head had been difficult, but he still remembered his surprise. And the way Star had searched his eyes for a reaction, but maybe not the one she had been hoping for.

"That's her son," Victor said.

His mother nodded.

He watched as Nate walked Star to the door, a dog rising to follow them. Victor moved closer to listen to their parting words.

"I want you to find someone," Star said. "I know you hate it when I bring him up, but I liked Kelly. If you can't be with him, then get out there and try again. You shouldn't be alone. It's not healthy."

No, it's not. Victor knew that from experience. He had isolated himself from the world. He might not have enjoyed society's rules and regulations, but the people themselves had been good. He had liked them.

Victor watched mother and son part ways, then followed Nate

back to the living room. The man walked to the sliding glass door, but he didn't open it. Instead he stood, staring out through the glass, the apartment silent except the whining of the dog. The light was fading from the day, but the man didn't switch on any lamps, leaving the room swathed in gray.

Oh yes, all of this was familiar. Such emotions had once been his own. Now they belonged to this person, and not by chance. He studied Nate's features carefully, recognizing some traits because Victor had seen them staring back at him in the mirror, and not just figuratively.

"Why didn't she tell me?" He swallowed painfully. "I can guess but... I would have tried. I really would have. Maybe I could have been a father."

"You were young," Rachel said from next to him. "And so was she."

Victor clenched his jaw, trying to consider the past from as many angles as possible. Fumbling in a young woman's bedroom after breaking curfew to do so. Getting arrested for theft and a concealed weapon. Months spent in a military academy, and all the chaos that had followed, including dropping out of high school. Of course Star hadn't considered him a potential parent because he hadn't even been a successful teenager. He'd failed to get even the basics right. Maybe she had been ashamed of him, that the father of her child was such a —

"She named him after you," Rachel said.

"What?"

"Your middle name." Rachel put a hand on his shoulder. "Nathaniel. That's what most people call him. Star's parents raised Nathaniel as their own. At first, anyway. You were both too young to be parents, and you might not like to hear this, but I think they did the right thing."

Victor glanced over at her. "I would have tried."

"I know, but it's difficult to provide for a child, and it takes so much more than just financial stability."

Victor had never managed any kind of stability. He didn't blame Star. In the same way he didn't agonize over the dumb decisions he had made when young, he saw no point in holding it against her. But still...

"I could have been something to him."

"You still can. He needs you. I've done what I could, but this isn't my natural calling. There are those who nurture and create, and others who are more skilled at guiding—"

"A guardian," Victor said.

"Yes! How did you know?"

"Jace. He helped me find you, but first he showed me the person he watches over. Maybe he can teach me the ropes. Damn, this is a lot to take in! I have a son!"

"Nathaniel is a good man," Rachel said. "You'll like him. Of course he does brood too much and get lost in thought more than is healthy. I wonder where he gets that from."

Victor chuckled nervously. "This is good news, right? We finally have a new member of the family. I never minded it being just you and me, but eventually, we'll have someone to invite over for Thanksgiving."

"Let's just hope that won't happen soon," Rachel said. "And you do have a bigger family. A father you never met and two sets of grandparents, just like anyone else. You can meet them, if you'd like."

Victor looked to her in excitement, then back to Nathaniel. "No. He needs me."

"So does your mother. Take a trip with me and see what it means to be a father by meeting your own. Then you can return here and put what you've learned to good use. Nathaniel will be okay in the meantime."

"Are you sure?" Victor asked.

"If not, you'll feel it and we'll return." Rachel smiled at him. "You've heard of a mother's intuition? Well, occasionally—" she tapped his chest, directly over his heart, "—a father feels it too. It's your calling."

He looked back to Nathaniel, at the despondent way he stared out the glass. Then Victor nodded with determination. "It's my calling."

Victor walked along the clouds at a leisurely pace. He'd gotten better at travelling. He could use emotional connections to appear where he most needed to be, but his personality hadn't changed. He enjoyed the simple life, even when dead, so normally he chose to walk. He had needed quite some time to reach Heaven again, letting his feelings for one person guide him.

His first impression of this realm had been of fluffy white

clouds, but he knew now that was just the front gate. Victor found himself in a busy downtown area, passing small art galleries and music shops as he walked. In the same way that Hell sometimes copied cities from the living world, so did Heaven. Victor wasn't quite sure where he was currently, the mixture of cowboy hats and dreadlocks leaving him thoroughly confused.

"Excuse me," he said, addressing an older woman outside a craft store. "Where am I exactly?"

"Texas," she answered with a twang.

Victor smiled. "Texas is a part of Heaven, huh?"

"Texas *is* Heaven," the woman replied. "They're the same thing!"

"Of course." Victor fought down a smile. "How silly of me."

He continued walking until the skyline was behind him. Eventually he entered a sleepy neighborhood, the trees large, the houses slightly worn down. Not so different from where he was raised. He found the right house by instinct alone, the door swinging open before he could knock.

Victor shook his head incredulously. "You wear the uniform even when you're at home?"

"Sometimes I take it off," Jace said, "but only on special occasions. Now might be one of them." He stepped sideways, making room.

"Now that's what I call an invitation." Victor went inside, finding the interior just as humble as the exterior. "Was this your house?"

Jace nodded. "Back in Austin."

"I like it," Victor said, flopping down on the couch. "Very modest."

"Not by choice." Jace sat at the opposite end. He didn't complain when Victor stretched out and put his feet in his lap. "It's all we could afford. How have you been?"

"Good." Victor grinned. "Amazing, actually! We've been travelling, my mom and I. We never got to do that in life, so we've been visiting the different realms together, or seeking out people we have emotional connections to. I got to meet her parents. I barely had any memories of them, so that was exciting. We even tracked down my father."

"Really?"

"Yup. And guess what? The guy is a total jerk. You would

think they wouldn't let assholes into the afterlife, but whatever. Mom told him he needed to reincarnate and try very hard to be more pleasant. That's seriously how she put it. She never was good at being angry. Anyway, I'm glad he ran off when I was young. Now his father, my grandpa, he's really cool. Full-blooded Native American and chief to his people. He's a real thinker. We had so many amazing conversations, sitting together by the fire and smoking. The way his tribe chooses to live their lives — it makes sense to me."

"Wow. I never thought I'd hear you say that about anyone!"

"No kidding," Victor said. "He's the best. So are the people surrounding him. I want you to travel there with me sometime."

"You and me taking a trip together?" Jace seemed amused. "Okay. I'll pencil you in."

"We also checked in on the living. People I still love. It's a short list for me, but uh… I made an interesting discovery. I have more family than I expected."

"Meaning?"

Victor took in Jace's uncertain expression and was reminded of their youth. Jace had always felt like he was competing with Star, and this new information certainly wouldn't help. Then again, Jace was a grown man. He probably didn't struggle with issues like jealousy anymore, but for the moment, Victor decided they could focus solely on each other. "It's complicated," he said. "I'm going to need your help, but there's time for that later. Anyway, all I'm doing is talking about myself. Show me around."

They both stood. Jace led him to the mantle, where a number of framed photos were lined up. Most depicted memories Jace and Ben had made together, although he had been generous enough to include one of Tim. Even if it wasn't the most becoming image.

"Tim's nose isn't exactly small," Victor said, "but I don't recall it being *that* big."

"Nobody's memory is perfect," Jace replied innocently. "It's the best I could do. Come see the kitchen. Believe it or not, I actually learned to cook. Nothing exceptional, but I've come a long way since our younger days."

"I always liked your cooking," Victor said. "Nobody could open a can of ravioli quite like you. So all these things are what you had in life? Is this house an exact replica?"

"Almost," Jace said. "I made one small change. To the bedroom."

Victor followed him down a short hall. Then he stood in the doorway and stared. "That's a ridiculously huge bed."

"Yeah," Jace said, scratching the back of his head and looking sheepish. "As you pointed out, it's going to get crowded at times. It's not meant to be anything kinky."

"No?"

"No! I'll want to sleep with Ben every night, by which I *only* mean sleep, because I'm sure Tim will want to sleep with him too. I figure Ben can snuggle up between us. And uh, you could sleep on the other side of me. If you want."

Victor snorted. "Are you asking me to move in?"

"You can't always live with your mother," Jace retorted.

"Hey, I've got my own clearing and everything. I'm *very* grown up."

"Obviously." Jace searched his face. "All I'm saying, is that if you ever want a place to stay—"

Victor grinned. "Like a sleepover?"

Jace nodded. "Sure. Technically we don't need to sleep, but it still feels good to dream."

Victor walked into the room. "You've got this all figured out, haven't you?"

"It was either this or add a few bedrooms to the house."

"You embroidered our names on the pillows."

Jace hurried forward to block his view. "Only to help me plan."

Victor stood on his tiptoes to see over his shoulder. "There's me, you, Ben, and Tim. You sure you don't want to add a few more places? What was the name of that guy you dated in college?"

"Shut up," Jace said. Then he laughed. "Maybe I went a little overboard with the planning."

"Just a little," Victor said with a smile. "Let things happen naturally. It'll work itself out."

Jace's posture relaxed. "You're right. I'll try."

"Not that it's bad to be prepared," Victor said. He walked around Jace, flopped on the bed, and rolled onto his back. "Have you tested this thing yet? As in a safety inspection. It would be a shame if your husband finally showed up and faulty bed springs sent him hurtling through the atmosphere."

"Heaven doesn't have an atmosphere," Jace said, "but maybe you're right." He pounced, landing on Victor and looking anything but angelic. "We better do some serious investigating."

"Definitely." He craned his neck forward for a kiss, but changed his mind because he had more to say. "I'm glad we found each other again. As far as endings go, I never expected mine to be so happy."

"Happily ever afterlife," Jace replied.

Victor groaned, determined to make sure Jace was too preoccupied to say anything cheesier. Their lips met, and no longer needing to breathe, they allowed the kiss to last a small eternity, knowing they would never need to part ways again.

The (not-so) Secret Files of Allison Cross

by ~~Jay Bell~~ Allison Cross

Hey, what's going on? It's me, the fabulous Allison Cross! I'm finally able to address you directly. Jay Bell usually keeps this from happening. He prefers to be the one to tell our stories, or "chronicle our lives" as he likes to spin it. Me? I say he's exploiting us, but I'll admit the attention is flattering. I balance things out by charging him twice as much for my counseling services. That's right, Jay Bell is often on my couch. The boy is troubled, let me tell you! During the most recent session, Jay was bemoaning how hard it is to keep track of us all. That's to be expected. The story of one life connects not just with another, but with countless others. Each of us have family and friends, who in turn have family and friends of their own. We're all connected in this way. Even you and me. One of my distant cousins probably has a best friend who went to college with your hair stylist. Who knows? Wouldn't it be fun to document all those lives, find out who they connect with, and how? And wouldn't this task be easier if I made my confidential patient files public? That's exactly what Jay asked me to do, the scoundrel. I'm much too professional to go along with such a scheme, but I made a counter proposal: What if I wrote new profiles for those I'm close to, and conducted interviews with those I hadn't yet met? Of course I would need to be compensated for my time, and reimbursed for all incurred expenses. Good thing Jay was already on the couch because he looked faint when I told him how much money I required, but in the end he agreed.

Below you'll find the results of my research. I decided to organize this list alphabetically by first name, since if you're reading one of the *Something Like...* books and need to look up a character, you'll probably only have a first name to go by. As much as I wanted to include *everyone,* Jay said he simply couldn't afford it. Because of that, I tried to limit myself to characters who appeared in multiple books, with some exclusions. Dr. Baker treated Tim's sprained ankle in both *Summer* and *Winter,* and despite his medical proficiency, I couldn't envision anyone needing to look him up or being eager to learn more about his life. Likewise there are exceptions for characters who appeared in only one book but who are of great importance regardless. Please note that these profiles do include some amount of bias, and in some cases required me to consult surviving friends and relatives. I hope you'll find them useful and perhaps even entertaining. At the very least, they allow us to catch up with some of these people to see where they are now.

Your friend,

Allison Cross
Austin, 2015

Aaron Osborn
Born: September 8th, 1980
Height: 5'10"
Build: Slim and prim, but not always proper. His words, not mine.
Other physical traits: Highlighted blond hair and a hint of eyeliner to add mystique.
Hobbies and interests: Looking gorgeous, avoiding conflict, and husband-hunting.
Noteworthy relatives: n/a
Motto/Quote: "Looking good is synonymous with feeling good!"
Bio: Aaron has a passion for beautifying the world. This includes himself, since he likes to primp himself for maximum results, and to others, because he loves the idea of helping people achieve this state of perfection. He was never fond of college and eventually ditched it to follow his beauty school dreams. This was made possible in part by a grant from Tim Wyman. Aaron makes this sound positive, when really, Tim paid him to write a letter and tape it to Jace Holden's door, but of course Ben Bentley was the intended recipient. I try not to think about this much because it makes me want to strangle Tim. Aaron didn't seem eager to focus on this either. He was much more interested in talking about the beauty studio he hopes to open soon, assuming the bank approves his loan. Good for you, Aaron!
Aaron appears in: *Summer* and *Winter*

Adam Bentley – See Benjamin (son)

Adrien York
Born: April 27th, 1973
Height: 5'11"
Build: Thin. His posture goes rigid when someone pisses him off, which according to him, is often.
Other physical traits: A tall forehead, dark swept-back hair that is graying, and lips that love to purse.
Hobbies and interests: Law, interior decorating, fine wine and food.
Noteworthy relatives: Caleb (husband)
Motto/Quote: "Being a bitch is easier than letting yourself be bullied."

Bio: Conflict has always been a part of Adrien's life. In his youth, other children would mock him for his effeminate body language or his tendency to lisp. This conflict became internalized when he began hating himself for traits he was incapable of changing. Only when Adrien was older did he decide he'd had enough and turned his anger on the world instead. This solution was hardly perfect since it made him defensive, his first instinct always to fight. In college, this was instrumental in bringing his relationship with Jace Holden to an end. After graduating, Adrien became a practicing lawyer, finally discovering a healthy outlet for his frustration. The anger that had once made his life difficult was now harnessed and instrumental in making him successful. After being devastated by the news of Jace's death, Adrien did some soul-searching and decided to focus on civil rights, wanting to ensure that gay couples have equality and access to resources when facing such difficult times. Even though the U.S. Supreme Court has now made marriage equality a nationwide reality, Adrien assures me that the good fight goes on. The laws might have changed, but that doesn't guarantee that attitudes have.

Adrien appears in: *Autumn* and *Spring*

Allison Cross
Born: March 1ˢᵗ 1979
Height: 5'10"
Build: Tall and thin, although hauling my son around has led to some impressive biceps. Watch out, Tim Wyman! Soon there will be a new muscled beauty in town!
Other physical traits: I asked Ben to describe me, and the first thing he came up with was "a wide smile and expressive eyes." Probably because when he's around, I'm either grimacing at his latest mistake or wide-eyed in disbelief.
Hobbies and interests: I love listening to music, singing, and believe it or not, I've been really into playing poker lately. This started when I caught the World Series of Poker on television, and since then, I've been sneaking online games in between sessions with my patients. Yes, I've been playing with real money, and no, I'm not in the hole. Maybe I have a shot at becoming the first female World Series of Poker champion!
Noteworthy relatives: Brian Milton (husband), Davis (son), Charles (father), Tonya (mother)

Motto/Quote: "If you need a sympathetic ear, go somewhere else. If you need a swift kick in the butt, then I'm your girl!"

Bio: My early childhood was idealistic, which I'm grateful for since the formative years can affect your entire life. When my mother died and my father turned to alcohol for comfort, I still had a strong foundation to help see me through. Helping people has become a habit of mine, so it's a good thing Ben Bentley and I met and became best friends in junior high. That boy needs all the help he can get! I love him dearly though. I might have lost my parents earlier than anyone should, but that void has been filled by other wonderful people, making me feel blessed; specifically my husband Brian, a recovering alcoholic. I admire him for being able to do what my father couldn't. It takes a tremendous amount of strength to fight off an addiction. Brian also gave me a wonderful son, Davis, who as I'm writing this, just spilled orange juice on the dog. We don't have a dog, so if you'll excuse me, I need to clean up this mess and track down the animal's owner.

Allison (that's me!) appears in: *Summer, Winter, Autumn, Spring, Fall, Lightning,* and *Tonight*

Amy Hubbard – see Caesar (brother)

Arthur Courtney – see either Sheila (mother) or Nathaniel Courtney (uncle)

Benjamin Bentley (aka Ben)
Born: October 27th 1979
Height: 5'9"
Build: Slender. I've witnessed him pack in a ridiculous amount of carbs, none of which seem to stick.
Other physical traits: His light-brown hair gets a tinge of blond in the summer, and I've seen those chocolaty eyes plead with me more times than I can count. I've always told him he's a handsome guy, and he always denies it.
Hobbies and interests: Love, boys, relationships, and trouble. Singing too.
Noteworthy relatives: Jace (first husband), Tim (second husband), Jason (son), Karen (sister), Adam (father), June (mother)
Motto/Quote: "It's better to have loved and lost than… Ugh. You know what? Loss sucks, but love is eternal."

Bio: Ben is brave. He came out of the closet at fourteen. In Texas. At a time when public opinion was generally negative about gay people. When he first came out, he did so rather naively, thinking the guys he messed around with would want to do the same. For them those experiences were the product of raging hormones. For Ben it was about love. If you need further proof of his bravery, once Ben saw the negative reaction and lost friends just for asserting himself, he didn't run back into that closet. He could have denied it or pretended he was joking. Not my Ben. He swallowed his disappointment and kept on searching. This led of course to Tim Wyman, who wasn't nearly as resolute. Ben had another tough lesson to learn: Not only were people not accepting of him, but some people aren't even accepting of themselves. Eventually Ben found someone just as wonderful and proud as he is. Jace Holden should have been his happy ending, but that's life. One minute a person is there, and the next... I have to say though, that I've slowly learned to respect what Tim Wyman has done, how he's tried to make up for the past and fill a much-needed role without exactly replacing it. I never wanted Ben to be alone. I'm happy that he no longer is.

Ben appears in: *Summer, Winter, Autumn, Spring, Lightning, Fall, Eternity,* and *Tonight*

Bernard Weber (aka Bernie)
Born: October 16th, 1928
Height: 5'10"
Build: He blames his gut on too many beers consumed on his boat, but he sure seems fond of microwave burritos too.
Other physical traits: Short grey hair and faded blue eyes that still manage to twinkle.
Hobbies and interests: Reminiscing about his Navy days, fishing (not only to catch dinner, but the occasional angsty teenager too), and finishing crossword puzzles. He's also pretty good at cards. As in I got my ass handed to me in a game of poker. Maybe I'm not ready for the big leagues just yet.
Noteworthy relatives: Brian Weber (son)
Motto/Quote: "I don't believe in no devil. Temptation is powerful enough without giving it legs."
Bio: Bernard sought adventure at a young age, which encouraged him to join the Navy. He was lucky enough to miss the ravages of

World War II and was involved instead with relief efforts. Toward the end of his service, when stationed in Pearl Harbor, he met a Hawaiian woman, Alani, who would later become his wife. They moved together to Bernard's hometown, Warrensburg, Missouri, where they had a son, Brian, and a daughter, Kala. Bernard dedicated himself to the happiness of his family, only faltering when he struggled with the emotional upheaval he felt when learning of his son's sexuality, a mistake that he says has haunted him for the rest of his life. Bernard provided for his family by opening Bernie's Stop and Shop, a gas station and convenience store. He was a father figure to Jace Holden, Victor Hemingway, and perhaps others, but Bernard is much too humble to discuss what else he has done for the community. He claims to enjoy the simple life, although that has nothing to do with retiring. Bernard might be pushing ninety, but he's not letting that slow him down.

Bernard appears in: *Autumn, Fall,* and *Eternity*

Bob Holden – see Jace (son)

Bonnie Rivers
Born: July 10th, 1992
Height: 5'7"
Build: Slight, although she has so much presence that you might not notice how small she is.
Other physical traits: She enjoys altering her appearance, whether through different hair colors, body piercings, or more elaborate changes.
Hobbies and interests: Playing the cello, pursuing romantic conquests, reading poetry.
Noteworthy relatives: Eli (sister)
Motto/Quote: "Identity comes from the inside and works its way outward, even though corporations would have you believe the opposite is true."
Bio: I'm hesitant to discuss Bonnie in too much detail. In the spirit of full disclosure, she is also a patient of mine. I *can* tell you that Bonnie is a wonderful friend. Kelly Phillips will attest to that. She is also passionate, as her longtime girlfriend, Emma Trout, knows all too well. Relationships are important to Bonnie. She is fiercely loyal to those she loves, although she would rather defuse conflict than choose a side. I've felt honored to assist her through

the different transitions of her life, and I hope someday her story is told, because I find myself admiring her vision and courage.
Bonnie appears in: *Spring, Lightning,* and *Thunder*

Brian Milton
Born: October 30th, 1974
Height: 5'11"
Build: I like a man I can hang on to, so those love handles? They're sexy!
Other physical traits: He's never had much hair, but what little he had was reddish-brown, and he's always been pasty pale. He's my little dough boy… which I promised to never call him in public. Oops!
Hobbies and interests: Brian loves theater and everything that surrounds that life, from actors to writers and even the techies who make sure everything runs smoothly. When Brian finds a subject interesting, he takes an interest in every aspect.
Noteworthy relatives: Allison Cross (beloved wife), Davis Milton-Cross (adorable son)
Motto/Quote: "What did I do now? Am I in trouble again? Please don't make me sleep on the couch!"
Bio: Brian is a good man. I mean it. People often say someone is good, or kind, or nice, but they do so while ignoring all of the evidence that proves otherwise. Brian is the real deal. I've never seen him get truly angry. Frustrated? Yes. But mostly he's a kind person who studied hard in school and never got in trouble with the law. He did everything right and by the rules, but people don't always respect that. Brian got walked on a lot in school, and taken advantage of when first setting out into the working world. Incapable of venting the way most of us do, he turned to alcohol, which led to his darkest years. Proving himself anything but weak, he overcame that addiction and started his own business. Now Brian is finally on top, and rather than get revenge on those who wronged him, he has decided to show them the kindness he always wanted to see. God I love this man!
Brian appears in: *Summer, Winter, Spring,* and *Tonight*

Brian Weber – See Bernard (father)

Bryce Hunter
Born: Who cares? Oh fine. January 1st, 1979
Height: 6'3"
Build: Huge. Like an ox.
Other physical traits: The guy is a monster. I hate to admit that he's sort of handsome, but any sex appeal is killed when he opens his mouth and spews ignorance.
Hobbies and interests: Drinking and staring into empty space.
Noteworthy relatives: He's the lovechild of a caveman and a Neanderthal.
Motto/Quote: "Durrrr. I'm Bryce and I'm a big stupid jerk."
Bio: Okay. Deep breath, Allison. It pains me to include people like Bryce and Darryl in my research, but they *did* play an important role in our lives. You can't have a good story without a villain, I suppose. Ben wouldn't be the awesomely strong person he is now if he hadn't learned to stand up to jerks like Bryce, and let me tell you, Ben looks *really* small next to this guy. That didn't stop Ben from picking a fight with him! Bryce was one of Tim's friends, which probably explains why I needed so much time to warm up to Mr. Wyman. I did try to reach Bryce for comment (or indecipherable grunting) but all I could discover is that he works construction these days. I like to imagine he pours cement. On himself.
Bryce appears in: *Summer* and *Winter*

Caesar Hubbard
Born: September 8th, 1989
Height: 6'
Build: Lean, but with a fair amount of muscle, which he casually flexed when he caught me looking. He also winked, but I pretended not to notice.
Other physical traits: The long waves of dark hair and golden eyes *are* a little hard to resist. I found myself reaching for my wedding ring more than once, just to remind myself of my commitment. This man is trouble!
Hobbies and interests: Wrestling, first aid, and anyone willing to give him the time of day, it would seem.
Noteworthy relatives: Todd Hubbard (father), Constance Hubbard (mother), Peter (brother), Amy (sister), Carrie (sister)
Motto/Quote: "Emotion robs all of us of free will, leaving us with neither options nor choices."

Bio: I have to admit to feeling puzzled after meeting Caesar. At first I thought he would be another Tim Wyman. Caesar comes from a wealthy family that expects him to meet the standards they set forth. He's also expected to be a good sibling to the many foster children his parents take in. Despite this, he has no qualms about following his romantic impulses. In fact, I'd say that's his greatest problem. My best friend, Ben, has always made love a priority. Caesar does too. He seems more capable of loving others than anyone I've met before. That might sound good on paper, but it has only brought turmoil to Caesar's life. Ben is content when he finally finds someone willing to love him back. Mostly. Caesar… I'm just not sure. I know Jason Grant once cared deeply for Caesar and still refuses to blame him for much, although hurt feelings still linger. And then there is Nathaniel, who isn't so forgiving about how his relationship with Caesar ended. I can't help but wonder how far back this trail of broken hearts extends, and what will eventually happen to Caesar's own.
Caesar appears in: *Spring* and *Thunder*

Caleb – See Adrien (husband)

Carla – I don't have much information about Carla. Tim was unwilling to tell me anything of substance, including her last name. I know that she was his girlfriend in Kansas, and that she was vindictive enough to spread lies about Tim after they broke up. I asked Ben about her, but even he agreed that some things are better left in the past. The most I could get out of Tim was that her little brother, Corey, factored into his realization of his own identity.
Carla appears in: *Winter*

Carrie Hubbard – See Caesar (brother)

Chinchilla (note: When Tim found out about this project, he insisted on writing Chinchilla's profile. It's hardly objective, but it did save me some work.)
Born: Never ask a lady her age!
Height: 13″
Build: She's my fat little sausage!
Other physical traits: She's brown and white. I think about her whenever I eat fried ice cream. Sometimes when Chinchilla is

nodding off, the tip of her tongue will stick out, which totally kills me.

Hobbies and interests: She lives to chase ball! Just don't expect her to fetch. She also learned to pounce bugs from Samson, so you'll often see her out in the yard, using her front paws to hop on stuff in the grass. I hope she doesn't think she's a cat!

Noteworthy relatives: Tim Wyman (dad, best friend), Benjamin (step mom, ha ha!), Samson (brother cat)

Motto/Quote: "Daddy gonna take me for a walk! Then he gonna rub my belly, because I'm his little princess!"

Bio: Chinchilla showed up in her dad's life at a time when he was… uh, a little misguided about how he expressed his love. The details don't matter. She had a job to do, and that was to keep her dad from feeling sorry for himself. Mission accomplished, because every moment spent with her is pure happiness. She's my little ray of sunshine, and I will never ever let her go. *Te quiero mucho, Gordita!*

Chinchilla appears in: *Summer, Winter, Spring, Fall,* and *Eternity*

Connor Williams

Born: January 30th, 1992

Height: 5'10"

Build: Intimidating, which he swears is all down to genetics and not hours spent at the gym.

Other physical traits: His eyes are intense, which along with the scar on his neck, can be a little off-putting. Connor admits to using this to his advantage at times.

Hobbies and interests: He has a passion for cooking, and although he took up truck driving because he wanted to fulfill his boyfriend's dream to travel more, Connor has found himself enjoying life on the road.

Noteworthy relatives: David Henry (future husband?)

Motto/Quote: "The only cause worth fighting for is protecting those you love."

Bio: I originally met Connor Williams when… Ahem. What happens in Galveston stays in Galveston. Let's just say he saved my bacon. When Brian and I took a trip down to Florida, I had a chance to get to know him better, and I discovered we have some things in common. Connor Williams originally hails from Kansas, and the beginning of his life was idealistic and secure. An auto accident changed this, and while Connor didn't lose his father in the same way I lost my mother, the outcome wasn't so different. He found himself relying on one parent, often needing to assist her. This protective instinct became a part of his personality, and in his late teens, encouraged him to intervene when a young guy named David Henry was being assaulted. Like me, Connor also needs to learn to take care of himself as much as he does others, but I feel a lot better having met the guy he hopes to spend his life with. David is a good person, and as long as they are together, I can't imagine their lives being anything but happy.

Connor appears in: *Kamikaze Boys* and *Tonight*

Constance Hubbard – See Caesar (son)

Corey – See Carla (sister)

Darryl Briscott
Born: June 4th, 1979
Height: About the right height for me to headbutt him, if need be.
Build: A self-assured sort of flabby that he carries like he's perfection.
Other physical traits: A smug expression.
Hobbies and interests: Conquest.
Noteworthy relatives: Asmodeus. Beelzebub. Lucifer. Take your pick.
Motto/Quote: "I thought you wanted to be someone. That'll never happen now."
Bio: Allow me explain that quote to you. Ben and I had the misfortune of going to the same high school as Darryl, where he was the ringleader of the popular kids. Darryl was also one of the biggest bullies there and a total sleazebag. He would use anyone foolish enough to date him before throwing them away. This meant he sometimes had to look outside his social circle. To my horror, he once briefly turned his attention to me. I wanted no part of that, which only seemed to encourage him. He asked me out, one hand on the locker behind me, all up in my personal space when he invited me to his place after school. Oh, and did I mention he called me Angela? The jerk didn't even know my name! I needed all my willpower not to vomit on him, but I still managed to shake my head and say, "No thanks." His response?

"I thought you wanted to be someone. That'll never happen now." Well that's a relief, because Darryl and his kind are the type of person I never wanted to be. I'm sad to report that Darryl is doing well, despite deserving the worst for picking on Ben so much. He's running his parents' company and living it up, but surely it's just a matter of time before a sexual assault lawsuit takes him down.

Darryl appears in: *Summer* and *Winter*

David Henry – See Connor (boyfriend)

Davis Milton-Cross –see either Allison Cross (mother) or Brian Milton (father) … I know what you're thinking. My own son and I don't give him a full profile? Personally, I'm hoping he doesn't become a major character in one of Jay Bell's books, since that requires a life overburdened by drama.

Doug Phillips – see Kelly (son)

Dwight Courtney – see Nathaniel (brother)

Ella Wyman – see Tim (son)

Emma Trout
Born: May 4th, 1995
Height: 5'9"
Build: Big and beautiful!
Other physical traits: Her longtime girlfriend, Bonnie, described her as handsome, which I found charming. And apt. I wouldn't say Emma is androgynous or masculine. Think Xena the Warrior Princess. That kind of handsome.
Hobbies and interests: Musicals, fashion, football, and telling the occasional fib.
Noteworthy relatives: Michelle (mother), Greg (father), Jace Holden (uncle), Preston (brother), Sylvester (brother)
Motto/Quote: "Whatever you say remains the truth until proven otherwise."
Bio: Before meeting Emma, I had heard plenty of stories about her from her mother, some of them proud, the majority exasperated, because she tends to get into trouble a lot. So when I was finally introduced to Emma, I was expecting a brat or

someone determined to go against her parents' wishes. As it turns out, Emma is a very bright girl and extremely personable. I found myself liking her almost instantly. Her intelligence can be disarming, especially for someone so young. She asked more questions than she answered, not that she held back exactly. Only the topic of her uncle, Jace, made her shake her head and hold her tongue, but I suppose that's understandable. Emma was much more eager to talk about Jason Grant, her best friend, or Tim and Ben, who are both honorary uncles to her. She seems to value family, which might be why she's so determined to seek out a worthy partner.

Emma appears in: *Autumn, Spring,* and *Lightning*

Eric Conroy (note: This is another profile Tim insisted on writing.)
Born: April 22nd, 1944
Height: 5'6" but he sure seemed taller when feeling happy.
Build: Thin, although once you saw him hauling around pans and stuff, you'd notice he had some muscle on him. Just not much. Not compared to me, at least.
Other physical traits: I loved his eyes. They were always so intent, like you could tell he was really listening to you. Or just paying attention to how you were, even during those silent times we spent together. He had a way of making you feel special. His hair was charcoal grey, and this one time he talked about dyeing it, but I wouldn't let him because it looked so dignified. I hope I'm even half that handsome when I reach his age.
Hobbies and interests: He loved art. Not like people who get snotty about what's good and what isn't. Eric knew his stuff, but he was open-minded. Likewise when it came to cooking and his appreciation of delicacies. That never stopped him from hogging out on pizza or a bowl of Lucky Charms.
Noteworthy relatives: He had a father (Mac), and a mother (Gina), and a sister, but I don't remember her name. They weren't real close.
Motto/Quote: I can't choose. He told me so many things that stuck with me, like how we never stop coming out, or how love never truly fades.
Bio: Eric was a native Texan who had some pretty awesome parents, because they accepted him in an era when being gay wasn't smiled upon. I thought I had it rough when I was growing up, but I'm pretty sure his situation was worse, or would have

been if the people in his life had been different. Eric managed to find love, and the way he told it, he felt like he was pioneering something new. The guys he was with didn't always appreciate him, which still pisses me off. Eric wouldn't want me to feel that way. He was so cool about the past, like he had accepted it and moved on. His feelings would still get hurt though, such as when I showed up in his life as part of a fraternity prank. I didn't realize what I was doing at the time, or that he would become so important to me. Eric always picked me up when I was down and made me feel worthwhile. Some of the stuff I did after he was gone, I don't think he'd be proud of, but without him I'm not sure I would have believed in myself. I might not have tried to become a better person. I still think of him all the time, especially when I need advice. I miss you, Eric. I never stopped needing you.

Eric appears in: *Winter* and *Yesterday*

Gabriel Porter
Born: December 15th, 1945
Height: 5'11"
Build: Trim and fit, especially considering his age.
Other physical traits: Gabriel carries and conducts himself like a gentlemen. His formal but stylish attire supports this image. I found myself taken by his easy smile.
Hobbies and interests: Fine spirits, politics, and sailing.
Noteworthy relatives: n/a
Motto/Quote: "Fight for change in your lifetime so that future generations can focus on more important issues."
Bio: I thought Tim might want to tackle this profile too, but he said he didn't trust himself, whatever that means. Having met Gabriel, I'm even more puzzled, because I found him to be charming. He had quite a few stories to tell, such as protesting the Vietnam War back in the sixties, or having adventures while in Canada where he fled to escape the draft. He seems to share Tim's love for Eric, having nothing but praise for the man. In fact, he even said that—although marriage between two men wasn't legal back then—he often thinks of Eric as his ex-husband. Gabriel is also capable of admitting his shortcomings, claiming that he isn't the relationship type, but the young guy smiling at his side seemed to think otherwise.

Gabriel appears in: *Yesterday*

Gina Conroy – see Eric (son)

Greg Trout
Born: November 15th, 1972
Height: 6'1"
Build: He's the Brawny man.
Other physical traits: No seriously, he's the Brawny Man. The newer one, not the truck driver with the mustache. I couldn't get that image out of my head the first time I met him.
Hobbies and interests: Much like the Brawny Man, he's an outdoorsy type, which makes it sort of ironic that he's a real estate agent for high-income homes. I bet he spends his entire weekend tromping around in the woods, then goes back to the suburbs on the weekdays.
Noteworthy relatives: Michelle (wife), Emma (daughter), Preston (son), Sylvester (son)
Motto/Quote: "A man is nothing without his family. They are his greatest treasure. … Make sure my wife reads this, okay?"
Bio: Greg hails from Warrensburg, Missouri, which he assures me is a little slice of heaven. While growing up there he met his best friend, Jace, and his future wife, Michelle, which just happened to be Jace's sister. He eventually moved to Houston because both he and Michelle wanted to be closer to Jace. While there, Greg found remarkable success in the real estate market, but he still dreams of returning to Warrensburg and developing land to help make the town as famous as he feels it deserves to be.
Greg appears in: *Autumn, Spring,* and *Fall*

Heath Courtney – see Nathaniel (son)

Jace Holden
Born: April 2nd, 1973
Height: 6'2"
Build: Tall and lean, but Ben assures me he had enough meat on him for some serious cuddling.
Other physical traits: He looked especially dapper in an airline uniform. I always envied those high cheekbones too.
Hobbies and interests: Reading biographies, eating fortune cookies, worshiping cats.
Noteworthy Relatives: Michelle (sister), Serena (mother), Bob

(father), Emma (niece), Ben (husband)

Motto/quote: "Hold close those you love most, especially if they're furry and grey or musical and gay." (Ben informs me that Jace came up with this one morning and spent most of the day laughing while repeating it. A talented poet he was not!)

Bio: Many people offered to write this profile, which itself is a testament to just how good a man Jace Holden was. Michelle, his sister, spoke about his upbringing in Warrensburg, Missouri, where he never got in trouble for bullying another student or for talking back to teachers. Pranks, on the other hand, or not paying attention in class because he was too busy dreaming of other places—those were the harmless sort of issues Jace had. When he met Victor Hemingway in his teen years, Jace was willing to break just about any rule to spend time with him. I'm sure that only helped cement their relationship because from what Michelle tells me, Victor disapproved of rules.

That Jace willingly broke off this relationship when it became too hurtful shows great maturity. Adrian, his college boyfriend, certainly seemed to think so. He described Jace as being inexperienced, but still an old soul. Adrien might have tutored him about life's finer aspects—food, wine, and culture—but he says that Jace already knew the most important of life's lessons: He understood people. He sympathized with them and treated them accordingly. Adrien says it was many years before he started realizing those same truths. He regrets that not learning them sooner led to the end of their relationship.

I can't say I share those regrets because I saw firsthand what a positive force Jace was in the life of my best friend. For most of the time Ben was growing up, he had an edge of sorrow that stemmed from feeling alone. A brief reprieve from this occurred when he and Tim were together, but not until Ben met Jace did he finally seem fulfilled. I was happy for him, and for myself too, because being around Jace was always a pleasure. He was a gentleman. Jace wasn't perfect, no matter what anyone might say. He was just as human as the rest of us. The only difference is how he conducted himself. Jace was a class act, no matter the situation, and no one made him happier than Ben. While I wish his life had been longer, I take solace in knowing that Jace lived out his days with the man he loved most. And for the record, Ben also volunteered to write this entry. You should have seen him sitting at the kitchen table, hands trembling above the keyboard, eyes watery. He did end up writing, and from what I understand it took the form of a letter, but in the end Ben felt it was too personal to share. I respect that, and hope you do too. I just don't want anyone questioning Ben's devotion. Have no doubt, Jace Holden was dearly loved.

Jace appears in: *Summer, Winter, Autumn, Spring, Fall, Eternity,* and *Hell's Pawn*

Jared Holt (Kelly kindly offered to handle this entry for me.)
Born: May 20th, 1990
Height: 5'11"
Build: Fairly average, really.
Other physical traits: His smile used to cause my stomach to do somersaults, and I loved how my bed would smell after he stayed the night.
Hobbies and interests: He was a big fan of those sports talk shows, and anything with Rowan Atkinson in it. And sadly, he was very interested in girls.
Noteworthy relatives: n/a
Motto/Quote: "It's totally possible to outrun failure. Just watch me!"
Bio: Straight boys. If you're a gay man, chances are you have one of these in your past. That guy you fell in love with when you were still awkward and lonely and thought that you would never meet another gay person. At least not one like you, still nervous about that first kiss or the idea of holding hands in public. I can't pretend to be so innocent, or use that as an excuse, because I *had* experienced many of those things. Still, he was my best friend. There was nobody in the world I enjoyed spending my time with more. It's only natural I should fall in love with him. Such things can't be helped. We all know nothing's going to happen—that no matter how bad we love our straight guys, it won't change who they are. I can give you some advice though. Once you get out there in the world and have a few relationships, someday you'll look back on that guy and feel a little puzzled that you cared at all. I understand why Jared and I were friends. That's easy. But now I get that he and I never would have made it, even if he had been gay. There are some amazing gay men out there, so stop chasing what you'll never catch and go find someone who can love you back.
Jared appears in: *Lightning*

Jason Grant
Born: March 18th, 1990
Height: 5'11"
Build: Extremely muscular, the handsomest guy you've ever seen, and tan all year round. (Jason promised to mow my lawn for free if I said this.)
Other physical traits: He's got messy hair, which is endearing, and intense eyes that drive the boys wild. And no, I wasn't bribed to say that!
Hobbies and interests: Jason loves horror movies, classic rock, and his guitar. He's an animal nut too.
Noteworthy relatives: Ben (father), Tim (father), Allison (honorary aunt)
Motto/Quote: "You *can* choose your family. Don't let anyone tell you otherwise."
Bio: Jason has been one big happy surprise for us all. Being an only child, I never expected to have nieces or nephews, or for them to be so white, but goodness do I love this boy! Jason had a rough start in life, being put into foster care at a young age. He spent most of his life bouncing from family to family, and as much as I sympathize, I'm glad this meant he eventually reached us. He fits right in. Much like Ben, who is one of his fathers, Jason is a fool for love. This manifested as unrequited crushes until he met Caesar Hubbard. When that didn't work out, he spent years pining over the guy, just like a certain someone did with Tim. And speaking of Mr. Wyman, he's not the only one who is prone to making tons of mistakes in the pursuit of love. Jason shares that attribute with him. They both tend to hide their feelings and rely on deceit to get what they want. That's two bad habits, and I'm proud to say that both Jason and Tim seem to have learned their lessons. Now if only we can get Jason and William to settle down together, but that of course has been a drama of its own. All I know is our lives are better thanks to Jason being in them. Welcome home, kiddo!
Jason appears in: *Spring, Lightning, Thunder,* and *Fall*

Karen Bentley – see Benjamin (brother) … Girl would have gotten a full entry if she hadn't ditched me back in junior high. But hey, I ended up with a much better friend in her brother, so no hard feelings. And no full entry. Ha!

Kelly Phillips
Born: November 22nd, 1990
Height: 6'
Build: He has a slender runner's build that he still maintains to this day. Hm. Maybe I should get out there and run some laps.
Other physical traits: Kelly was a model, but that doesn't tell you much. Female models fit into a fairly generic template, but male models get the job because of something exceptional about their appearance. In Kelly's case, I think it's the way he can cut through the air with a razor sharp stare, or make a sneer seem like the sexiest expression in the world. The boy has fiery passion and it shows.
Hobbies and interests: Photography, competitive sports, and travelling.
Noteworthy relatives: Royal (brother), Laisha (mother), Doug (father)
Motto/Quote: "When anger stops serving a purpose, it's time to start forgiving, beginning with yourself."
Bio: Some of my clients I like so much that I feel guilty for charging them. Kelly is chief among these. I met him when he was a troubled teenager on the verge of a serious drug addiction. He was also suffering from post traumatic stress due to a horrific accident. Most of all, he was angry. That can be beneficial when appropriately directed, but not in this case. Kelly, despite how comfortable he is with expressing his frustration (vehemently at times), is an extremely self-reliant person. If he has a problem with someone else, he expects no one but him to fix it. This usually means driving them away with sharp words, or torturing himself trying to find an impossible solution. Any relationship, no matter the nature of it, requires both parties to communicate and work together to solve issues. Especially romantic relationships, like the one he had with William Townson, which went on much longer than it should have. Kelly is just as smart as he is athletic and artistic. He learns from his mistakes, and with a little guidance, he left his next boyfriend, Nathaniel Courtney, at a much healthier interval. As complicated as his relationships with others have been, I've seen Kelly thrive over the years, moving from one passion to the next and never letting any of life's setbacks keep him down for long.
Kelly appears in: *Spring, Lightning, Thunder,* and *Tonight*

Krista Norman
Born: July 2nd, 1979
Height: 5'4"
Build: She was always a wispy little thing.
Other physical traits: Blonde and perky with a deer-in-headlights expression.
Hobbies and interests: Whatever you like. Seriously.
Noteworthy relatives: n/a
Motto/Quote: "What's that supposed to mean?" (not meant rhetorically)
Bio: I've been awfully hard on the people Tim Wyman used to hang out with back in high school. Considering that Krista was his girlfriend much of the time that Tim was also involved with Ben, you would probably expect me to hate her. But let me tell you another story. I shared a social studies class with Krista, and we were partnered up once. None of her friends were in this class, which made her seem a little lost. Some people are born leaders. Krista was born a follower. Away from the influence of her friends, she was a lot nicer. I could tell from the beginning that she was watching me for signals of what I expected from her, but I tried to keep these minimal, and I felt I got a glimpse of the real her. A little insecure, but gentle and able to laugh at her own shortcomings. I even started thinking of her as a friend. That all changed when I saw her in the hall with her usual posse. Suddenly I was invisible, but despite that slight, I wish her well. Some Facebook stalking revealed tons of photos of Krista with her children, and one post where she talked about being a single mom, but she sure looked happy in all those images. Good for her!
Krista appears in: *Summer* and *Winter*

Laisha Phillips – see Kelly (son)

Layne – He attends the same youth group that Jason and Kelly do. He has a notorious sense of humor and a flair for the dramatic. Frankly, I found out a lot more than that about him, but Jay Bell asked me to keep this one brief. Why? I could speculate, and if I'm correct, it means Layne should probably head for the hills before his life gets any more dramatic than it already is.

Lisa – A shy but personable girl from the youth group Jason and Kelly attended. I've been asked to keep this one brief too. Poor kids. They won't know what hit them!

Mac Conroy – see Eric (son)

Marcello Maltese: Ah, excellent. Are you recording?

Allison: Yes, although just focus on talking to me. I'll extract all the relevant information later on.

Marcello: Extract? This isn't an interview?

Allison: No. I'm writing profiles on all the people who—

Marcello: If it's profiling you want, you might as well contact the police or any number of intelligence agencies. They've already done the work for you.

Allison: Ha! Wait, you're not kidding, are you?

Marcello: I'm the most solemn person you'll ever meet. Now if you don't mind, there is much that demands my attention.

Allison: Wait! Would you be willing to do an interview instead?

Marcello: I thought you'd never ask. First question, please.

Allison: Okay. Um… When were you born?

Marcello: Next question, please.

Allison: Seriously? I need to know this. Everyone else has answered.

Marcello: Although I do not employ it often, I am not beyond discretion.

Allison: I could contact the DMV, if you would prefer. I have a client who works there, and they owe me a favor. I'm sure they could provide me with your date of birth. Then I'll publish it for everyone to see.

Marcello: Fine, fine. If you must know, my fiftieth is coming up soon. Oh how I dread it!

Allison: That's funny, because I've been to one of your birthday parties, and if I recall, *that* was supposed to be your fiftieth.

Marcello: Ah yes! Roughly ten years ago, wasn't it?

Allison: Exactly.

Marcello: Then you must be mistaken and attended my fortieth. Numbers don't lie.

Allison: No, but I'm starting to think you do.

Marcello: Wonderful! We've gotten to know each other already!

Allison: Moving on. How tall are you?

Marcello: That depends on slipper or shoe, sandal or sock. I'm rarely barefoot. Too many fetishists around, eager to objectify me. Story of my life, really.

Allison: We'll get there. But first... Oh, never mind. I'll do it myself.

Marcello: What are you writing?

Allison: I'm describing your build.

Marcello: What did you put down?

Allison: Voluptuous.

Marcello: Oh, I like you! Now I regret having you thrown out earlier. Complete misunderstanding. Tim was so kind to call and clear it all up, don't you think? Anyway, be sure to include that I have a full head of thick silky hair that reaches my shoulders. Mention my movie star good looks too. Rock Hudson! Compare me to him! People will believe anything so long as it's in print.

Allison: So, any hobbies or interests?

Marcello: Where to begin? All aspects of beauty appeal to me, but none more so than the masculine form. This encompasses all mediums; Canvas... Clay... Flesh... Especially flesh. I'm sure you've seen a painting that inspired you to declare, "My goodness! It's so lifelike!" Well, why not go to the source? Live nude models! Just picture them standing around galleries and museums, bringing much-needed warmth to an otherwise frigid environment. What better way to get the blood pumping and the eye excited for art? You know, I might be on to something!

Allison: Or on something. What can you tell me about your family?

Marcello: Only that they had exceptionally bad taste.

Allison: Meaning?

Marcello: They chose to be rid of me shortly after I was born.

Allison: You're an orphan? I'm sorry. Not that there's—

Marcello: It's fine. Everyone should have a family. That's how nature intended our species to develop. I'm less concerned with the beginning of the story though. I'd rather know how it ends. That's what I've been waiting to see, although I hope I have a few chapters left in me yet.

Allison: But if we could go back to your childhood momentarily and—

Marcello: You're heard the expression, life begins at forty?

Allison: Yes.

Marcello: Let's keep it that way.

Allison: Okay, the present. If I'm not mistaken, you run a successful media business.

Marcello: Studio Maltese, yes.

Allison: And this is how you met Tim. He modeled for you, right?

Marcello: I met Tim through my dear friend Eric. Oh, how I loved Eric! There was a kindred spirit, one who understood that in life you should not only stop to smell the roses, but the champagne, the fine food, and the skin of anyone willing to let you get close enough. Of course his appetite was never as vigorous as mine. Like a bird in all things, Eric was, able to savor even the smallest delights, despite having so much.

Allison: You sound as though you admired him.

Marcello: Greatly. Oh yes.

Allison: And speaking of love, do you have anyone special in your life?

Marcello: Yes. Would you like a list? I keep one, you know, dating all the way back to my very first fumblings at summer camp.

Allison: That's not exactly what I meant. Is there anyone you love on a more emotional level?

Marcello: Have you met Nathaniel Courtney? I bet you haven't reached him on your list quite yet. You seem the type to go in alphabetical order, and you're much too informal to give priority to last names. Am I wrong?

Allison: Um… So anyway, tell me about Nathaniel.

Marcello: I see in him a young man so dissatisfied with the cards life dealt him that he stood up, knocked over the table, and punched the dealer. Nathaniel is ruthless in business and kind in all other arenas. That's a rare combination. He'll do well for himself. I'll see to that.

Allison: I'm not sure that makes sense, but none of this really has. Is there any sort of motto you live your life by? Anything you would like written on your tombstone?

Marcello: How about: "If you're going to piss on my grave, at least make sure you're facing the right direction so I can watch. And don't forget to shake." What do you think?

Allison: Try again.

Marcello: Very well. "We live in a world of give and take, but that's not necessarily a bad thing. Give others your time and confidence, take away their concerns and loneliness when you can. Give them a piece of yourself when feeling brave, and take their love and cherish it when offered. Life is an exchange, an open market, so get out there and start living before the store closes permanently."

Allison: That's… That's surprisingly good advice!

Marcello: Thank you. Now then, why don't you join me for a drink? I've got something delightfully bubbly to tickle your nose!

Marcello appears in: *Summer, Winter, Spring, Lightning, Thunder, Fall,* and *Yesterday*

Michael Schwartzer – I'm afraid I couldn't find out much about him, other than he used to date Eric Conroy back when they were in college. Tim gave me a grumpy face when I asked for details, sort of like he did when I was trying to figure out who Carla is. I'm tempted to tell Ben and get Tim in trouble, but knowing my best friend, he'll only find it sexy that Tim is being so mysterious and withdrawn.

Michelle Trout (born: Holden)
Born: August 14th, 1974
Height: 5'10"
Build: She's slender and tall, but she still has curves in all the right places. Not that I'm into her like that! She's my friend. We've got a female bromance going on. Homance? Er…
Other physical traits: People often comment that she and Jace look alike. It's true, and yet that somehow works to both their advantages.
Hobbies and interests: She has a PEZ dispenser collection that is slowly getting out of control, and she's crazy about coming-of-age movies, but aside from those two things, she's mostly sane.
Noteworthy relatives: Jace (brother), Greg (husband), Emma (daughter), Preston, (son), Sylvester (son)
Motto/Quote: "If we all agreed to take care of each other, it would end all suffering."
Bio: Michelle has a good head on her shoulders. Sometimes she chooses to use it. Ha! I like to give her a hard time, but really, she's one of the coolest people I've ever met. She grew up in Warrensburg, Missouri, had an awesome brother, and married

a handsome guy with a well-paying job. If she wanted, she could have had a fairy-tale life free of worry, but instead she works in one of the most emotionally taxing jobs imaginable—child welfare. My clients come to me for help by choice. Child Protective Services is the complete opposite. Nobody wants this agency in their life, but that doesn't discourage her, because she wants all children to have the same quality of life she provides for her own. People often focus on her brother and how perfect he seemed, but come on! Michelle is just as amazing. Perhaps even more so. BFF!

Michelle appears in: *Autumn, Spring, Thunder* and *Tonight*

Nana (I asked for her real name, but she just patted my hand and said "I am your Nana")
Born: January 26th, 1936
Height: 5'1"
Build: She's a grandmother, meaning she isn't exactly skinny. I suppose she would need muscle to carry around someone like Tim, which honestly, I can still picture her doing even though he's all grown up.
Other physical traits: She piles her hair high on her head, perhaps to make herself appear taller, and she still dresses like someone in her thirties. I think she looks fabulous!
Hobbies and interests: Crocheting, foreign languages, and soap operas (during which she refused to listen or speak to me).
Noteworthy relatives: Tim Wyman (grandson), Ella Wyman (daughter)
Motto/Quote: "Good things happen, bad things happen. That's life. You decide if you want to be happy or not. The rest is in God's hands."
Bio: Tim offered to write this entry, but my journalistic integrity wouldn't allow it. I insisted on flying down to Mexico City to be with her, and I could hardly leave my child and husband behind, right? I don't understand why Jay Bell threw a fit when I asked him to reimburse my expenses. Anyway, I first met Nana at Ben and Tim's wedding, and I found her unforgettable. Disney should base a fairy godmother on her because that's what she reminds me of, albeit one with modern sensibilities. Nana has had a lifetime of love and loss, but she hasn't let it wear her down. She seems to have learned from each experience and allowed them to

make her stronger. I sometimes wondered how Tim managed to turn out all right, but after meeting Nana that question has been answered. If he's got some of her somewhere in his DNA, no wonder he found his footing. I've met older people who shake their heads at the world and complain about how things used to be better. Nana would rather hug the world. She treats everyone she meets like one of her children, and trust me when I say that's a wonderful feeling.

Nana appears in: *Winter* and *Spring*

Nathaniel Courtney
Born: June 6th, 1986
Height: 6'2"
Build: He's one giant hunk of a man, that's for sure!
Other physical traits: Nathaniel has a tendency to scowl when feeling defensive, or angry, or thoughtful, or maybe even calm. The only time I saw him not scowl was when he was looking at Kelly.
Hobbies and interests: All aspects of film-making.
Noteworthy relatives: Star Courtney (mother), Dwight Courtney (brother), Heath Courtney (father), ??? (biological father)
Motto/Quote: "Don't let anything stand in your way. Shove it aside, even if that includes facets of yourself."
Bio: I've only had one professional session with Nathaniel, which I obviously can't divulge the details of. I will say that some people are so resistant to the idea of counseling that sessions become counterproductive. I do feel comfortable in relating something that happened later, when I asked for more details of Nathaniel's past for the profile. He wasn't comfortable discussing his biological father, which explains the dramatic triple question mark above, but he did talk enthusiastically about his mother. His fondness for her helped break the ice, because soon Nathaniel was discussing his strained relationship with his brother, and how many of his relationship issues can be traced back to what he and Caesar Hubbard had together in their youth. None of this seemed to matter as much as Kelly does. The level of dedication and love Nathaniel feels for him is undeniable, so I made one more request: Try sitting on my couch one more time. He declined, which has me concerned for their future together.
Nathaniel appears in: *Spring, Lightning, Thunder,* and *Eternity*

Peter Hubbard – See Caesar (brother)

Preston Trout – See Michelle (mother)

Rachel Hemingway – See Victor (son)

Rebecca Obst – Rebecca came up in conversation when I was speaking with Nathaniel. She was his best friend in high school and college until some event caused them to become estranged. She declined to meet, but she did ask me to pass on her apologies to Nathaniel, and to say that she misses him still.
Rebecca appears in: *Thunder*

Royal Phillips – See Kelly (brother)

Ryan Hamilton
Born: September 12th, 1984
Height: 5'10"
Build: Ryan wasn't looking so good when I met him. I'm not sure he's eating enough.
Other physical traits: I can tell he was handsome once, and could be still if he didn't look so tired. The prison tattoos are slightly off-putting, with the word "love" tattooed on one hand, a letter for each knuckle.
Hobbies and interests: He used to party all the time and had a thing for drugs. Whatever his interests are now, they are limited to what a person can do behind bars.
Noteworthy relatives: n/a
Motto/Quote: "They say forgiveness starts with yourself, but that would be easier if others would forgive you first."
Bio: I have to admit, this was the profile I was dreading most. Sure I had to write about some high school bullies and such, but this guy… He pointed a gun at my best friend. Had things played out differently, it chills me to think what might have happened. I had never met Ryan before, and when visiting the prison, I wondered if I might come to sympathize with him. Surely something in his past drove him to drugs and violence. He was open to discussing it all, his hands clenching as he spoke. His family had money growing up, they put pressure on him

to be successful, and they weren't accepting of his sexuality. That's about it, and sure, it's rough to have unsupportive parents. But so what? Few of the people I've written about in these profiles had perfect upbringings, but none of them are junkies or violent criminals. Hell, Tim comes from almost the exact same background, and he's doing fine. Ryan noted this too. He spoke a lot about Tim—how they have so much in common and how that was the reason Tim took him in. "He was trying to fix himself." Or so Ryan claims. I'm not sure it's true. I think Tim saw someone young and vulnerable and simply wanted to help. Tim didn't deserve what he got. At least it's all in the past now. Or should be. Ryan asked me over and over to reach out to Tim on his behalf, insisting that they needed to speak, that it was an important part of his healing process. I don't care if it is. He isn't getting to Tim through me, that's for sure.

Ryan appears in: *Summer, Winter,* and *Spring*

Samson
Born: October 2nd, 1995
Height: 9"
Build: He always looked a little chunky to me, but it's never a good idea to tell a pet owner that their animal is overweight. They're blind to the facts and will respond as if you're being cruel.
Other physical traits: He was definitely cute. Grey fur and orange eyes.
Hobbies and interests: He's a cat. They just eat and sleep. Right? I've never had one, so I don't know.
Noteworthy relatives: Jace (father)
Motto/Quote: "Meow! Purrr purrr purrr." Geez. I can't believe I just wrote that!
Bio: (note: Ben felt the poem on the following page should be included here. He found it tucked away in one of Jace's books, in his handwriting. Ben also made sure to point out that Jace never wrote *him* a poem, but he's trying not to take it personally.)

Ode to a Cat
by Jace Holden

Always claiming the best seat, a furry self-crowned king,
Always sleeping until I need rest, then suddenly demanding.
Playing hissing jumping, leaping clawing thumping.
Then to the litter box, stinky smells and gleeful kicking.
No need for restraint, father will do all the sweeping!

Why do I put up with such abuse, you thoughtless creature with no use?
That's it, I'm finished, I'm through! There will be no more me and you!
Then gentle feet pad across the floor, one brief hop into my lap for more.
This time love, a tickle behind the ear. Oh how I love when you are near!
Rest assured, my purring little friend, for you and me there is no end.
You're my son and I your dad, your kneading paws make us both so glad.

Samson appears in: *Summer, Winter, Autumn, Spring, Eternity,* and *Hell's Pawn*

Serena Holden – Jace (son)

Sheila Courtney
Born: September 8th, 1987
Height: 5′6″
Build: Some mothers give birth to a child and look like they spent the previous nine months in a fitness gym. In other words, I'm jealous.
Other physical traits: She has a bright smile, like every day is a good one.
Hobbies and interests: Martial arts. This seems to be a recent passion.
Noteworthy relatives: Nathaniel (brother-in-law), Arthur (son)
Motto/Quote: "Leaving yourself vulnerable can make those you love vulnerable too."
Bio: I suppose what you really need to know is that she's Nathaniel's sister-in-law, but I could tell there was more to the story once I'd met her. I see a lot of women like her in my line of work. The best of them learn to be strong and happy on their

own. Oh, and it's always a relief to spend time with a mother with a child who is about the same age as mine. Once they get past the bashful introduction, the children play together, giving us a much needed break.

Sheila appears in: *Thunder*

Stacy Shelly
Born: Somewhere in 1979, I presume
Height: I sure felt like she was seven feet tall.
Build: Perfect.
Other physical traits: See above.
Hobbies and interests: Making people cry.
Noteworthy relatives: The thought of there being more people like her in the world terrifies me.
Motto/Quote: Imagine the most terrible thing a person could say. Then imagine the most beautiful woman in the world saying it to you.
Bio: Ben was harassed by quite a few bullies in his high school years, some of them really big guys. I never felt afraid, mostly because none of them would ever physically harm me. They might have been jerks, but even they knew better than to hit a woman. I didn't have that assurance with Stacy Shelly. She wasn't just mean and gorgeous, she was also brilliant. I remember her giving a science report once, rattling off information that even the teacher struggled to keep up with, a smirk on her face the entire time. If Stacy Shelly entered the girl's room, you left. Unless you had a death wish. I was one of the lucky ones. She only made me cry a handful of times. I knew other girls who changed schools or dropped out entirely. So sorry, Jay Bell. I won't be following up on this one to find out where she is now. I'm scared to even Google her name!

Stacy appears in: *Winter* Just one book so far. Please keep it that way!

Star Courtney (born: Denton)
Born: May 19th, 1970
Height: 5'7"
Build: Considering how big her son is, I expected her to be a lot bigger. She appears to be of average size though.
Other physical traits: I'll admit that sometimes when I see hair

that blonde or teeth *that* white, I sometimes draw some very unfair conclusions, but the articles Star has written online range from spiritual issues, cultural differences by country or region, and the inner workings of a healthy marriage. This implies Star is as sharp as she is good looking.

Hobbies and interests: Yoga and travelling.

Noteworthy relatives: Nathaniel Courtney (son)

Motto/Quote: "Love 'em and leave 'em, but only if you can't get them to love you back."

Bio: Star also hails from Warrensburg, Missouri. Small world! But is it *that* small? This woman just happens to come from the same town as Jace, his sister, and also Greg and Victor. I can't help but wonder if she has some connection to one of them. And why did Jay Bell insist that I create a profile for her? It's not like Ben's mother or either of my parents have gotten entries. Unfortunately, Star is located in the northern part of the country, and the only information I gleaned is from a Facebook profile and a blog that hasn't been updated recently. I intend to get to the bottom of this though, and soon.

Star appears in: *Autumn* and *Thunder*

Stephanie Kokkinos (aka Steph)

Born: November 4th, 1989

Height: 5'8"

Build: Hard to say from the photos I saw online, but she seems to keep herself in shape.

Other physical traits: She has wonderful curly hair.

Hobbies and interests: Love and languages. She's a polyglot!

Noteworthy relatives: n/a

Motto/Quote: "If at first you don't succeed, dump his ass and find someone more worthy of your time."

Bio: An interesting side effect of conducting these interviews is how eager some people were to find out what happened to old friends and lovers. I spoke to Steph over the phone, and she spent most of the time asking *me* questions. She wanted to know what happened to Caesar, her high school sweetheart, the only guy she was foolish enough to date repeatedly, even though they obviously weren't compatible. She also asked after Jason Grant, who became one of her closest friends. Sadly they lost touch, but I gave her his contact information. Who knows, maybe these profiles will be responsible for a few reunions! As for Steph herself, she seems to know what she wants and is determined to get it, no matter how many times she has to try. Sounds like there are a few broken hearts in her past. Maybe she has more in common with Caesar than she cares to admit.

Steph appears in: *Spring* and *Thunder*

Sylvester Trout – See Greg (father)

Thomas Wyman – See Tim (son)

Tim Wyman
Born: August 24th, 1979
Height: 6′
Build: He's got muscles, and boy am I tired of hearing about them.
Other physical traits: What Ben calls a winner's smile, I call a shit-eating grin. One thing we agree on—those silver eyes are out of this world!
Hobbies and interests: Painting, jogging, homewrecking. Ha! I kid, I kid…
Noteworthy relatives: Ben (husband), Jason (son), Ella (mother), Thomas (father), Nana (grandmother)
Motto/Quote: "First impressions and second chances? If you keep ruining those, then it's time to take a long hard look in the mirror."
Bio: I like Tim. Let's get that out of the way because I flip-flopped so many times over the years. When he first met Ben, I was wary but also happy for my friend. I saw Tim making an effort, despite still being in the closet, and I was won over completely right about the time he ruined it all. I wasn't thrilled to meet him again in college, and I did my best to keep Ben and Tim apart. Was I wrong? It might seem like it now, but things were complicated back then because whenever Tim got near Ben, he made a mess. Then came a dark time in all our lives, but especially so for Ben. A shadow hung over him for years, and things got bad enough that while I was browsing through old photos, I saw one of Ben looking happy and realized than it had been ages since I'd seen him smile. Tim was in this photo too, lying on the same bed that Ben was perched on, and even though Ben was looking at the

camera—at me—I knew the real reason he was grinning. So I figured what the hell—he couldn't get much sadder. I contacted Tim, not knowing what to expect. Definitely not the mature man I soon met in person. Perfect and well-rounded like Jace had been? Not even close, but Tim was different now. He had the makings of... Brace yourself because this is really cheesy. I felt Tim had the makings of a hero, like he could be the one to sweep in and save Ben from his quiet misery. And he did. Flexing and smiling and strutting around like a peacock, but that had always worked for Ben, and some things never change. Life has only gotten better since then. Ben always insisted there was a side to Tim that no one else saw, that all the love and adoration he felt for him was justified. As time goes by, I keep seeing more and more glimpses of that legendary man, enough that what I feel most for Tim Wyman these days is gratitude.

Tim appears in: *Summer, Winter, Autumn, Spring, Lighting, Thunder, Fall, Yesterday,* and *Eternity*

Todd Hubbard – See Caesar (son)

Victor Hemingway (note: Star Courtney did finally respond to my messages, and despite being nice, she's just as guarded about her past as her son is about his. I was only able to add a few basic facts to her profile above, but while speaking with her, I took the chance to mention the other people from Warrensburg. She reacted strongest to Victor's name and agreed to write down her thoughts about him. What you see below is the result.)
Born: March, 13th, 1972
Height: 5'9"
Build: Victor had little respect for regular mealtimes and rarely seemed concerned about food, so it was a miracle he weighed anything at all.
Other physical traits: He had mismatched eyes, one green and one brown. I thought I was mistaken when I first noticed them, but when I brushed his hair aside—it was longer back then, and without thinking, I just reached out, the tips of my fingers bumping against his forehead before I swept his bangs back, just so I could see better. That was the first time I ever touched him, and I don't care how ridiculous it sounds, I knew then we were meant to be together. In retrospect, maybe I was wrong.

Hobbies and interests: I'm tempted to say "debating" and leave it at that because Victor was the most contrary person I ever met. He loved ideas, and his favorite way of exploring them was to argue every little point.

Noteworthy relatives: His mother's name was Rachel. He also had a cousin named Donny, who must have come from somewhere. I'm afraid that's all I know.

Motto/Quote: It's hard to choose, so I'll go with one that haunts me. After one of our heated debates, I was feeling both exhausted and stupid because I couldn't keep up with him. I said as much, and Victor just shook his head and said, "You'll do more in your life than I ever will. Actions are permanent; everything else is fleeting." He seemed genuinely proud of me when he said this, and at times I tried to live up to his expectations, but now I look back on that moment with an edge of sorrow because he was right. I just wish he hadn't been.

Bio: Once upon a time, I met a guy at a party, except it wasn't much of a party. Just a bunch of teenagers hanging out in an unfinished basement. The guy was really just a boy, but I didn't know it at the time. Victor was only thirteen when we met, and when I found out his true age the next day, I was embarrassed to have fallen for someone so young. I was fifteen, which seemed a great deal older at the time. Looking back, we were both just children. Regardless, I fell for him on that first night, so no matter how embarrassed I might have been, for me it was too late. Victor was a thinker. I'm sure you've met someone like him before. Loves to talk, has a number of weird ideas you've never considered. Chances are he or she smokes a lot and mostly ignores their environment, not worrying about things like dusting or vacuuming or staying fit. I can't help but wonder if these people have it right. Our thoughts and connections with each other matter most, don't they? That should be our priority? I'm sure if Victor were still here today, he would tell you. You can tell by now that this story doesn't have a happy ending. Victor's troubles only increased the older he became, but I like to think back to those early months he and I spent together. We stole so many moments, just for us, and at times we stopped talking and our bodies took control. I loved being in his arms, and I often wished it would last forever. The world had other ideas, but Victor was right. Actions are permanent, and he did more than just talk with me. In that way his legacy lives on. So the next time you meet one of those strange people who so easily challenge your ideas while neglecting everything around them, cherish your time with them, because as much as it saddens me to say it, this world isn't meant for philosophers.

Victor appears in: *Autumn* and *Eternity*

William Townson
Born: September 30th, 1990
Height: 6'1"
Build: He might be in the Coast Guard, but he sure has the body of a Marine!
Other physical traits: Just picture the ultimate Boy Scout. If you need more than that, imagine a blond guy with green eyes who swims all the time. Now take away the tan, because this boy is always pale.
Hobbies and interests: Swimming, and something called the Beast Wars. Is that like the Pokémon? I should ask Davis. He would probably know. Oh, and you would think a sailor would be good at cards, or maybe I'm getting better because I totally robbed William blind over a game of poker the other night.
Noteworthy relatives: n/a
Motto/Quote: "Deny the darkness inside yourself or face it head on. Either way you'll find yourself haunted by it."
Bio: I heard about William long before I met him. Mostly from Kelly, who spent many sessions on my couch trying to make sense of their relationship. I can't say I got the best impression of William then. Kelly had plenty of good things to say about him, but reading between the lines is part of my job. When they decided to go their separate ways, it didn't take long before another guy was heartbroken over him—this time my nephew Jason. Once, before he moved out on his own, I found Jason sitting out by the pool. He was fully dressed, sitting cross-legged and perched on the very edge like he intended to plunge in and needed to work up the courage. He wasn't even dangling his feet in the water, so I asked him what he was doing. "Smelling the chlorine." That's all he said. I thought maybe it was some new way of getting high, so I went inside and asked Ben, who explained: William smells like chlorine, and William is far far away, so that's the closest Jason could get. Sad, I know. Perhaps

because of this, I imagined William to be something of a heartbreaker. When I finally met him, I discovered a soft-spoken, polite, and genuinely nice person. It didn't take me long to warm to him, especially since he seemed determined to make up for lost time in regard to Jason. I even joked with him that he'd soon be my nephew-in-law. Life sure is full of twists and turns, and now that possibility doesn't seem so likely. I'm still holding out hope, because William really is a nice guy. At least I think he is...

William appears in: *Spring, Lightning, Thunder,* and will tell his story in *Rain*

Zero (note: All I was given was a name and a point of contact. The following is a transcript of the telephone conversation.)

Allison: Hi, Nathaniel. Thanks for taking another of my calls. What can you tell me about this Zero person?

Nathaniel: Seriously?

Allison: Yes.

Nathaniel: He's a dog.

Allison: Oh.

Nathaniel: Why are you profiling animals? I thought you were a therapist, not a vet.

Allison: I'm just running down the list I was given. So anyway, when was he born? How tall is he?

Nathaniel: He's a dog.

Allison: We've established that. Do you always have to be such a grump?

Nathaniel: How would you react if someone called you and started asking about your pets?

Allison: I don't have any pets. My son Davis goes feral at times, so I suppose that's close. And if someone called to ask about him and I knew they weren't some creep, I'd be happy to talk because I love him.

Nathaniel: I love Zero. A lot. You wouldn't believe how much.

Allison: More than you love Kelly?

Nathaniel: Heh. Ummm... I don't have to answer that, do I?

Allison: Give me a little more on Zero, and Kelly will never hear about this.

Nathaniel: He's a Siberian Husky, and at one point in my life, he had the unenviable duty of keeping me happy. These days, it's all about him, because he's done his time. You really don't have pets? I can't imagine being without them.

Allison: I have more than enough living souls to take care of, believe me. You've been very helpful. Thanks.

Nathaniel: Wait! Can you put in Zero's profile that he's the best dog ever?

Allison: I could, but another guy already asked me to say the same thing about his dog.

Nathaniel: I'll give you five bucks.

Allison: No deal. But if you would agree to meet me one more time… Just to talk. Kelly loves you. He just wants to make sure that you'll be okay.

Nathaniel: I don't belong in therapy.

Allison: I'm a counselor. Sometimes it helps to have someone to talk to. A neutral party. And even if you think it won't help you, I'm pretty sure it will help Kelly.

Nathaniel: Well, when you put it like that… Yeah. Okay. Just don't forget—best dog ever. And while you're at it, make sure to put that Kelly is the best boyfriend ever. Actually, when will this be published?

Allison: Months and months from now.

Nathaniel: In that case, you might as well make it fiancé. Or husband because if he says yes, I'm not waiting any longer than I have to. So yeah. Put that Kelly is the best husband ever. Just don't ruin the surprise for him. Okay?

Allison: My lips are sealed.

Zero appears in: *Lightning* and *Thunder*

The *Something Like...* Timeline

Hello! Jay Bell here. The more convoluted the *Something Like...* series becomes, the more messages I get asking for an official timeline. I would love to present you with one that uses fancy graphics, or better yet, an online version that lets you select from various options to alter the way you view the data. Maybe that will happen someday. Any programmers out there? In the meantime, here you'll find a rather primitive list of key events and the corresponding dates. The timeline below documents the year main characters met their romantic partners and—depending on how things played out—when they got married or split up. It also includes deaths and a handful of other significant happenings. The approximate age of each character is found in brackets after their names, although I did try to take their birth month into consideration. That's why some characters might appear to be the same age during some events, or a year apart in others. You'll also see, written in italics, where each full-length novel begins. I make no effort to avoid spoilers here, so be warned. While this isn't the super-deluxe timeline I'd like to offer you someday, I hope you'll find it interesting regardless, especially when realizing what simultaneous events occurred in the same year, albeit in separate books. It's strange to think that Victor took his life in the same year Ben and Tim first met, or that when Ben is finding love with Jace, Tim is also finding a comforting presence in Eric.

1965
Eric [21] meets Michael [20]

1966
Eric [22] and Michael [21] breakup

1967
Eric [23] meets Gabriel [22]

1977
Eric [33] and Gabriel [31] start dating
1985
Star [15] conceives with Victor [13]

1990
Beginning of Autumn
Jace [17] meets Victor [18]

1991
Jace [18] and Victor [19] breakup

1994
Eric [50] and Gabriel [49] split up

1995
Jace [22] is reunited with Victor [23]
Jace [22] breaks up with Adrien [22]
Jace [22] meets Samson [0]

1996
Beginning of Summer
Beginning of Winter
Ben [16] meets Tim [16]
Victor [23] takes his own life
Jace [22] applies to be a flight attendant

1997
Ben [17] breaks up with Tim [17]

1999
Jace [26] meets Ben [20]
Tim [20] meets Eric [55] and Marcello [??]

2000
Jace [26] moves to Austin to be with Ben [20]
Tim [20] runs into Allison [21]

2001
Eric [57] passes away

2002
Ben [22] and Tim [22] meet again in their final year of college

2003
Tim [23] meets Ryan [19]

2004
Beginning of Thunder
Ben [24] and Jace [31] get married
Nathaniel [18] and Caesar [16] break up for the first time

2005
Ben [25] and Tim [25] meet for the third time
Tim [25] and Ryan [21] break up

2006
Beginning of Spring
Jason [15] meets Caesar [17]
Jason [16] meets Jace [33]
Jace [33] passes away
Nathaniel [20] and Caesar [18] reunite

2007
Beginning of Lightning
Kelly [16] meets William [17]
Nathaniel [20] and Caesar [18] break up permanently

2008

Ben [28] and Tim [28] meet again for the final time
Kelly [17] and William [17] are in a car wreck

2009

Jason [18] moves in with Ben [29] and Tim [30]
Jason [18] meets William [18]
Emma [14] meets Bonnie [17]
Kelly [18] meets Nathaniel [23]
Kelly [18] and William [18] break up

2010

Samson [15] passes away
Kelly [19] and Nathaniel [24] break up

2011

Tim [32] proposes to Ben [32]
Ryan [27] reappears

2013

Caesar [24] and Jason [23] meet again
Jason [23] and William [22] reunite
Kelly [21] and Nathaniel [27] reunite

2014

Ben [33] and Tim [34] get married

Hear the story in their own words!

Many of the *Something Like...* books are available on audio too. Listen to Tim's tale while you jog with him, or ignore your fellow airline passengers while experiencing Jace's story again. Find out which books are available and listen to free chapters at the link below:

http://www.jaybellbooks.com/audiobooks/

Also by Jay Bell
Kamikaze Boys

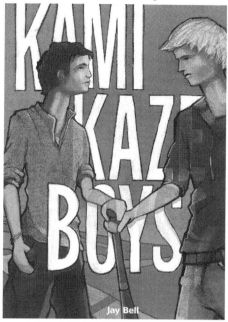

True love is worth fighting for.

My name is Connor Williams and people say I'm crazy. But that's not who I am. They also think I'm straight, and mean, and dangerous. But that's not who I am. The stories people tell, all those legends which made me an outsider—they don't mean a thing. Only my mother and my younger brother matter to me. Funny then that I find myself wanting to stand up for someone else. David Henry, that kind-of-cute guy who keeps to himself, he's about to get his ass beat by a bunch of dudes bigger than him. I could look away, let him be one more causality of this cruel world… But that's not who I am.

Kamikaze Boys, a Lambda Literary award winning novel, is a story of love triumphant as two young men walk a perilous path in the hopes of saving each other.

For more information, please see:
www.jaybellbooks.com

Something Like Characters: Series One

Now you can own art worthy of hanging in the Eric Conroy gallery! This first series of cards features five original illustrations created by Andreas Bell, the same hunky guy who does the cover illustrations for the *Something Like...* books. Each card depicts one of your favorite characters (we hope!) with a selected quote by them on the opposite side. The sixth card features unobscured cover art from the first four books in the series, and will be personalized to you and autographed by Jay Bell. (That's me!) Find out more details at our store. We've got T-shirts and all kinds of stuff too!

http://www.jaybellbooks.com/merchandise/

Made in the USA
Las Vegas, NV
13 March 2023

69002116R00189